4/2²

HOPE AND GLORY

HOPE AND GLORY

A novel

JENDELLA BENSON

WM

WILLIAM MORROW

An Imprint of HarperCollins*Publishers*

HOPE AND GLORY. Copyright © 2022 by Jendella Benson. All rights reserved. Printed in Canada. No part of this book may be used or reproduced in any manner whatsoever without written permission except in the case of brief quotations embodied in critical articles and reviews. For information, address HarperCollins Publishers, 195 Broadway, New York, NY 10007.

HarperCollins books may be purchased for educational, business, or sales promotional use. For information, please email the Special Markets Department at SPsales@harpercollins.com.

Published as in the United Kingdom in 2022 by Trapeze, an imprint of the Orion Publishing Group Ltd.

FIRST U.S. EDITION

Library of Congress Cataloging-in-Publication Data has been applied for.

ISBN 978-0-06-308057-7

22 23 24 25 26 FRI 10 9 8 7 6 5 4 3 2 1

I

Glory was home, she felt it instinctively. But there were a few sleepy seconds, after Faith had killed the car engine and before Glory opened her eyes, when she thought for a moment that she might still be in LA, and Daddy might still be alive.

Faith opened the driver side door and a gust of damp January air startled Glory to full consciousness. She heard the car boot click open and was easing herself out of the passenger seat when Faith arrived in front of her, handing over the one and only suitcase Glory had brought back from nearly two years on America's furthest coast.

Packing away her American dream had been easier than she thought it would be and, despite the circumstances, when the Boeing finally left the tarmac at LAX, Glory had felt relief wash over her.

Faith cast a critical eye over her younger sister, her immaculate brows creasing as she took in Glory's disheveled state.

"Allow me, Faith," Glory said with an exhausted sigh, reading her sister's mind. "I literally just stepped off an eleven-hour flight."

Faith tutted.

"She's not going to be alone. Just put on a brave face for her, it's hard enough as it is."

"This *is* my brave face!" Glory said impatiently.

She hadn't cried yet. Since Faith had called in the middle of the night to break the news, she had only been feeling anger. That anger had guided her fingers as she hastily typed out a resignation letter a few hours later and booked a flight back to London.

Her manager's response arrived in her inbox at 7 a.m.

Whatever the circumstances that have led to this, there is a mandatory notice period as outlined in your contract. I expect to see you in the office this morning and we can discuss.

But her suitcase was already packed, the rest of her belongings were in a pile with a note for her flatmates—*Take whatever you want, the rest can go to Goodwill*—and once again it was in anger that she responded curtly, *That won't be possible,* before deleting her work inbox from her phone.

And now Glory was angry at her sister who cared more about her presentation and had not once asked how she was feeling.

She pulled a baby wipe from the thick packet that Faith held out to her. Glory wiped her face down, and followed Faith up the stone steps that led to their childhood home, a three-bedroom maisonette in one of the few remaining blocks from the era of sprawling council estates. She waited in front of the dark, weathered door to Number 23 while Faith picked through her keys and felt a wave of nausea descend upon her. She took a deep breath and reached a hand out to steady herself on the railing. She was about to enter the house she grew up in, the house her father died in, and the house she would never see him in again.

"Faith, I can't," Glory managed to choke out between breaths.

Faith whipped her head around ready to reprimand her, but when she saw the strangled look on Glory's face, her irritation was overtaken by concern.

"Glory? What's wrong?"

"I can't, I—"

Glory bent forward, rested her hands on her knees and tried to suck cool air into lungs that felt shallow and tight.

"Breathe, Glory, breathe."

She felt Faith's hand on her back, rubbing in circles.

"Don't say anything," Faith said when Glory tried to speak again. Glory squeezed her eyes shut, and felt the events of the past twenty-four hours finally overtaking the numbness that had enveloped her since Faith's call.

"I can't go back," Glory said again, managing to swallow enough air to speak.

"We have to go in, we can't not go in," Faith said, her hand still working soft circles on Glory's back.

"No, I can't go back to LA." Glory lifted her head to look at her sister.

Faith's face changed from concern to confusion.

"Glory, forget LA! You're in London now!"

Glory shook her head and pulled herself up. She rested her hands on her hips and arched her back, letting her lungs expand and fill with more air. Faith watched her, tapping out an anxious rhythm on the railing.

When Glory finally felt her breath slow to a bearable pace, she closed her eyes and allowed herself one last deep inhale.

"OK, I'm fine now."

Faith nodded, turning back to the door and slipping in her key.

The door opened on to a short corridor then a small living space. Familiar smells of camphor, palm oil and chili welcomed Glory, smells she had hated as a teenager, dousing herself in layers of cheap body spray to mask the scent of her house. But now Glory was grateful that everything had remained more or less the same. The same crucifix was nailed to the inside of the front door, guarding the entrance, the same cream textured wallpaper ran through the room, the same brown leather sofa and armchairs. Glory's fingers found all these textures like they were talismans. She reached up and ran her fingertips over Jesus's emaciated metal body, before tracing one of the wallpaper swirls and pressing her fist into the soft give of the sofa.

The living room was host to older women of various sizes. They cackled and talked over the television, the tonal song of their Yorùbá colliding with the news anchor's clipped English. Seated in their father's armchair, Auntie Dọtun was the first to see the sisters enter.

"Ah! Mama Ìbejì!" she called out, rushing to her feet to give Faith a hug. "Where are my twins? And how is Michael? I haven't seen you people for so long!"

Faith dipped into a discreet curtsy before their mother's old friend crushed her in a tight hug. Glory continued kneading the edge of the sofa. For a moment, it felt like the room was frozen in time, all the older women looking on Faith with open adoration as if she was the blessed Virgin Mary incarnate. But the moment didn't last long enough because as soon as Faith stepped to the side, Auntie Dọtun's gaze pinned Glory down.

"And the prodigal daughter has returned."

It was an observation, not a welcome, and Glory didn't offer a deferential greeting nor did Auntie Dọtun swaddle her in a grateful embrace. Instead the older woman offered both cheeks for Glory to kiss awkwardly, before she presented her to the room.

"Celeste, this daughter of yours has not been eating!" Auntie Dọtun called out to their mother, who wasn't actually in the room.

4

Glory did the round of greetings, collecting loose hugs and clumsy pats on the shoulder. She could hear Faith, now in the kitchen, scolding their mother for cooking instead of getting the rest she needed. She began making her way to join them, but as soon as her back was turned, she heard a comment slip out behind her, a sly whisper chased away by a snicker: "Na dis one, ọmọ britico!"

British girl. Glory bristled at this illogical insult—each of these women had chosen to raise their own children in Britain, only to take issue with her generation's Britishness—and kept walking, past the cluttered table where the family computer had once lived, and down the steps into the narrow kitchen at the back of the house.

The woman stirring a large pot of jollof rice was smaller than she remembered, her face was sunken around the eyes and her skin hung slack around her jawline, but Glory's entrance drew a smile, and a flicker of the mother she once knew briefly appeared.

Glory walked into the arms held out to embrace her. The hug was tight but not warm, as though her mother was trying to confirm her physical presence rather than convey affection but, caught in her mother's arms, Glory thought she might finally cry.

Celeste released Glory and rested a hand on each of her daughters.

"My children," she said quietly, looking from sister to sister. "How was your journey?"

"Fine, Mummy."

"And where are my twins?" Celeste continued, turning now to Faith.

"With the childminder."

Celeste nodded, saying no more. The air around them was as heavy as their mother's hands.

"How are you doing, Mummy?" Glory asked meekly, and her mother sighed, her chest heaving with the effort.

"I'm coping," her mother replied, turning back to the pot in a businesslike fashion.

"Have you eaten?" Celeste asked over her shoulder.

Glory thought it was not the time to mention her flirtations with plant-based diets, and how white rice was really the worst of all carbs known to man. But as the cocktail of jollof spices filled her lungs, she realized that in that very moment there was nothing she wanted more than a mouthful of American long grain and tender goat meat.

"I'll go and put my suitcase upstairs," Glory began, thinking she would hide in her room until the food was ready.

"Oh!" Her mother snapped open the oven door and bent to look at the cubes of roasting meat. "I've just prepared your room for Auntie Búkì, she's arriving in the morning."

"So, I'll stay in Victor's room?"

"Tèmi's mum is staying in that one."

Glory sighed.

"So where should I sleep?"

"We can put a mattress on the floor next to the desk in my bedroom."

That was not the answer Glory wanted. There was no way she had quit her life in LA to sleep on the floor in her mother's bedroom. Faith saw Glory's face drop and harden, and intervened.

"Or you could come and stay with us!" she said. "You haven't seen our new house yet, have you? We've got a spare room—*two* guest rooms in fact!"

Glory thanked Faith, relieved to be rescued from the indignity of sleeping on the floor, but also from the prospect of waking up beneath her father's desk, his ghost hovering over her while she slept.

But now, with no place to escape to while she waited for this to be over, Glory reluctantly slipped back into the skin of the second daughter. She served heaped plates of rice and meat to the council of aunties. The irony of waiting hand and foot on the people who were supposed to be supporting her family did not escape her, but she forced her scowl into a smile for her mother's sake.

"Our sister Celeste has been through *so* much," Glory overheard one of the aunties commiserating with another as she was summoned to shift a side table. "Her only son . . . well, you know what happened, àbí? And then for her husband to die as well, all within eighteen months!"

"Yes, she's been through enough," Glory repeated to herself when she was told to collect empty glasses to be refilled, or questioned about things she would rather not speak on. No, she did not know when she would be flying back (*her mother had been through enough*), and she was not thinking of marriage at the moment (*her mother had been through enough*).

There was no response to the comments about her weight or her appearance, and as long as she had danced this dance with her elders she had never worked out how to defend or deflect the jibes (and, of course, *her mother . . . her mother . . . her mother . . .*).

By the middle of the afternoon, all that was left were empty plates streaked with stew, and discarded bones stripped of all edible elements. Balled up in the corner of the sofa, Glory dozed and half dreamed of a shower and a comfortable bed. A Nollywood film now bellowed from the TV, vying for airspace with laughs that cracked through the room like thunder. Eventually, even Faith tired of everything, and made a show of checking the time on her rose gold wristwatch.

"I need to go and collect the twins," she said to the room.

The women clucked "of course." Glory dragged herself out of her nest, said her goodbyes, and limped out to the car with her suitcase.

The temperature outside had dropped, and the blueness of night crept around the corners of her vision as she reloaded her luggage and got into the passenger seat. Faith was peering at her phone. She sucked air through her teeth viciously and started the engine.

"What's wrong?" Glory asked.

"Michael was meant to pick up the twins today, but, of course, he can't do that any more for one irrelevant reason or the next."

Faith threw the car into reverse.

Glory realized that since Faith had picked her up from the airport, she hadn't once thought to ask after her brother-in-law.

It wasn't that Glory didn't like him. Michael was the perfect son-in-law in the same way that Faith was the perfect daughter: compliant and respectful; knowing exactly when and how to speak. But he lacked Faith's personality. All Glory knew about him was that he worked in corporate law and supported Arsenal, two facts so nondescript Glory thought they weren't even worth mentioning. Dislike felt like too active an emotion; Glory preferred to think of herself as indifferent.

"How is Michael?" she asked. She could at least feign polite interest given she would be staying in the house paid for by his salary. As though she was suddenly aware of her mask slipping, Faith straightened up and smiled.

"He's fine, actually, really good!" Faith nodded to herself. "Work is going really well, he's just so busy at the moment, but that's the world of law, I suppose."

The lines sounded stale and well rehearsed. Faith's efforts to maintain an appearance of togetherness verged on pathological at times. She often reminded Glory of a Stepford Wife.

A flicker of genuine excitement crossed Faith's face as a thought occurred to her.

"You're going to *love* the new house, by the way! It's in the cute bit of Bromley—proper nice, proper suburbs."

Yes, thought Glory as Faith went on about house prices and catchment areas, *she's a fucking Stepford Wife*.

But to Faith's credit, the house was nice. It was gorgeous, in fact. A family house on the end of a terrace in a newly built gated development. Of course, it was nothing like the gated communities in the suburbs of LA, but it was nice all the same. The edges were clean and sharp and the street lamps, a dazzling clear white instead of the usual murky yellow, made Glory feel like she was on a movie set. Through the windows of the houses and flats they passed she could see kitchens and living rooms that would not be out of place in a showroom. They pulled into Faith's driveway—she had a driveway *and* a garage—and Glory noticed the neat square of grass out in front of the house, small, but a marker of family bliss nevertheless.

2

That night, sleep came to Glory in feverish waves. When she wasn't awake, staring into the dark corners of Faith's guest room and feeling grief settle in her body, exhaustion pulled her into stretches of thick, dreamless sleep. But then sleep receded and tears took its place, soaking Faith's memory foam pillow until Glory felt empty and hollowed out. Finally.

Glory willed herself to sit up and do something useful. She collected her wash bag and towel then padded down the hallway, prodding gently at white-paneled doors until she found the bathroom.

In the shower she cranked up the temperature until tiny pinpricks of heat scattered over her shoulders and back. She let her hair loose from its bun and scrubbed through her curls until the water ran clear and the follicles squeaked against each other. She soaped up her body and scoured her skin with her washcloth, imagining she was washing away the remnants of her Los Angeles life: the golden glow of sunshine; the glossy smile and corporate personality she adopted for work. It all slid off her body and spiraled into the drain.

The irony was that the main thing that had kept Glory chained to her American ambition was not wanting to disappoint her father by returning to London with nothing to show for herself. In his death he had not only provided her with the perfect get out clause but also avoided having to see Glory fail at something else.

"In all things we give thanks." Glory could imagine Daddy gruffly saying that from wherever he currently resided. That was enough to push her over the edge again and she turned her face upward, directly into the flow of water. The stream mixed with her tears, washing the salt from her face like tropical rain. She sighed audibly, feeling cleansed and baptized, before finally turning off the water and wrapping her body in a towel.

She opened the door, only to jump back when she was met by Faith waiting outside.

"Sorry!" Faith said as Glory yelped and clutched the towel to her chest. "I heard the shower running and I thought it was Michael."

Glory stooped to pick up the bundle of clothes she had dropped.

"I'm going to make some tea, do you want any?" Faith asked as she backed away.

"What time is it?"

"About 5:30."

"Faith, why are you up?"

"Michael's not back yet."

"Back from where?"

Faith shook her head and sighed. "Work thing, maybe. I dunno. There's always something. I'm going to make tea."

Faith drew her dressing gown tight around her before walking down the hall.

Glory dressed quickly, stopping only to pull back the navy curtains and look out into the back garden, the grass impossibly green in the low light. A trampoline and playhouse were tucked in the back corner of the tidy lawn, and from the window Glory could see into four other back gardens, all pretty and neat, but Faith's was by far the neatest. Glory remade the bed, arranged her wash bag carefully on the nightstand and left the room, closing the door gently behind her.

The hallway walls showcased pictures of Faith, Michael, Esther and Elijah, hugging and tumbling over each other in a stark white studio. They were a stock picture family, smiles so bright you could practically hear their laughs tinkling, dark brown skin glowing under the studio lights.

The door to her niece and nephew's room was ajar, and Glory peered into the darkness, imagining their lives filled with the kind of toys that she and her siblings had lacked as children. The door to Faith and Michael's room was shut tight, but Glory could picture a king-size bed, an en-suite bathroom, built-in wardrobes and maybe even a mirrored dressing table for Faith.

Downstairs, in the artificially bright kitchen, Faith leaned against a countertop, her fingers wrapped around a mug of steaming tea. Her sullen face seemed oblivious to all the good fortune that surrounded her, and she was still as Glory maneuvered around her to make her own cup of tea. When Glory released a yawn so wide she could barely cover it with her hand, Faith snapped to attention, as if seeing her sister for the first time.

"Jetlag?"

"Yeah."

"Sorry."

"You're turning in to Mummy."

Faith glanced up from her mug with a strange look on her face. "What do you mean?"

"Apologizing for things you've got no control over."

"Oh," Faith said, pulling the corner of her lips into a smile that didn't reach her eyes.

"So, Michael's really busy, huh?"

"Yeah, you know how law is," Faith said flatly.

"That's what you said yesterday."

"Because it's true."

"Right."

Glory nodded, struggling to find the appropriate platitudes to soothe her sister. "I'm here if you need any help."

It was weak, but it would do.

The two of them stood in an unfamiliar silence, until Glory asked the question she had been working up to since leaving their mother's house the night before.

"How's Victor doing?"

"He's OK. Well, as OK as he can be." Faith tried another lifeless smile.

"Will he be allowed to come to the funeral?"

"No."

"What? Don't they get, like, compassionate leave or something?" Glory asked.

Faith looked up, a pained expression on her face.

"He's in *prison*, Glory. There is no compassion or leave."

Glory took a sip from her mug and swallowed hard, not daring to meet Faith's eye.

"How was he?" she asked meekly. "When you told him, how did he take it?"

"I didn't tell him, so I don't know."

Glory looked up at her sister now, dropping her penitent act.

"Why would you let someone else tell him *that*?"

"Do you understand how prison works?" Faith asked, her tone sharp. "You can't just contact him whenever you want.

13

I called the prison, told reception and then they said someone in the chaplaincy would break the news to him."

"And?"

"And what?"

"Have you spoken to him since? Is he OK? What's going on?" Glory asked, her tone verging on frantic.

"He's fine, Glory," Faith sighed. "I mean, he's OK. He called me later that day. He's OK."

Glory nodded and cast her eyes back toward the floor. "I should probably go and see him soon or something."

"He'll need to add you to his visit list first."

"His visit list?"

"Yeah, it's a list of people he wants to receive visits from. You can't just turn up at the prison and ask to see him. Once he's added you, then you can book a visit."

"I'm not on there already?" Glory asked, her tone sour. She had no right to be offended, but she was.

"Why would you be? You've not been here."

Glory swallowed another gulp of hot tea.

"So what needs to be done for the funeral?" she asked after a while.

Faith visibly relaxed.

"Well, venues have been booked, photographer and videographer too, catering is more or less sorted, I'm dropping the lace off to the tailors tomorrow morning, so I'll need your measurements for that." Faith rattled off the list on her fingers. "Ah, you can do the program, actually, I'm sure you can put your creative skills to good use."

Faith picked up her mug and took a satisfied sip.

"You've done all of that already?"

"Yeah, Mummy's friends have actually been really useful for once."

Glory twisted her mouth around her face, trying to work out the most nonconfrontational way to pose her next question. She chewed at the insides of her cheeks.

"What color is the lace?"

"Blue."

"Daddy's favorite color was green."

"He liked blue too."

"But green was his favorite."

Faith closed her eyes and tipped her head back.

"I'm just saying, it would have been nice to have a little more input," Glory mumbled into the rim of her mug.

"We had to move quickly, there wasn't time to waste."

"But still . . ." Glory trailed off with a shrug.

"To be honest, I wasn't even sure if you were going to make it home for the funeral," Faith said after a pause, keeping her eyes on the ceiling.

"You what?" Glory frowned.

Faith breathed out slowly, bringing her eyes down to rest on Glory.

"Forget it."

"Nah, say what you're saying," Glory insisted, maintaining steady eye contact.

"Well, you missed two Christmases—"

"So?"

"—and Victor's entire trial and sentencing."

Glory set her jaw, jutting her chin out slightly while trying to keep her tone even.

"You honestly thought I wasn't going to come to my own father's funeral?"

Faith turned her back to her sister and soaked her mug.

"You managed to organize a whole funeral in a couple of days and didn't think I'd want to know what you're doing?"

"It's not all organized, I've still got to meet with the caterers, still need to distribute the aṣọ ẹbí to Mummy and Daddy's friends, there's the order of service to be finalized—there's plenty to be done."

"But you just started planning this without me?"

"What's this actually about, Glory? Because I know you can't really be upset that I never waited for you to go around Liverpool Street looking for cloth!"

Angry tears began to build behind Glory's eyes. She flared her nostrils, trying to fight the pressure.

"He was my dad too, I thought my opinion should at least be considered."

Faith opened her mouth, ready to respond, but snapped it shut almost immediately.

Above them tiny feet pattered across the ceiling and a sharp "Mummy!" peeled through floorboards. Faith rubbed a weary hand across her brow.

"Look, Glory, I'm glad you're back, I really am, but just don't make this any harder than it needs to be, all right?"

Glory sniffed hard and stared into the dark circle of her mug.

The quick little footsteps moved down the stairs, and soon the words "Auntie G'oryyyy" were ringing through the kitchen. Elijah and Esther ran toward her, winding their arms around her legs, and Faith laughed as the force of her children sent Glory off balance.

"How long are you here for?" Faith asked as she picked up each child and wrestled them into their booster seats. "When's your flight back?"

"I don't know yet," Glory lied.

Faith paused, her fingers still working at the clasp around Elijah's waist.

"You don't know?"

"I've got extended leave, I'll just let them know when I'm ready to come back."

As Faith went to buckle Esther in, Glory could see the cogs whirring in her sister's mind. She gripped her mug tighter, braced for an inquisition.

"Well, you can stay here as long as you need to," Faith concluded. "I could use the company."

Faith landed a loud kiss on Esther's round cheek. "Yes, we'd like that, wouldn't we?" she asked her daughter in a sing-song tone. She straightened up, massaging the skin under the eyes.

"OK then my little munchkins! What do you want for breakfast?"

She clapped out each word with the energy of a children's TV presenter and the twins responded appropriately. Esther and Elijah were enamored by their mother's performance, as she opened and closed cupboards pretending to hunt down their breakfast cereal, but to Glory her sister's voice sounded just a little too shrill and a little too bright.

"Faith, whatever you need me to do for the funeral, I'll do it, OK?" Glory said as a peace offering.

"You can start taking some of these calls from Nigeria, if you want—absolutely everyone has an opinion on this funeral, even if they couldn't get a visa!" Faith said as she poured out the twins' cereal.

"You know that's probably not a good idea, Faith. You are much better with elders than I am, I will just offend everyone and then Mummy will have a headache from random uncles and aunties complaining about me."

Faith laughed at that, a genuine chuckle that Glory didn't realize she had missed until that moment.

"You're right, I'll handle the aunties and uncles, you can deal with the program—and the food actually, could you meet the caterers for me?"

"Of course," Glory said, glad to feel needed.

"You know what else? Would you be able to go to Brixton later and get some rosary beads for Mummy from that religious shop in the market? That's the only shop she wants them from."

Faith set two brightly colored bowls of Cheerios in front of her children.

"Rosary beads? Since when are we Catholic?"

Faith sighed.

"A lot has changed around here, Glory. Believe me."

3

The days after Glory's arrival collapsed into one long, meticulous to-do-list, overseen with military precision by Faith. So when the day of the funeral arrived, they were both relieved. All that could have been done had been done, and everything else wouldn't matter by tomorrow.

At their mother's house, Glory waited outside. The cold winter air was an antidote to the claustrophobic activity taking place inside the house. She waited by the hearse, averting her eyes from the walnut-paneled casket that lay behind the glass.

She had been wrestling with the image of her father's waxen face since the final viewing of his body at the funeral home the night before. She had fought it all through the night, trying to remember what Daddy had looked like the last time she had seen him in person. But the details of the day had been displaced by the excitement. She had looked at her family as she hugged and kissed them at the airport, but she hadn't really *seen* them; her vision was already focused beyond them and beyond London, on Los Angeles and everything she believed it had to offer.

Guilt. She could feel it again, pushing the contents of her stomach up into her throat. She tried to focus on one of the photographs she had selected for the program: the skinny young man on his first day at university; the stiff groom in a tuxedo looking nervously into the camera lens; the nineties version with a thick black moustache and arms full of children. But the specter of his jaw, wired shut in a grimace, swum back into frame and Glory found herself hobbling to the back of the limousine, where she vomited a sickly, yellow stream into the gutter. One of the drivers rushed to her, pushing a packet of Kleenex into her hand. She straightened up and leaned weakly against the side of the vehicle, wiping her mouth with a balled up fist of tissue in time to see her mother emerge, supported by Faith on one side and Auntie Dòtun on the other.

Celeste's face was ashen and her mouth set in a tight line, but the sequins on her blouse shimmered in the weak morning light. Gripped in one of her hands was a handkerchief, and she clutched it so hard her knuckles were pale. Celeste walked slowly toward the first limousine parked behind the hearse, but stopped in front of Glory, pressing another folded handkerchief into her hands without a word. Glory looked from the handkerchief to Faith who rolled her eyes, before Auntie Dòtun whispered, "It's been blessed by Pastor Owódùnní. It's for protection for today."

"What's wrong?" Faith asked, spotting the tissue and the arm Glory wrapped around her stomach.

"Nothing—I just threw up."

Faith's eyes widened.

"It didn't get it on you did it?" she asked. "I won't have time to redo your makeup if it did."

She clasped Glory's chin in her fingers, turning her sister's head this way and that.

"No, I did it down the drain." Glory pulled herself out of Faith's grip.

"OK." Faith nodded grimly. "Drink some water but we need to leave."

Glory remembered the somber sight of funeral processions when she was younger, and she remembered stopping to gawp as the long black cars snaked through traffic. But now she resented the audience the scene produced. Strangers stared with no sense of embarrassment while others averted their gaze and made the sign of the cross. Glory closed her eyes for the rest of the journey, praying for the day to come to a swift and successful end.

At the church, it was apparent that everyone who had ever known their family had turned out to pay their respects. People whose calls Glory had been avoiding waved to her as the family got out of the cars, and what felt like hundreds of eyes carried her into the church building. Glory held on to the hand her mother wrapped around her forearm, and kept her gaze trained on the floor in front of each careful step Celeste took, but she couldn't help thinking that her return to London was not meant to be like this. She was not meant to be an object of pity for everyone she had been so eager to leave behind. This was not how the story was meant to end.

The family waited in a small side room while mourners were ushered into the hall. Celeste sat between Faith and Glory, vibrating with the low hum of another desperate prayer. Faith took out a white handkerchief—also blessed by Pastor Owódùnní—and pressed it into the crease of her nose, blotting away nervous sweat.

The hall doors shut behind the last set of well-wishers, then the undertakers brought the casket into the church foyer. Michael and the mix of relatives and business associates who were pallbearers assembled around the casket, preparing themselves to shoulder the weight of Glory's father's mortal remains.

The PA system squeaked as the minister asked the congregation to stand, and the musicians struck up chords. Glory, Faith and their mother slipped in front of the queue of mourners in matching fabric that had lined up behind the casket.

"Remember, this is a celebration of life!" Glory's mother hissed at her daughters who stood either side of her, their backs stiff and straight. It was the first sentence she had said all morning. The shrill notes of a Nigerian chorus started, the doors of the hall swung open, and the family of the late, great, Adékúnlé Ọlárótìmí Akíndélé swayed into the hall.

A strong undercurrent of family politics had steered much of the funeral planning and even the day itself. Otherwise irrelevant cultural expectations escalated in importance, but the only battle that mattered to Glory had been won: she had been the one to give her father's eulogy.

For those slighted by no official slot in the program, the minister opened the floor for tributes. Glory could see that her father was well loved, but she still watched cynically as well-wisher after well-wisher lined up to underscore their proximity to the family. Glory let their words swim past her, nodding an "amen" at the appropriate moments and clapping when required.

As she stood at the graveside with Faith and her mother, the finality of the occasion came into sharp focus. She still had so much to tell Daddy. As the casket was lowered into the open grave she wanted to jump into the hole with it. She distracted herself from this irrational urge by propping up her mother, who leaned on her heavily, shoulders shaking in deep silent sobs, while behind them Auntie Dòtun repeated, "It is well, my sister, it is well!"

At the wake the atmosphere changed from somber to festive. Plates of fish and meat were served while music bubbled from speakers in the community hall. Faith was dipping her way around tables attending to older guests, ensuring they had enough plantain or the softest portion of stewed beef. The twins ran in circles and Celeste sat at the center of the room, holding court with friends who fussed over her while she piously refused plates of food.

"Sister Celeste," one of her friends pleaded. "You can break your fast to honor your husband now!"

But Celeste pressed her lips firmly together, accepting only water, though the weight with which she had leaned on Glory at the graveside suggested she could have done with some sustenance.

One of her mother's friends eventually came over to the corner where Glory had planted herself, glowering at those who had so readily replaced sorrow with mouthfuls of food.

"Your mother wants you to come," the woman said, and Glory followed her back to the thicket of aunties.

"Glory, you remember Ọmọlará's mum?" Celeste said, holding an arm out to a woman around her age whose face was folded up in pity.

Glory mumbled something noncommittal as she was wrapped in a desperate hug.

"Glory, don't be rude. Greet your elders properly, at the very least!"

"It's OK, Mama Faith," the woman said. "My dear, I'm so, *so* sorry."

She released Glory for a second before drawing her to her bosom once again.

"And Lará wanted to be here, but she couldn't get the time off work. I'll get your number from your mum and she'll call you. She really wants to speak to you."

Glory nodded but said nothing, waiting for her chance to leave before she did something else to irritate her mother.

"It's been years, but you are like family, ehn?" the woman continued, now holding Glory's hand between her damp palms. *Family*.

When the woman turned back to Celeste, Glory made her exit. The earnestness in her tone was too much.

Finding her previous corner occupied, Glory floated around the hall, trying to avoid making eye contact while looking for another nook to hide away in.

To their credit, she saw that Victor's friends had made a late appearance. They were dressed appropriately enough, each of them sporting matching guinea brocade, cut into slim-fitting tunic tops, worn with dark jeans and the obscene patent glare of their designer trainers. She watched Faith attend to them, dispensing hugs and chilled bottles of Supermalt, and even managing to laugh as the young men blushed under her big sisterly charm. Resentment filled Glory's stomach. Everything was too bright and too loud.

Glory left the hall and escaped to the ladies' bathroom, barricading herself in a stall. She perched on the closed lid of the toilet, and gathered up her lace skirt so she could rest her feet against the back of the door. Voices followed her in shortly after, and it was her brother's name that pricked her ears.

"You know what happened with Victor, right? And now this sudden death . . ."

The other voice tutted in agreement and entered the stall next to Glory.

"To be honest," the first voice continued, "the tragedy started a long time ago. You know they had another daughter, right?"

Glory's throat tightened and she curled her fingers into tight fists, feeling her nails dig into her palms.

"Oh, really?" the second voice piped up. "What happened?"

"So sad, really, so sad. I can't even remember how it happened, but it was when the girls were very small."

The cubicle door was a foot or two in front of Glory's face, but it was swimming in the distance. She pressed her head into her lap, fire building in her throat.

"What was her name?" voice number two asked, flushing the toilet and leaving the cubicle.

"I can't even remember now—I didn't know the family at that time, actually, it was my sister's husband who told me."

Rage coursed through Glory and she wanted to scream at the anonymous voices. The audacity of these witches gossiping about her family at her father's funeral and they didn't even know the name of her dead sister! Glory grasped her thighs through the material of her skirt, digging her fingers in as deep as they would go and letting the pain flood her senses in place of pure indignation.

She waited until the whirr of the hand drier quieted down and the door slapped shut before she got up, slowly, feeling dizzy and unsteady. She took a deep breath and hurried from the stall, past a group of women gathered in the outer corridor.

"Glory?"

She spun around to see Michael with the group she had pushed past. He towered over them and the way they looked at him in sickening admiration made Glory feel even angrier. *They probably all wanted their daughters to marry a man like him*, Glory thought darkly. *If only they knew.*

"What?" Glory shot back at her brother-in-law.

"Faith was looking for you—"

"I just need a minute!"

One of the women standing near Michael audibly gasped. "You should not be talking to your older bro—"

Glory turned her back on the group and walked away.

"It's OK, ma." She could hear Michael placating his groupies. "She's grieving, it's a hard day for all of us."

A cold gust of air hit her as she left the building and rounded a corner. Out of sight from the entrance she pressed her hot body to the cool outer wall. Running her hands over the brick, she zeroed in on the rough texture beneath her fingers, counting to ten and swallowing air. When she felt she could finally breathe freely, she bent over and let out a guttural sob.

The sound crashed around inside her head, so loud she didn't hear the person approach. She felt a careful hand on her shoulder before she heard her name being whispered, and she looked up to see a shadow in front of her. The light filtering from the windows high up in the building's walls revealed a worried face.

"Stand up," the voice gently said. Glory studied the stranger's face, which felt familiar, as he fumbled through his pockets.

"Let's sit over here, and I'll get you some tissue, yeah?"

He led her by the arm to the low wall that surrounded the community hall before disappearing into the night. When he returned, Glory had calmed down. Embarrassment eclipsed the grief and panic that had wracked her body a few minutes before. She accepted the wad of toilet paper he held out to her, wiped her eyes and blew her nose.

"I'm sorry . . . *Julian*."

His name came back to her. He was Faith's age, the son of a family friend, and she vaguely remembered childhood birthday parties from photo albums, pictures of kids squashed together behind a caterpillar cake.

"Sorry for what? It would be weird if you weren't upset."

"I know, it's just . . ." She waved a weak hand in front of her, letting her sentence fade into the evening air.

"If you wanna be alone, just say. I saw you rush out and just wanted to make sure you were OK."

"It's fine," Glory said quietly, "I just need a minute."

"OK, I'll give you some space." Julian backed away and then stopped.

"Listen, I know we ain't spoken in time, but if you ever need anyone to talk to—and I'm sorry about what happened to your brother too . . ." Glory flinched. ". . . but I know what it's like—I mean, I've got a couple people inside, so, y'know, if you ever want to talk, come and find me."

"Find you where?" Glory asked. Julian looked through his pockets again and held out a card.

"I'm usually at my shop but my phone number's there too."

Glory turned the business card around in her hand and looked up at him with a quizzical expression.

"I'm not trying to move to you," Julian said with a self-conscious laugh. "I'm serious, yeah?"

He dug his hands into the back pockets of his trousers and looked at the floor.

"We basically grew up together," he said, by way of explanation. "So if you need anything just holler."

"Thanks, I appreciate it."

"Cool."

Julian turned around and went back inside.

4

The day after the funeral was an anticlimax, of sorts. The relief Glory had been hoping for was lost under advancing tides of emotional and physical exhaustion. Downstairs, Faith was splayed across the dark gray corner sofa, Esther and Elijah bouncing around her while they watched kids' TV and showered each other with sticky crumbs of toast.

Glory stood outside the living room, watching the little world that the twins created for themselves. Unintelligible syllables and cryptic gestures passed between them, their mother oblivious to the debate the two of them were engaged in. Jealousy shot through Glory and then she remembered the words of the women from the bathroom—*so sad, really, so sad*—and a familiar ache resurfaced.

Faith groaned in response to Glory gently prodding the top of her head, and pulled herself up to make room for her sister.

"Do you guys have Postmates?" Glory asked.

"Post what?"

"Postmates. It's an app where you can get anything delivered. We could get a full English delivered to the house in like thirty minutes." Glory clicked her fingers.

"Now *that* would be amazing." Faith sighed.

"Do you think if I asked nicely Michael would pick us up some breakfast from McDonald's?"

"Leave him. He's having a lie-in."

"A lie-in?" Glory pulled a face. "Was Daddy's coffin that heavy?"

"Don't start, Glory."

"Me? I'm not starting anything!" Glory brushed her palms together in the manner of their mother, the corners of her mouth pulled down. "He's not my husband to be starting any—"

"Glory!" Faith barked, then sank back into the sofa and closed her eyes, as if the energy it took to reprimand her sister had physically hurt her. The television chirruped away in the background as Glory watched her sister's chest rise and fall.

"I'll whip something up."

In the kitchen, she found two blackened plantains and an unopened pack of bacon behind a stack of tupperware filled with leftovers in the fridge. After opening and closing many cupboard doors she also discovered a forgotten packet of flour just within its use-by-date and the last remaining eggs.

The recipe was haphazard and untested, but Glory presented the food to Faith with a flourish.

"Ignore the presentation, couldn't find any icing sugar or maple syrup to really make it look nice."

"Bacon and pancakes?" Faith asked, inspecting the food with a skeptical look.

"But not just *any* pancakes," Glory responded with a playful smile. Faith looked unconvinced, as she turned the plate around to look at it from another angle, before cutting a portion of pancake with her fork and chewing thoughtfully.

"Now take a bite of the bacon!"

Faith carefully picked up a rasher with her fingertips, and took a bite.

"What is this?" she asked.

"Plantain pancakes!"

Faith gave Glory a long look, before pushing another forkful into her mouth.

"You learned this in America, innit?" Faith said between bites. "Americans have weird taste, always mixing salty and sweet, peanut butter and jam, all that nonsense."

"But it's nice, right?" Glory settled down to begin on her own portion.

"You know, I once saw a man on TV put gravy and syrup on his waffles—*gravy and syrup*, Glory! But this is the kind of thing all those hipsters moving into Peckham would love," Faith said as she finished off the final bit of bacon. "What do they call it when you mix two different styles of foods together?"

"Fusion cuisine."

"Fusion cuisine." Faith nodded. "So, have you thought any more about when you're going back?"

"I'm not gonna be freeloading off you for too much longer, if that's what you're worried about."

"No, it's not even that—I mean, in theory you can stay here as long as you like, Michael's never home anyway, but I'm just thinking about Mummy, really." Faith changed position, folding her legs underneath her. "I'm worried about her being all alone in the house when everyone goes back to Nigeria, you should go and stay with her for a bit, before you go back to LA."

Faith watched Glory eat, waiting on her response.

"Yeah, I could . . ." Glory began.

"But?" Faith leaned forward.

"Well, you know what me and Mummy are like, innit?"

"She really needs someone there."

30

"Yes, she needs someone, but does she need *me*? We frustrate each other, you know this better than anyone."

Glory tried a wide, cheeky smile, but Faith remained serious.

"You've not been here, Glory, she's changed," was all that she said.

"Changed how?"

Faith chewed her bottom lip.

"She's become really antisocial."

"Her husband just died, that's normal," Glory said, but Faith shook her head. Her gaze was fixed in the middle distance and she pulled at a loose lock of hair.

"No. She changed after Victor . . . went away."

Glory waited for Faith to continue.

"Her superstitions . . . you know those handkerchiefs she made us hold yesterday? They were sent by one of her *holy men* in Nigeria. She spends hours on the phone to these random pastors and prophets who say they can get her a miracle or have a word from God for her. I don't even wanna know how much she paid for those scraps of cloth."

"Paid?" Glory thought back to the cheap squares of cotton stained with oil.

"Oh yes, paid. Holy men for hire. Daddy used to argue with her about it. I was late to court the day the verdict came back because she asked me to send money for some special holy fire prayer that was meant to get Victor acquitted. Two hundred and fifty quid down the toilet!"

"Wow. I didn't know."

"Of course you didn't."

Glory shifted in her seat. "That's a lot of money. Daddy must have been pissed."

Faith shot a sharp look from Glory to the twins, whose attention was firmly fixed on the television.

"Sorry. Angry. Daddy must have been very angry."

"Oh, he was," Faith said, her eyes wide. "He called her a madwoman." She whispered the word behind her hand, shielding her children from the slur.

"He said that to her face?"

"Yes! Their arguments were bad, Glory. Vicious. You don't even know the half of it."

Glory tried to imagine what a vicious argument between her parents might look like. She could count on one hand the times that her father had raised his voice—or at least raised his voice at her. Drama was their mother's domain; Daddy took pride in being more measured. Glory tried to skate over the thought of her parents' marriage falling apart while she was in LA, willfully oblivious.

"Then just as things felt like they were getting better . . ." Faith sighed and Glory could see tears begin to form in her sister's eyes.

When tragedy loomed as large as this, going over a sequence of events that could not be changed felt like a pointless exercise. But now, for reasons she couldn't really explain, Glory needed to know the miserable details.

"What happened?"

Faith locked eyes with Glory, her eyes glassy.

"What happened that day?" she asked.

Faith drew in a long, labored breath, pushing her head back into the sofa. Her eyes scanned the air in front of her as though she was reading an autocue. Then she began.

"I had a dream," Faith said. "It was a week before Daddy passed. I was climbing a mountain, high up on this snowy ledge and then I looked down and started getting extreme vertigo. It felt so real. I looked up the meaning online afterward— like, *what does it mean when you dream about climbing a mountain and getting vertigo*—and it said that means something tragic is going to happen to someone close to you. I thought it was about you."

"Me? What did you think was going to happen?"

"I don't know," Faith said. "I just thought . . . anyway. A week later, it happened. A pulmonary embolism, I told you."

"I know that, but *how* did it happen?"

"What do you mean how? That morning he was getting ready and he just passed out. Mummy was trying to revive him and then she called the ambulance, then she called me."

"What did she say when she called you?"

"I— I can't remember, I just went to the hospital and met them there."

"Did you see him when you got there?"

"He was already gone."

"So where was he? In A&E?"

"No, he was in a room."

"A room?"

"Yes, Glory, a room. He was on the bed. It was really cold in there. There was a sheet over him."

"Why was it cold?"

"A fan was on or something. There was a sheet over him, it was moving up and down, and I thought for a second he was still breathing."

"Did you check?" Glory asked, panic rising at the irrational thought her father could have been buried alive. But she had seen him in the funeral home. He had not been alive.

"Of course I checked, I went right up to him and put my hand on his face, but—no. It wasn't his breath. It was the fan."

Glory was about to ask her sister what he felt like when she had touched his body, but she saw that Faith had started silently crying. It was only when Glory felt two fat drops land on the back of her hands that she realized she too was crying. She sniffed hard and turned away from her sister.

"Who else was there? At the hospital?"

"Auntie Dọtun. When I came out of the room, Mummy was basically having a breakdown. I thought they were going to sedate her because she was babbling and saying all these crazy things."

"What was she saying?"

"She was saying . . . sh-she . . ." Faith floundered, cleared her throat and started again. "She said, *They'll say that I killed him.*"

Glory spun back to face Faith.

"Who was saying that?!"

"No one was *saying* that, Mummy was just . . . you know how people gossip."

Glory thought again of the women at the funeral. She thought to tell Faith what she had overheard, but instead swallowed hard and allowed herself to cry out loud. Then Faith cracked, trying in vain to stifle her cries through shaking hands. Furious what ifs cycled through Glory's mind: had their mother called the ambulance fast enough? Did the doctors try hard enough? Who just got up in the morning and dropped dead? It couldn't be that simple.

Esther turned around to look at her mother and her aunt, a questioning look on her face. She turned to her brother.

"Mummy's sad again," she said in a flat tone. Elijah pulled his eyes away from the TV screen to survey the two adults for himself.

"I'm sorry, my babies," Faith sniffed, rubbing her eyes and beckoning her children to her. "Don't worry, Mummy's OK, she's OK."

"Why are you sad?" Elijah asked his mother.

"I miss Grandpa."

"When's Grandpa coming back?" Esther asked.

The innocence of the question made Glory sob harder.

The twins looked alarmed.

"Why's Auntie G'ory sad?" Elijah asked.

"She misses Grandpa too," Faith said, gulping down air in a bid to force the crying to stop. Esther broke away from her mother and placed a pudgy little hand on Glory's knee.

"It's OK, Grandpa will be back soon. People go away but they come back. Like Daddy."

The sweet simplicity of her toddler logic was enough to draw out a smile through Glory's tears and she wrapped her arms tightly around her niece, planting a firm kiss on her forehead.

They stayed like that for a while, Faith holding on to Elijah and Glory hugging Esther. Eventually, Elijah got bored and prized himself from his mum to turn his attention back to the TV and Esther followed him.

Glory watched them sitting next to each other, their shoulders lightly brushing as they sat much too close to the screen. She couldn't have been much older than Esther and Elijah when it happened, too young to understand what she had lost.

"Do you think we're cursed, Faith?" Glory asked impulsively.

"Cursed? Why would you ask that?"

"I was just thinking about something someone said at the wake."

Faith sat up.

"They said our family was cursed?"

"No, they were just talking about all the different things that have happened. Daddy, obviously, Victor and, er, Hope."

Faith went rigid. The name felt strange in Glory's mouth. Her tongue was thick and heavy as she formed the vowel, so little had the name been spoken between them.

"People need to learn how to mind their own business," Faith said, her voice taking on a hard edge. "They were only called to mourn and eat rice, not analyze our family history like they don't have their own secrets and skeletons. Who was it?"

"I didn't see them, I was in the toilet cubicle."

"Useless people!" Faith spat out the words, her lips curled into a snarl, and Glory couldn't help herself.

"Oh my days, Faith, you are proper turning into Mummy!" Glory laughed.

Faith kissed her teeth and tried to send a cutting look Glory's way, but when she saw her sister falling backward with laughter, a smile escaped her lips. She threw a cushion in Glory's direction and readjusted her posture.

"Speaking of Mummy, what can we do?" Faith asked Glory. "I think she improved a bit in the run-up to the funeral when she had people staying and the planning to focus on, but when everyone goes, what then? No husband, no son, an empty house full of a lifetime's worth of rubbish. Do I move her in here? Do we bring someone from Nigeria to stay with her for a while? What can we do?"

Glory stopped smiling and sat up, feeling the weight of responsibility press her into submission.

"I'll go stay with her, but just give me a bit of time, OK?"

"Sure," Faith said with a smile, satisfied at this conclusion.

"So what happened in LA then?" she ventured after allowing the technicolor yelp of Saturday morning children's TV to fill the silence between them.

"What do you mean what happened? Why do you think something happened?" Glory's ears began to feel hot.

"Come on, Glory—you loved LA! I could barely get you on the phone to tell me how much you loved it. I saw your Instagram, you were having the time of your life while we

36

were . . . here . . . anyway! You were so excited to move there, I'd have thought you would be on your way to the airport right now."

"I just needed a break," Glory said casually, although she had been working her way up to this conversation ever since the panic attack outside her mum's house on the day she landed.

"From what?"

Faith waited for an answer as she stroked the head of Elijah, who had returned to nestle against her, but the moment was cut in two by the shrill ring of the landline. Esther brought the phone to her mother, who answered. The call was brief.

"We've got to go to Mum's," Faith said as she hung up the phone. "I need to give her Daddy's death certificate among a million other things."

She stood up and stretched.

"Will you watch the twins while I have a shower, please?"

As the opportunity for a heart-to-heart with her sister slipped away, Glory was shocked by her own disappointment.

"No problem," she said, picking up a gray flocked cushion and hugging it to her chest.

5

Celeste was on the phone making promises she couldn't keep. There were the school fees of extended relations that needed to be paid, a cousin who wanted to start a business, and someone's daughter who was due to get married in a few months.

In the run-up to the funeral the house had been vibrating with activity and guests, but just one day later it felt deserted. The creaks coming from above suggested an auntie still lurking, perhaps packing her things for her flight back or planning how to make the most of the remaining weeks of her visitor's visa, but apart from their mother spouting pledges into the landline, the Akíndélé residence was still.

The twins resumed the TV marathon that had been interrupted by the drive to Peckham, while Faith hovered in the center of the room, passing the envelope containing the death certificate from hand to hand while she waited for her mother to end the call. Glory slid past and into the kitchen to find a drink.

She was no stranger to clutter. She had grown up in the house of a first-generation immigrant whose survival instincts saw potential in every piece of bric-a-brac or pound shop find. She was used to benign hoarding, but the assortment of ruin that filled the passageway between the living room and the kitchen was quite different. Glory could make out piles of shattered crockery, a row of empty plastic milk cartons, and, curiously, a nest of knotted video tape that she assumed came from the broken VHS tapes heaped under a pile of newspapers. Less a calculated stockpile, more the debris of an unsettled mind.

In the kitchen, she ran the tap and drank a glassful of water without stopping to take a breath. She could hear Faith's voice getting louder and more agitated in the living room, so she lingered, filling another glass and pushing each new gulp around her mouth as she leaned up against the counter. When this second glass was finished she headed back into the fray.

". . . but you can't afford to. We haven't even finished paying off the funeral and you're—"

"Is this how you talk to your mother? I've just buried my husband but you want to kill me too—"

"*Mum!*" Faith threw her hands in the air, exasperated. The twins paused their mild bickering for a moment to look up, eyes darting between their mother and grandmother. Celeste snorted and turned her back to her eldest daughter, pushing past Glory toward the kitchen. Faith followed her.

"Your father had life insurance through his work, when that comes through that will help."

"That's meant to pay off the *mortgage*, Mummy, to take the pressure off of *you*. It's not meant to be distributed to every family member who comes begging. They're taking advantage!"

Celeste held up a hand, an attempt to silence Faith that went ignored.

"We really need to sit down and look at the finances, I don't want you to lose this house on top of everything else.

You might need to get a lodger to help with cash flow around here. Especially if you're going to take more time off work—"

"Lodger, kọ́?" Celeste snorted again. "So that a stranger will kill me in my bed?! I've watched that show on Sky—what's it called?" Celeste clicked her fingers in the air trying to recall whatever true crime series she had seen last, but gave up.

"Anyways, Olọ́run má jẹ ẹ́—God forbid!"

Faith sighed, admitting defeat in this instance, and left the kitchen.

"Where do you want the death certificate?" she called behind her, but when there was no response, Faith tossed the envelope onto the coffee table and slumped into an armchair.

"I'll put it in Daddy's folder," Glory offered. She picked up the envelope and headed up the stairs taking them in a leap, two at a time.

To her right she could hear the bed creaking in the room she and Faith shared until Faith left for university. Further down was the family bathroom and across from that Victor's small bedroom. To her left was the largest bedroom, where her parents had slept side by side for nearly three decades. It looked out into the street, so as a teenager any thought of sneaking out and back in at night, the way her peers boasted about, was ridiculous.

From their bedroom her parents could hear everything happening in the living room directly below, from whispered quarrels between the siblings to the theme tune of forbidden TV shows. When they were smaller their mother would tell them that even when she wasn't watching them, God never stopped, and he fed her information when she prayed. When Glory reached secondary school she realized that her mother's omniscience had more to do with the thin floors of their 1970s home, but the feeling of being watched never quite left her, especially when she was out in and around Peckham, where anyone in a sprawling network of family friends and church members could gather intel.

When she had lived at home, the most common reason for Glory to visit her parents' bedroom was to be disciplined. Outside of that there was rarely any other need to cross the threshold between her life as a child and the mystery of her parents' interior lives. At her most curious, she would press an ear against the closed door to listen in on muffled arguments and tense discussions before whatever verdict Daddy had come to, and her mother eventually agreed with, was delivered to the children like a commandment carved in stone.

As she pushed open the bedroom door now, she marveled at how hard it was to shake these associations, even as a woman in her twenties. She half expected to find her mother sitting on the bed with a stern expression and a Bible open on her lap, ready to rebuke the middle daughter who gave her so much trouble. But the bed was empty and unmade, the air was stale, and the heavy curtains were drawn tightly. They looked like they hadn't been opened in weeks.

Glory switched on the light and an offensive yellow filled the room from the bare bulb in the center. The side of the bed on which Glory's father had slept was piled with clothes in the vague shape of a body. Most available surfaces were covered in books, or tattered copies of Nigerian society magazines, and plastic bags—lots of plastic bags filled with rubbish, and other mysterious things that contributed to the fermented smell in the room.

The only surface that remained unadorned by junk was

Glory's father's desk. It was pressed against a wall but its size made it impossible to ignore. It was the kind of desk that belonged in a drawing room. Whenever she saw her father sit at it to write, he'd roll back the cylinder cover and unfold the desk to reveal a writing table of dark, polished wood.

"It's an antique bureau," he would tell Glory when she asked about its strangeness, and he took great pride in it. No one else was allowed to touch it, not even their mother. Glory's hand hovered now as she kneeled before the drawers, waiting for a disembodied voice to rebuke her. She knew that Daddy kept an official record of their lives in a folder, somewhere, everything from her parents' certificates of naturalization to exam results and school reports. But she had never actually seen where he kept it. She took a deep breath and opened the top right drawer. It contained letters, pens, and loose paper clips, and her heart fluttered at seeing her father's handwriting scrawled across an old envelope. She quickly pushed the drawer shut.

The following two drawers were fruitless, containing documents to do with his work and a collection of newspaper clippings. It was the second drawer down on the other side that contained the old accordion file, bent and bulging. Glory released the latch and it sprang open. Each compartment was meticulously labeled, but there was no label for death certificates. She took her father's certificate out of the envelope and held it gently in her hand. She didn't want to cry again, but she felt she needed to do something. A prayer, perhaps? Or a final word to her father's spirit as it waited above her, making sure she didn't mishandle this, his precious desk?

Glory sighed and sat back on her heels, reading the certificate's declaration. It was strange to think that the official record of a person's whole life was confined to a single sheet of paper. The rich details of existence compressed into a few boxes detailing name, date of birth, place of death and other arbitrary notes.

She opened the file again and found the compartment that contained their birth certificates. She passed over Faith's and Victor's, and picked up her own. There was a sheet of paper clipped to the back of her certificate and when she pulled it away she felt something cold land in the pit of her stomach. Of course, it was her other sister's birth certificate—or at least a photocopy of it. Her name, "Hope Kẹ́hìndé Akíndélé," leaped from the page.

Hope must have had other names—Glory had at least three more than the two that were recorded on her birth certificate—but now they were lost to time. Maybe her mother remembered them, or maybe they had been swallowed by the silence that surrounded her twin sister's death.

Glory filed away the documents with a catch in her throat, closing the lid on the quiet order of her father's desk and returning her attention to the chaos around her. It was beyond her how her mother could live among all of this, and the lump in her throat was replaced with mild disgust. She hurriedly left her parents' bedroom, almost colliding with Auntie Búkì at the top of the stairs.

"Good morning, Auntie," Glory said solemnly.

"Good morning, my dear," Auntie Búkì said warmly. "How are you?"

Auntie Búkì folded her hands, resting them on the soft round hump of her stomach, waiting for Glory's answer.

"I'm OK, Auntie," Glory said, trying to smile.

"Pẹ̀lẹ́, my dear," the older woman said, patting Glory. "I wanted to ask you, when are you going back to Texas?"

Glory swallowed hard.

"I was in Los Angeles, Auntie, and I'm not sure yet."

"Mmm," Auntie Búkì said with a thoughtful nod. Glory

recognized this listening look, and knew that some piece of unsolicited advice was sure to follow.

"You know, your mum only has you now," Auntie Búkì continued, lowering her chin with a meaningful look in her eye.

"What do you mean?" Glory asked innocently, although she could work out the direction this conversation was going in.

Auntie Búkì cleared her throat and looked up to the ceiling. She exhaled through her nostrils, pressing her lips together. Glory thought she could see water collecting in her mother's friend's eyes, but Auntie Búkì quickly blinked and when she met Glory's gaze again, her eyes were clear.

"You know, the Bible says that children are a heritage from the Lord, and your mother has tried so much with all of you. She has sacrificed so much, she is strong, but she needs you, ehn? With your brother and your sister gone, and Faith has her own family now, she only has you. You must honor her—*Honor your father and mother so that it may go well with you*—that's what the Bible says, ehn?"

Glory nodded, trapped by the expectation of Auntie Búkì's words.

"It's what your father would have wanted," Auntie Búkì said, suspecting the Bible verses had not been enough. The older woman smiled kindly, and moved past Glory to make her way down the stairs.

Glory closed her eyes. She could feel the walls closing in around her, and if she opened them she might find herself buried under piles of rubbish and all her mother's broken things.

She drew in deep breaths and willed her legs to move. She took one shaky step forward and then another, before skidding down the stairs and straight out of the front door, into the evening air.

Glory could hear Faith calling her name from inside the house, but she needed distance. There was too much death, too much misfortune. Faith stood at the front door calling down into the street, but Glory carried on walking away.

6

"How often do you get them, the panic attacks?"

"Don't know."

"You should probably go see a therapist or something."

It was the morning after and Faith and Glory were at the supermarket. When Glory had finally returned to the house, her face damp with perspiration and her breath ragged although she hadn't run, she had expected a wall of questions and concern. But their mother and Auntie Búkì had been oblivious and Faith had looked Glory over, but said nothing.

"Did you hear me? I said—"

"I know. I was seeing one before. In LA."

"Oh." Faith frowned slightly before adding, "So you'll do it then?"

"When I can afford to."

"If you ever need to borrow money—"

"Do you remember anything about Hope's funeral?"

Faith looked up from the multipack of children's yogurt she was studying.

"Why are you asking me that?"

"I was too young to remember it and I've just never

heard you or Mummy or Daddy ever talk about it. I guess with Daddy's funeral it just made me think what happened at hers?"

Faith took control of the trolley, scooping up Elijah and balancing him on her hip. She marched ahead and Glory found herself skipping alongside like a child.

"I've never seen any pictures or anything, I don't even know where she's—"

"Can you grab some crackers from that shelf?"

Glory handed Faith the box. "But don't you think it's weird, Faith? No one ever talks about it."

Faith had stopped walking and was scrolling through the shopping list on her phone, mumbling to herself as she ticked things off of her list. She shifted Elijah from one hip to another.

"That's not something you talk about, you know how our culture is. In Nigeria, if a child dies, they don't even allow the parents to attend the funeral."

"So did Mummy and Daddy just not go then?"

"Glory, you know how half of our family still thinks you finished uni? If our parents can't bear to admit that one of their children is not a *graduate*, do you really think they're going to start having heart-to-hearts about their absent daughter?"

She did have a point.

"Anyway, dwelling on the past isn't helpful. When I want to talk about Mummy, you don't want to know, but you're here asking me questions about something that happened twenty years ago?"

"Faith—"

"I'm not interested, Glory! Talk about it with your therapist!"

Faith pushed off ahead and Glory spent the rest of the trip trailing her sister around the supermarket.

When they reached home, Glory unloaded the car, put the shopping away and retreated to the guest room without saying another word. She slammed the door behind her then pressed her face into the pillow, replaying the conversation from the supermarket over and over in her head until her phone chimed and she took it out of her pocket.

It was an Instagram notification: *bossman_j started following you.* The profile was private, but in a few seconds a flurry of further notifications popped up. bossman_j was working his way through her feed, liking pictures from months and months ago. Glory squinted at the tiny circle that made up the user's avatar but couldn't make out a face, just the top of a tattooed shoulder. Intrigued, she sent through a follow request. It was immediately accepted, followed by a private message:

"*Thought I'd have to like all your pics to get your attention.*"

The message ended with a winking emoji.

Glory clicked through to the user's feed. It was Julian.

On the night of the funeral she had been too busy dealing with snot and tears to really try and take him in, but in the gym selfies and carefully but casually posed shots with his friends, he cut a striking figure. He wasn't particularly tall but he was broad, with muscles rippling across his back and arms. His tattoos curled over his shoulders and down his back, intricate shapes etched on his rich, brown skin. Glory's stomach tingled at the attention he was giving her, but she played it cool.

"*Hey.*"

No emojis, no kisses.

"*How you doing this evening?*" he typed back.

"*I'm good,*" Glory lied, "*you?*"

"I'm cool, but I don't like chatting on Insta. You still got my card? Text me. :)"

Glory waited awhile, enjoying the mild thrill of him knowing that she had read his message but had not yet responded.

"Can't find it, but here's my number."

She typed in the digits and hit send.

A few minutes later a FaceTime call came through on her phone. She panicked, staring in horror at the screen displaying her own face at an unflattering angle before the call abruptly ended. A text then appeared:

"Accident. This is Julian, though. You cool?"

"You already asked me that," Glory replied, this time with her own winking emoji.

"My bad. Anyway, you looked like you were enjoying."

A jolt of panic shot through Glory at the possibility that the FaceTime call had somehow connected without her realizing.

"What do you mean?"

"Your pics on Insta."

Relief.

"Ohhh. Yeah. LA can be fun."

"What was your favorite part?"

What a question. Was it the isolating loneliness? Or perhaps it was the long hours, poor vacation time and relentless requirements of work?

"Don't know, too much to choose from. You'll like it though."

"Maybe one day you could show me around."

And so they continued. Julian politely asked after Glory's family and she did the same of his. They talked about his barbershop, and Glory imagined him lounging in one of his barbers' chairs, watching the weekend rush clear.

"*Can I call you?*" Julian asked after awhile. "*I've got an idea I want to run past you, but it's easier to talk over the phone.*"

Glory consented. Julian rang immediately.

"I'm thinking about opening a salon next door. What do you think?"

His voice was low, almost husky.

"That's a good idea. His and hers right next to each other. If you get some beauticians and nail techs in there too it can be like a one-stop shop for the glow up."

"I like how you're thinking. You could make a good business partner."

"Well, I do have a year and a bit of a business degree, but I'm not interested in all of that."

"So what are you interested in?"

This was better than the usual "So what do you do?" line of questioning, but still, Glory felt the pressure to impress. There were answers that she knew would make her sound exotic or intelligent, but then there was also the truth. She could always just try telling the truth.

"Food."

Julian chuckled.

"You like to eat?"

"I love to eat."

"Does that mean that you like to cook too?"

Glory could feel where this was going, but she hoped for Julian's sake that he would divert.

"Yeah . . ."

"So when are you going to cook for me then?"

With anyone else this would signal the point where her interest would begin to wane, but she didn't want to let this small misstep taint her impression of Julian. She was enjoying this too much to dismiss him so quickly. It reminded her of the early days of her LA life when she had felt almost delirious with the possibilities of each day. Each lingering look with a handsome stranger suggested the start of a whirlwind romance and she bounced into her workplace each morning imagining that she was the star of her own romantic comedy. At least that's how it had been before it all turned sour. Or maybe it had been sour from the beginning, but the flirtations and the parties had been enticing enough to keep her distracted.

"Wow, so you still don't know how to cook at your big age?" Glory teased.

"Nah, I know how to c—"

"It's OK, y'know. I can send you some YouTube videos and simple recipes. We'll start with boiling rice and move on to seasoning chicken."

"Nah, don't try it! I know how to cook," Julian insisted, rising to Glory's bait.

"OK, if you're sure." Glory acted the part of a concerned skeptic. "Big strong guy like you can't be living off chicken shop and Maccy Ds."

Julian's laugh was warm and deep. "You're funny. Anyway, what you doing tomorrow?"

"Not much. What are you doing?"

"I'll be at the shop. You should come by actually, it's not too far from your mum's house. I could give you a tour."

"You think you're slick, innit?" Glory said, unable to stop smirking.

"What do you mean?"

Maybe it was the way that Julian wore his desire so plainly, or perhaps it was just the feeling of having nothing to lose, but Glory felt bold.

"First you followed me on Instagram, then you told me to text you, then you asked if you could call me and now you're telling me to come to your barbershop."

Julian didn't say anything.

"If you wanted to see me again, you could've just asked me when you first messaged me on Insta."

"Wouldn't have been as convincing though, would it?"

And of course, he was right.

"Well, what time shall I come by tomorrow?"

"Anytime. I'll be there all day."

"I'll let you know when I'm on my way."

The house was dark and quiet when Glory emerged from the guest room flushed with the excitement of something new. She crept downstairs to get a snack and passed the living room where Faith and Michael were on the sofa wrapped in the blue light of the TV screen.

"What you watching?"

"Some spy thriller thing—you wanna join us?"

Glory would usually feel like a third wheel, but in her current mood she felt charitable enough to join them.

While a car chase flashed across the screen, Glory watched Faith and Michael out of the corner of her eye. Taken in isolation, this scene suggested the perfection everyone else seemed to see in the young couple. But Michael's recent absences weren't Glory's only problem, the real issue was everything that came before. In the end he had "done right" by Faith with the groveling proposal, and the lavish wedding made everyone else forgive and forget, but Glory could do neither.

She stood up from the sofa. The descent of unpleasant memories made it impossible to sit for a second longer. Faith and Michael turned in unison to look at her.

"You OK?" Faith asked.

"I'm going to bed. Got plans for tomorrow."

"OK," Faith hummed. She settled back against Michael, who pulled his wife into him, as if it was the most natural thing in the world.

7

Peckham had changed, or at least it was in the process of changing. There was still the swell of churchgoers on the high street on this brisk Sunday afternoon. Members of the Cherubim and Seraphim Church bundled their billowing white garments beneath winter coats, while the brightly patterned outfits of other African Pentecostals fought the dull hues of British winter.

But if you left the station from a different exit, you found yourself in another world. Blunt-bobbed women smoked cigarettes at tables set out on the pavement, the whir of coffee grinders accompanied straight-faced baristas sorting different types of nut milk, and bleary-eyed art students in worn denim told tales of the night before.

The join between Old Peckham and New was abrupt and awkward. It was like crossing from one planet to the next as the elongated vowels of easy brunch conversation switched to the jubilation of afternoon church services, wafting out of windows left open to accommodate poorly ventilated buildings. Women tightly bound against the cold stood outside hair and beauty shops, promoting their services.

"Darlin', you want to do your hair?" one woman called to Glory as she passed.

Glory declined and kept walking, self-consciously fluffing her twist-out into shape. She had spent most of the morning constructing a suitable outfit from the remnants of her wardrobe, which actually worked in her favor because she didn't want to look like she was trying too hard. She hadn't told Julian that she was making the journey from Bromley to see him, so she needed to look as if she truly had "just swung by."

She passed the butchers and fresh produce shops, the shouts and smells as familiar as the soundtrack to her favorite film. She walked past the corner where Woolworths used to be, past the JD where the object of her teenage infatuation had worked every summer, and ducked past the shops selling fabric and jewelry, where friends of her mother might be shopping or selling, always ready to ask after Celeste even if they had seen her only yesterday.

Glory left the throng of the high street and wove her way through the quiet back roads. Thankfully Julian's shop wasn't one of the more conspicuous barbershops on Rye Lane or Peckham High Street because, even as a grown woman, Glory didn't want stories of her "talking to a boy on the street" to find a way back to her mother. But she did have to walk past two other barbershops before she made it to Pharaoh's Barbershop and Grooming (Fit For A King).

The signage was black with an assortment of hieroglyphics either side of the gold lettering. The inside was black and chrome, with a mural at the back showing a pharaoh being attended to by a harem of beautiful women. The shop was empty except for two barbers. One was attending to a client; the other sat in his chair spinning around and around, half watching a flat screen TV showing sports highlights. All three looked up at Glory as she entered.

"Hi, is Julian around?"

"*Julian?*" the idle barber asked. "You mean, Jay?"

Glory nodded, her face hot.

"Ay, bossman!" he hollered from his seat, angling his head toward the back of the shop. "You've got a pretty lady out front!"

Then to Glory he added, "Take a seat, princess, he'll be out in a bit."

Glory sat on the pleather sofa. In front of her was a low glass coffee table scattered with men's magazines. Her seat was slightly cracked, a sign of regular use, but everything else about the shop was polished and gleaming. Against the wall where the mural was there were two glass cabinets with grooming products, natural beard oils and hand-blended pomades. This was a far cry from the barbershops she had been forced to take Victor to when he wasn't old enough to go by himself. They were loud and smelled of disinfecting alcohol, sheen spray and the musk of old men in summer. Glory was impressed.

The idle barber continued to spin, but every time the seat swung back around his eyes landed on Glory. She shifted in her place and turned her full attention to her smartphone.

"I like these girls with their natural hair now," the barber said to no one in particular. Glory smiled tightly, her eyes briefly glancing up at him. "Yeah, man, it's good. None of this relaxer, weave an' wig business—queens don't need no artificial crown." He enunciated the word "artificial," seeming very pleased with his little quip.

Glory carried on scrolling blankly.

"You don't need none ah dat, ya hear me? You got *good* hair you know, don't mash it up with that fake white woman business."

Glory cleared her throat, annoyed by the stranger's lecture.

She looked over to the other barber, who was deep in debate with his customer about football squad formations, and out onto the street where a group of children whizzed by on scooters and trainers with wheels set in the heel.

Eventually Julian emerged from a door labeled "office," phone in his hand as he ended a call.

"I shoulda known suttin' was up when man turned up to the shop looking all smart an' that!" Idle Barber leaped from his seat, pointing his finger in Julian's direction with a knowing smile. Julian was wearing a slim-cut fine-knit jumper that clung to him. His long silver chain and earrings gleamed. He looked good.

"I thought man was coming from church, ya nuh?!" Idle Barber turned to look at the other barber, while Julian beckoned Glory to leave with him.

"Wait—you not going to introduce your friend, nah?"

"If you had any manners you would have introduced yourself," Julian said coolly over his shoulder as he held the door open for Glory. The door shut on the laughs of the men in the shop, as Idle Barber swore to himself and landed back in the chair.

"Sorry about that."

"It's all right," Glory said. "He was telling me how much he liked my hair."

"He was?" Julian didn't seem to like the sound of that.

"Yeah, he said queens don't need an artificial crown."

"Well, he's right about that one." Julian smiled.

"So you agree I'm a queen?" Glory asked, but Julian just laughed and dodged her question with one of his own.

"Where did you want to go?" He stopped and surveyed the residential street they had strolled onto.

"Well, I *did* come to look at your shop, innit, but you were so quick for us to leave."

"Do you really want to spend your afternoon with those clowns?" Julian said.

"Oh, I see. You want my undivided attention."

Julian looked at her like he was trying to work her out, a smile playing on his lips. Despite her banter Glory now felt self-conscious under the directness of his gaze. She bit the insides of her cheeks and looked away.

"The shop's really nice, though. How long you been open?" Glory continued walking and Julian followed her lead.

"About five months—still early days."

"Are you into all that Egyptology stuff as well?"

"Me? Not really, that's more my business partner."

Glory nodded, keeping a careful distance between them as they walked side by side.

"So where are you leading us to?" he asked.

"We could go to one of the new cafés. We could sit in and have a coffee."

"One of those white places?" Julian had stopped again.

"Yeah, you not feeling it?"

He screwed up his face and looked back toward the barbershop.

"What's wrong with white people?" Glory was amused at his reluctance.

"We're gonna sit down, be minding our own business, and I swear someone's gonna come up to me asking if I've got any weed."

A burst of laughter escaped Glory's lips.

"I'm being serious, man," Julian said in earnest, but with a smile. "Couple months ago I was parked up and I saw my friend walking past, we were just talking through the window and some white man interrupted our conversation to ask if I was selling."

Glory was laughing properly now, any self-consciousness forgotten.

"And it wasn't like a nitty, either! Man looked like a teacher or something, even had a little scarf on, everything, he could have been an undercover fed." Julian pulled himself tall, pretending to ask for cannabis in his approximation of a posh accent.

Glory was still laughing, dabbing at the corner of her eyes.

"Don't worry, no one will ask you for drugs while I'm around." Glory's eyes twinkled at Julian with mischief. "Plus drug dealers don't go for lattes on a Sunday afternoon, do they?"

"Wouldn't know, would I?" Julian smirked.

"And it's cold out here, can't have you freezing to death in your church jumper."

Glory let her fingers pluck at the fabric on Julian's arm and he fell into step next to her, their bodies closer than before. She led them to a café that had sprouted up on the ground floor of a previously disused building. Julian held the door open and allowed her to enter the dimly lit shop before him. The furniture was typically mismatched, reclaimed wood and repurposed secondhand pieces. The dark green walls pulled everything closer together, and Glory's eyes moved over the low sofas hosting a handful of customers and their laptops to the servers moving in mechanical motion, banging jugs of steamed milk against the countertop.

Glory squinted to read the menu chalked up on the back wall and Julian waited behind her, as if waiting for direction. She let out a low whistle at the price of a bagel—"*Eight English pounds?!*" as her father would remark—and ordered a peppermint tea.

"What d'ya want?" Glory asked Julian who was still hovering behind her.

"Erm, I'll have a Coke or something."

"We've got organic root cola?" said the woman behind the till.

"Yeah, one of those." Julian took out a roll of notes from his back pocket.

"It's on me," Glory said, waving away his money. "I'm the one that dragged you here."

But he brushed her to the side with one sweep of his arm and Glory didn't protest.

Julian allowed Glory to lead them to a corner table. He squeezed into the chair across from her. At first he sat tall then he changed position, leaning back into the chair and stretching one leg out. Glory sat properly, carefully arranging her coat on the back of the chair and stirring her tea. Julian poured his root cola, took a deep sip and held the glass up to examine it, frowning.

"Is it nice?"

Julian licked his lips. "It tastes like them sweets, like Black Jacks."

Glory thought how strange it was that she was sitting across from him. They had grown up in proximity of each other, but not really together. Julian was older than her so, once they had outgrown children's parties, she would only glimpse him in throngs of teenage boys. Then he might acknowledge her with a curt nod or flicker of recognition, but they had never been close, so there was nothing really to catch up on.

"So, what made you decide to open a barbershop?"

Julian began to explain, but Glory wasn't really listening. She was watching how his large hands moved as he spoke, how he almost but not quite met her gaze as he told his origin story to the window to her left, his eyes briefly grazing hers before they looked away again. It was so different to the frank stare of American men. They would always hold her gaze, every conversation feeling like an audition, especially in a city where beauty and charm came to compete and make their fortune.

". . . but anyway, how are you doing after the funeral and that?"

Glory set down her cup and exhaled. Julian looked directly at her now, his face open and unassuming. She remembered his kind presence next to her as she sobbed and heaved in the dark just a few days before, and she felt heat rise in her face as her eyes began to water again. She blinked furiously and looked away.

"Sorry, man, we don't need to talk about it, I just want to know you're all right."

Julian pushed a napkin across the table and Glory took it, lowered her eyes and released a little laugh.

"I'm not gonna lie, this is so awkward," she said as she wiped her eyes. "I can't remember the last time we spoke but I'm here crying for the second time."

Julian didn't say anything, he just watched her, before looking down at the table and clearing his throat.

"If you're embarrassed about crying, don't be," he finally said. "But just so you know, I'm shit at small talk." His tone was serious and Glory appreciated the fact that he was so forthright. She felt herself lower her guard as she pressed the napkin into a tight ball in her hand.

"I used to be too, but then working in LA I just learned how to waffle. *Hey sweetie, how are you? What have you been up to? Do you want a coffee? I'm just about to grab one!*" Glory's exaggerated Valley girl accent amused Julian. "I think I've forgotten how to have a real conversation."

"I'll allow you for now, can't have you crying in here and people thinking we're having domestics." Julian looked around the shop in mock suspicion, making Glory smile.

"So, Glory, what were you doing when you were working out in LA?" He clasped his hands together and set them on the table as if he was conducting an interview.

"Well, I *was* working in a digital agency, mainly on the collaboration side, working with influencers on specific campaigns and activations." The spiel still came easily, and Julian looked mildly impressed.

"So you could give me advice on social media stuff for my shop? I'd pay you of course."

Glory hesitated. "I mean, I could in theory, but I don't want to do that any more."

"Why?"

"I'm over it, to be honest—I dunno." Her voice sounded as uncertain as she felt.

"So what are you gonna do when you go back?"

"I'm not going back."

"For real?"

Glory nodded and took another sip of her tea to avoid Julian's attentive eyes.

"You didn't like it or what?"

"Erm . . . I . . . nah," Glory confessed. "I actually didn't."

Julian's eyes widened.

"Don't look at me like that," she said with an uneasy laugh, turning to hide her face with a hand. "LA just wasn't me, y'know? I tried, and it all looked good from the outside, but, well, I was just struggling."

Saying it out loud released something inside her.

"Boy," Julian exhaled, "it didn't look like you were struggling."

"I work in social media, I know how to make things look good." Glory let her eyes linger on his face for a second before looking into her cup. "I started getting panic attacks, had to see a therapist and everything."

"Sorry, man. That sounds mad."

"Don't get me wrong, when I first got there it was great. It's just like how it looks on TV, y'know? All wide open spaces, the sun is always shining, palm trees lining the road—"

"We have palm trees in Peckham too!" Julian said with a grin.

"*Proper* palm trees—not those stubby little things near the bus station!" Glory playfully threw a sidelong glance in Julian's direction before she continued. "It felt like a dream, like I'd done it. I'd made something of myself after dropping out of uni and disappointing my parents. I wasn't married like Faith, but I'd done what they did, just picked up and gone to another country and made it work."

Julian couldn't help but look impressed as he nodded along to Glory's words and she let herself remain in that moment with him, in the version of her LA life that lived on social media and in reports back home to her family.

"Then it stopped working," she said abruptly.

"What happened?"

Glory hummed, hesitant to pour her heart out any further on their first date—if this could even count as a date.

"When you're partying and around people all the time, it's easy to believe that you're not lonely. You think you can't be, you shouldn't be, but I didn't have any real friends, just housemates and colleagues. I dated a few people but the whole dating thing is just weird over there. I couldn't get with it. Then there was all this work drama—I just wasn't in a good place."

"What work drama?"

"Boring politics—it doesn't matter. But after Faith called me about my dad, the first thing I did was email my manager and resign. I didn't think twice—obviously, I was upset and everything but there was this little part of me that felt relieved I could finally leave."

"Woah, it was like that, yeah?"

"Honestly? I wanted to leave ages ago. I just needed a reason that didn't feel like—like I'd failed or something. The worst thing is, the person that I stayed for, the one who I cared what he thought the most was my dad."

Glory bit her tongue, knowing she could go on and on. All the thoughts that she had held in her head were now competing to be spoken and made real.

Julian nodded awkwardly and swirled the ice around his glass before he finished the last of his root cola.

"Did you . . . date a lot?"

Glory didn't answer immediately, sizing him up from across the table.

"I mean, I can't believe anyone would go on a date with you and just let you go."

"Everyone's stunning in LA. The best thing about me was my accent."

"I doubt that." Julian looked away, his tongue rolling over his bottom lip. "I think you're underselling yourself."

"You sound like my therapist."

"Really? Should I be charging you for this?"

"I don't have any money."

"An IOU is fine, or you could do something for me in exchange—nah, nah, nothing like that!" Julian's hands shot up in defense as Glory's expression changed. "I mean, you could apprentice at my shop if you're looking for a change of careers."

Glory snorted.

"I don't think many men would trust a woman in a barbershop."

"You know what? I've always said that a female barber would make a lot of money—if she's good of course—men

64

would be lining up to get their trim from a pretty woman, all that close proximity, the feminine touch, it would be a big USP."

"You're a proper entrepreneur, innit? Always thinking about business."

Julian looked pleased with himself. Glory really liked his smile and, as his body language began to open up, hers did in return. They ordered more drinks and talked until the sky began to darken.

When they eventually left the café, Julian hunched his shoulders against the chill and Glory graciously offered him her coat. When he declined she linked an arm through his, rubbing a hand up and down his sleeve. Despite the cold his body felt hot through the jumper and Glory found herself leaning into him, imagining how warm she would feel if he wrapped his arms around her.

"I enjoyed our small talk," he said.

"Yeah, it was a nice distraction from everything."

"Let me distract you again, but next time we go out to eat."

"Can't say no to a free dinner."

"Who said I'm paying?" Julian stopped and Glory looked at him before he broke into a cheeky grin. "OK, it'll be your *welcome back to London* meal."

Glory could feel her phone buzzing in her pocket. She stopped and took the call.

"Where are you?"

It was Faith.

"I'm . . . just out and about, why?"

"How close are you to Peckham? Can you get to the house?"

"What's wrong?" Glory felt a wave of nausea overtake her.

"Mummy's having some kind of breakdown, I don't know,

I've been trying to call you, I'm on my way but I don't know how quickly I can get there," Faith said in a breathless ramble.

"I'm around the corner in Peckham, I'll go now."

"Oh, thank God!" Her sister sounded like she was about to cry.

When Glory ended the call, worry twisted its way across her face.

"What happened?" Julian asked her.

"I need to go to my mum's, something's wrong."

"You want me to come with you?"

"No—thank you, though—I just really need to go."

"Send me a text later to let me know you're all right though, yeah?"

Glory nodded and squeezed his arm before walking off quickly in the direction of her mother's house.

8

Auntie Búkì opened the door before Glory had finished knocking, a panicked look in her eyes and the cordless phone in her hand.

"What happ—?" Glory's question was cut short by the sight of her mother babbling in incomprehensible Yorùbá from her place on the floor. She was rocking back and forth and cradling her own arm. Glory could see red seeping from a deep gash. The glass coffee table was shattered and tipped on its end.

"Have you called an ambulance?" Glory asked Auntie Búkì, crouching next to her mother but scared to touch her.

"No!" Celeste barked, breaking from her murmurings.

"She won't let me," Auntie Búkì said helplessly, waving the phone in her hand.

"Auntie Búkì, call the ambulance!" Glory said, trying not to sound as hysterical as she felt. "Mummy, lift your arm above your head, we need to slow down the bleeding."

As Auntie Búkì began dialing, Celeste shouted again, trying to pull herself up from the floor as if she was going to take the phone from the trembling woman's hands. But when she put a palm down to steady herself, a shard of glass pierced her and she yelped.

"Mummy, stay still! Put your arm above your head!" Glory gently tried to take her mother's arm and guide it into an elevated position but Celeste snatched her arm away and continued with her rocking.

Auntie Búkì had stopped dialing the number and now looked at her friend, fear and pity in her eyes.

"What happened?" Glory asked.

"Th-the phone rang—I was upstairs and I heard the phone ring, and I don't know who it was but then I heard a crash and I came downstairs and she was like this!"

Glory could make out snatches of pleading English among Celeste's Yorùbá—"My God, my God, why have you forsaken me?"—and as the stain on her mother's boubou turned from a shocking red to almost black, Glory felt weak.

She took out her phone and called Faith.

"Have you called an ambulance yet?" Faith asked, her voice echoing through her car's Bluetooth.

"She keeps shouting at us if we try," Glory said pathetically.

"Well, is it bad? What happened?"

"I don't know, Faith! She won't let me touch her, she just keeps saying stuff—Auntie Búkì said she got a call before it happened."

"Check her phone and see who called then!" Faith's voice was reaching higher and higher in pitch and Glory prayed her sister would be able to make it to the house in one piece.

"It was the house phone, Faith!"

"Well, check the number or call them back or something!"

Glory took the phone from her ear and turned to her mother.

"Mummy, you need to tell us what happened. We need to understand what's going on," Glory said in a low, steady tone. Celeste snapped out of her trance for a moment and simply said, "Victor!" Then to Glory's horror, her mother began to cry.

68

"Something's happened to Victor!" Glory relayed to her sister and she heard Faith swear under her breath.

"I'm nearly at the house, but I'll call you back."

A knot of dread formed in Glory's stomach, threatening to push itself up into her chest and induce a panic attack, but this was not the time to panic. Glory stood up slowly and went to the kitchen, opening cupboards and drawers until she found clean tea towels. She ran the kitchen tap and filled a mixing bowl with warm water, soaking the tea towels and carrying the bowl back through to the living room.

This time she didn't ask. She wrung out a towel and pried her mother's arm away, carefully cleaning the area around the wound and then winding two more damp towels around Celeste's forearm. Glory's actions snapped Auntie Búkì to attention, and she rushed to replace the bloody water with a fresh bowl, then went upstairs to get a change of clothes for her friend.

They carefully helped Celeste out of the bloodied house dress. Her mother's skin felt papery and delicate as Glory supported her weight, noting her stooped shoulders and the fine web of stretch marks and scars that covered her mother's stomach. This body that had held and birthed four children, that had once felt as solid as an oak tree, that Glory would throw herself against when upset, would burrow into looking for comfort, now felt like a hollowed out husk.

When Faith arrived, Celeste was lying on the sofa, her arm propped up by cushions. Her mutterings were replaced with a distant stare. Auntie Búkì had set the coffee table to the side and was sweeping up broken glass.

"How is she?" Faith asked briskly as she led Esther and Elijah into the house.

"She's OK," Glory said, looking at her niece and nephew with apprehension. "You brought the kids?"

"Yeah? Where was I supposed to leave them?" Faith said, defensive.

"Er—with Michael? If you had come earlier there was broken glass and blood everywhere!"

"Michael isn't at home."

"On a Sunday?"

"Well, you've done a good job clearing up here," Faith said, before adding in a lowered voice: "Do we still need to call an ambulance?"

For all her appearance of being zoned out, Celeste sat up when she heard the word ambulance.

"No one should call an ambulance!"

"Mummy, you need stitches at the very least," Glory said, the pleading voice she had been using turning more impatient.

"Celeste, she is right," Auntie Búkì added, performing one last sweep of the space where the coffee table used to be.

"Then Faith can drive me to the hospital," Celeste said with resignation, turning away from her daughters.

"What's that?" Esther asked, pointing a tiny finger at the deep crimson patch on the carpet pile.

"Ah!" Auntie Búkì exclaimed. She hurried to the kitchen returning with a damp tea towel, laying it carefully over the incriminating spot. *Nothing would shift that stain*, Glory thought, *and there would be a patch of brown carpet that would mark this day, this new family low, for as long as that carpet remained.*

"Let's go to hospital," Faith said, sounding too upbeat.

"Do you want to leave the children with me?" Auntie Búkì asked, looking warily at the fidgeting toddlers hanging on to their mother's legs.

Faith looked around the living room, properly taking in the scene for the first time.

"Erm, no, it's OK. Glory will be with me, she can help me manage them."

"In that case, I will finish cleaning."

"Are you ready to go, Mummy?" Faith gently asked.

"I must use the toilet first," Celeste said, shifting to get up from the sofa. Faith bent to assist, but was shrugged off by her mother.

"I am not an invalid!"

Faith watched her mother carefully climb the stairs, clenching and unclenching her fists as if she were coaching herself to stay put and not rush to her mother's aid. When Celeste reached the landing and began shuffling toward the bathroom, Faith exhaled and turned back to Glory.

"Victor is in the hospital wing."

"What?! Why?!"

"He got into a fight. He's been there since Saturday night. They should have called *me*, not Mummy. *I'm* on his file as next of kin!"

"Is he OK?"

"Well, he's alive," Faith said with a mean laugh.

"Don't say that, Faith," Glory said, feeling nauseous again.

"It's true though! What was it that Daddy always used to say? *In all things we give thanks.*"

9

In the family room of Maudsley Hospital the walls were a sickly peach and the table in the center was sticky. They had been there for what felt like hours, but according to the white plastic clock it had only been ninety minutes. Only.

The chairs were uncomfortable and the armrests prevented them from lying down, which was all Glory wanted to do after spending three hours in A&E waiting for her mother to be stitched up, and another ninety minutes in a psychiatric hospital waiting for whatever else. Faith struggled to accommodate her dozing children, each toddler perched on one of her legs.

It had been a fight to get them in as the tough-faced security personnel tried to flex what little authority they had and insist that no children were allowed to visit.

"It's not a social visit, it's an emergency admission." Faith had battled on at the reception desk until finally they were permitted down the labyrinth of corridors, into the tiny lift and up to the floor that Celeste had been put on. Then they were corralled into the small room next to the nurses' station. Glory had been out to check how things were progressing but she was promptly marshaled back inside the room with a sigh and sharp look from one of the nurses.

A selfish thought snaked through her mind: *this would have been easier to bear if she was eight hours behind in Los Angeles.* She was angry at how helpless she felt watching her oldest sister doze off with her children, knowing Celeste was just a few feet away but completely out of her reach, and with no firm knowledge of what exactly had happened to Victor or why he was in hospital. Her mother spent her time and money on so-called spiritual men in Nigeria because she thought there was something seriously wrong in her family. Taking everything into account, Glory was inclined to agree.

Faith's head fell forward. She whipped it back and opened her eyes.

"What's going on?" she asked, blinking hard.

"Still waiting. You can go home if you want, I'll wait until this is all sorted."

Faith shook her head.

"Can Michael come and take the kids at least?"

Faith closed her eyes.

"Not being funny, Faith, but Michael is always missing when you need him most."

"Now is not the time, Glory."

"It never is, but seriously, what's the point in getting married if you're living like a single mum? It's only natural to wonder what's such a big distraction for him."

Faith's eyes flew open and pinned Glory down with a hard stare.

"Who the hell do you think has been helping me through all this while you've been off doing whatever you like halfway across the world?"

Glory's ears burned and she opened her mouth to respond, but Faith ploughed on.

"Who was it that helped get Victor a lawyer? Who has been

73

listening to me go on and on about Victor and my selfish little sister who doesn't give a toss about anyone besides herself? You don't get to pass judgment on Michael, Glory, because where were *you*? You never came home once! For Christmas, for New Year, for birthdays, for Victor, for *nothing*! The twins wouldn't even know what you looked like if I hadn't shown them pictures of you nearly every damn day!"

Esther and Elijah began stirring on Faith's lap, fumbling themselves awake under the harsh fluorescent lights. A sharp rap sounded at the door, which opened wide enough to let a nurse slip her head in.

"I understand that this must be distressing for you, but it's late, and I don't want you disturbing my other patients."

Faith hushed her fussing children and settled them in to individual chairs. She then stood up and stretched.

"Michael's not perfect. And I wish he was home more and all of that, but at least he never put me in a mental hospital!" She pointed in the direction of the ward. "God rest his soul, but Daddy was not easy to live with, especially these last two years."

"How is this Daddy's fault when he's dead?"

Faith looked at Glory, weighing up what she was about to say next.

"Despite what you think, your father was not a saint."

She spoke evenly, but the look in her eyes as she held Glory's gaze felt menacing.

"But will you take me seriously, now? When I say that she needs someone in the house with her?"

Glory nodded, a lump in her throat constricting her vocal cords. Faith wasn't one to snap or break, and these new fraught edges on the two women Glory had always trusted to have everything together meant something had gone seri-ously wrong. But Glory hadn't been around to find out what.

Glory cleared her throat.

"I'm not going back to LA, Faith. I'll move back home."

Faith looked confused. "You're not?"

"No. I'm staying here."

Faith released a deep sigh, her face softening into a smile, before closing her eyes, folding her body forward, and resting a heavy head on her crossed arms.

10

"She's trying to poison me," Celeste said when Faith asked why she refused to drink from the cup of water that a nurse had brought.

"Mummy, if you keep talking like that, they won't let you out of here, they'll say you're having paranoid delusions."

Celeste sniffed, but pushed the water to the side.

"By the grace of God I will be discharged tomorrow, but if not remember to bring me more bottled water."

It was on the third day of her stay in hospital that Celeste had realized where she was. The first two days were spent in a confused stupor, the combination of sedation and emotional exhaustion clouding her understanding and slurring her words. Faith passed those two days wringing her hands and not sleeping, eaten alive by the fact that she had allowed her mother to be admitted to a mental hospital.

"It's not like we sent her away to live in a care home," Glory reasoned.

"She just shouldn't be in that place!"

Now that Celeste was alert, Faith visited daily, bringing toiletries and food their mother would actually eat, and she sat mute while Celeste channeled all her energy into being both mortally offended by the situation and stoically aloof from it.

With the nurses Celeste adopted the accent she used for answering unknown numbers, her version of a clipped, nasal British tone. She was determined to show them that she was sane, and this was all a terrible misunderstanding. There was one nurse, however, who she took a particular dislike to. This nurse was the only black woman on staff and Celeste's distrust of her was intense and acute, fueled by the certainty she was logging information, to pass on to unknown mutual acquaintances. If water was brought by this nurse she would refuse to drink it.

Celeste's six days in hospital were proving too long not only for her but also for the hospital's staff and Faith, who was fielding calls from concerned relatives when the phone at the house went unanswered.

Glory had nearly a week to move back into her mother's house, and although it wouldn't take more than a day, she procrastinated.

Once Auntie Búkì had packed her loads and left, Glory had the wild fantasy that she would clean the house from top to bottom so her mother could come back to order. Rather than begin with the more obvious areas that needed attending to, Glory's curiosity about her sister's funeral sent her looking for the family photo albums. She found three faux-leather tomes on a shelf, obscured by a pile of unopened letters but realized the 6 × 4 prints only chronicled events as far back as Victor's birth. The earliest photograph she could find was one of Celeste looking tired as she cradled newborn Victor, with a young Faith and even younger Glory by her side. Daddy stood over them looking protective and proud. Hope was not in that photograph.

She tried to piece together any scrap of information that could have leaked out over the years, but Glory was drawing blanks where she felt memories should have been. It was hard to conjure up scenes without photographic evidence to inspire them. Glory closed her eyes tight and tried to remember something, a place or a smell before Victor was born, but it was as if life hadn't existed before then.

Eventually something came to her: it was a nightdress that her mother used to wear, yellow with tiny flowers embroidered on it. She remembered her mother coming to collect her from somewhere, nursery it must have been, and she was wearing this nightdress under a brown coat. It felt like the middle of the day and Glory had been looking forward to something else, but her mother had come too early. She remembered being upset, she remembered her mother getting upset and, like an old celluloid reel, the memory cut out.

Glory stopped turning pages and put the volumes back where she had found them. She was going to turn her attention to the task at hand. But as she stood in the passageway, the clutter in the house felt even more oppressive, alive in itself as it feasted on the remains of the wild ambitions and boundless hope of a family of five—which should have been six—that lay broken under thin layers of dust.

Glory went back into the living room and lay down on the sofa. She was tired but wanted to avoid sleep and the dreams she had begun to have about her father each night. She dreamed of him sitting at a table, walking through a door, smiling and speaking to her but she couldn't remember what he was saying, where they were and she wasn't sure if these were obscure memories or nostalgic fiction. But the dreams felt so real that when she woke it took a moment for her to remember that she had been asleep and Daddy was still gone.

She couldn't sleep, she couldn't clean, but, remembering Faith's vertigo dream, Glory thought that perhaps her own dreams were a sign, a message for the present from the past. *What would Daddy do now?* she asked herself. For him, duty was the highest form of love and she was failing in one of her primary obligations: she should go and see her mother again. She checked the time and made the trip to Camberwell.

During the day, the hospital looked less intimidating. Without the ominous glow of street lamps, the building's stately pillars looked less like the entrance to a Victorian asylum and more like the military hospital the building had been at one point. The night Celeste had been admitted the foyer was deserted and the lights were dimmed, but today she was met by a bright and breezy receptionist who directed her to her mother's ward.

Glory waited for Celeste outside the nurses' station. The security door had to be released by a staff member each time someone passed. Through the small panes of rectangular glass, Glory could see dazed patients in dressing gowns shuffle up and down a row of chairs in front of a TV.

Celeste was draped in a cardigan, her head wrapped with a silk scarf. She was engaging two members of staff in a serious discussion. After a while she left and returned looking sullen, fastening her coat tight around her. A nurse released the door with a quiet whoosh.

"They are insisting I must go out," she said with a pout. "Is it raining? I told them it was raining, but they said it was just wet."

Glory's mother tugged the belt of her coat tighter and wound a large scarf around her neck. Her skin had taken on a paler hue and Glory agreed a walk outside would do her good. But she knew her mother's primary reservation would be bumping into someone down in Camberwell.

"Let's go to the park across the road, it will be quiet there."
Glory offered her mother an arm and Celeste took it, her
movements stiff and unrehearsed as they walked to the lift.

Outside, the air felt fresh despite the traffic cutting up and
down Denmark Hill. Her mother paused for a moment and
took a breath, filling her lungs before continuing her steady
pace at Glory's side.

"So, how are you doing, Mummy?"

"I'm OK," Celeste said. "I hope they discharge me soon,
this place is enough to make a sane person mad!"

Glory said nothing.

"There are some very sad people on that ward," Celeste
continued, making a clucking sound at the back of her throat.
"There's one young girl there, not much older than you or
Faith, and they've taken her children away from her. So sad.
She cries all night."

"What's wrong with her?"

"Wrong? They say she has bipolar something, but it is
that place that is making her mad!" Celeste jabbed her finger
violently in the air, as if the hospital was in front of them
instead of behind as they walked deeper into the park. As
Glory had hoped, the park was empty on this weekday afternoon, but the benches were damp so they kept walking.

"She's a very nice girl. I don't think she's Nigerian, but
she's very respectful. She calls me 'auntie' and every evening
she will come and ask me to pray for her and her children."

"That's nice. What did the doctors say about you, though?"

"What do you mean?"

"Do they know what happened? What caused you to—well,
y'know what happened at the house that day, after the call,"
Glory stuttered.

"Me? I'm fine. I will be even better when they discharge me."

Her mother held on to the word "discharge" like a charm.

"But it was quite serious. We were very worri—"

"Don't worry yourself," Celeste grunted.

Glory gave her mother's statement a moment to sit in the damp air before she tried one last time.

"Mummy, I don't want to upset you, especially as you're looking so much better than before, but they don't just section people for no reason. Maybe you're forgetting what happened that night, but you were very upset and you even hurt your arm when you fell. I was scared—and Faith was too."

Celeste stopped abruptly and Glory turned toward her. Her expression was stern but not angry, and she punctuated each word with her forefinger and thumb pinched together, as if she was plucking them from the air.

"Let me tell you something, Glory. I was not sectioned. Nobody signed a Section 3 paper in my name—I know what I am talking about, ehn? I work in a care home, I know about these things. I went to the hospital *voluntarily*, I can leave whenever I want, but I am listening to the doctors and will leave when discharged so as not to cause problems. I am not mad, and God forgive you for talking to your own mother as if she was."

"Sorry," Glory said quietly.

When she was satisfied that her words had sunk in, Celeste took Glory's arm once more, her hand resting in the crook of her daughter's elbow, and continued forward.

"It is even good that I am there, not for my own sake, but for some of the others on the ward. There is one old English lady called Vera, we have good conversations. The nurses say that they hadn't heard her say more than a sentence before I came. These people are sad, but they are not crazy. They just need company, they need someone to talk to. It is like the old people in my care home, they just need companionship.

This country kills its old people with loneliness." Celeste clucked dismissively and Glory mumbled her assent.

"Anyway, my dear . . ." Celeste lightly tapped Glory's arm. "Faith tells me that you're not going back to America."

"No, I decided to stay."

"Oh, why? I thought you were enjoying California."

"I was, but I want to come back. Back home."

"Home" felt heavy, weighed down by so much expectation.

"So what will you do now?"

"Honestly, Mummy, I don't know. So much has happened, I have a lot of questions, there's a lot to process, y'know?"

"What questions?"

Nothing helpful, Glory thought, but that was Faith's voice stuck in her head. She hoped Faith was wrong, and her mother would take kindly to Glory's questions about her other sister. But, as fine as Celeste seemed, things still felt precarious. Now was not the time.

But she did not remember when last she had spoken alone with her mother. With the path looping them through Ruskin Park and back, and an open ended afternoon ahead of them, Glory allowed herself to relax under her mother's touch, letting the steady rhythm of their footsteps soothe her.

"I don't know what I'm doing right now, Mummy. I want to be here, back in London, but I don't know what my purpose is right now. When I consider all my options I just think, *What's the point? Where am I going?*"

Celeste nodded knowingly, as though she had sensed this quiet turmoil all along. Glory braced herself for suggestions of returning to university or considering something safe and predictable like nursing.

"Purpose," her mother said with a chuckle. "You know I pray for you every day."

Of course Glory knew.

"But you know what my number one prayer has always been? For wisdom for you. *If any of you lack wisdom, let him ask of God, that giveth to all men liberally.* Do you know where that is from?"

"The Bible?"

"Of course it is from the Bible!" Celeste scoffed. "Where else would it be from? But do you know *where* in the Bible?"

"Proverbs?" Glory asked after a pause.

Celeste kissed her teeth and continued, brushing aside Glory's ignorance.

"The questions you have are big, and you will need wisdom to answer them. Wisdom comes with time, ehn? But while you wait, you can find something to do. Don't be idle."

"Well, did Faith tell you that we spoke about me moving back to the house? I can help out and keep you company and stuff."

"I'm not an old woman with nothing to do, I have a job. I don't need your pity!"

Her mother's words stung, but Glory continued.

"I can't live with my sister and her husband forever, I *want* to move back home," she said, hoping that if she said it with enough conviction she'd feel like she meant it.

"Oh, really?" Celeste's tone changed slightly. "You know, my house is not California. You cannot just be living how you were living there."

Glory snorted. "Living how, Mummy? Do you have a secret Instagram account I don't know about?"

"I'm not on any gram. Anyway, I think that's a good idea, yes—I think it would be good for you to come home."

Celeste straightened up and pulled Glory's arm in close as they continued their slow loop of the park.

II

Glory moved back home the morning her mother discharged herself from hospital. It was the type of cold, wet day that seeped into the bones. Faith dropped her at the house early so that she could turn on the heaters and chase out the chill before Celeste arrived. As the old boiler groaned into action, Glory sat on the sofa in her coat and caught up on the latest, tapping through newsfeeds, time lines and notifications.

She was typing out a message to Julian when she was interrupted by a call from an unknown number.

"Hi Glory, it's Lará—Ọmọlará."

Glory remembered Lará's mother, the woman her own mother had introduced her to at the funeral, and her tight, anxious hug.

"Oh, hey Lará. How are you?"

"I'm all right. I'm so sorry I couldn't make it to the funeral. My mum said it was good—well, not good, like, really nice—well, she said that your dad would have been proud."

"No, don't worry about it, it's fine, and thanks," Glory said and an awkward beat passed between them.

"How are things? I mean, that's a stupid question . . ." Lará sighed heavily down the phone. "I'm sorry, Glory. I'm probably chatting shit right now, but I was so shocked when I heard the news. Been thinking about all the time we spent together when we were younger and how we fell out of touch and—I'm just sorry, that's all I can say, I guess."

"It's OK, Lará. Really. Believe it or not, this is not the most awkward conversation I've had since my dad passed."

Lará laughed with relief.

"Well, it would be nice to hang out before you go back. Where is it you live again? New York?"

"LA—well, it was LA. I'm not going back, so, no rush!" Glory said, trying to sound carefree.

"Oh, OK then. Are weekends good for you? Or Tuesday evenings? I know it's a random day in the week but—"

"Can I get back to you on that? I'm still trying to adjust to everything, and I'm not really going out or feeling sociable right now. Sorry."

"No, of course! Shall I check in in a few weeks then? Or you can just send me a message when you're feeling up to it."

Glory exhaled, feeling freed by her honesty and the ease with which Lará received it.

"Yeah, sure thing. But I really appreciate you calling. I really do."

When they'd said their goodbyes, Glory returned to the message she'd been drafting.

"*You owe me dinner. Don't forget.*" She hit send and soon after Julian responded.

"*How could I? What you on tonight?*"

"*Not tonight. My mum is coming home from hospital. But soon?*"

"*Because it's mumzy I'll accept the rejection.*"

"*Delay is not denial.*" Glory ended her message with a winking emoji before putting down her phone and deciding to get to work—this time, no distractions.

She shed her coat, turned down the heating and took her suitcase upstairs to the old bedroom that no longer felt like hers. Glory stripped the bed linen and sat on the edge of the sagging mattress, facing the one mint green wall in the pale pink room.

When Faith left for university, Glory had decided to stake her sole claim on their bedroom. She only got as far as painting one wall before giving in, leaving paint splattered on the carpet and splotched across the ceiling. It was a story her father would tell to anyone willing to listen, a young Glory sneaking out of the house, not to party or meet boys, but to go to the B&Q on Old Kent Road.

She was caught staggering home, a large tub of Dulux cutting ridges in her palms, but her bemused parents were not sure how to punish her, as to banish her to her room would only allow her to complete the mission she had disobeyed rules to begin. In all her conniving she had forgotten to budget for rollers and Daddy decided that a fitting punishment would be to allow his daughter to attempt to paint the entire room with the one small brush to be found in the house. He had stood in the doorway watching his industrious child complete one wall, her scrawny arms shaking with exhaustion.

The burden of this memory made Glory's head hang for a second, but then she shook it off and began to bundle up the bed linen. She tucked it under her arm and moved to her mother's bedroom, collecting an empty laundry basket along the way.

In the master bedroom, she drew back the heavy curtains and forced open the stiff windows, allowing crisp air and weak daylight to pour in. The human-shaped pile of clothes on the bed turned out to belong to her father, but Glory ignored the catch in her throat and collected them into a black bin bag which she packed into the bottom of the wardrobe to be dealt with later.

She stripped her mother's bed and tossed the linen into her laundry basket, before stacking glasses filled with cloudy water. Glory found a plastic bag full of old supermarket recipe cards that she remembered her mother would bring home after a big food shop. They were curled with age, the gloss fusing them together, so when Glory tried to peel them apart, they crumbled in her hands. Under this plastic bag she found a cheap white microwave that she recognized from her childhood. The casing was cracked and discolored, the reason for its presence in the master bedroom not immediately obvious.

Celeste was clearly a hoarder, but Glory wasn't sure if she had always been this way, if her bedroom had always looked this chaotic. Her habit of purchasing things for later or "just in case" was a habit Daddy was not fond of. Her mother would buy things and "lose" receipts, hoping that by the time the bank statements came, her impulsive purchase wouldn't matter any more. But Daddy was an accountant, record-keeping was his thing, on paper or in memory. Anyway this hoarding of sad broken things was different to buying a bread oven on a whim.

Record-keeping. A thought occurred to Glory and she put the rubbish she had been collecting to the side and approached her father's desk. She opened it carefully and took out the accordion file, slowly thumbing each labeled compartment. When she couldn't find what she was looking for, she began again at the beginning, carefully flicking through each section, reading each label aloud, looking inside each compartment, just to be sure. But what she was looking for was not there.

There should have been a compartment labeled "death certificates," because that is where Hope's death certificate should have been. But there wasn't, so Glory reopened the compartment that contained their birth certificates, picked up the photocopy of Hope's and read it carefully, as though the other certificate would appear if she just paid enough attention. It didn't.

Glory returned the paper to its rightful compartment, closed the file and set it down on the floor. She began searching through the desk, pulling open drawers and rifling through their contents, tossing old letters and newspaper clippings to the side, catching a nail on loose staples and stabbing herself with dried-out ballpoint pens. Still nothing.

She kneeled on the floor in front of the desk, resting her head on an open drawer. Her heart was racing. She took three long, deep breaths before lifting her head and readying herself to return everything to its place, just as her father would have wanted. Then she rose to her feet with her bin bag in hand. The death certificate had to be somewhere in this house full of junk and, if she worked through the house room by room, she would have to find it.

12

Glory soon realized she had taken her leisurely days at Faith's house for granted. There, her only obligations had been a bit of babysitting, cooking and acting as a sounding board for Faith's trains of thought and complaints. But at her mother's house there was no polite Polish lady who came once a week to clean, and Celeste had no appreciation for Glory's kitchen experiments. She took it upon herself to critique Glory's most basic creations. The texture of her rice was too this or that, her stews had too much onion, not enough Maggi, and since her chicken was not boiled and fried *and* baked, it was undercooked and flavorless.

"When are you going to get a job?" Celeste had taken to asking this at the most irritating moments.

"When one falls from the sky," Glory mumbled through a clenched jaw.

"Pardon?"

"I'm still looking," Glory lied, louder than before.

"Well, I need you to go to Catford to collect something for me."

"Catford? Today?"

"Yes," her mother replied with a look that said, *it's not like you're busy doing anything else.*

"Or if you need that time to look for a job that's fine. The clock is ticking, the sooner you get a job, the sooner that everything else will fall into place, I'm sure—a husband, a house, some children."

Glory had to grind her molars to stop herself responding.

"So, do you want me to move out? I thought you wanted me to move back home but now it sounds like you can't wait to get rid of me!"

"Me? No," Celeste said, a pained expression on her face. "I just want the best things for you. I see how your generation is just waiting, waiting—waiting while life passes them by!"

But Glory was only waiting for her mother to get better so that she could get on with her own life, and she told Julian as much on the phone one morning.

"Have you decided what that life looks like yet?" he asked, his voice echoing through his speakerphone.

"Where are you? I can call you later—the line's really bad."

"Ah, classic Glory. Answering a question with a question."

"You haven't known me long enough to be talking about *classic Glory*."

"You're acting pissy today. Don't worry, I'll come and rescue you, Cinderella."

"Don't patronize me! And I can rescue myself. You're just too busy for me these days," Glory said, dropping her voice in an exaggerated sulk.

"Sorry, I'll make it up to you. I don't know where I can find a pair of glass slippers, but I'll get you some new creps if that'll cheer you up. What size are you?"

"Seven. Are you driving?" Glory asked, hearing the unmistakable tick-tick-tick of the indicator.

"Yeah, I don't think they make glass slippers that big anyway."

"You're rude."

"Sorry, Bigfoot."

"What size are you?"

"Ten, but I'm a man. Aren't girls supposed to be like size four or five or something?"

"Girls, maybe. *Women* on the other hand—"

"Yo, Glory? I need to just . . . Let me call you when I'm back on ends in a bit. OK?"

"Err, OK then," Glory said, her attitude returning, but Julian had disconnected the phone before she could say bye.

She kissed her teeth, checked the time and left her room to go and check on her mother. She pushed the bedroom door open wide enough to tuck her head around the door.

"Mummy?" she whispered into the gloom. "Mum?" The room was still and quiet.

Once upon a time it had been Celeste who was pushing her head through Glory's bedroom door on a Saturday morning, rousing her violently and ordering her to Peckham to buy tinned tomatoes or spices for the rice she was cooking for so-and-so's party later that day. Now Celeste met every social invitation with disdain and excuses.

Glory went downstairs feeling listless. Saturdays in London were so boring. Lará's invitation crossed her mind, but then the landline rang. In contrast to the low hum of mobile phones on silent mode, the noise of an actual phone ringing felt intrusive. Glory waited to hear the springs in her mother's bed shift as she rolled over to reach for the handset by her bedside, but there was no movement above.

"Hello?"

"Faith?" Victor said.

"No, it's Glory."

"Is Faith there?"

"No, she's not."

"Where's Mum?"

"Sleeping."

"OK."

She could hear shouts in the background, a raucous noise that reminded her of school playgrounds. They let it fill the space between them for a while.

"How are you doing?" she asked finally.

The flat buzz of a tannoy obscured his response.

"Huh? I missed that."

"I've got to go. Not got much credit."

"Oh, OK." Glory's throat closed up. "It's good to hear your voice?"

It came out like a question, laying the ground for him to reply "same here" or similar, but he sounded like he was already in the process of putting down the phone, his voice melting into the noise behind him.

"Yeah, bye."

Glory hung up and flopped onto the sofa, switching on the TV and idly flicking through channels, trying to stop Victor's indifference from darkening her mood. Her brother's grudges were legendary, but they came from the same bloodline—if she wanted to, she could be as stubborn as him.

The day Victor was sentenced an old school friend sent her a private message on Instagram, a picture of the front page of a tabloid. Victor's mugshot in a row with his co-defendants. The only message the silly girl sent was "OMG!" and the heartbroken emoji. Glory didn't reply.

But, remembering the shame that descended on her in that moment, she was filled with guilt. If that's how she had been feeling thousands of miles away, how did her parents feel, still waking up and walking through a community who had no doubt devoured and dissected their public disgrace?

In hindsight that would have been a good time to leave America. She would have been able to support her brother, spend time with her father and avoid the beginning of everything going wrong. But Daddy never pressured her to come home, lulling her into a false sense of security, and when her mother did not take kindly to Glory's excuses about work commitments, she thought she was being dramatic.

"Glo-ry!" She had shouted each syllable down the phone. "You don't think that we have suffered enough? You want to punish us by staying away? I did not kill my own mother, o! But this daughter of mine wants to bury me!"

But in the end, it had been Daddy they had ended up burying.

Glory settled on a Saturday afternoon cooking show. When Faith arrived at the house, unlocking the front door and half pushing, half dragging her squabbling toddlers through, she found her younger sister on the living room sofa making mental notes about the qualities of different types of sweet peppers.

"Victor called looking for you." Glory didn't look up from the TV or bother to greet her sister.

"Why did he call you looking for me?" Faith asked, ushering the twins to the foot of the stairs to remove their coats and shoes.

"He called the house phone and I picked up. He thought I was you."

"Oh. How is he—? Esther, darling, don't lean on your brother like that please!"

"Wouldn't know. He didn't want to talk to me."

"Did he say that?"

"He didn't have to."

"Maybe his credit was low, nothing to worry about— Esther!"

"Who told you I was worried? Anyway, what's new with you?"

Faith removed her own coat, hung it on the banister and pushed Glory's feet from their place on the sofa, taking a seat next to her.

"Michael's gone to Croatia for a stag party. It's his colleague's thing. He's trying to be seen as one of the lads but it feels like we're getting a bit old for all of that, to be honest. I heard Croatia's the new Ibiza."

"That workplace takes up all his time during the week and now it's taking up his weekends as well? Babylon t'ing!" Glory said, passing the remote to Faith.

"Yeah, well . . ."

"Bit ridiculous though, isn't it?"

"That's just the nature of the job."

It sounded like a line fed to Faith by Michael himself, and if it hadn't been so obvious Glory might not have asked her next question.

"Do you trust him, though?"

"Of course!"

"At least someone does," Glory mumbled into her nail. But the comment was out before she could consider what she was saying.

"Esther and Elijah, why don't you two go upstairs and see if Grandma's awake?" Faith waited until they had clambered up the stairs and were creaking across the landing before she continued.

"You don't like Michael," she said eventually. "Why don't you just tell me the real reason why?"

Glory finally tore her eyes away from the TV.

"Remember when you got pregnant—the first time? He abandoned you then and it feels like he's abandoning you now."

Faith's pregnancy had landed like a grenade in the middle of her second year at university. But in the face of accountability,

Michael—then in his third and final year, with his mind set on law school and training contracts—broke up with her. After Faith miscarried, he continued to keep his distance.

Miraculously, Faith went on to complete her degree, landing a place on a graduate scheme. She was making her way in life when Michael came back and somehow managed to convince her to give him a second chance. While it was enough for everyone else, Glory could not forgive nor forget.

A muscle in Faith's jaw jumped.

"You can't hold the past against people. If I'm happy to move on, why can't you?"

"You say he was there for you before when I wasn't—OK, fine. But I can only judge him by what I've seen with my own eyes. I've lived with you both and he's a ghost, Faith."

A ghost that had somehow still managed to derail Faith's life if anyone cared to ask Glory for her opinion. Faith had been a data analyst with an economics degree and now she was a trophy wife.

"I'm really not about to get into this with you, Glory, OK? Michael is not your problem, he's mine."

Faith got up from the sofa and made her way up the stairs.

Interpreting this exit as a dismissal, Glory shouted after her sister's back: "Well, I'm going out!"

She got up, grabbed a coat from the bottom of the stairs and headed out of the door. She had no destination in mind, but walking off her frustration was a coping mechanism she'd learned in LA, which, as a bonus, had helped her to get to know her neighborhood.

On the advice of her therapist she even attended a few hiking meet-ups, and one of her favorite Instagram shots was her silhouetted against the dusky skyline at Griffith Observatory, taken by a Japanese teenager she had befriended on the Mount Hollywood hike. There was an awkward selfie of the two of them in front of the Hollywood sign from earlier in the day. That image had not made it on to Instagram.

On this walk, Glory settled for a few laps around the lake in Burgess Park, the movement distracting her from wasting even more time glued to her smartphone. Shamefully, she found that when the lives of others stopped being interesting to her, she would scroll through her own Instagram feed, finding a strange solace in each perfectly composed square filtered through golden light.

With each step, Glory's thoughts began to order themselves. She needed a plan forward—a job, something to get her out of the house and away from her mother for a few hours a day. The digital agency life had less allure when the view from her office was likely to be the Gherkin and a gray London sky. *Maybe*, she thought, *she needed to take a leaf from Julian's book and start something new.* Her current circumstances were the stuff rags to riches tales were made of, she had listened to enough podcasts to know that much. Faith had said something about a hipster restaurant when she had first arrived, but she knew nothing about running a restaurant, and food was something fun for her, turning it into a business would probably change that. But Julian had also mentioned the beauty salon thing. That could work.

Glory reached into the pocket of her coat to look for her phone, but instead she found Faith's car keys. When the phone in the other pocket turned out to be Faith's as well, she looked down and saw Faith's coat instead of her own. Her phone was probably still on the sofa back home. She swore under her breath, noticing a WhatsApp notification on the lock screen. It was from Michael, and she could read the beginning of the message:

"*I need you to forgive me. Call me when—*"

Glory's thumb hovered. She could find out what Michael had done now, but if Michael had pissed Faith off, Faith had had the opportunity to tell Glory earlier. Glory wasn't about to fight a battle for someone who didn't want saving.

She dropped the phone back into the coat pocket and headed home, taking a detour that took her past Pharaoh's. The waiting area was filled with men and boys and both barbers were busy, with a third one joining the ranks for the afternoon ahead.

Glory hovered at the doorway, hoping one of the barbers would look up and see her and she wouldn't have to announce herself to the whole shop. Eventually the previously idle barber looked toward the door.

"Is Ju— is Jay about?"

"Nah, doubt he'll be back today," the barber said, holding a razor between his teeth as he narrowed in on his client's hairline with the buzzing clippers.

"Do you know where he's gone?"

He paused from his task, looking up and glancing from Glory to one of the other barbers. This other barber made eye contact and shrugged.

"Can't help you there, princess," the formerly idle barber said.

Glory turned and left, feeling a few bored stares graze over her as she walked past the shop window.

13

When Glory arrived back at her mother's house, Faith, Esther and Elijah were in the living room.

"Is that my jacket?" Faith asked as Glory entered, the earlier tension forgotten. "I was wondering where I left it."

"Sorry," Glory said, taking it off. "I picked up the wrong coat when I left." She hung it back on the banister.

"Is that Glory?" Celeste called from the kitchen. "Did she remember to get the rice?"

"You never asked me to get any rice, Mummy! And anyway, I told you we shouldn't eat long grain any more. I can make jollof with bulgur wheat, it's just as tasty."

"She's telling the truth," Faith said. "Glory cooked it when she was at ours, it's really nice!"

Celeste walked through from the kitchen, standing at the threshold of the living room with a frown on her face and her hands planted on her hips.

"Whatever you want to eat in your house is fine, whatever you want to eat in America is your business," she said sternly. "But as for me and my house, we will eat rice!"

Faith sniggered and reached into her coat pocket and took out her phone. Glory watched her sister stare at her screen, her hair falling forward to obscure her expression. Faith huffed, slipping it into her back pocket. She then reached into the inside pocket of the coat and brought out an envelope.

"I need to put this back upstairs before I forget," Faith said, checking the contents of the envelope. "I've scanned it, so I won't need it again."

"Pass it, I'll do it," Glory said, reaching out to take it. Inside was their parents' marriage certificate, delicately worn, the paper furring at the folds.

As Glory read over the details, the date leaped out at her.

"Mummy, I didn't know you got married *after* Faith was born!"

"We were married in Nigeria before we came to England," Celeste said, looking up.

"But this certificate says you got married in 1988—Faith was born in '87!"

"We were married before," Celeste insisted. "We had the traditional at my parents' compound, it was a very big affair."

"But you had the white wedding here?"

"It wasn't a wedding—it was a *formality*."

"England doesn't recognize traditional weddings, Glory, you know that," Faith interjected.

"I know *that*. But I didn't know *this*, I didn't know . . . never mind."

Celeste tutted and, irritated by her mother's offense, Glory turned and climbed the stairs.

Her progress on clearing and tidying the house had been a predictable dance of two steps forward and one step back, with her mother finding reasons to hang on to every other item that Glory proposed was donated to a charity shop or thrown away.

Celeste's bedroom was the one room that remained in a permanent state of disarray. Entering it now, Glory could see that the file of all important documents was balancing precariously on the closed lid of her father's desk.

As Glory reached out she knocked it from its perch, and it tumbled to the ground, documents escaping and scattering. Stooping to pick up the file, Glory stopped abruptly when she saw a picture of herself with her two sisters among the loose leaves. All three of them together, complete.

Hope was next to Glory, and Faith stood behind them, while on either side of the three little girls was a white man and a white woman. Faith's hair was braided in tight rows and she stood upright in a denim pinafore with pink flowers embroidered around the collar. Glory and Hope were shoulder to shoulder in matching outfits. The woman's hand rested tenderly on Faith's shoulder and the man had his hands crossed behind his back, looking serious but not unkind.

Glory turned the photograph around in her hand, the paper creased with time but still as glossy as ever. Written on the back in her father's handwriting was, "Joan and Edward Marksham with Faith, Hope and Glory, March 1993." Glory had never heard her father once utter her twin's name, but seeing "Hope" in his handwriting practically summoned his voice back from the grave. The smudged memory of her sister's existence came into sharp relief as she looked at the little girl wearing the same powder-blue pinafore as the tiny version of herself. While Glory's face was a suspicious frown, holding the gaze of the camera lens at a careful distance, Hope's was open and inviting. She looked so pure and helpless. A wave of nauseating grief shook Glory and sent her to her knees.

When Glory collected herself, the first thought that burned through her was *why?* Why had she never seen this picture before? And were there more photos like this hiding somewhere? She picked up the accordion file and tipped it upside down, emptying the remaining documents onto the floor. Her hands frantically searched the papers and opened envelopes, tossing them aside as she looked for more pictures—more evidence of this version of her life. Then she turned to the file itself, her hands searching the corners and pulling at the cover, her fingers finding the cardboard edges, probing, hoping for a hidden compartment into which it may have slipped.

"Glory? Can't you hear me calling you?"

Faith walked into the room, interrupting her sister who was wild-eyed and bent over the jumbled pile.

"What are you doing?"

"I knocked it over," Glory said, trying to sound innocent, even if she felt like a thief, desperately scrabbling for something forbidden. "Why were you calling me?"

"We were talking about Tabitha's wedding. You know she's having a traditional? Are you coming?"

"She hasn't invited me."

"Why wouldn't she invite you? She practically lived with us that summer her mum went to Nigeria."

"We just don't talk."

"Since when?"

"Since LA? Maybe before? I don't know."

"You don't talk to *Tabitha*? Do you have *any* friends any more?" Faith said with a good-natured laugh. But Glory said nothing, moving her hands over the documents on the floor, pretending to sort them.

"Er, OK then," Faith said, and turned to leave the bedroom.

"Faith, have you ever . . . ?" Glory was about to ask Faith about the photograph, but something made her change her mind.

"Have I ever what?"

"Did *you* know that Mummy and Daddy weren't officially married when you were born?"

"Glory," Faith said, her voice tired. She rested one hand on the doorknob and another on her hip. "Why do you fixate over these things? I knew, yes—well, I found out later, but I knew."

"It's just . . . weird. I didn't know," Glory repeated, her mind catching on this fact like the needle of a record player skipping on a scratched groove.

"Did you even read it properly?" Faith asked. "It wasn't some lavish ceremony, it was at a registry office. Like Mummy said, it was just a formality."

Glory nodded and let her head hang. She was upset, not for her parents' pathetic registry office wedding, but for all the things her family thought were fine to leave unsaid.

"OK?" Faith asked.

"Yeah, fine. No big deal."

Glory cleared her throat and looked up. "I'll tidy this up and come downstairs in a bit."

Faith left and Glory slipped the picture inside the waistband of her jeans. She collected the rest of the scattered contents, slotting them solemnly back in their rightful homes. Then, just as she was about to close the file and put it back in the desk, she decided to do one last check. Still no death certificate for her sister, and though she hadn't expected to miraculously find it, its absence turned her gloom into a stony rage. She was done tiptoeing, she deserved answers. Glory went back downstairs, the hidden photo burning hot against her stomach.

But when Glory entered the living room, she saw her mother with Esther sitting on her lap. Celeste was comforting her granddaughter as she breathlessly explained some injustice Elijah had unleashed upon her.

"Elijah," her mother called with a soft force. "Come and apologize to your sister."

Elijah whined stubbornly, keeping his back firmly toward his grandmother and sister, until he was gently coaxed into turning around and standing next to them.

"Sorry, Estie," he finally said, his pink bottom lip pushed out, his eyes low and sad.

Esther threw her pudgy arms around her brother and Celeste clapped and encouraged them both, before planting a kiss on each of their foreheads. Esther kissed her grandmother back and Elijah shyly pushed himself into Celeste's bosom. Her mother was lost in the gentle intimacy of her grandchildren and Glory's own words echoed back to her: *Your mother has been through enough.* Now was not the time for confrontation.

14

An evening with Esther and Elijah had lifted Celeste's spirits, and praise songs echoed around the top floor of the house as she showered the next morning. Glory was reminded of the Sunday mornings of her childhood, the house buzzing with energy as the family got ready for church.

Back then church had felt like the center of everything. It was the social lynchpin of life, where the children of your parents' friends became family, making up for the absence of blood relations on British soil. It was where Glory had first met Lará after their mothers became fast friends, and even though the family's church had chopped and changed as Celeste fell out with pastors' wives or acquired a taste for services that didn't exceed three hours, the web of connections remained, and her mother's diary had always been full.

Glory's father complained continuously about the mounting costs of lace and damask, bought according to the designated color schemes for each function. But when it suited him, he would rise to the occasion, pressing crisp twenty-pound notes into the hands of young couples whose names he could barely remember, and toasting them with imported Nigerian Guinness. There were official portraits of him at these celebrations—birthdays, weddings and naming ceremonies—his billowing agbádá and commanding presence holding everyone around him in orbit.

Sundays were an opportunity to show up and show off for the whole Akíndélé clan. As children, Faith and Glory would be buttoned into matching dresses. Victor had a collection of little waistcoats that could put a grown man's wardrobe to shame. The first victory of adolescence was getting to wear whatever you wanted to church; the second was being able to opt out of Sundays altogether.

Glory's mother rapped on the door to her room.

"I hope you're ready, o! We need to leave!"

"Leave to go where?" Glory said from under the duvet.

"Church! Or did America make you godless?"

"You never mentioned going to church to me."

"It's Sunday, what else would we be doing on a Sunday?"

"I'm not going to church, Mum."

"You haven't been to church since you've been back."

"Neither have you!" Glory heard the low hiss of her mother sucking the air through her teeth, before Celeste walked away singing with renewed vigor to cover her annoyance.

Glory leaped up from her bed and into the hallway.

"Mummy?"

Celeste turned back to her daughter; Glory's heart crawled into her throat and she twisted her fingers in her sleeves like a child.

Celeste raised an eyebrow. "What is it?"

"Erm, you know, Hope? My twin sister?"

The name landed between the two women with the weight and force of an anchor and Glory watched her mother's face close up as she drew into herself.

"When I went to put away Daddy's death certificate I saw

a copy of her birth certificate, but I couldn't find her death certificate and I don't remember her funeral and I've never seen any pictures. Not even Faith remembers, and it's weird that we've never spoken about it."

It all came out in a rush of breath, so fast that Glory wasn't even sure her mother understood her babbling, but the way Celeste's face turned from blank distance to darkened rage suggested she had understood enough.

"Is this what you've come to speak to me about?" Flecks of saliva shot from her mother's mouth like poison darts. "Kí ló ń dàmú ẹ?! And on the Lord's day! Instead of you going to church you've come to test me? *On the Lord's day?!*"

She almost shrieked the last question. Glory's heart dropped from her throat to her stomach and she set her jaw against the tears that threatened to fall.

"What is wrong with you?" Celeste repeated in English. "Why do you like trouble?" She turned away from her daughter.

"It was just a question. A simple question," Glory said in a small voice.

Her mother spun around.

"Kíni question?! Keep your stupid questions!" She slammed her hand on the banister sending a pile of towels tumbling onto the stairs below, before pointing a trembling finger in Glory's direction.

"You are an ungrateful child! I didn't raise you this way! So selfish!"

The second outburst broke whatever resolve Glory thought she had, and she fled back to her room, pushing the door shut behind her as her tears ran free.

"Selfish, selfish girl!" her mother ranted as she went to her own room, throwing open drawers and clattering around in a temper. Glory lay in her bed, listening to her mother's rage ricochet around the house until eventually the front door shut and all was silent.

She lay still, a familiar weight settling into her body and pressing her in place. She replayed her mother's outburst, substituting her dumbstruck silence with counterpoints and her own accusations, shouting back until the imagined version of her was hoarse with fury. At some point she dozed off, her thoughts transforming into a confused dream caught between LA and London.

When Glory awoke, the afternoon was sliding into evening and she could hear the television blaring below. Her head felt tight with dried tears and snot and, after going to the bathroom to splash her face with cold water, she went downstairs.

Her mother was in the kitchen, talking loudly on the phone to compensate for the volume of the television that cast its glow across the empty living room.

"You're awake," she noted over her shoulder, the phone cradled against her cheek. "There's rice in the fridge." Then she turned away, throwing rapid-fire Yorùbá down the mouthpiece before breaking to emit a bellow of laughter.

Glory took the plastic tub from the fridge and spooned out a small portion of the yellow fried rice, still warm from its cooking. This passed as a peace offering in her mother's world.

Glory took her plate back upstairs and settled on her bed, the sensuous comfort of the food warming her from the inside out.

When her phone rang she fished for it beneath the tangle of covers, exhaling when she saw Julian's name light up the display.

"Sorry, meant to call yesterday but got caught up with stuff."

"Did you get my glass trainers?"

"Shit. Knew I forgot something."

"Another disappointment."

"What's wrong?" Julian asked, sensing something in Glory's tone.

"Everything's wrong, but that's nothing new."

"What happened?"

"I'll save that for when you take me out. I know you don't like small talk," she said, but really Glory was thinking about her mother overhearing the conversation.

"OK. Where you wanna go?"

"Let's get some dim sum at Yam Bui or something."

"Dim what?"

"Never mind. Surprise me."

Julian let out a low whistle.

"No pressure then."

"It doesn't have to be fancy. I've not had Nando's in a while actually."

"Nando's? Wow, you really don't rate me do you? One sec!"

Julian's voice got further away from the phone while he held a muted conversation with someone else in the background.

"Glory, can I call you back?" he asked when he returned.

"You'll probably forget again."

"I won't—but if I do, we're definitely going out this week. But not Nando's."

"Cool."

Glory ended the call and set her empty bowl down on the side table next to her bed. She noticed the photograph that she had taken from her father's file on top of a bank statement, and picked it up gingerly.

The second viewing didn't feel as earth-shattering as the first, although she felt the blood vessels in her chest constrict a little as she studied the sweet faces of her sisters. She looked carefully at the background, a suburban hedge slightly out of focus, a clear blue stretch of sky, but it held no other clues. The wrinkles around the eyes and mouths of the white couple suggested they were older, and they were both dressed conservatively. Joan's cream blouse had a large pussy bow and her dark blue skirt was long, flared ever so slightly at the hem. Edward was wearing a dark brown patterned jumper and gray trousers, a sharp crease pressed down the front of each leg.

"Who are you?" Glory whispered to the photograph, but Edward kept his slight frown.

She decided to put the photograph back. Keeping it would do her no good. The memory of her mother's ire was still fresh. She wished Daddy was here, although she could not say with certainty that his reaction would have been any different.

In her mother's bedroom she opened up the desk, found the file and slipped the photograph into one of the back pockets. She returned it to its drawer and was pushing it shut when the bedroom door swung open, nearly hitting her. Celeste stood silhouetted in the doorway.

"What are you doing there?" Celeste asked sharply, one hand on her hip and the other holding open the door.

"Just putting something away. Faith gave it to me yesterday, but I forgot to do it."

Suspicion shadowed Celeste's face as she watched her daughter shut the drawer and stand up.

"That's all!" Glory added, her hands up in surrender, and she sidled past her mother, who turned and watched her leave.

15

Julian didn't call Glory back, but he did turn up to take her out later that week on a drizzling Thursday evening. He arrived in a black Mercedes—not his own, but a happy accident in the Uber lottery. As Glory settled into the leather seats, he presented her with a large brown bag holding a distinctive red shoebox. A white Nike swoosh was splashed across the lid. Inside the box were a pair of white and silver Air Max 95.

"Closest I could get to glass."

"Oh my days, you didn't *actually* have to get me anything!" Glory said, embarrassed by his generosity.

"Do you like them?"

"They're really nice."

"That's all that matters."

The car pulled out of Glory's street and Julian made small talk with their driver. He seemed nervous, constantly pulling at the cuffs of his shirt and stealing glances at Glory who was enjoying the view of London through black tinted windows.

When they reached their destination, the driver jumped out of the car, opening Glory's passenger door with a slight bow.

"Did you ask him to do that?" she asked Julian as the car drove off.

"Nah, he's just working extra hard for those five stars."

As they approached the restaurant, Glory recognized the small gold logo debossed into the black granite signage immediately.

"Oh, Maijhun. Nice."

"You know it?" Julian asked hopefully, pulling open the heavy glass door.

"Yeah! This must be the baitest Michelin star restaurant in London. Isn't this where all the fraud boys take their links?"

Glory laughed, but Julian had missed the joke. He stood aside to let Glory enter first.

"But it's nice, I love it. There's a branch in LA as well. I used to eat there all the time. You know it's owned by the same woman who owns Yam Bui?"

Julian grunted and gave his name to the host at the door.

"This is nicer than the LA one though!" Glory tried again as they were led through the restaurant to their table.

The interior was dark and glossy and the bar glowed with row upon row of backlit liquor, the blue lights refracting through creatively crafted bottles. They were taken to a table in the corner and Glory slid into her seat. The chairs were half circles, practically armchairs, big and comfortable enough to curl up in. Julian sat across from her taking in his surroundings. Above the table hung a light that doubled as a hanging basket, the deep green foliage glowing from another invisible light source.

"This is really nice, thanks for bringing me here," Glory said after ordering a glass of wine. Julian finally made eye contact with her and nodded before studying the menu.

"You reckon they do special fried rice with sweet and sour chicken on the side like the Chinese in Elephant?" he said after a moment. Glory looked up from her own menu and found Julian smirking at her horrified reaction.

"I'm playing! But seeing as you're the expert in these things, what should I order?"

"You've not been here before?"

Julian shook his head.

"What made you choose here then?"

"I asked around, innit. Tried to find something that would impress you."

Julian tossed the remark out casually but he was staring very closely at the wine list in front of him.

Glory ordered for the both of them, starting with a spread of starters. She took great pleasure in explaining the dishes to him as if she had prepared them herself, and was not just trying to remember what was written on the menu. Still, Julian was the one impressed, unable to hide his surprise when she picked up the sleek black chopsticks.

"It's easy really," she said, clicking them together in her hand. "I can teach you."

"I'm fine with a fork. Glad to see you're in a better mood, though."

"What do you mean?"

"On the weekend, you were upset. You said everything was shit, or something like that."

Glory was already halfway through her second glass of Merlot and her brain was cushioned in its warm fuzz. She could feel her words beginning to slide into each other and she wanted to enjoy this feeling.

"Oh that? Don't worry, I'm over it—now *this* is dim sum!" Glory exclaimed as their waiter brought a tray of steamed dumplings. She picked one up with her chopsticks and offered it to Julian across the table.

"This is the lobster one, it's amazing."

Julian eyed the little package and shook his head.

"I don't eat seafood, like prawns and lobster and crab and all that."

"Why?" Glory said before she sank her teeth into the soft, fragrant parcel.

"If you think about it, they're just giant insects that live in the sea."

Glory spluttered, covering her mouth with the back of her hand.

"OK, have this one, it's chicken." This time she set the dumpling down on his plate.

Julian obliged her with a small bite of the dumpling. He swallowed, shook his head and mumbled something under his breath, looking at the other patrons as the low rumble of conversation continued around them.

Glory's eyes traced his profile. His trim was immaculate, of course, and his skin was clear and smooth. She could see the glint of his chain tucked inside his black shirt, the top two buttons carefully undone. She remembered how he had smelled when he hugged her in the car, and again how his face had dropped when she made the comment about Maijhun and fraud boys. She wanted to reach across the table and take his hands in hers and apologize again. But maybe that was the wine.

"How's business?" she asked.

Julian kissed his teeth and leaned back in his chair. "Full of problems."

"Like, *mo' money mo' problems*?" Glory asked, smiling at her terrible New York accent.

"I wish," Julian said with a sigh. "Let's talk about something else."

"You tell me your problems and I'll tell you mine."

"You go first." Julian leaned toward her and for a second Glory thought he was about to take her hand.

She set down her glass and ran a tongue thick with alcohol over her teeth.

"Did you know I had another sister, a twin?"

"Had?"

"She died when we were little."

"How?"

"That's the thing, I don't know. I don't know anything. My family doesn't talk about her, but I've been thinking about her a lot recently, I guess with my dad and everything, and I found a picture of us that I'd never seen before. I tried to speak to my mum about her on Sunday, and she switched on me. Went fully crazy, shouting and cussing me and all sorts."

"Shit, man. I'm sorry."

Glory swallowed hard and looked down.

"I dunno what to say, man. I'm sorry."

"You don't have to say anything. There's nothing to say," Glory said with a sad laugh. "My family's fucked up and that's the end of it."

She wanted him to take her hand now. She could feel herself losing her grip on the emotions spinning within.

"Have you spoken to your sister—your other sister—about it? You said her and your mum are really close, maybe she can help."

Glory shook her head and looked up, willing tears not to fall. She had drunk too much too quickly.

"I tried before and Faith just said something about me always running away, or avoiding the issue, or dwelling on the past or something."

"Would madam like to order her main?"

The waiter had appeared at Glory's left again, after clearing away the small plates, but she was suddenly no longer in the mood for a proper meal.

"I'm OK—Julian, do you want anything?" Glory asked as she finished off her wine.

"We're good, thanks." Julian looked at Glory as he said it. "Just the bill."

The waiter glided off and Julian reached into his pocket, bringing out a thick wad of notes folded tight.

"Haven't you heard of a debit card?"

"Didn't get the chance to go to the bank," he said, and Glory watched him peel off some notes and lay them on the table in plain sight. When the waiter returned, she quickly picked up the leather bill folder, stuffing the money inside as Julian stood to leave.

"You don't want your change?"

"That's for the tip, innit? C'mon, Glory. This ain't Nando's!"

His trademark smirk split into a wide grin as he waited for her to collect her coat.

The rain had stopped but the pavements gleamed slick under the street lamps. Julian pulled out his phone to summon a cab, but Glory linked an arm through his and began walking. It was still early and she wasn't ready for the night to end, but she was grateful that Julian read her cue and didn't force her to say it out loud.

"You know, when you tell an American that you're from London, this is the London they imagine," Glory said as they walked past luxury car showrooms and Georgian townhouses with white pillars and sash windows.

"What do they say when you tell them you're actually from Peckham?"

Glory didn't answer.

"Or did you let them think you sip tea with the Queen on weekends?"

"They don't know where Peckham is."

"I don't blame you to be honest. What good has Peckham done for anyone? Besides rappers."

"You know, in America, as big as it is, people are shocked that you can be both black and British. It literally blows their mind."

"Did you beg it though? Start talking posh and everything?"

"Would you judge me if I said I did?"

"Nah, like I said, I get it. This place is proper claustrophobic, I wouldn't mind escaping. You done well."

Without a doubt Glory had leaned into the privilege of reinvention, enjoying the possibilities it offered. She modified her accent, rounding her vowels and pitching her tone slightly higher. She liked the double takes from shop assistants who had already decided to ignore her, or the confusion that clouded the faces of tech bros, whose neat categories of condescension were shaken up by an accent they only associated with Hugh Grant.

"So where would you want to escape to?" Glory asked Julian.

"Dunno. America seemed like the place until they started killing black men in broad daylight. There's always the Motherland, I guess. Or Cuba? I could link up with 2Pac."

They laughed and Glory ran a finger down the inside of Julian's arm.

"I'm sorry about your sister, I didn't know."

"You sure you never heard aunties gossiping about it when we were younger?" Glory began to laugh but it quickly turned to a mournful sigh. "I don't think anyone knows, to be honest. I think I need to go back to therapy, though. If I can't talk to my family about this stuff, I need to talk to someone."

"Have you and Victor had a chance to talk yet?"

"He's still avoiding me."

"Sorry. I should be distracting you from all this sad shit, not making you think about it."

"It's not your fault, you've done a lot. You bought me new creps, took me to Maijhun, I'm living my hood dreams right now!"

Glory flung out a tipsy arm, the bag with her new Nike trainers swinging dangerously into the road.

Julian responded with a small, hollow laugh and they continued walking, the only sound the wet crunch of car tires rolling by.

"You said you'd been to Maijhun bare times."

"I said a few times, not bare."

"Nah, you made it sound like you were a regular! Best friends with the head chef, the guy at the door knows you by name and that!" Julian said, teasing Glory with his flirtatious half-smile once again.

"I didn't! But carry on," Glory said, giving him a light-hearted push.

"Who were you going to Maijhun with?"

The question caught Glory off guard.

"Why are you asking? Jealous?"

"Curious."

"No one important," Glory said, and when Julian waited for more she added: "His name was Adam and he was a prick."

"Guess you don't miss him then," Julian said, not even attempting to hide his relief.

"He was a prick and I should have known from the start. The first time we met was at the launch party for this micro-brewery that my agency was working with and he pushed in front of me in the queue to taste the beers, and when I said something, guess what he said?"

"What?"

"*I thought black people don't like beer anyway!* What a prick!"

"Rah," was all Julian said in response, and Glory felt that she had let herself say too much.

"So why did you go out with him?"

"Loneliness."

"Oh."

Glory waited for it, for the uncomfortable realisation to sink in that she wasn't this jet-setting, confident adventurer. She waited to feel Julian pull away. She could usually feel when the cold set in, but after allowing a few seconds for the truth to settle, she still felt him there, as warm and close as before.

"Do you know where we're going?" he asked after a while.

"There's a park near here."

"We've passed two parks already."

"Those aren't parks. They're just patches of grass to break up the concrete. We're going to the actual park."

They continued walking, but Julian kept his phone in his hand, his thumb poised over the Uber icon.

"If you could be anything you wanted to be, with no limitations or anything, you could just click your fingers now and make it happen, who would you be and what would you be doing?" Glory asked excitedly. "No small talk, right?" she added when Julian looked amused by her question.

He considered his answer for a few paces.

"I'd be me, doing what I'm doing now, just with more money. Maybe I'd open a chain of barbershops across south London, or something. I'd have the money to do it, so probably, yeah."

"Seriously?" His answer had shocked Glory. "That's how you really feel?"

"Yeah, what's wrong with that? I said I wanted to escape Peckham, not myself."

"No, nothing's wrong with that. It's nice actually. Refreshing."

"*Refreshing*. OK, then. What about you?"

"I've been trying to work this out since I got back. Hey, if you're thinking about a chain of barbershops, what about the beauty salon idea you mentioned before?"

"Oh, that," he said, all enthusiasm gone. "Yeah, gonna have to postpone expansion until I sort a few things out."

"What things?" Glory asked.

"Erm . . . Just other aspects of business that aren't going as smoothly as I thought."

"Barbershop business?"

"Kind of related. Is this the park?"

The black gates of St. James's Park had appeared before them, the wet gold crests over the entrance glistening in the dark.

"This feels unreal," Julian said, unsure. He looked both ways down The Mall, Union Jacks lining the wide street. "If you were any other girl, I'd think this is a set up."

"A set up?"

"Who goes to the park in the dark? My mum used to tell us that's when the witches would gather to do their juju."

Glory's laughter echoed around them.

"Maybe in Burgess Park, but I don't think witches gather at St. James's."

Glory started walking back toward him, taking confident strides until they were face to face, their bodies almost touching.

"Do you trust me?" she whispered. They were so close she went cross-eyed trying to focus on his face. Impulsively she drew a line across his bottom lip with her finger.

"You're drunk."

"No I'm not."

"You're drunk," he said again, running his tongue over the path her finger had traced.

"Tipsy, perhaps."

And Glory broke away with a giggle, holding her hand out to lead Julian into the park.

He grasped it and with a sudden jerk he pulled Glory back, his other arm encircling her waist.

"We're not going to the park, Glory," he said into her ear and Glory felt his voice rumble through her body. She squirmed out of his arms but kept hold of his hand.

"Fine," she said, exhaling slowly. "Let's go home."

She allowed him to take the lead. He was going in the wrong direction, but she didn't mind at all.

16

Glory slept well that night, and she woke up with possibility fluttering in her stomach. When she closed her eyes she could still feel the pressure of Julian's arm pulling her in, confident and decisive in his intention. She could feel the firmness of his body against hers and the surge of electricity that passed between them as he whispered into her ear. It took every ounce of pride within her to not message him, "*So what are we then?*" Without a doubt she wanted him, but a message like that would be very off brand.

She had better things to be doing anyway. There was the job hunt that she had promised her mother was well underway when in reality she had barely gone over her CV. Every time she thought about opening up that Word document she was filled with despair. She didn't want another job, she wanted money, a reason for her mother to get off her back and for her to stop feeling useless. She didn't want to be tap dancing in interviews, trying to explain her questionable choices and haphazard career to someone whose job she could do blindfolded. Her charm and determination had seen her walk into the LA role before her body had a chance to adjust to the new time zone. That was gone now. She was tired. All of that optimism had been burned out long before her return. But thinking about Julian made her feel hopeful again and, as foolish as she felt as a woman in her mid-twenties daydreaming about her crush, she could allow herself this one indulgence.

She stayed in bed for a while, savouring the silence now that her mother had returned to work. Over the years Celeste had had many jobs, everything from the fabled cleaner of immigrant lore through to receptionist and carer for vulnerable adults. In between those jobs she had had countless hustles, trying her hand at catering (but she much preferred attending parties to serving at them), importing small quantities of lace and Swiss voile to sell to her friends (but she got tired of chasing debts), and when she discovered a cheap supplier of trinkets and household items, she had gone into business with Auntie Dọtun, providing Chinese fans and bottle openers in bulk as party favors.

When Celeste got promoted to management at the elderly care home she had been working at for nearly a decade, she zeroed in on the opportunity, tolerating the tedium for the steady benefits it provided. Until Victor's trial and her husband's death, Glory doubted she had missed more than a day of work at that place, and she was grateful that Celeste's attention would now be directed somewhere other than her.

A message appeared on Glory's phone from Lará, who had been quietly persistent in keeping her word about meeting up.

"Random, but I won dinner for two at this fancy place in my work's raffle. Let me know if you're up for it x"

Glory was not, but she didn't have the heart to turn down Lará again.

"*Congrats!*" she typed back. "*I'll let you know x*'

Glory decided it was time for a shower. When she noticed blood spotting the smooth surface of the bathtub she realized it was not possibility she had been feeling in her stomach. She finished showering quickly and hobbled to her mother's bedroom, trying carefully not to leave a trail of red in her wake. As she rummaged through drawers she feared Celeste's menopause may have already started, meaning an uncomfortable walk to the corner shop with tissue wedged between her legs.

Thankfully, she found a packet of Kotex pushed into the back corner of the wardrobe. When she pulled it out, it brought with it a bundle of paper that had been tucked tightly beside it. The bundle contained a photocopy of Hope's birth certificate, taken from her father's file, it seemed, along with the photograph of the three sisters and the white couple, and some other pictures she had never seen before.

In one, Faith sat on the lap of the woman, whose light brown hair was buffed into a haphazard halo. The pose was disarmingly intimate for a stranger or casual acquaintance, with both faces upturned to the lens. The other photograph was of a frowning little girl in school uniform who looked like Glory, but something told her that she wasn't looking at herself. The little girl clutched a blue bag, her stare piercing through the gloss of the two-dimensional print.

Glory held the photographs until they began to buckle beneath her tense grip. She could feel a panic attack approaching, the force of it encroaching upon her like waves breaking on a beach. The air seemed to dissolve in her chest as her breathing got shallower and shallower, and her pulse began to quicken until she could feel it in her neck, throbbing violently.

The steady descent of a bead of blood down the inside of her thigh brought her back to the present. Its sticky trail forced her back to the bathroom, still clutching the photographs, and in the shower for the second time, Glory's thoughts sorted themselves. She needed to speak to Faith.

17

That afternoon Glory got on the bus to Bromley. The journey was long enough to role-play the conversation she was going to have with Faith, and she was braced for a showdown.

After a few rounds on the doorbell, Faith answered, sleeves rolled up and lightly dusted in flour all over.

"What's happening here then?" Glory asked as she followed her sister through to the kitchen.

Elijah and Esther were in their high chairs playing, covered in flour and sticky dough.

"We were making gingerbread men, but I think I messed up the dough, so we're making non-edible decorations."

"I don't think Elijah got the memo," Glory said as she confiscated a piece of slick dough that was dangerously close to her nephew's mouth. "I thought they went to the child-minder's today?"

"Yeah, but I was bored."

"Bored? You know you could always go back to work."

"Says the unemployed one."

"Do you enjoy being a housewife?" Glory tried to make the question sound casual.

"This works for us, this was our deal."

"Your deal?"

"Every married couple has a deal—like, an understanding of how things are going to be, what's important to them, what their priorities are."

Glory rescued another lump of dough from Elijah's mouth and he began to kick at his seat and whine, furious that his preferred method of play was being denied.

"Ugh, stay here with Estie, while I get him cleaned up."

Faith released her son from his harness and carried him upstairs. Esther was using a shape cutter on her roll of dough, cutting each star into smaller, misformed chunks. Glory gathered the pieces and reshaped the dough.

As she watched her niece's pudgy fingers work over the imperfect stars, Glory thought back to when the twins had been born. She had marveled at the newborns, their skin wrinkly and bodies still contorted from their confinement. The fact her sister had produced these little humans out of nothing was mind-blowing in its truest sense. The idea one of them may no longer be a physical force, full of desire, tantrums and fury, was unthinkable.

But that was what had happened to Hope, and knowing she had never really mourned her sister filled Glory with guilt. But her parents must have, and maybe Faith, with a childish understanding of loss, had as well.

"I found some old photographs today," she told Faith when her sister reentered the kitchen with Elijah.

Faith sat him back in the high chair and began wiping down the tray table as Glory carefully took the photographs out of her pocket, making sure to leave the photocopy of Hope's birth certificate well hidden.

Faith took them and flicked through with an impassive look, but when she returned the prints to Glory she watched her younger sister carefully.

"You just *found* them?"

"Yeah, I was looking for a pad in Mum's room and found them at the back of the wardrobe, next to the Kotex."

Faith paused, decided that explanation seemed plausible, and continued with the clean-up operation.

"Do you recognize that white couple?" Glory asked, picking out one of the prints and holding it up for Faith to see again.

"They used to babysit us for a while. I can't remember their names—

"Joan and Edward?"

Faith gave Glory a strange look, but eventually she nodded and said, "Yeah, that sounds right."

"So, were they like our neighbors or something?"

"No, they lived quite far, out in the countryside. Kent or Essex, or something like that. I can't remember."

Faith began clearing up around Esther now. The idea of decorations seemed far from her mind as she rolled the dough into a ball and dumped it in the bin. Her actions were quick and impatient. Glory could feel her line of questioning veering closer and closer to a brick wall.

"Why would we go so far out every time they needed babysitting?"

"OK, well, maybe it wasn't babysitting, as such, but we lived with them for a while out in wherever it was. Like maybe a year or something."

Glory stopped, looking Faith straight in the face even as her sister avoided eye contact and unbuckled Esther from her seat.

"*Lived* with them?"

"Basically." Faith shrugged. "Mummy and Daddy were both working long hours—actually, I think Daddy might have been studying then. I guess it's like full-time childminding—one sec, let me wash Esther up."

The only sound in the kitchen was Elijah talking to himself. He stopped to regard his aunt with a blank stare before continuing his monologue.

This new information didn't bring the same blow as the photographs but, on a very basic level, Glory's understanding of her family mythology had changed. She wasn't sure what that meant yet.

"Don't go talking to Mummy about any of this."

"Why?"

"There's no need to unnecessarily upset her."

"Why would it upset her?"

Faith sighed. "Are you coming to see Victor with us next week?"

"First I'm hearing about it."

Faith put Esther down and released Elijah from his high chair, directing them both to the living room. She turned toward Glory.

"You know, it'd be great if you showed as much interest in your brother as you're showing in these two old white people from a photograph."

"It's actually my brother who has no interest in me. Have you asked him why he won't add me to his visit list?"

Faith followed the twins out of the kitchen and into the front room. She took out a jigsaw puzzle from a chest of toys underneath the window and scattered the pieces on the floor.

"He won't even speak to me on the phone."

Glory stood, one foot in the living room and one in the hallway.

Faith switched on the TV and began cycling furiously through the channels, the screen flicking so quickly from scene to scene that it must have been impossible for her to process what she was seeing.

"Maybe you're not trying hard enough."

"Why are you so protective of Mum?" Glory sounded more pitiful than she had intended.

"*Someone* needs to be."

"Did she tell you about the other day?" Glory asked sheepishly.

"Of course she did, but she didn't need to. I know you, Glory. You just won't let this go, will you?"

"Let this go? You mean just forget about *my twin* like everyone else in this family?"

"No one's forgotten about anyone, Glory! Just because we aren't documenting our every thought on social media doesn't mean we aren't thinking about people and things!"

"Well, does Mummy talk to *you* about Hope?"

Faith continued to mechanically click the remote.

"When it comes to family, your priorities are pretty strange," she said after awhile.

"Could say the same for you."

Faith stopped channel-hopping and slid onto the floor to help her children with the jigsaw puzzle.

Glory decided to change tack. "You know, if I just got answers to my very basic questions, I would stop pissing you and Mummy off," she said in a brighter tone. "There's no need for all this secrecy."

"I don't know anything, Glory," Faith said, sounding tired.

"OK, but what's your earliest memory? Let's start there."

Faith stopped arranging puzzle pieces and closed her eyes for a moment, breathing deeply and letting her head drop back. Glory watched, excited that she might actually be getting somewhere, but suddenly Faith's eyes snapped open.

"I don't know anything, sorry."

"I just asked—"

"If that's the only thing you came to talk to me about, you might as well leave now because I can't help you," Faith said without looking up.

Glory stayed ten more minutes before she made her excuses and left.

18

When Glory reached Peckham she knew she wasn't ready to go back home. It was the beginning of March and the promise of warmer weather was in the air. The streets were beginning to fill with Friday afternoon traffic and Glory wasn't conscious of where she was heading until she saw the black signage of Pharaoh's. She could see Julian in the doorway, leaning against the frame in conversation with a couple of men who were just outside. As he saw her approach, he excused himself and walked up to meet her, a smug smile crawling across his face.

"Fancy seein'" you 'ere!" he said in an exaggerated Cockney accent. He ran his tongue across his teeth trying to hold in a laugh.

Glory could only force a smile that felt like a grimace, aware of all the eyes on them.

"What's up?"

"Nothing," Glory said, trying and failing at a convincing smile. "Are you busy?"

"Come, let's go for a walk."

He began walking in the direction of Burgess Park.

"Can we go somewhere private?" Glory asked after a few

steps, and Julian stopped, digging his hands into his pockets and looking back to his barbershop.

"My yard ain't far," he said with a casual shrug.

"Who's there?"

"No one."

"Good."

Julian led the way.

"So let me guess," Julian said, trying to keep things light. "You've come to tell me how much you enjoyed last night and want to return the favor by cooking for me."

"Unfortunately not," Glory replied, deadpan.

"Ah, you're breaking my heart, Fredo," Julian said in a raspy voice.

"What?"

"Never mind."

"Are you quoting *The Godfather*?"

"Yeah, sorry."

"It's OK," Glory said, easing up. "I like *The Godfather*."

"Swear down?" Julian said, a little surprised. "Well, I guess everyone likes *The Godfather*."

"I like them kinds of films though," Glory said, bothered by Julian's comment. "Them Mafia ones."

"Really?" Julian sounded unconvinced. "*Goodfellas*? *Casino*? *Carlito's Way*?"

"Yes, yes, and *Carlito's Way* isn't a Mafia film, it just stars Al Pacino."

Julian considered this. "Fair enough."

He stopped in front of a small paved walkway leading up to a squat, three-story tower of flats. It was one of the newer buildings that had sprung up when the old North Peckham Estate, with two-story maisonettes like Glory's family home, had been torn down. The newer buildings were smaller and more compact than the old estate had been, the luxury of two floors replaced by boxy rooms that clustered around one central corridor. Julian juggled through a large set of keys until he found one and then he continued up the path.

"Here we are," he said as he turned the silver key in the entry door to the building. "As the Mafia says, *mi casa es su casa!*"

"That's Spanish."

"I know," Julian said with a sigh. "I was just tryna make you laugh."

Glory didn't say anything else until they had gone up a flight of stairs and were inside the flat.

"You live here by yourself?" she asked as she looked at the pristine shoe boxes that lined the length of the hallway, like the storeroom of a Foot Locker.

"Yeah, you remember my sister, right? She got married and lives in Milton Keynes now. My mum went back home a couple summers ago."

A few family pictures remained on the walls of the hallway. Glory looked closely at one of Julian and his sister as teenagers, posing at their mother's graduation. She remembered his sister quite clearly as one of the older, bossy girls who could intimidate a younger girl with a judgmental look or icy glare. Left under Julian's care, the rest of the flat was in a determined state of transition, from family home to the quintessential bachelor pad. In the front room an enormous flat screen TV and shiny black sound system dominated, while on the coffee table lived an array of remotes and consoles.

Glory got comfortable on the sofa as Julian went around the room tidying away abandoned glasses and clothes flung across furniture.

"You smoke?" Glory gestured to an ashtray and a few discarded sheets of rolling paper.

Julian looked at her, trying to gauge what the correct answer would be.

"Sometimes. You?"

"Nope."

He collected the ashtray and errant Rizlas and took them through to the kitchen, before calling through the open doorway to offer Glory a drink.

"Do you have any herbal tea?"

"No tea, what else you want?"

"What else you got?"

His drinks selection was poor; fizzy drinks she didn't like and spirits she would not accept. In the end she settled for a bottle of chilled water and he did the same, sitting next to her on the sofa with a respectable distance between them.

"So tell me what's going on."

"Faith just pisses me off!" Glory said, twisting the top off her bottle roughly.

"What did she do?"

"Nothing! That's the point."

Julian let silence linger for a few seconds before saying, "I don't follow."

Glory sighed and took out the photographs, laying them out on the coffee table.

"I found these pictures this morning hidden in my mum's wardrobe. I've never seen them before so I took them to Faith to see what she might know."

Julian leaned forward and examined the photographs. "Is that you?" he asked, pointing at the picture of Hope.

"No, that's my sister. Hope."

"Oh shit!" he said. "You really are twins. Who are these two?"

"Well, apparently, we used to live with them for a while! Some random white people that I've never seen before or heard mentioned, but apparently us three lived with them for like a whole year!"

Julian looked confused. "I don't get it."

"Neither do I to be honest," Glory said, slumping back onto the sofa. "But Faith said I'm not allowed to ask my mum about it."

"Faith said that? You know you're a big woman. You can ask your mum whatever you want."

"In theory . . ." Glory chewed on a finger. "You know how Nigerian mums are, ask them something they don't like and they'll be acting like you spat at them and tore their wig off. Too much Nollywood."

Julian chuckled, leaning forward again to look at the photographs, picking up the picture of the three sisters with Joan and Edward.

"So this is you, yeah?" he asked, pointing at the tiny scowling Glory. "And that's your sister?"

Glory nodded.

"I knew it! Even mini Glory has attitude."

Glory nudged him with her thigh and he pushed her knee back, letting his hand rest on her leg longer than necessary, before turning back to the photographs.

"What primary school did you lot go?" Julian asked, holding the picture of Hope by herself close to his face.

"Grove End."

"Their uniform is green right?"

"Yeah."

"So what uniform is your sister wearing?"

Julian handed the picture back to Glory and she peered into the photograph.

"I don't know." On a more careful glance, what Glory had assumed was the dark green of her uniform actually looked more navy. She tried to make out the gold stitching of the school emblem on the little girl's cardigan. The text below the crest was long, definitely longer than "Grove End Primary School," and the first two letters looked like they might be "St."

Instinctively she took out her phone to call Faith, then remembered their earlier conversation. She'd give Faith a chance to get over herself and then she'd approach the topic from another angle.

The room fell into silence again, the only sound the quiet hum of electronics on standby.

"What are you thinking about?" Glory asked Julian, who had sat back against the sofa, resting both hands behind his head.

Julian grinned sheepishly, avoiding eye contact. He looked younger all of a sudden.

"There's this thing that's been playing on my mind bare . . ."

"Go on."

"You done me dirty, y'know? Last night, after Maijhun."

"What are you talking about?"

"You know," Julian said with a smile.

Glory's pulse quickened.

"I don't know."

"When we were walking to that park and I pulled you in . . ."

"Oh yeah, we were hugging, right?"

"And then you ran away."

"I didn't run away," Glory said, trying to stifle the smile that was breaking across her face.

"Well, I want another one—a proper one."

"Another hug? No problem."

Glory unfolded herself and leaned over to Julian, who wasted no time as his lips met hers. They were soft, as was his grip around her waist, and Glory feared that if she let herself go completely, she would melt into him. His fingers began to slip underneath her top and slowly up her back. Her skin was hot and tingling and she pressed herself into him as they kissed. She felt his hands slide around to her front, his fingers dancing across the skin of her stomach when she pulled away abruptly.

"You all right?"

"I'm fine. I'm just, erm." She shifted awkwardly. "I'm on my, erm, y'know."

"Your period?" he asked in a low tone, as if someone might overhear him. She nodded. He wiped the edges of his mouth with a thumb and a finger.

"Oh, calm," he said. He put his arm around her shoulders and they settled into a comfortable position side by side, both staring at the blank rectangle of the TV.

"Let's watch a film," Glory said, the familial tension of the day forgotten.

"What you wanna watch?"

"Anything."

Julian opened one of the cupboards below the television and began rifling through Playstation games, albums and DVDs.

"You should really organize that, you'd be able to find stuff quicker."

Julian looked at Glory over his shoulder. "Listen to me very carefully. There are three ways of doing things around here: the right way, the wrong way, and the way that *I* do it. Y'understand?"

"All right," Glory said, a little put out, "I was just trying to be helpful."

"No, Glory," Julian said, turning to her. "That's from *Casino*—remember?"

Glory shook her head.

"OK, we're watching *Casino*! Actually, scrap that. We're watching *Goodfellas*."

Around half an hour into the film, as Ray Liotta was leading Lorraine Bracco through the back entrance of the club, handing out twenty-dollar bills and shaking hands like a corrupt politician, Julian's phone started ringing. He picked it up, looked at the screen and sighed, turning it facedown on the coffee table and sitting back. But when it wouldn't stop ringing he paused the film, apologized to Glory and answered the call.

"Now? . . . Today?"

He stood and left the room. Glory waited, adjusting her clothing self-consciously, the question that had been buzzing in her head that morning resurfacing. There was no time to play it cool, because if she hadn't gotten her period this morning, the sensual kiss they had just shared would probably have gone a lot further.

"Everything all right?" she asked Julian when he finally returned.

"Yeah, someone wanted a favor but I managed to long them off 'til tomorrow. You still wanna watch *Goodfellas*?"

"Yeah, but . . ." Glory hesitated, mentally egging herself onward. "I want to ask you something."

Julian dropped down on the sofa beside her.

"Yeah, what's up?"

"Well . . . what are we . . . doing here?" She managed to say, feeling somehow weaker for needing to ask the question.

"Doing here?"

"I mean, like, are we dating or what?" Glory said, her face burning with embarrassment. "Last night was a date right?"

A satisfied smile now appeared on Julian's face and he relaxed back into position.

"Yeah, wasn't it obvious?"

"Just checking—I don't know how things . . . work . . . here."

"Sorry, I forgot you were used to the American way of doing things," Julian said wryly.

"No, not tha— Look . . ." Glory shifted in her seat to face him, now holding his gaze earnestly. "I just want to make sure that we're both on the same page because I've made this mistake before."

Julian nodded, sitting up slightly, ready to reciprocate Glory's forthrightness.

"I hear that, well I like you, innit—if that wasn't clear enough before, then let me lay all my cards out. I like you and I wanna see where this goes."

"Are you seeing anyone else?"

"No," Julian said quickly. "Are you?"

Glory shook her head.

"All right then."

"So we're exclusive?" Glory said pedantically.

"Yes," Julian said with a laugh. "Unless you don't want to be? I dunno, do you want an open relationship? Is that what people do out in LA?"

"No, I just wanted to be absolutely sure."

"OK then!" Julian said. "Do we need to shake on it, is there any paperwork to sign or can we get back to watching *Goodfellas*?"

Glory kissed her teeth and swatted at him, before turning to face the TV.

"You know I learned how to chop garlic from *Goodfellas*," Glory said as she got more comfortable, lifting Julian's arm to wrap it around her shoulders. "The guy cutting garlic with a razor in the prison scene really left an impression on me, and it works, it actually makes the garlic dissolve into the oil in the pan."

Julian looked at her for a moment.

"You're really different, y'know?"

"You'll get used to it," Glory said, bringing her legs onto the sofa and resting her head against his chest.

19

Glory stayed late at Julian's flat. So late that his barbers began calling him, asking him where he was because after getting everyone else ready for their Friday evenings, they wanted to close up the shop and go about their business. Julian and Glory walked back to Pharoah's, Glory waiting while he checked over the shop floor and locked up, and then he walked her back to her mother's house.

It was late enough that Glory didn't hesitate to kiss Julian goodbye on her doorstep, convinced that her mother would now be asleep, but when she unlocked the front door and entered the living room, she found Celeste sitting upright in Daddy's armchair, hands folded across her lap and a stern expression on her face.

"Where have you been? It is late!"

"I was at Faith's house and then I went to see a friend," Glory said, trying to keep guilt from taking over her voice.

"You left Faith's house hours ago. She told me."

"You could have just rung me to find out where I was, Mummy," Glory said, irritated that her sister and mother were again talking about her behind her back.

"I am not going to be running up and down the streets looking for my daughter!"

"No one's sayin'—Glory sighed. "I'm a grown woman. If there was a problem you should have called me, if there's not, why are you stressing?"

Celeste kissed her teeth and rose from her seat.

"Insolent girl. I'm going to bed."

Glory watched her mother's back retreating from her, feeling like a scolded child. She wanted to say something that would be sharp enough to grab Celeste's attention, something that would make her mother take her seriously as the adult she was, but she scrambled to find something that would be harsh and piercing enough.

"Mummy!" she began abruptly. "What primary school did we go to?"

Celeste stopped halfway up the stairs and turned around looking tired and annoyed.

"Did we go to any other primary school besides Grove End?"

"No," Celeste said. "Why are you asking me that?"

"Nothing—no reason," Glory replied, her mind skittering over facts and thoughts. She waited until she heard the creak of the mattress signal her mother's presence in the main bedroom, then Glory rushed to the shelf with the photo albums.

She flipped it open to the first page, the earliest photographs she had found—Victor's birth. She checked every photograph from that day, but only Glory and Faith were present.

She then called Julian.

"Hey," Julian answered the phone warmly. "Missing me already?"

"I just thought of something!" Glory said, feeling her heart pound against her rib cage. "That picture of Hope, she was in primary school! But Victor was born before I started primary school. But Hope died before Victor was born!"

"Wh-what? Start again."

"Until I found those photos I showed you, I had never seen any pictures of me or my sisters before Victor was born. The pictures we have at home are all from Victor's birth onwards—but Hope isn't in any of them!"

"OK?"

"But in that picture, Hope is in primary school! I was four when Victor was born but I hadn't started primary school yet!"

"Wait!" Julian exclaimed. "What are you saying?"

Glory took a deep breath and started again.

"I always thought Hope died before Victor was born, but she couldn't have! Because she went to that primary school, whatever that primary school was! But Victor was born *before* we would have started primary school, but she's not in any pictures when Victor was born!"

Julian didn't say anything, no doubt trying to piece together Glory's excited, but jumbled explanation of time lines.

"So you're saying that Hope couldn't have died when you thought she died, because she was still alive after Victor was born?"

"Yes! Exactly!" Glory said, struggling to keep her voice low enough not to disturb her mother. "I need to find her death certificate to find out exactly when she died, but it's not here. Faith won't help me!"

"Check online," Julian said. "You'll find it online."

"A death certificate?"

"Yeah, birth certificates, marriage certificates, death certificates, they're all available online."

"Since when?"

"Since always—they're like public records or something."

"I didn't know that, isn't that like a data protection issue?"

"Yeah, you'd think."

"Wait, how do you know this?"

"You don't want to know—but just check, innit. You can find it there."

Glory ended the call and opened her browser. She typed in "lost death certificate" and the first result was the government website where she could order copies of these "personal" public records.

She clicked on the website and skim-read all the information, creating an account with trembling fingers and opening a new search query.

Which index would you like to search? She clicked "Death."

When was the death registered? Glory clicked on the first menu and highlighted "1994" before clicking on the second menu and adding "+/- 2 years."

More text boxes appeared and Glory filled them in. "Surname at Death," "First Forename at Death," "Sex." When asked "Where was the death registered?" she typed "Southwark" and clicked search.

No Matching Results Found.

The room began to spin. Glory stumbled over to the sofa and sat down heavily. She rechecked the details entered and changed the option next to the name text box from "Exact matches only" to "Phonetically similar variations."

This time the page took longer to load, and Glory held her breath as she watched the progress bar inch its way forward until a message appeared in red text: *500—Internal server error.*

Glory's face began to feel hot. Maybe Hope's death hadn't been registered in Southwark at all, maybe she was searching the wrong borough's database. She began to fan herself with her hand, stopping momentarily to hold a sweaty palm to her cheek.

Kent or Essex, that's where Faith had said they were living with that Joan and Edward, maybe Hope had died while they

were living there. But those counties were impossibly big—
what town had they been living in? Which district would
have claimed Hope's death?

Even as Glory desperately sorted through the possibilities, she felt the reality of them slipping through her grasp.
Hope's death certificate wasn't in the house and it wasn't in
the government index. Hope's death didn't exist officially in
the same way her family had never acknowledged the loss.

Glory lay flat on the sofa, her heart still hammering away,
hot flushes and nausea threatening to overwhelm her. She
felt her phone vibrating by her side and remembered she had
told Julian she would call him back, but she couldn't bring
herself to speak to him. She wasn't ready to sit up yet, and
she wasn't ready to confront Faith and her mother with the
results of her search. So while she waited until she felt ready
to do something, she counted slowly in her head, praying the
air would continue to flow through her lungs and her blood
would continue to pump through her body. She prayed she
wasn't dying despite everything her brain was telling her.

20

"You slept downstairs?"

It was positioned as a question, but was actually a statement. Impatient and cutting, Celeste was already irritated with her daughter before Glory could wake up and properly orientate herself.

"Sleeping in your clothes like you're homeless!" Celeste kissed her teeth and threw a contemptuous look in Glory's direction before leaving the front room and heading toward the kitchen.

Glory pulled herself into a seated position, the fitful and uncomfortable sleep she had eventually fallen into making her feel more delirious than well rested. She checked her phone, it was Saturday morning.

"No job! No husband—heh!" Celeste shouted to the living room, clapping loudly to punctuate each indictment. "Going out late at night and then sleeping around the house like a drunkard! I told you, my house is not America! It is not wherever you think you have come from!"

Celeste was in a particular mood, the kind that projected whatever irritated her on to whatever was in her vicinity, coating her immediate surroundings in her prickly anger, while she looked for a reason to fight.

Glory covered her head with her hands, as if her mother's words could be stopped by a physical barrier. She then stood up and made her way to the bathroom. ·

"So my mouth is smelling? Is that why you're ignoring me? Glory!"

As she sat on the toilet, the events and revelations of the night before came back to her. She checked her phone again. Three missed calls from Julian and a text message. She opened her browser and saw the timed out page of the government website.

She then finished in the bathroom, making her way downstairs with more determination than before, following the sound of her mother's tirade until she was standing in front of the woman in the kitchen.

"Where's Hope's death certificate?" Glory asked, as evenly as she could muster.

Celeste took a step backward, as if she had been struck. "Who are you talking to?!"

"You tried to hide her birth certificate and these pictures." Glory brought out the photographs and the now well creased photocopy. "Have you hidden her death certificate as well?"

"S-so you have been going through my things?"

"It's not there. It's not in Daddy's folder or his desk and I looked for it online and it's not there. Does it even exist?!" Glory asked, her voice rising as she threw the photographs on the kitchen counter.

"Are you all right?" The question was rhetorical, delivered with half a breath, a cocked head and a squint that would have been a precursor to physical punishment when Glory was a child. "You have forgotten how to address your mother, àbí?"

"Just tell me what the hell is going on! There are no pictures of Hope until I found these hidden in your wardrobe! I thought she died before Victor was born, but in this picture she's in a school uniform! A uniform that belongs to a school I didn't go to! What happened to my sister?"

Celeste stared back in open-mouthed shock. It felt like all the air had been sucked from the room for the few seconds that it took Celeste to find her footing again.

Her mother's hand cut through the air and slapped Glory across the face. Glory gasped and time stopped, as Celeste looked in horror between her hand and her daughter's cheek. Tears filled Glory's eyes and began to spill, though it wasn't to do with the pain. The slap had been a shock, but it hadn't been that hard, and when Glory lifted her head to look at her mother she could see tears on the older woman's face as well.

"I am a God-fearing woman," Celeste began, her voice trembling with emotion. "But s-see what you have caused, Glory?"

Celeste looked at her hand as if she was seeing it for the first time in her life. Glory was still too stunned to speak. She began backing away from the kitchen, not sure if her mother was going to slap her again. She hadn't been smacked since she was a child, and even then her mother had never hit her in the face, it was always a few light smacks to her bottom or the back of her hand. The woman standing in front of Glory was clearly unhinged.

"You don't know what I've had to sacrifice for this family, for your father, for all of you."

Celeste's voice was pleading and she advanced slowly toward Glory, who was continuing to back away.

"I had to go against my own instincts as a mother, you

don't understand. God forbid you ever have to understand what it means to give up your own child!"

"Give up?" Glory's voice was quiet and feeble.

Celeste broke down, her wails scaring Glory more than the violence. She knew she should stay with her mother, make sure she didn't hurt herself again; the stitches from the last incident had only just dissolved.

Celeste was now speaking in Yorùbá, as she often did when English words seemed to fail her. Her voice was thick with emotion and the words morphed into sounds that collided with one another and crashed over Glory.

Glory left the kitchen, quickly dialing Faith's number.

"Your mother attacked me!" she said in a hushed shout when Faith finally answered.

"Glory? What are you talking about?"

"She attacked me! She slapped me in my face and now she's having another breakdown."

"What?!"

"Come and get me because I can't stay here!"

Celeste continued to wail and moan from where she had finally fallen to the floor.

"Glory! You cannot leave her!"

Glory sniffed and sighed. Faith was right.

"She slapped me, Faith," she said again, her voice breaking. "She slapped me straight in my face."

"What happened, Glory? I'm coming, but tell me what happened!"

"I was asking her about Hope's death certificate, and she just lost it and slapped me."

There was a deep sigh on the end of the phone. "For fuck's sake, Glory!" was all Faith said before she hung up the phone.

21

Despite everything, Glory didn't leave her mother as she had told Faith she would. Of course she stayed, eventually returning to the sobbing heap of a woman and helping her to stand, supporting her to the foot of the staircase, then up the stairs and back into her bedroom.

"Glory—má bínú. I'm sorry, ehn? Má bínú," Celeste had repeated over and over again as Glory assisted her to her room.

When she sat on her bed, she reached out to cup Glory's face, but her daughter ducked reflexively away from her.

"Ọmọ mi," Celeste cried in a trembling voice. But Glory was not moved by her mother's contrition. As soon as Faith came, she was leaving. Maybe for good.

Faith arrived just over half an hour later, and for once she was unaccompanied.

"Where are Estie and 'Lijah?" Glory asked from her place on the sofa, still wearing the same clothes as yesterday, still nursing her cheek although the pain had gone.

"With Michael—where's Mummy?"

"In her room," Glory said, standing up and preparing to leave.

"Just wait. Let me go check on her first, OK? I'll come back down. Just wait."

Glory fell back onto the sofa, bringing out her phone to scroll through the uncomplicated lives of others. Faith went upstairs.

Julian was calling again, but Glory let the call ring out. A simple Google search had turned into chaos and may see her mother admitted back into Maudsley. She had no energy to explain that to him over the phone.

Faith eventually came back downstairs. "Mummy wants to speak to you."

"I don't have anything to say to her unless—"

"Just come upstairs, Glory."

Faith turned on her heel and went back up to their mother's room. Glory reluctantly followed.

Celeste was propped up in bed, a Bible open across her lap, looking mournful. Glory felt like she had arrived at her own exorcism.

"Please, sit," her mother said, sounding strangely formal.

"I'd rather stand," Glory said, and Celeste sighed, her eyes swiveling to the ceiling.

"I am not a bad person," Celeste began, but her voice broke, so she cleared her throat and began again.

"I am not a bad person. I am God-fearing and my conscience is clear, but I have not been honest with you."

Glory said nothing.

"My daughter, Hope, is not dead. She is not. She is alive but she lives with another family."

From the moment Glory discovered that the death certificate may not exist, this possibility had presented itself, but hearing her mother say it out loud was different.

Glory coughed, choking on her own spit and shock.

"Where? Who is this family?"

"They are the English people in the photographs you saw."

Celeste still wasn't looking at Glory, but Glory could not tear her eyes away from her mother.

"Mummy," Glory choked again over that word. "Where is she?"

Celeste dropped her eyes from the ceiling and into her lap, smoothing a hand over the thin Bible pages.

"When I came here I worked all the hours that God gave me." Celeste's voice was strained but she kept her tone measured, trying to hold herself together. "When it was just Faith it was fine. She would stay with a woman who went to the church we attended at the time. But when you came, Glory, with your sister, it was harder. She couldn't take all three of you, especially with the little money I could afford to pay her, but she knew of another woman, Mama Wawo, who said she could find someone to look after you all. So when you, Glory, were just a few months old, all three of you went to them, the Marksham family, a very nice English family in Kent, who would look after you and I would send them money and come to see you whenever I could."

Now Celeste took a gasp, it was rasping and shook her whole body. Faith reached out a steadying hand to her mother and Glory remembered for a moment that she was not alone in witnessing this, Faith was here, silent and calm, seemingly unfazed by the secrets spilling from their mother's mouth.

"It was not meant to be that long. No, that was not the plan, but what choice did I have? What mother voluntarily leaves her children for so long? But I had to work for you three. So that I could move from the hostel to a house, and then we could live as a family in a proper home. But when we went to collect you all, finally, your sister was screaming like we were trying to take her from her mother."

Celeste broke. Her mouth collapsed, each word came out in ragged, uneven breaths, and she began to wring her hands.

"We brought you all home but she wouldn't eat, she would just cry all the time, like she was being tortured. She would cry and cry. So we took her back to Kent for a while, I thought that would help. What was I supposed to do?" Celeste's eyes fell on Glory with a pitiful stare.

"Even then when we brought her back again she would cry, you don't remember because you were young, barely older than Esther and Elijah now, but all she would do was cry."

Celeste's voice began to falter.

"Then Kúnlé came back one evening and he had had enough. He beat her. With a coat hanger. The marks were very bad and I was scared. I called Mama Wawo and got her to drive me to Kent that evening. I took your sister there but when I got back, Kúnlé said that I had made my decision. That was it. She would stay there until she was old enough to know better, to want her real family instead of them. I tried to keep in touch, but he wouldn't even hear her name in the house. She had disgraced him, that small girl had disgraced him, and he would not hear of her again. Then they moved. The family moved to the Midlands and I let her go with them."

Glory had never heard her mother refer to her father by his first name. It was always "your Daddy" or "your father." To others it was "my husband," but now the name "Kúnlé" sliced awkwardly through the air, as if her mother had forgotten who she was addressing. It felt as foreign to Glory as the description of the man who had beaten her twin so much that his wife feared for her child's life.

She could not imagine her father beating her. He blustered and shouted and ranted on, but she could not remember a time when he had raised a hand to strike her. In college, when her peers would regale each other with tales of childhood beatings with slippers, wooden spoons and spindly branches collected from the garden by the offending child, Glory would laugh and holler with the rest of them. But she had no tale of her own to contribute. Her father didn't beat her. Her friends would raise their eyebrows and their mouths would gape in disbelief, but it was true.

"Why did you let them go?" Glory asked, her cold tone masking the turmoil she felt within. Glory felt like she had been torn wide open and was tumbling through a tunnel of questions about the story, about her parents, about herself.

"What could I do, Glory?" Celeste said in a quiet wail. "What could I do? I continued to go and visit her while she was still in Kent, but she didn't want to leave Joan. And there was no money! It was hard!"

Celeste cleared her throat.

"And then I got pregnant with Victor and it was still hard. I was managing my pregnancy and you two, and Kúnlé was so tired with his work, and I couldn't cope with all of that and then a crying child who wants to return to her white mother—it was just me!"

"Bu—"

"You do not understand, Glory! You are not a mother! You will not understand until you are a mother! It's not like back home where you have people around to help you manage. I had no one but Joan! She and Edward offered help and I took it because who else was there?"

Celeste's nostrils flared, and Faith muttered, "Mummy, please don't get upset."

Glory's mouth snapped shut, her sister's words another strike. She couldn't believe how calm Faith was through all of this. She felt like someone had crushed her rib cage, squeezing all the air from her, but Faith was barely reacting.

"But where is she now?" Glory asked carefully, her voice barely above a whisper.

"They moved to the Midlands. We kept in touch for a while, but then . . ." Celeste fluttered her fingers, as if a child was like a scarf you lost on a windy day.

"But then what?"

"Glory," Faith said carefully.

"Faith, we have a sister out there somewhere and we don't know where?! This is insane, Faith, how are you so calm?"

Celeste's sobs started, a shaky low whine cutting in between each gasp.

"Glory," Faith said through gritted teeth. "Go downstairs!"

"Faith, I'm not a child. This is wild—what if this was Esther or Elijah? How could—"

"This isn't helpful, Glory! Go downstairs! I'm coming!"

Faith glared at Glory, her eyes, dark and hard as stones, telling her sister not to utter another word.

When Faith finally followed, Glory was pacing the living room, just like their father used to.

"Faith, what the *hell?!*" Glory intoned in a loud whisper.

Faith held up a hand, trying to silence her sister, but Glory ignored the gesture.

"Did you hear anything that Mummy just told us?! Hope is alive and always has been, but she just lost touch with her like she was a dog that ran away?!"

"You got the answers that you wanted, all right? So just drop it, and I swear to God if you continue pushing Mummy on this I will slap you myself!"

"Are you sick?!"

"Glory, you have literally no idea what you're talking about," Faith said in a patronizing tone. "Do you know how ill Mummy was after having Victor? She was damn near psychotic with postnatal depression, of course she lost touch with them!"

"I didn't know that," Glory said, humbled.

"Of course you didn't, you were a child and you still act like a child now!"

The memory of her mother in the yellow nightdress returned to Glory, sharper and more significant than before.

"How did you know? You were a child too."

"She told me after I had Esther and Elijah, when I was struggling with depression myself."

"You had it too?! I didn't know, Faith! I didn't know!"

"No," Faith said. "You didn't. And despite whatever you think you know now about what happened to Hope, you've only got half the story, but keep going on about it with Mummy and you will put her back in hospital and I promise you, I will *never* forgive you!"

Faith's eyes were dangerously bright.

"Faith," Glory began, trying to keep her voice soft and non-confrontational. "You can't expect me not to have questions. You can't expect me to hear all of that and not have more questions. She was *my* twin!"

Faith's eyes roamed over the front room, eventually resting on the portrait of their father that Michael had hung over the TV.

"Well," she said finally. "You'd be asking the wrong person."

22

"Wow, she's alive!" Julian said, when Glory finally called him back. "I thought you had changed your mind or something."

"Changed my mind about what?"

"You know, what we agreed on yesterday—we didn't shake hands or sign any papers so I thought you were backing out."

"Oh," Glory said. "No, but maybe I should think twice after your little piece of advice got me into a whole load of trouble."

"What?" Julian's jovial tone dropped and Glory felt guilty for blaming him for something that probably would have happened anyway.

"Sorry—no, it wasn't your fault, I just did that thing you said, I looked online for Hope's death certificate. Turns out it doesn't exist."

There was no sound on the other end of the phone until eventually Julian said, "So, what does that mean?"

"Do you want the long version or the short version?" Glory said, turning over in bed where she had been laying low since Celeste had calmed down and Faith had returned to her family, with another strict reminder for Glory to keep her mouth shut.

"Give me the conclusion and then you can fill in the details after."

"Well, Hope is alive. She lives with that white couple in the pictures. My mum lost contact with the family after she went crazy after having Victor—no, that's mean—she had some issues after Victor was born and then lost contact with the family. So, yeah."

"Shit," Julian said under his breath. "Fackin" 'ell, Glory. That's mad, still."

"You're telling me!" Glory managed to force a laugh.

"So what now? Have you looked her up?"

"Googled her, you mean? So I can land myself in another mess when I discover some other fucked up family secret?"

"Well, yeah . . ."

"Yes, of course I have!" Glory said.

It had been the first thing she did when Faith had left. She had opened up her laptop and typed "Hope Akindele" in to the search bar, scrolling through a page of results related to the Nollywood actress, Funke Akíndélé—no relation as far as Glory knew. She had then tried "Hope Akindele UK" and scanned over articles about a doctor called Gbénga, an entrepreneur called Vanessa and international students giving glowing testimonials for British universities.

She then tried "Hope Marksham," and when that proved fruitless she had allowed the search engine to autocorrect to "Markham" before moving on to Facebook. But the site only returned variants like "Akindele Hope Gbade" (living in Ibadan, Nigeria) and "Alice Hope Marksham" (from Shropshire, working in Edinburgh).

She was so desperate, she almost considered risking a hailstorm to ask her mother if she remembered which town the family had moved to. But remembering Faith's threat, and not for one second doubting the protective zeal of her older sister, Glory let her idle fingers call Julian instead.

"Actually, do you know someone called Mama Wawo?" Glory asked him.

"Mama Waro?"

"Wa-*wo*. Mama Wawo."

"Nah, don't think so—why?"

"Someone my mum used to know, she might be able to help me find my sister," Glory said, feeling more and more deflated as she realized that, despite the revelation, Hope felt as far away as she had done before her continued existence had been confirmed.

"Oh, nah, sorry, babe," Julian said, softly.

"*Babe*? Are we giving each other nicknames now?"

Glory was trying to distract herself from the mood that was settling upon her.

Julian snorted.

"Yeah, what's mine?"

"Hmm . . . The Mayor of Peckham."

"The Mayor of Peckham?"

"Yeah, you know everybody."

"You mean everyone knows me."

"Either way, you're bait, Mr. Mayor. Wow, never thought I'd be going out with a bait one—yuck!" Glory made a wretching noise down the phone.

"Well, I know it's probably not the best time, but there's a house party tonight if you want something to take your mind off everything. I can introduce you to my constituents."

Glory could hear Julian smiling through the phone and she allowed herself to be convinced that a party would make her feel better. At least, it would be better than wallowing at home in silence while Google sent her in circles.

"What's the dress code?"

"Er—it's a house party, so whatever, but look sexy, innit."

"Damn, no pressure."

"First Lady of Peckham sexy, you see it?"

Glory was beginning to regret Julian's nickname already. "OK, I'll see what I can find."

"A'ight! Cool!"

When she ended the call, the Facebook app popped up on her screen and in the search results she saw the name "Hope Kehinde." The tiny profile picture showed the side of a woman's face, most of it thrown into shadow. Glory sent a friend request and closed the app.

23

"Man liiike!"

"Yes, my bruddah!"

Julian clapped his hand into a firm handshake with the tall figure standing at the door. Glory waited patiently behind him for the pantomime of compliments to get played out before his attention would be turned back to her.

"You're looking good, my g, life is treating you nice!"

"Just tryna be like you, bruddah!"

"This is Glory, by the way," Julian finally said, and Glory turned to face his friend with a gracious smile and demure "hi."

"Is that you, yeah?" the friend said, the alcohol and bass forcing his whisper into an indiscreet shout. Glory turned away, giving Julian a moment to bask in his friend's admiration without Glory making him self-conscious.

It turned out "First Lady of Peckham sexy" was hard to achieve with the clothes Glory had at her disposal. She regretted leaving the majority of her possessions in America. When she was leaving, her wardrobe had felt like the least of her problems, but if she had known she would be unemployed for this long, but with a popular boyfriend and parties to attend, she might have packed at least one nice dress and a pair of heels.

Glory turned back to the two men in time to see Julian handing over the bottle of Courvoisier he had brought for the occasion.

"Vossi, bro? You know this liquor gets man in *trouble!*" The friend burst into salacious laughter. "Oi, remember that time in West—" But Julian cut him off with another friendly clap on the back.

"We all know you don't need any Vossi to misbehave, bro!" Julian said with a laugh. "Glory, you ready to go inside?"

He held out his hand, guiding her through the doorway.

The three-story house in Rotherhithe was teeming with people, and the layout of the other houses meant the music echoed around the cul-de-sac, amplifying drum patterns a few seconds off beat. Glory could see through the darkened kitchen to a back garden where more people were, and others sat on the stairs and leaned against banisters, some bubbling to the music that was coming from the living area, others engaged in animated conversation that made them spill their drinks and apologize to whoever was on the stair below them.

"Where are the drinks?" Glory said into Julian's ear. She had already finished off a can of Coke spiked with a miniature of Wray & Nephew, thinking it would be enough to loosen her up and push the cares of the day from her mind. But she should have bought the pocket-sized bottle instead, it would have carried her through the night.

"Kitchen," Julian said over the music, and he took her hand in his, leading her through the crush of bodies to the back of the house. His firm, guiding presence eased her mind. It felt so good to be wanted, to be claimed so publicly, even if the room was dark and everyone around them was too drunk or engrossed in other matters to notice how he positioned her in front of him at the drinks table, his hands resting lightly on her hips as she selected a white rum and some tropical juice.

As childish as his friend's comments had been at the door, it felt good to be the kind of girl that her boyfriend's friends would secretly ogle at—someone a man could be proud of. "A trophy?" a critical voice piped up within, but she pushed any thoughts of hypocrisy and Faith from her mind with a mouthful of KA and rum.

When Glory heard the opening ad-libs to "Whine & Kotch" her hips began to move of their own volition.

"You want to dance?" Julian said, spinning her around by her waist so she was facing him.

"Yeah, you?"

"I don't dance darlin,'" Julian said, his silver tooth winking.

"Don't be dry," Glory said, pushing out her bottom lip.

"OK, I *can't* dance. But you can dance on me if you want?"

He looked down at Glory's hips, which were moving in little circles, accentuating their rocking rhythm with his hands.

"So I can look like a video vixen in a rap video?" she asked with a tut. "No, thanks."

"You got your drink?"

Glory nodded, and Julian took her by the hand again, leading her back through to the hallway and then into the front room, where the music was loudest and the crowd was thickest. Julian nodded and saluted along the way, finding a window ledge to lean on next to people he recognized.

He wrapped a protective arm around Glory's waist while he leaned away to participate in half shouted, half gestured conversation. Glory watched the room react to hit after hit, jealous and bored as she downed her drink quickly in the hope that the effects of the rum might stop her caring about dancing by herself.

"Where's the bathroom?" she shouted in Julian's ear when her drink was done, and he pointed in the direction of the stairs.

Glory picked her way through dancing couples and encouraging friends whooping and hollering as one of them showed off an intricate dance step. She climbed the stairs and joined the queue.

"I like your hair!" a young woman said, joining the queue behind her.

"Yeah, the little buns are cute!" her friend chipped in.

Glory said thanks and instinctively touched the two bantu knots at the front of her head, making sure they hadn't unraveled.

"I hope the neighbors don't call the police," the first friend said.

"I think Dorian said he told them all beforehand, so it wouldn't happen again."

"Were you at the last party?"

This question was directed at Glory, who hadn't realized she had been drawn into the circle of their conversation.

"Oh? Me? No, first time."

"Oh cool, how do you know Dorian?"

The two girls trained their attention on her, smiling warmly.

"I don't, my—I came with one of his friends."

They both nodded, and Glory turned back in the direction of the bathroom door.

"Was it Jay you was with? Jay who owns the barbershop in Peckham?"

Glory tensed, now sensing some ulterior motive behind their innocent toilet-queue chatter.

"Yeah, I did," she said, trying to maintain a casual tone. "You know him?"

"Just seen him around," was the response, and Glory smiled at the women and turned back around.

She buried her attention in her phone, and when it was finally her turn she slipped into the bathroom quickly, making sure the door was firmly locked behind her.

She changed her tampon, and was dismayed to find there was no bathroom bin. She would have to find some creative way to dispose of it. The women waiting on the other side of the door made the whole endeavor feel more conspicuous, and she ended up wrapping her rubbish in a thick wad of tissue, and packing it tightly in a balled fist.

She left the small bathroom and threw an easy smile at the two-woman inquisition team that waited its turn. They flashed back thin plastic smiles as she squeezed past them, back down the stairs, and out the front door.

Faith was right, she needed friends and, after discreetly disposing of her package in an outside bin, she took out her phone and sent a message to Lará:

"Hey, what are you up to tonight?"

She saw a message from Julian:

"I'm in the garden."

After a few minutes allowing the night air to cool her down, Glory turned to go back inside.

The music was only getting better, but the rum hadn't made enough of an impact to push Glory toward the dance floor. She forced her way back through the kitchen and into the garden where a smokers' circle had formed with Julian at the center, taking a long pull on a spliff. When he saw her approach he quickly pushed a thick plume of smoke out of the corner of his mouth, looking like a child caught with their hand in the biscuit tin.

"Hey!"

"Hi," Glory said, lowering her voice a little. "You're driving us back, remember?"

"Yeah, don't watch that—I know my limit," Julian murmured through tight lips.

"Ay, don't let us get you in trouble with the missus!" came a mocking cry from one of his friends.

Julian laughed it off, introducing the circle of men one by one to Glory, before they continued their conversation.

Glory checked her phone again. No response from Lará.

"You're Victor's big sister, right?" the one introduced as Sims asked, interrupting her endless scroll.

"Yeah, well, one of them," Glory replied. "You know him?"

Sims took a toke on the spliff.

"Nah, but my BM's little brother was his co-defendant and got wrapped with him," Sims said, his voice thick and nasal from holding in the smoke. He finally exhaled, and a cloud of white hovered above his head. "It's fucked how they did 'em."

The men chorused their agreement.

"That's how they tried to do M Dot as well, remember? They tried to say it was a joint enterprise because a witness said he was with the man who did it. But then they checked the CCTV and saw that he was with them before, left for a while and then bumped back into them three hours later. But I bet if the CCTV wasn't there he would be in Wanno right now with the rest of them. The system's fucked!"

The group murmured again, but Glory looked at Julian, her eyes questioning.

"The system works the way it's meant to work," Julian said after a few moments of the group smoking in silence. "That's the point of joint enterprise, more prisoners means more money for private prisons, more slaves for private companies, inflated conviction rates. Everyone wins apart from us!"

"That's why I'm saying we all need to get our money up and get the fuck outta here!" Sims said, holding the spliff out for Julian who made a show of refusing it. "Every man take his savings and return to his motherland—build our people up rather than paying taxes to a system that would rather see you in the jail cell or underneath it! Jay—your dad's in Naij ain't he? You're set my bruddah!"

"Yeah, I guess so," Julian mumbled, the mention of his father making him shrink.

"Return to where, Sims?" one of the other men said. "I was born right here! This is my motherland!"

"Well, this fuckin" mother don't want you, bro! Truss me!"

Scattered laughter broke out among the group, before someone began telling a story about an uncle who returned "back home" and lived like a king.

"You all right, Glory?" Julian asked, breaking away. "You wanna go inside?"

"What's joint enterprise?" Glory asked sheepishly. Julian looked stunned then confused.

"That's the charge that Victor got convicted on. Didn't anyone tell you?"

"No," Glory confessed. "I thought it was something else."

"You mean Faith or your parents never explained anything about the case?"

Glory shook her head.

"Your family just don't talk about stuff, huh?" Julian rubbed a hand on his chin.

"This is what I've been telling you!"

"And you've never spoken about it with Victor either?"

"Victor hasn't spoken to me full stop. He drops the phone whenever I answer and then calls back later hoping my mum will pick up."

"What did you do?"

"What do you mean what did *I* do?"

"Usually when you go to prison you don't care about anything but your family and getting out. If he's beefing you then there must be a reason."

Glory sighed, there was no use protesting.

"I never came home for his trial," she said, dropping her voice as low as it could go. "I didn't want it to be real and it was easier to pretend that it wasn't when I wasn't here. It was hard to get my head around the fact that he got charged and convicted for something like that. *Manslaughter*, Julian. Someone's son died."

"Don't get me wrong," Julian's face was serious and still, "it's proper sad that he died, but Victor got bagged on a joint enterprise charge. That's bullshit!"

"But what's joint enterprise? You haven't explained!"

Julian looked back at his friends.

"It's basically guilt by association. When you hear 'joint enterprise,' it's a fancy way of saying 'all them little shits are gang members!' An easy way to increase conviction rates, but—shit, Glory." Now it was Julian's turn to sigh. "I'm meant to be taking your mind off family drama and here we are talking about your brother's case. You sure you want to talk about this now?"

Glory noted the way he looked so concerned even in the dim light of Dorian's garden. There was so much family drama, of course she didn't want to talk about it now.

"We'll talk more about it tomorrow, OK?" she said, smoothing her fingers over the crease between his eyebrows.

"Tomorrow? What's happening tomorrow?"

"I'm staying over tonight, didn't I tell you? My mum will lose it if I come back late again and seeing how we're official and that . . ."

Glory winked, biting coyly on her tongue. Julian smiled wide, pulling her in close and tucking his thumbs into the waistband of her skirt.

"Don't let your fan club see this," Glory said, pressing two hands to his chest and pushing him away. "They've already cornered me once."

"Fan club?"

"Yeah, two girls asking me questions about you while I waited to use the toilet. *Did you come with Jay? How do you know him?*" Glory mimicked the women's questions in a mocking voice.

"Who were they?" Julian asked, pulling Glory back toward him.

"They didn't say, but I knew dating a bait guy would be trouble."

"We can go back to mine right now, y'know?" Julian looked serious again. "I don't mind."

"But I really wanted to dance," Glory said.

"You can dance at mine, I might even buss a two step with you in the privacy of my own yard."

Glory laughed, then nodded and Julian turned back to the smokers' circle.

"Ay, you man! I'm out, yeah!" he called, throwing a hand up over his shoulder.

Someone wolf-whistled and the others jeered, and Julian waved them all away while leading Glory back into the house and toward the front door.

"Julian, you know I'm still on my, erm, y'know," Glory said cautiously as Julian said quick goodbyes to all the familiar faces he passed.

He didn't answer until they were out in the cul-de-sac walking back to where he had parked his car.

"What, you're not done already?" he asked, keeping up a brisk pace. "I'm not dumb, Glory, I know—so what, I can't chill with you while you're on your period or what?"

"Nah, it's just—I dunno, like, your friends were all like . . . I dunno."

Julian leaned both arms on the top of his car, tapping the fob against the roof.

"I'm not really tryna find out the details of your last relationship or anything, but you keep asking me these questions which makes me think that whoever he was, he was a bit of a dickhead."

Glory couldn't deny that, but then she also couldn't count whatever she and Adam had as a relationship.

"I don't even like parties, I'd rather chill at home with you in your pyjamas with your period, your hot water bottle, your satin bonnet and alla that—any day!"

"Wow, you're so romantic, and what do you know about hot water bottles and satin bonnets, anyway?" Glory opened the car door and got in. "Or is that what you learned from all your previous girlfriends?"

Julian sat in the driver's seat and closed the door, but he didn't start the car.

"I know you're joking, but I don't like all of that other girlfriend talk. Forget anyone else, I'm with you, yeah? I don't know who those girls were in there asking about me, but they don't matter because I'm with you."

His face was stern but it made Glory feel like a wall within her was dissolving.

"You know . . ." Julian began, but then he stopped, looking down into his lap with a little chuckle.

"What?"

"I've liked you from time, y'know."

"Since when? From when we were *kids*?" Glory frowned.

"Since, I dunno, we were teenagers. I always used to see you around and you had this little attitude going on, and I used to think, *Yo, she's kinda nice!*"

Julian's voice was soft and self-conscious.

"Why didn't you say something?"

"I did . . . when I saw you at your dad's funeral."

Glory spluttered.

"*Ten* years later?!"

"Listen, I didn't have anything going for me back then. A skinny little yout" with a hot temper. Now I'm a man with something to offer."

He finally looked up at Glory and smiled. She turned her body toward him, reaching a hand around the back of his neck and drawing his head toward her. They kissed, and when she felt the gear stick pushing into her she broke away.

"Push your seat back," she told him.

"What?"

"Push your seat back—all the way back."

He obliged, and Glory maneuvered herself up onto the passenger seat and eventually onto his lap, managing to straddle him in the cramped front seat of his BMW.

"What are you doing?" Julian asked with a glint in his eye.

"I just need to get this out of my system, then we can drive."

She took his bottom lip into her mouth, biting gently on it and feeling his body respond. His hands found her skin beneath her clothes, running up the length of her torso, his fingers dancing over her rib cage before he finally cupped a hand around her breast. His lips kissed a trail down from her mouth and along her jaw, and she threw her head back, pressing on to the steering wheel and sounding the car horn.

They both jumped, and then started laughing uncontrollably. Someone passed the window and tapped on the glass shouting "Oi! Oi!," making them both laugh even more.

Glory slowly and awkwardly extricated herself from Julian's lap and back into the passenger seat, pulling down her top and readjusting the cups of her bra.

"We can go now," she said when she was settled, putting on her seat belt and checking her phone again.

"Just give me a minute," Julian said, clearing his throat and looking out the window. "Let me, er, yeah!" He flicked his eyes down at his lap, where his erection was straining against his jeans, and Glory laughed again, even harder than before.

24

Glory woke up in Julian's bed, wrapped in his smell. To think only a couple of days ago they had been on their first proper date, and now she was watching him sleep. She felt sick with how much she liked him, amazed by how they had been thrown together so intimately by the circumstances of their meeting and everything that came after.

She liked him so much she might even end up cooking for him. Glory started planning a Sunday brunch menu, and got up to see what Julian's cupboards might have to offer and what she would have to buy.

She was bent over, looking into the top freezer compartment when Julian entered the kitchen.

"Now this is what every man dreams of waking up to," he said, watching Glory from the doorway. "What you going to cook for us?"

"Nothing," Glory said, turning around and shutting the freezer door. "Julian, you have nothing in your kitchen apart from leftovers and frozen boxes of rice that I assume your auntie cooked for you. Don't you cook at all? Not even Indomie?"

"I'm a busy man," he replied with a shrug. "I'm a *busi*nessman!"

"Well, there's nothing for me to cook, so what do you wanna do? Do you want to go out to eat?" Glory leaned against the fridge and folded her arms.

"I'd love to but I've actually got errands to run this morning," Julian said, running a hand over his head and looking apologetic.

"Oh." Glory could not hide her disappointment. "On a Sunday?"

"Yeah, if I'd known you were staying over I could've planned differently."

"No problem, I'll probably head home then."

"You can stay here. I won't be that long."

"No, it's fine," Glory replied. "I need to have a shower and eat something proper!"

Glory kissed Julian on the cheek, more to prove to herself that she wasn't pissed off than for his benefit, and went to gather her things.

She found her phone in the bedroom and saw a message from Lará:

"*Sorry, I'm only responding now. Was at a boring dinner. You free today?*"

"*Perfect!*" Glory typed back. "*Just need to get ready but tell me when and where.*"

"All right, I'm going, I'll speak to you later, yeah?" Glory called from the hallway as she slipped on her shoes.

Julian came to stand in the doorway.

"You don't have to leave you know?" he said, resting an arm on the door frame.

"It's fine, I'm gonna meet a friend."

"Who?" Julian said, frowning.

"Lará."

"OK. Cool."

As quick as she had been to leave, Glory didn't actually want to go back to her house. As long as she didn't open that door, whatever complications lay behind number 23 did not exist—at least, for the night.

Before she reentered she actually prayed, bargaining with God that if she opened the door and her mother was OK, then she would go to church one day soon. She made her pact on the doorstep, allowing a few seconds for it to process, before swinging open the door and seeing what she might find.

The front room was empty and dark; the house was quiet.

"Mummy?" Glory called, but there was no answer. Maybe she had gone to church.

Glory climbed the stairs and called again into the still darkness: "Mummy?"

"Yes?" came the hoarse response and Glory walked across the landing and into her mother's bedroom.

Celeste was sitting on the edge of her bed in a flimsy nightdress, her shoulders stooped and her head down.

"Mummy what's wrong?"

"I'm fine," Celeste said weakly.

"Are you sure?"

Glory reached to touch her mother's shoulder, but Celeste shrugged away her hand.

"I said I'm fine, jàre!"

Glory let her hand drop, not sure what to do.

"Do you want me to call Faith?"

"No. Where have you been?"

"I stayed with a friend."

"Which friend?"

"You don't know them. I'm meeting up with Lará though."

"Oh!" Celeste's suspicions dissolved. "Greet her for me."

"I will . . . Are you sure you don't want me to do anything for you before I leave, Mummy?"

"No, go and see your friend."

Celeste waved her daughter away, so reluctantly Glory left to have a shower and change into fresh clothes, stopping by her mother's room to check in on her one last time. But her mother was not there.

Instead Glory found her in the kitchen, wrist deep in a bowl of water as she prepared dried beans for soaking and peeling.

"I thought I would make some àkàrà for us," Celeste said with a warm smile. "Do you remember when I used to make it for you when you were a little girl? You would always ask for àkàrà and ògì for your birthday breakfast. Do you remember?"

Celeste's eyes were swimming with nostalgia, but Glory was sure she was mistaken. She couldn't remember ever asking for àkàrà and ògì for breakfast. She was definitely a Coco Pops girl.

"Mummy, I'm going out—remember? With Lará."

Celeste's face clouded over for a brief moment.

"Oh, of course," she said, removing her hands from the bowl of beans and wiping them on her nightdress. "I need to let these beans soak for longer, anyway. Greet Lará for me, ehn?"

"I will, Mummy," Glory said, watching her mother for a moment with weary concern, before turning to leave.

25

Glory met Lará in front of a gray and black glass building in Shoreditch. Glory had studied Lará's WhatsApp profile picture carefully on the bus, making sure that she'd recognize her child-hood friend, but against the milling crowd of mostly white people, Lará would have stood out anyway. Her braids were piled onto the top of her head, studded with silver clasps and rings. She was wearing square, thick-rimmed glasses and her lips were a bright orange that matched the geometric print on her oversized shirt, stylishly unbuttoned and tucked into a pair of high-waisted, stonewashed jeans. She effortlessly fit in with the creative crowd that Shoreditch drew, and Glory felt drab and invisible in her signature monochrome athleisure. In LA she had adopted this style as she thought it spoke to the life of easy health and sophistication she wanted, but looking at Lará, absentmindedly checking her phone and playing with a loose braid, Glory felt she might have to update her look.

"Glory!" Lará exclaimed as Glory approached. Genuine joy lit up her face and Glory forgot her aesthetic misgivings and felt glad she had agreed to meet her old friend.

"Thanks so much for coming with me!" Lará said after they had exchanged a short obligatory hug. "I should have seen this exhibition weeks ago but just need to catch it before it closes."

"No problem, is it here?" Glory asked, looking through the glass front of the building. She could see large white panels marked with black lines.

"Yeah, just around the side."

Glory followed Lará to the entrance of the gallery.

"So is this for work, or?" Glory began, realizing that she didn't actually know what Lará did.

"Kind of—well, just general inspiration really," Lará said, smiling at the attendant who greeted them at the door.

"What do you do?" Glory asked, hating herself as soon as she finished asking the question.

"I'm a junior designer at a creative agency."

"Oh, cool," Glory said. "I used to work in marketing back in LA."

"I never knew—would I recognize the agency?"

Glory felt the irrational pressure that came with unspoken competition—even though she was sure it wasn't Lará's intention.

"It was a boutique agency specializing in influencer partnerships and niche social media campaign activations."

"That sounds interesting! I can't wait to move somewhere smaller when I've got a bit more experience. Working in a big agency has its perks but it's all a bit faceless and I get stuck with the boring projects."

"Mmm." Glory nodded, but the words "big agency" stuck in her head, and she realized that even if Lará dressed like a carefree art student who shopped at vintage stores and charity shops, she still had her life together in ways that Glory did not. Maybe she should try to get back to America and salvage whatever career she had left.

They were now at the entrance to the main hall of the gallery and Lará stopped to take out a small notebook and pencil from her bag. She began to carefully read the exhibition notes pasted on the white wall in black vinyl letters, pausing every now and again to scribble quick notes in her book. Glory skim-read the information then stopped in front of a TV mounted on the wall. A woman in white, the exposed parts of her body covered in white paint, kneeled next to a plastic bucket filled with what looked like black soot. She had a braided whip in her hand and crushed soot up and down its length before rising and approaching a blank canvas on a stand. After sizing up the rectangle, she drew back her arm and snapped the whip against the canvas with such force that the stand rocked back and forth. The muscles in the woman's lean body rippled with the effort.

The sound and violence made Glory jump and gasp out loud. Lará glanced in her direction, her pencil frozen in the air.

"You OK?" she asked, and Glory swallowed, pushing her lips into a feeble smile.

"I think I just need some fresh air," she said, as if they hadn't only just entered the gallery. "I'll wait for you outside," Glory continued, as another thwack of the whip made her skin crawl.

Glory went back to the entrance, and leaned against one of the bollards that lined the street. From her position, she could watch Lará walking around the gallery, silent and studious, her face fixed in reverent concentration as she inspected sooty marks etched on each canvas. From here, Glory couldn't hear the force of the whip colliding with the canvas or the grunt of the woman exerting herself so violently in the name of art. From here it was easier to forget what her mother had told her about her father and Hope.

When Lará emerged, she was still finishing off a written thought.

"Hope I didn't take too long," she said apologetically, dropping her notebook into her bag. Glory jumped at the word, thinking for a moment that Lará had read her thoughts.

"No, it's fine. Did you get what you needed?"

"Yeah, the mark-making technique is incredibly interesting—like how brutal it is, but how delicate the results actually look. I guess, it's kind of a metaphor for how we exist as black people in Britain, right? We were forced into this country's history so violently—through slavery and colonialism—but they whitewash history, minimize our impact and instead we're just these delicate black lines on a white landscape. Interesting and decorative in one sense, but also inconvenient and dirty in another."

Lará stopped abruptly. "Sorry! You probably think that's all waffle."

"No, actually, that's helpful. I don't really get art like that, but you explained it really well. I can kinda see how it makes sense now."

"You didn't like it though?"

"It's just . . . violent, innit. Like, to think that that's how they used to whip slaves and stuff. Like that whip would be cutting into someone's back, and children's backs too."

Glory shuddered, trying to shake off what she was feeling, the panic attack that was advancing on her.

"You want to go grab something to eat?" she asked hurriedly.

Lará looked up and down both ends of the street they were on.

"I've been craving Mexican food recently, but I dunno if there's anywhere near here that serves it—wait, what? You don't like Mexican food?"

Glory hadn't realized her face had revealed her thoughts so plainly.

"Nah, it's not that. I love Mexican food, but—argh, I'm gonna sound like a proper snob, but after eating the Mexican food they make in LA, I don't think the food here is gonna cut it."

Lará laughed, throwing her head back.

"I get it, that's like after I went to India last year, I can't eat Indian food anywhere else!"

Glory joined in with the laughter, but felt quietly disturbed by Lará. The shy and timid wallflower from their childhood had grown into this worldly and experienced woman who could explain modern art like she was giving directions to the train station. *I can't let her meet Julian*, Glory thought, irrationally. If Glory's projection of culture and sophistication impressed him, Lará would probably sweep him right off his feet.

"Shall we just go get a drink or something instead? Something light?" Lará asked when she had righted herself and stopped giggling.

"Yeah, sure," Glory answered, thankful for the cheaper option and remembering her mother making àkàrà back at home. She wanted to return with enough appetite to eat it.

"How long were you in India for?" Glory asked as Lará led them to a nearby coffee shop.

"A couple months, it was a holiday masquerading as a research trip," Lará said with a sly smile.

"What were you researching?"

Lará thought for a moment, twiddling her braid around her finger in a way that Glory was beginning to recognize as a cute tic.

"I really want to be a type designer—that's what I actually want to specialize in—so I was looking at different types of scripts and writing systems while I was there. I was playing around with doing a Masters in type design and for my thesis I was gonna develop a specialist typeface for Yorùbá, one that's more tailored to the tonal nature of the language and not based on the Latin script with all the diacritics."

Glory nodded slowly, although she felt like she only understood half of what Lará had said.

"So you're going to do a Masters?"

"Nah, too expensive. And I think I can effectively DIY it, but that also means that I have to 'work my way up' in the design world."

Lará pushed her glasses up her nose and pulled a face.

"My mum would love it if I did a Masters," Glory said as they took a seat in the café. "Well, she'd love it if I actually went back and finished my degree first."

"What were you studying?" Lará asked, inspecting the menu on the wall.

"Business management. What did you study?"

"Graphic design."

"Your mum *actually* let you do an art degree?" Glory asked, her impression of Lará turning from begrudging admiration to awe.

"Yeah, I know." Lará chuckled. "No one can believe it, but it's true. My ultra-Nigerian mother let me go to art school. What do you want to get? I'll order for us."

Glory made a few half-hearted objections and slowly reached for her purse, but, as she had hoped, Lará shook her head and headed toward the counter.

By the time Lará returned to the table with a tray of teas and gluten-free vegan biscuits, Glory's assessment of her had completely changed. She needed friends and who better to have as a friend than Lará, someone who seemed to embody the self-assurance that Glory pretended to have, and someone who had managed to convince her Nigerian mother to study art as a full-blown, very expensive degree.

"Did I already ask you when you were going back to LA?" Lará said, nibbling the end of a biscuit.

"Um, I'm not going back," Glory said brightly, cradling her cup in her hands and blowing into the fragrant tea.

"Oh, well, if you need a job here, I can see if anything's going at my agency."

"Thanks, but I don't want to work in that industry any more. It's not for me." Glory averted her eyes from Lará's. There was a lump caught in her throat and she was starting to feel emotional. How many times would she have to explain—and not really explain—this to people? Why did everyone care so much about what people did or didn't do?

"Are you OK, Glory?" Lará asked gently, and to her horror, Glory felt a single tear slip loose and roll down her cheek.

"Shit!" she said, holding a hand to her face. "This is so stupid, I shouldn't even be crying about that stupid job."

Lará handed her a napkin.

"Did something happen? Is that why you don't want to go back?"

"Office politics!" Glory tried to laugh, but the noise got trapped in her throat and came out as a strangled sound. "It was my own fault anyway."

"What was?" Lará asked, refusing to remove her eyes from Glory.

"It's so dumb and it's my own fault really," Glory repeated. "I made a very stupid decision to start dating one of my colleagues and when things ended, it got messy."

"Messy how?"

"I really shouldn't have gone out with him anyway, he was a complete dickhead—the warning signs were there! But then when we broke up I found out that he and a couple of his tech bros had, like, this rating system for all the women in the office they'd slept with. It was an actual spreadsheet on a company laptop!"

"*Fuck!*" Lará said under her breath. "Were you on it?"

Glory bit her lip and nodded. Everything about her had been rated out of ten, from her physical attributes to her position on the "freak" scale down to the quality of any nudes she had sent. Thankfully she had only sent Adam one picture, and it wasn't technically a nude, so that had tanked that rating at the very least.

"Did you tell anyone?"

"Yeah, not my manager or anything, but someone else and they basically said that's why I shouldn't *shit where I eat* and that kicking up a fuss about it could jeopardize my job and my visa status and . . ." Glory let out a heavy sigh. "I thought that job was everything at the time. But then it turned into a nightmare."

"You know you could have reported them to HR or something? I swear that's sexual harassment at the very least. What the fuck?!"

"I could but—anyway, it's done now. I've learned my lesson. Don't shit where you eat, innit."

Glory flashed Lará a sarcastic smile and gulped down some of the still-hot tea. Lará was shaking her head, breaking her biscuit into smaller chunks and eating them in quick succession.

"I'm so sorry, Glory."

"No, it's fine—"

"It's not!"

"No, seriously. I feel better now that I've actually told someone. Everyone thinks I'm crazy for leaving LA, I'm sure. Your reaction reminds me that I'm not. That's all I needed."

Glory smiled across at Lará again, and this time it was a real smile.

"You've not told your mum or sister or anyone?"

"Hell no! First of all, my mum doesn't know that I've even had sex and second, there are more pressing family dramas to attend to."

"Yes, of course. Your dad."

Glory stopped mid-sip, thinking that once again her mind was being read but realized that Lará was talking about Daddy's death, not the fact that he was the reason she had believed her twin was dead for all these years.

26

Faith and Celeste went to visit Victor the following week as planned, but Faith's face wore the results of an unsuccessful day when she dropped their mother back to the house.

She pulled Glory aside as she was leaving. "Is she taking the prescription the hospital gave her?"

"What prescription?"

"Glory! I need you to pay attention to people besides yourself!" Faith clicked her fingers a few times. "She was given a prescription that she was meant to be taking. Little orange and white capsules to keep her mood stable."

"Would Mummy even take them? You know she only believes in prayer and blessings from holy men."

"Well, *something* was working for all these weeks. How do you think I managed to convince her to go back to work?"

"What were the pills?"

"Some antipsychotics or something—I can't remember the name."

"Mummy's psychotic?"

"No, Glory! You sound like one of the aunties from Nigeria. *Are you trying to tell me that my sister is mad?* She's not mad, or psychotic, she just needs mood stabilizers. It's just medication for her mind. That's it, OK?"

Glory nodded.

"So what happened on the visit?"

Faith sighed and massaged her temple with two fingers.

"She just started acting weird. As soon as we were searched she started getting agitated. Then when we finally got in to see Victor, it got worse. She was acting like she wanted to climb up the walls and go out the window. Soon as the hour was over Victor practically ran out of the hall."

Faith pinched the bridge of her nose and all Glory could do was contribute a sympathetic grunt.

"There was this horrible moment when we left the hall and they had us waiting in this little room for a while, Mummy pushed to the front of the queue and started banging on the door! It was so embarrassing, I thought she was going to smack the officer in the face when he finally came. And then she's been talking under her breath the whole drive back. I'm really worried, Glory."

Truth be told, since Celeste had confessed about Hope and the Markshams, Glory had noticed that their mother had been in a constant state of irritated distraction, not even having the presence of mind to scold and rebuke Glory as she normally would. But not only was this a self-serving silver lining for Glory, she didn't want to admit that Faith had been right, and that talking about Hope had only caused further upset for their mother, and nothing else.

Glory checked Facebook often, but Hope Kehinde had not accepted her request or responded to the follow-up message she sent a day later:

"*Hi, sorry to bother you, but I'm looking for a long-lost relative and wonder if she might be you? She was born in London but grew up in the Midlands, I can give you more details if you want them."*

"Just keep an eye on her, please?" Faith said as she walked out to her car.

Celeste spent the rest of that evening in her bedroom, so all Glory could do was eavesdrop through the sealed door. The conversation was muffled, but Glory could work out that her mother was on the phone and not talking to herself as she had first thought in alarm. When Glory came to say goodnight, the conversation was still going.

At three o'clock in the morning, Glory was woken by her mother standing over her bed in the dark.

"You must pray with me," she said in a hoarse voice.

Glory began to protest, but Celeste cut her off.

"I had a dream!" she hissed, and Glory was dragged out of her stupor and through to her mother's bedroom.

The harsh light in the room made Glory blink stupidly. At the foot of the bed, Celeste pushed a heavy hand on her shoulder to prompt her to kneel. Celeste began to speak in tongues, unintelligible syllables flowing unceasingly from her mouth, and then she pressed a thumb smeared with oil onto Glory's forehead, wrapping the rest of her fingers around Glory's skull in a tight grip and praying so hard that Glory's own head began to shake with fervor.

It was only when her mother commanded her to pray that Glory took full stock of what was happening.

"Mum—"

"Pray!"

"But—"

Celeste began to drown Glory out with more tongues, a steady drone as she reapplied oil to her daughter's forehead until it began to drip down the bridge of Glory's nose.

That's when Glory did begin to pray. She repeated variations of "Oh God, what's happening?" over and over under her breath, but that seemed to satisfy Celeste who began to call out instructions and encouragement.

"Yes, amen! Those who call on the Lord will be saved! The prayers of the righteous availeth much! Whatever is bound on earth will be bound in heaven! Whatever is loosed on earth shall be loosed in heaven! Shonda-robbo! Blood of Jesus! Iski-baba!"

And it continued, Glory muttering under her breath and Celeste exhorting until her voice began to crack with exhaustion.

"This is good," she said as her strength eventually began to flag and she dismissed Glory.

Glory woke up later that morning, her pillowcase stained and forehead still greased with oil. She tiptoed around the house while her mother slept.

She called Faith. No answer. So she showered and dressed and when she finally crept into Celeste's bedroom, she found her mother spread eagle on the bed, mouth open as she snored softly. The bottle of oil from the night before had tipped over, and its contents had seeped across the side table and onto the floor.

Glory carefully picked up the bottle and read the now translucent label. All it said was "Holy Anointing Oil" in a medieval-looking font, under which was the address of a church in Lagos. Glory mopped up the spilled oil with tissue from the bathroom and disposed of the bottle.

She called Faith again, then sent her a message. Then she called the family GP and made an appointment. The type of private therapy that her American health insurance had afforded her was not an option, so she would have to swallow her pride and settle for an NHS referral. Either way, in the haze of last night's frantic prayer session she had resolved that she was not prepared to let her own madness catch her unawares.

When Glory finished that call, she checked her phone again. There was still no response from Faith but she could not wait any longer. She neither wanted to be alone in the quiet house, nor did she want to be around to find out what mood Celeste would wake up in.

She pulled on her coat and shoes and left, letting the door carefully click shut behind her.

27

Glory rang the doorbell three times before Michael answered.

"Oh!" Glory said as the door swung open. "Hi."

"You look surprised to see me in my own house," he responded coolly.

"Just wasn't—I thought you'd be at work."

"Well, I'm not."

"OK, is Faith in? I texted her to let her know I was on my way."

"She's in the kitchen," Michael said over his shoulder as he walked away.

The atmosphere in the house was tense. The absence of the children left a vacuum, and it felt like Glory could hear every sound made by Faith in the kitchen echo through the emptiness.

"Where's Estie and 'Lijah?" Glory asked. Faith was opening and shutting cupboards, rearranging the already spotless space. The cleaner must have just been. When Faith turned around, her eyes were raw and bare without their usual carefully applied adornments.

"What's wrong?" Glory asked, and her sister self-consciously dabbed at the skin around her eye sockets.

Faith shook her head and smiled weakly.

"I didn't know you were dropping by."

"I texted you. What's wrong? Where are the kids?"

"Upstairs."

Faith leaned against the countertop and exhaled, throwing her head back. Glory approached her and lowered her voice.

"What's going on?"

Faith beckoned Glory through to the utility room and pushed the door closed behind them. The washing machine was whirring away, finishing off a spin cycle, but Faith still spoke in half whispers.

"We just had a massive argument. He's going away for work, again. He's hardly ever here during the week and now he's volunteering for work trips like he doesn't have a family."

"Are you scared of him?"

"What?! No!"

"Then why are we hiding in here and whispering?"

Faith drummed her nails against the top of the washing machine. "You don't get it."

Glory marched from the small room at the back of the kitchen through to the living room, where Michael sat on the sofa, his feet up on the coffee table and the TV tuned to Sky Sports.

"Long time," Glory tried to begin casually, although there was nothing casual about the way she stood over him.

Michael turned down the volume on the TV. "Yeah, it's been awhile. How have you been?"

"All right. You?"

"Yeah, you know how it is, same old."

"Mmm," Glory nodded as if she knew. "Work still busy?"

Michael dragged his eyes from the TV, pausing the action to give Glory his full attention.

"As always. Did Faith send you to tell me off?" His mouth was stuck in a smug half smile, which sent bubbles of irritation through Glory's blood.

"Just asking."

"Right."

He turned back to the TV and hit play.

"You get why Faith's not happy though, innit?"

"Why don't you tell me."

His eyes were fixed on the players jogging up and down the pitch.

"It's kind of unfair that she's basically housebound with Esther and Elijah all the time while you're out and living your life."

"Unfair?" Michael now turned his full attention toward Glory. "Did *she* say that?"

"Sometimes it seems like you're preoccupied."

"Preoccupied with what?"

"You tell me."

Glory folded her arms, ready for a fight.

"I'm working. Someone's got to pay for Faith's Barbie house."

"Why are you saying it like that? *Barbie house.*"

Michael shook his head, dismissing Glory with a little laugh.

"Are you really though?"

"Am I really what? Working? Of course—what else would I be doing?"

Glory shrugged. In her peripheral vision she saw Faith enter from the kitchen. Sensing her presence, Michael turned around.

"Is this what you've been telling your sister? That I'm doing something else? What do you think I'm doing then?"

"What? No! All I said was we—"

"Is that what the real issue is? You think I'm lying? You don't trust me?"

"Michael, I never—Glory? Why did you say that?"

"It's a fair question to ask!" Glory said, looking from Michael to Faith and back again. "He's always staying the night at his mate's place in Battersea and going away for weekends. Whose job requires *that* of them?"

"A job that pays well! That pays for this house, that means that Faith can live in comfort and not have to work and be fifty-something still managing a care home!"

"But who told you that my sister wanted to be some idle fucking housewife?!" Glory bit back.

"Who told you that she didn't?!"

Glory opened her mouth to respond, but shut it immediately when she saw Faith's eyes throwing daggers at her across the room.

"Is that what this is about, Faith?" Michael asked, catching his breath.

Faith stammered.

"N-no, I-I never—"

"Why can't you just tell me how you feel like an adult instead of playing these childish games?"

"What? Glory?! What did you say to him?"

Caught between her sister and her brother-in-law, Glory suddenly felt lost for words.

"I just—I mean, like . . ." and she trailed off when she realized she no longer knew what she had meant.

Michael tossed the control onto the sofa and stood up.

"Going for a drive," he said, and Faith stayed glued to her spot until she heard the front door shut behind him and the car engine start up.

"What. Just. Happened?" Faith asked, taking angry steps toward Glory, her eyes blazing and nostrils flared.

Glory flopped onto the sofa and picked at the edge of a cushion.

"Why don't you speak up for yourself with Michael, though?"

"Speak up about what? About stuff that I don't care about? Why are you so fixated on this housewife thing?" Faith's voice was growing hoarse with emotion.

"Our mum wasn't a housewife though, Daddy didn't let her just stay at home idle," Glory said in glum defiance.

"Are you even listening to what you're saying? Mummy isn't Anna Wintour editing *Vogue*! She works in residential care where her senile patients call her a golliwog or spit at her. And *let her*? You're talking like either of them had a choice! Do you know how much the mortgage costs after they remortgaged a couple of years ago? Do you know how many times Michael's salary covered it to stop them falling behind? Do you know how much outstanding council tax they owe?"

Glory said nothing. She couldn't bring herself to look at Faith so she concentrated on a loose bit of stitching.

"You've got to start seeing things for what they are, Glory! You're not a child any more."

Faith took a breath and waited for her sister to say something. When a response didn't come, she turned on her heel and stomped up the stairs.

28

Glory waited in the living room for Faith to come back, her mood restored, goodwill replenished, chatting about something inconsequential, while she juggled her babbling children. But time passed, the TV unit slipped into standby, and the light faded around her in the room.

She got up and left.

As she waited for the bus to come, a notification came through on Instagram. It was a direct message from one of the barbers at Pharoah's:

"Are u with J? Tell him to come to the shop now. Feds are here."

Glory immediately called Julian's number, but it rang and rang, eventually connecting with his voicemail. She ended the call and tried again, but this time it didn't even ring. It had been turned off.

Glory opened the Uber app on her phone, ready to request a ride and get back to Peckham as quickly as possible. But the app told her that she could not use it until she had settled her previous balance. She opened the banking app on her phone and checked her account, swearing into the winter sky when she realized she was at the limits of her overdraft once again.

The wait for the next bus was long and chilly, and when she finally boarded she sat right at the front on the top deck, watching the street lights through the condensation on the windows.

Glory changed buses when she reached Peckham, then began the short walk to Pharoah's. As she approached she could see the flashing blue lights of a police car casting the long shadows of spectators across the road. She hurried through the small crowd that had formed outside and into the bright light of the shop front, where her path was blocked by a burly officer.

"What happened?" she called past him to one of the barbers who was sat in his chair, a wad of paper towels wound around a hand he held elevated. Another officer was crouched in front of him with a notepad.

"What's going on?" Glory shouted again. This time the barber looked at her, his face weary.

"Where's Jay?" he asked her gruffly.

"I don't know, he's not answering my calls."

"When you find him, tell him he needs to get down here. Some dumb yout's tried lick off the shop."

"Did they take anything?"

The barber grunted and turned back to the officer at his feet.

"Are you OK?" Glory asked him. "Has someone called an ambulance?"

The paper towels around his hand were growing bloodier.

"We've got things under control, miss," the officer said, and she backed away from the shop in a daze, her heart pounding.

Nearby she could hear someone, who claimed to have been in the shop at the time, recounting what had happened in bursts of excitement.

". . . my man grabbed the yout's knife you know—with his bare hands! I think that shook them up because when he saw that, the yout" just dropped the knife and ran out the shop and all his likkle pussyhole friends followed."

The guy was jumping about energetically.

"Did they take anything?" Glory asked him, thinking of Julian's preference for thick rolls of hard cash.

"What?"

"Did the yout's take anything?"

"Oh, no! When Tony grabbed the blade they realized what kinda badman they ah deal wid! Ya simme?" The boy preened with pride as though he was the one who fended off the robbers. "I dunno who called the feds but they didn't need to. T's not gonna tell them nothing. We'll deal with that ourselves, ya feel me?" He pounded a fist into his open palm and Glory walked away, sickened by his enthusiasm.

There was no answer at Julian's flat and his phone was still turned off. She backed away from the entrance to the block of flats and began walking to her house. At the end of the road ahead she saw a black van pull up. The door opened and a man hopped out, hands buried deep in his pockets and his head bowed, but as he walked toward Glory, engrossed in whatever thought, she recognized his gait.

"Julian!"

He looked up, confused by the sight of her, then he looked caught out, pushing his hood back in a guilty sweep.

"Glory, what's going on? What are you doing?"

"Where have you been? I've been calling and calling and then I went to the shop and there's police there!"

"Police?"

"Someone tried to rob the shop and Tony the barber got stabbed in the hand or something, I dunno, but he said you needed to get down there."

Julian kissed his teeth.

"Crabs in a fucking bucket, I swear!"

Julian piled his hands on top of his head. As he stood just shy of a streetlamp, Glory could make out half circles of dirt embedded under his nails.

"Do you know who might have done it?"

"Probably," he replied grimly. "I need to get to the shop."

He began walking in the direction of Pharaoh's.

"Shit!" He stopped and looked down at the loose tracksuit he was wearing, his feet sporting a pair of muddied work boots instead of one of his immaculate pairs of trainers. "I need to change first." He turned back around and headed in the opposite direction.

"You want me to come with you?" Glory asked, turning to follow him.

"No, just go home, Glory. I'll call you later, yeah?"

And he picked up his pace, breaking into a slow jog up the road.

29

When she got back to her mother's house, Glory could hear laughter leaking through the front door as she put her key in the lock. In the living room she found her mother, Auntie Dọtun, and Auntie Dọtun's ten-year-old granddaughter, Olivia.

Olivia was small and spindly, with oversized glasses and quiet tendencies. She sat folded away in a corner, her face peering intensely into her tablet. When Glory greeted her, she glanced up, mumbled a shy "hello" and went back to whatever was on her screen.

"Ah, Glory! I would have thought you'd be back in sunny California by now! You missed the cold, ehn?" Auntie Dọtun boomed from her spot on the sofa.

"She's not going back now, I thought I told you?" Celeste answered on Glory's behalf.

"Eh-hehn! You are finally going to settle down in one place? Soon you will be inviting us to eat rice at your wedding, àbí?"

"Wedding, kọ́? This one finds it hard to settle on anything!" Glory's mother snorted.

"Ah? Why now?" Auntie Dọtun turned to Celeste with her palms upturned, as if Celeste held the answer to Glory's great malady. "By her age we were married and had multiple children!"

Auntie Dòtun turned back to Glory with a somber look.

"You are young but time flies, o! Don't waste your youth, pregnancy gets harder as one gets older—and don't you want to give your mother more grandchildren while she still has the energy to babysit?"

Auntie Dòtun laughed and slapped Celeste's shoulder.

"I keep asking Yẹmí when he will give me more grandchildren. Olivia is nearly a teenager, we need more!" Auntie Dòtun clapped her hands and Celeste nodded along sympathetically.

Her mother's generation had short memories. Glory could remember the scandal and disappointment that surrounded Olivia's birth ten years ago, when Yẹmí, Auntie Dòtun's first son, was nineteen and unmarried but found himself the father of his Portuguese girlfriend's unborn child. It was hard to discern which was the biggest scandal—the teenage pregnancy, or the European mother—but either way, Auntie Dòtun and her husband had refused to accept their unborn grandchild as their flesh and blood until the baby was born and a DNA test could be administered. As young as Glory had been then, the ugliness of the situation had not escaped her. And although Auntie Dòtun doted on her intelligent and polite granddaughter now, as far as she knew, the relationship with Olivia's mum had never been repaired. Apologies were not a strong suit among Celeste's peers.

Glory contrasted that with how her own parents responded to Michael and his sins, readily accepting him after all the scandal and drama he wrought in Faith's life, and happily overlooking his obvious shortcomings even now. Was it the double standard held against sons and daughters? Or was it the fact that Michael was Yorùbá and Inês, Olivia's mother, wasn't? Whatever the answer, Glory found the hypocrisy hard to stomach while everyone else was content to sweep such things to the side and carry on: unity for unity's sake.

"I'm just waiting for the right man to come along, Auntie Dọtun," she eventually said, trying to remain good humored.

"Like she is just waiting for the right job!" Celeste laughed, and Auntie Dọtun smiled knowingly at her friend. Glory's face dropped. "Maybe a miracle will happen and one day she'll finish her education."

Glory knew all control over the conversation was lost when her mother began talking about her as if she was not there.

"She was studying a good degree—business management! And she just couldn't stick with it."

"But a husband wants a wife that can put her mind to something and finish it!"

"And that's what I've been telling her—is that not what I've been saying to you, Glory?"

"I think it's this feministin'—"

"Feminism," Celeste corrected her.

"Yes, feminisms. I think that's the problem that they have."

"It's true now, they think they don't need a husband, they don't want to serve him—I even heard that Mama Ṣèyí's daughter-in-law refused to kneel at her engagement!"

"Heh!" Auntie Dọtun exclaimed as she shook her head solemnly. "But Faith did well, by God's grace."

"She did. Anyway . . ." Celeste clapped her hands and dusted them off. "They don't know that we worked and had children, àbí? They don't know that we served our husbands and made our own money, àbí?"

"See!" Auntie Dọtun said, addressing Glory once again. "Your own mother did well, didn't she?"

It took all that Glory had within her to swallow the words that sat fat at the front of her tongue, fighting to burst out and wipe the self-satisfaction from their faces. *Did well?* Sure, her mother had done well, if well included leaving one of her children with strangers. And yes, she had definitely served her husband, but what did she have to show for it?

Glory chewed at the inside of her cheeks until she thought she could taste the salt of her own blood, then she smiled, her lips taut and strained, nodding a little and excusing herself from the room. She could still hear her mother and Auntie Dòtun congratulating themselves as she ran up the stairs, and by the time she reached the landing, her eyes were burning.

Glory went to her mother's room, briskly opening her father's desk, not caring if Celeste were to come and find her snooping again. There had to be something else, another clue that could take her closer to finding her sister. She found Hope's birth certificate and examined it again, reading over every detail even though by now she had basically memorized it. But when she turned it over she noticed a handwritten note she had missed all this time. It simply read "Markshams" and a telephone number.

Glory quickly typed the string of digits, checking twice to make sure she had transferred them accurately. Then she took a breath and made the call before she could change her mind.

"Hello, Jade Garden."

"H-hello? Jade who?"

"Jade Garden. Are you phoning for collection or delivery?"

"Er, no—no, sorry, I think I've got the wrong number."

The line clicked as the other person hung up the phone.

30

The brittle winter was breaking into a pleasant spring, London warming up and transforming. The city was a whole different beast when the oppressive gray sky began to turn blue and, to Glory, Los Angeles felt like a lifetime away.

Faced with dead ends on every front, Glory took Faith's advice and turned to the here and now: reconciling with Victor became her goal.

Julian suggested she write a letter, but at first Glory was not convinced. Even when they were close, before Victor got arrested, if she ever sent him a message longer than two lines he would not respond. But Julian assured her that prisoners liked receiving letters, even if they didn't reply.

The first letter was a long and rambling confessional written in one sitting, and even though she didn't expect a response, the silence still stung. But with Julian's encouragement she kept writing little notes—nothing too heavy, just thoughts she'd write on the back of postcards and put in envelopes.

Then one day while she was on Brick Lane with Lará she saw street art on a building. It was a reimagining of the cartoon *Wacky Races*, each team's car replaced with a sleek black luxury vehicle. Instead of the bright hodge-podge of cartoon characters, Dick Dastardly, Penelope Pitstop and the rest were now slickly coiffed poseurs, using selfie sticks as they reclined on the bonnets of their Bugattis and Ferraris. Glory snapped pictures and printed copies out at the Boots in Liverpool Street Station.

When they were children, Victor was obsessed with the show, sketching the characters over and over then designing his own racing cars and drafting in Glory as his imaginary teammate. When Glory got home she wrote a quick note to him and posted it along with the prints.

The day Victor received them, he called the house phone. Glory was on her way out the door when her mum called her back in to speak to her brother.

"Gotta be quick 'cause it's bang-up, but I got the pictures."

His voice was deep, cutting through the clamor around him.

"When I saw them, I immediately thought of you," Glory said, grinning into the receiver.

"Thanks."

"What for?"

"For thinking of me."

A tannoy squawked.

"Of course."

Victor called a few more times, their conversations stretching longer and longer. When Glory made him laugh out loud twice in a row, he finally suggested she come and see him.

"Send me your deets and I'll add you to my list."

"What do you need?"

"Ask Faith, she knows. I've gotta go."

And that's how Glory found herself pressing her thumbs onto a fingerprint scanner one morning, before being thoroughly patted down by a thin-faced woman wearing blue vinyl gloves.

The first waiting room was a small square, edged by worn chairs bolted to the floor. Everything in the room was a dull, institutional pea green, and the small TV mounted high on the wall showed an episode of *The Jeremy Kyle Show* that was getting especially rowdy. Children kicked and fidgeted, while their mothers and grandmothers chatted among themselves. Everyone seemed to know each other and the conversation moved from the banal to the impatient as time rolled on and the small room filled up.

Almost all of the people waiting were women, apart from an older gentleman with blue tattoos bleeding up his forearm and under his polo shirt sleeve. There was also a group of legal representatives, in pinstripe suits and shiny shoes. They tapped on the marked floor as they waited, shifting folders and laptops from one arm to another and checking the time on their wristwatches.

Finally a buzzer sounded. The door they had entered through slid shut and another clanked open. An officer guided them out of the small box and across a driveway. They waited while one door was locked and the next gate was opened and then trooped up a narrow stairway. It was a repetitive motion, this stopping and starting, and Glory counted six occasions when the group was locked in one confined space before being released into another. By the time they were emptied into the visiting hall, the children were tight balls of energy that tore across the open space, ignoring the adults shouting after them.

Faith had prepped Glory on the procedure, and she joined the queue in front of the booth that served as a command station. At the front of the line she gave the officer Victor's name and he scanned down a seating chart until he found it, directing Glory to a table in the center of the hall. Everything was fixed to the floor, and if it wasn't, it was fixed to three other things that made it impossible to move.

Glory wedged herself on one of the seats and looked around. One side of the room was taken up by a children's play area, complete with a padded obstacle course and mini playhouse. There was a little cubby that served as the kitchen, from which another queue snaked as visitors waited to buy sausage rolls and styrofoam cups of coffee.

Prisoners entered from a small door behind the command station. Glory could see them lining up to get patted down and receive fluorescent vests that marked them out as inmates. She watched as three children raced across the hall at the sight of their dad, dodging the officers standing on either side of the door and ambushing him as he received his vest. The officers pulled them apart, and the children were sent back to the other side, hopping from foot to foot as they waited for permission to hug their father again.

A young woman who had spent the entire waiting period adjusting and readjusting her cleavage rose to meet her partner. He scooped her up in a burly bear hug, and she tottered on her heels when he placed her gently back on the ground. For the whole wait her face had been tense, as she smacked her lips and examined her nails, but now, across the narrow table from the man she was here to see, she was transformed. She giggled and flicked her hair, planting sloppy kisses on her partner's neck as he watched the officers on duty out of the corner of his eye.

Glory was engrossed in the scene, in particular the striking contrast between the joy of the family reunions and the scuffed but sterile environment they were taking place in. She didn't realize Victor had made his own way out into the hall until he was loping toward her. His movements were controlled by a band of muscle across his chest and arms that also kept his posture ramrod straight, and he nodded stiffly at a few other prisoners before sliding into the seat across from Glory.

"I swear, don't start crying, bruv!" he said with a laugh, looking away as Glory's eyes welled up.

She hadn't expected the emotion to overtake her so suddenly and so thoroughly. Her brother had just looked like her brother before, but now he looked like a man. Prison had aged him.

"Can I hug you?"

"Yeah."

They stood and embraced.

"So . . . any new tattoos?" Glory joked nervously.

"Only this one." Victor pointed to a scar on his jaw, presumably from the fight that had landed him on the hospital wing.

"I'm sorry."

It was weak, but it was all she could think to say. She wasn't sure how to reach out to someone who had been through so much. She didn't even have a frame of reference to begin to understand what he had gone through. The brother she knew before never fought physically, and she felt as if she was trying to break beneath the institutionalized exterior to reach the boy she once knew. So instead she made small talk about the food on offer and the other women she had been waiting with. Halfway through talking about the man with the blurry tattoos, Victor stopped her.

"Your energy is jarring."

This new version of her brother was also much more direct.

"I'm still getting used to this."

"Well, I'm gonna be here for a long time, so you better get comfortable."

Glory swallowed, unnerved by how accepting Victor was of his situation—although, he didn't really have any other choice.

"Well, there's not much new with me to be honest. I'm sure Faith has kept you up to date with everything else . . ." Glory began feebly.

"Why are you still here? I'd have thought you'd be back in America by now."

Glory shrugged.

"I wanted to stay."

"What's here for you?" Victor asked plainly.

"Everything," Glory said. "Did you read my first letter? I'm sorry, Vic. I'm sorry for not coming sooner when your trial began. I just couldn't—I'm sorry."

"Did you think I did it? Is that why you didn't come?"

Victor's jaw was set, defiant. His eyes dared Glory to say what she would not. Maybe he was looking for a fight and had only allowed her to see him just to break her down. Perhaps this was a sort of revenge for her absenteeism. She couldn't say she didn't deserve it.

"No! I just didn't understand. I do now, I think."

Victor held Glory in his steely gaze, still silent.

"Not enough though. I don't actually know what happened."

"What do you *think* happened?"

Glory pushed imaginary specks across the table in front of her.

"All I know is I got a call saying you were arrested, but you hadn't done anything. Then I got a call saying they wouldn't release you on bail, but you still hadn't done anything, then the trial, then you were . . . here."

Victor's eyes flicked over Glory's face, taking stock of how sincere she was. Then he nodded to himself, cleared his throat and began to talk.

209

"It was summer innit, so me, Theo and Délé were just chilling. Bored. Then Délé got a call about a BBQ in Palace. So we got in Theo's car and went. When we got to the house, everything was calm, just food, drink and vibes."

Glory could picture it. The type of summer's day when the heat filled everything. The friends arriving at a house, greeting familiar faces, music spilling into the street and everyone waiting until the sun got a bit lower, and the alcohol ran a bit warmer in their blood, before they really committed themselves to the bassline.

"We weren't even there that long when Theo got into it with . . . Jojo." Victor's voice strained to say the victim's name, his cool exterior breaking for a second. "I don't even know what happened, but they were squaring up and everyone was trying to separate them, so I was telling Theo to allow it, innit, and then he was like, '*OK, let's go.*' So us men left now with Délé and we were driving to somewhere else when someone at the party started calling Theo saying that Jojo was calling him a pussy because he ran and all this shit. Theo just pulled the maddest U-turn and started heading back, I swear to God I thought we were gonna crash, he was driving like a madman. So I told him now that I'd drive innit, 'cos I ain't tryna die. Big mistake. That's how they stuck it on me, 'cos I didn't have a license but I was driving his car, they said it showed intent or some bullshit."

Victor broke off from his story, incensed all over again by the details of his conviction. Glory waited for him to continue, watching the muscles in his jaw jump as he ground his back teeth together.

"You all right?" Glory asked. Victor let the pause drag on before kissing his teeth.

"Yeah, man, this is . . . Anyway." He sat up and continued at a quicker pace than before. "So we get back to the party and Theo jumps out the car before I can even slow down properly, Délé follows him but I have to park up, innit, so I don't reach the house until after them man. I get into the back garden and I just see Theo with a Henny bottle in his hand."

"Was it empty?"

"Nah."

Glory winced instinctively, imagining Theo wielding the narrow neck and wide bottom like a hammer.

"Theo swung at Jojo and he just slumped on the floor, there were all these girls screaming and like, everyone closed in on Jojo because he was just lying there on the floor. So, I'm thinking in a minute everything's gonna sink in and Jojo's boys are gonna turn around and come for Theo so I'm pulling him back to the car, I don't even know where Délé is but by the time we get to the car he's with us. The last thing I see . . ." Victor trailed off. He swallowed.

"The last thing I saw was Jojo's feet, they were moving so I thought he was still . . . I thought he had just been knocked down and was like recovering or something. I swear, I thought . . ."

Victor sighed and though his stare went through her, Glory refused to look away. He was not a monster. She would not look away.

When he had made it clear that he had finished, she nodded, as if to formally conclude this part of the visit, before letting her eyes fall from his, to his jaw, to his hands.

"There's tissue at the counter," Victor said, nodding toward the little cubby. Glory breathed out a desperate "ha!," pushing her fingers into her lower lids to stem the threat of tears, and offered to buy him something.

"Nah, they force us to eat enough shit as it is," he said, leaning back in his chair and smoothing his hands over his stomach, "I'm not going to voluntarily eat that."

"You still eat pork? I heard a lot of guys turn Muslim or Rasta when they come here." She smiled, an offering of normality to apologize for the display of emotion she knew Victor didn't want. He snorted and twisted his lips into a mischievous smile.

"Still weighing up my options. Don't tell Mum though."

Glory wiped a stray tear away as she queued up. The woman in front of her was talking with an inmate. He wore bright green trousers and thick black work boots, holding a tray of food for another woman at the front who was trying to balance a child on her hip as she sorted through coins. The woman and the inmate laughed heartily together. He appeared to be working, a red lanyard around his neck and a bottle of surface cleaner tucked into the waistband of his trousers. As their conversation tailed off, the woman turned, the remnants of a laugh still dancing on her face, and seeing Glory, she let out a compassionate whine.

"First visit?"

Glory nodded.

"I remember mine, love. It does get easier though, if that's any consolation. Are you here to see ya fella or a relative?"

"My brother."

The woman nodded.

"Who are you here to see?" Glory asked.

"Today it's my uncle. My fella was here for a bit, but he got shipped out not long ago to the coast. You should tell your brother to get transferred there as soon as he can, much nicer than here."

The woman's lips curled as she gave a sidelong glance at the officers.

"Anyways, we have to stay strong for 'em, don't we? If they think we're doing all right, they'll be able to get on with it.

Stay strong, yeah?" she said with a warm smile before turning to place her order.

Glory ordered a black tea and a bottle of chilled water. While she waited for her tea, she thought over the details of Victor's story, and the scar on Victor's jaw inspired questions of its own, but Glory didn't want to turn their reunion into an interrogation. She wouldn't risk pushing him further inside himself than he already was. But when she got back to the table it was her that Victor wanted to talk about.

"Why didn't you go back? For real."

Glory handed him the bottle of water before taking a seat. Victor wrenched the cap off the bottle and she watched her brother drink, trying to log every small change in his face.

"I didn't wanna go back to work. I got into a mess with a colleague—Lará says it was like sexual harassment or something, but I dunno. I messed up."

Victor paused, then nodded slowly, digesting what had been said.

"When did that happen?"

"Ages ago to be honest. I should have left before. It's funny, if I'd have actually come back for your trial, I would have avoided all that mess but, it's just . . ." She hung her head. Victor watched her steadily.

"Just what?" he asked.

"You wouldn't understand."

"Probably not, but you might as well explain."

Glory tossed a few words around in her head, opening and closing her mouth as she tried to work out the best way to phrase what she wanted to say so it didn't sound so terrible. But if there was a way she could explain herself without it sounding bad, she would have done so a long time ago.

"Fuck's sake, Glory. The visit's only an hour." Victor looked at the clock at the back of the hall. "I'm sitting in the fucking can, I'm wasting enough time as it is."

But he smiled.

"Do you remember in primary school, when I took those coffee pods to the spring fair?"

Victor screwed up his face, trying to pull a memory out of somewhere, but eventually he shook his head.

"Well, we all got told to bring stuff to raise money for the school or something, and Mummy was working as a cleaner at the time and she gave me these two stacks of coffee pods."

"What are coffee pods?"

"Those aluminum packets that you put in coffee machines? Like in offices and that."

"Oh yeah."

"Yeah, remember how she used to come home with random cleaning things?"

"I remember. Like rubber gloves and blue paper rolls and that?"

"Yeah, exactly. Well one day they must have been changing the coffee machines and they had all these old coffee pods that didn't fit in the new machines, so they gave them to Mum for some reason—"

"And obviously she won't throw anything away, even if having it don't make sense!" Victor rolled his eyes and for a split second he looked like Faith.

"Yeah, yeah! So obviously we didn't have a coffee machine at home, so she gave them to me to give to the spring fair and my teacher, Miss Harper, said, '*Did your mum nick these from her workplace?*' I was so young but I swear down, I've never forgotten how embarrassed I was."

"I remember Miss Harper. She smiled like she was trying not to hit you. Patronizing bitch."

Victor spat out the last word with a harshness that made Glory flinch. He never used to speak this way.

"Mmm. Well, ever since then I feel like I've been watching myself from the outside, wondering how things will look to other people, how they'll interpret them. Mad, innit?"

"You can't live your life like that though."

"I don't know how to stop."

Victor shrugged and puffed out his cheeks, at a loss for what to say next.

"Did you know that Mummy has been calling and sending money to these prophets in Nigeria?" Glory said. "She thinks our family's cursed, and that's why all these bad things have happened."

Victor frowned and looked at his hands.

"I used to think she was being all dramatic, but I think I believe it too on some level."

The silence pooled between them.

"I mean, look." Glory took a deep breath and started again. "I don't know if you really remember when we were little, when Mummy was doing her cleaning and Daddy was working and doing tutoring and other things on the side. It was a struggle, but even as things got better, the struggles didn't go away. I remember having to give some of my student loan to help pay the mortgage at one point. Then I went and dropped out of uni and Daddy was so upset and Mummy was angry, but I wanted to prove to them that I knew what I was doing. The plan was to go to America, make some money, get some success then come back and help you all. Pay off the house and their debts—do all of that. Then when everything happened with you, I was in no better position than when I first landed. I didn't even have money to help get you a good lawyer. I felt like shit because I was on the other side of the world and not even there to help physically. It's stupid and it doesn't make sense, but that's what it is. I was ashamed that I was so useless and thought maybe if I stayed something would get better, and everything would still work out the way that it was meant to. Then Daddy . . ." Glory cleared her throat.

"I get it. I get it, it's OK."

Victor drummed his fingers on the table and looked around the visiting hall. "It's cool, don't worry about it. Don't cry again." He rested a gentle hand on Glory's forearm.

"Do you forgive me?"

Victor sat back. "I will eventually."

"Forgiveness is a process, even to forgive yourself—that's what my therapist told me."

"You're seeing a therapist?"

"Yeah."

"Do they make you talk about your childhood and that?" Victor asked sarcastically.

"Nah, not really, I talk about my anxieties, unhelpful thought patterns, basic stuff really."

"Does it help?"

"I guess," Glory said. "Better than pissing off Faith and pushing Mummy over the edge."

"They've got counselors here who we can go and see if we want to."

"You gonna see one?"

"Nah, I'm not tapped like that."

"You're saying I'm tapped?" Glory asked, pretending to be offended. Victor laughed.

"I dunno, Glor." It was the first time he'd said her name and her heart leaped. "You've been moving mad these last couple years, can't lie. Anyways, what else is happening outside?"

They found their way back into easy conversation. Glory filled him in on daily minutiae, what everyone they knew was up to. He seemed to drink in the details, even the stories about people he could only vaguely put a face to, and then out of nowhere he interrupted Glory.

"I wish I never got in that car."

He was peering intensely at a piece of flesh he was peeling away from his finger. He looked like a small boy, covered in scars, some razor thin, criss-crossing the back of his hands, traveling over his veins, and others not physically tangible but evident in the crease between his brows as he narrowed his focus on this minor act of self-mutilation.

"You can't torture yourself thinking about the past."

"The past is all there is in here. Even what I'm going to eat tomorrow has already been decided. The future is a foreign concept, it's like asking what exists in another dimension."

Glory didn't have an answer, so she just made a noise in the back of her throat.

"Another thing." This time Victor looked at Glory, his eyes draining of the hardness. "We all fuck up, but family is the only thing we've got. The only fucking thing."

Glory nodded, her chin yo-yoing desperately. She had been wondering when was the right time to tell Victor about Hope. She was wondering if he would react the same way that Faith had, but this was the sign she needed.

"I know, Vic, I know. I'm so sorry. I know."

They sat for a while, then she leaned forward, lowering her voice a little.

"Vic, I need to tell you something. It's about our other sister."

Victor's eyes widened, first in confusion then in curiosity. He leaned in toward Glory as she began to rapidly recount everything, starting with the discovery in their father's desk.

According to Celeste's time line, Victor had never met Hope. Hope was even more abstract to him than she was to Glory. She had been expecting an eruption of righteous anger that would stoke up her own indignation once again. But Victor listened to the revelations in silence, not moved by Celeste's tearful confession nor shocked by their father's uncontrollable anger. In the end, when Glory explained the dead-end phone number and the fruitless internet searches, all he said was, "Well, you have to look a bit harder for her, innit?" As final shouts from the officers corralled the visitors from the hall.

Glory interpreted that as an order, but if only it were that simple.

31

"I need another lead besides my mum or Faith," Glory explained to Julian in the back office of the barbershop.

"Mmm," Julian said, distracted. Since the attempted robbery, Julian had fitted a new security system that included CCTV and iron security grilles on his office door and the back entrance. It had cost him a lot.

"If I could find that Mama Wawo at the very least, she might be able to help."

"Mmmm."

"Julian, are you listening?"

He sat up, snapping his attention back to Glory. His disappearances and unanswered calls were becoming more and more frequent, and when he told her he was "handling business," she noticed that "business" often had nothing to do with the shop. She wasn't stalking him but Pharoah's was only around the corner from her mother's house, and he seemed to be spending less and less time there.

But finally Glory had him all to herself—kind of. The door to the office was closed and she swung around like a child in Julian's squeaky chair while he sat on the edge of his desk, falling in and out of their conversation as his thoughts drifted this way and that.

"What about the school uniform in the picture? If you can work out what primary school Hope went to, maybe it would lead you to something else."

Glory stopped spinning, shocked that he had been paying enough attention to come up with a sensible suggestion. Then a shout sounded from the shop and Julian leaped to attention, reaching for the baseball bat he now kept under his desk.

"Stay there," he told Glory, and he opened the door with one hand, keeping the weapon down low by his side as he peered around the doorframe.

He relaxed, tossing the bat back under the desk then leaving the tiny office. Glory got up to see for herself what was going on.

Julian stood in the doorway talking with a group of men wearing the uniform of youth, thick dark puffa jackets and layered tracksuit bottoms, despite the sun that had begun to warm up the day.

One of them seemed particularly agitated, pacing in front of Julian, his arms flying around sharply to animate whatever he was saying. Julian said little, nodding occasionally and putting his hands out in a gesture that asked the young man to calm down. This carried on for a while, and eventually Glory returned to the office chair, spinning around and around until Julian reentered, reaching for his jacket and keys.

"Listen, Glory, I need to head back to my yard real quick, but go home and I'll call you when I'm done."

"Done doing what? I can come with you."

Glory rose from the seat.

"Nah, just wait at yours."

Julian looked toward the front of the shop, where the group had dispersed apart from the agitated one who was still rocking on his toes.

"What's going on?" Glory asked, following his eyes. He had caught whatever nervous energy was powering the boy outside, she could feel it.

"I just need to let Telly in to mine, get him settled then I'll come get you."

"Settled? Is he going to be staying with you?"

"For a bit."

Julian threw on his jacket, motioned for Glory to stand, and pushed the chair back into position at his desk. He checked around, confirming he had everything he needed, and locked the door behind him.

"What's happened, Julian?"

"I'll explain later, just go home."

Of course they didn't live together, but the thought of this unknown volatility invading Glory's world via Julian's flat made her uneasy. But with no real grounds to object, she left with Julian, his goodbye trailing behind her as she turned in the opposite direction and walked back to her house.

She knew that he wouldn't call her later. Or at least not during daylight hours, and she wasn't going to wait until the sorry text or sheepish call that would come at some point between sundown and midnight.

As she turned onto the end of her road, a car cruised past, the unmistakable bassline for Junior M.A.F.I.A.'s "Get Money" rumbling from its subwoofer. "*Fuck bitches, make money! Fuck niggas, make money!*" Glory found herself mumbling along to the track and given the circumstances, it seemed sage advice.

As her mother never tired of pointing out, she was not working and, besides having no money, this also meant she had too much time on her hands to wait for Julian to fill. It was time for her to expand her horizons workwise—or perhaps lower her sights.

When she reached home, Glory went straight to her room. Sitting on her bed, she took out her phone and in the Notes app began listing every possible job she could do that wouldn't completely kill her spirit. The list was short and the only realistic option was working for the silver service agency she had spent a summer at, before her aborted stint at university.

The pros were it was flexible work, she would be working private functions with little chance of being spotted on the job, and sometimes the tips were really good. The main con was that one small step for a healthy bank balance was another giant leap into the past. *At this rate*, she thought, *she might as well trade in her iPhone for a Sony Ericsson and go back to tying multicolored shoelaces in her hair.*

Glory laughed, despite herself, thinking back to a picture that Lará had sent her soon after their reunion in Shoreditch. It was the two of them with a few other teenage girls, posing on the top deck at the back of a bus, their hair tied with shoelaces, color matched to their outfits. Glory thought they looked like Power Rangers, each girl a carefully coordinated block of color. She was all in green, Lará was in blue.

"Was this from your Bebo page?" Glory had typed back, throwing in a few laugh-cry emojis for good measure.

"Yep! I think we were going ice-skating in Streatham or something." If Glory wanted to go ice-skating now, she wouldn't be able to afford it unless she borrowed money from her sister or Julian. She had less money at her disposal than when she was in college on EMA, and that thought alone shamed her. Her father would be mortified.

Her parents had never had family to rely on when they arrived in England. She knew the stories of the indignities of low paid jobs they were overqualified for. She knew the insults leveled at them as if she had been the one to swallow them herself. But despite that, they had provided more than a stepping-stone; their blood, sweat and tears were the foundation that her life was built on. And, yet, she was agonizing over whether to do something useful or to keep doing whatever she was doing, which was nothing, and was clearly taking her nowhere. So, of course, she put her pride to the side and submitted her CV to the agency's website.

Grimly satisfied, Glory lay back on her bed and checked social media for the umpteenth time that day.

When she opened the Facebook app she sat up like a jolt of electricity had run through her. She had a private message from Hope Kehinde. She waited a long time to open it, trying to decipher the feeling that made her delay reading the message she had been waiting on for weeks. What she felt most was fear: fear it was her long-lost twin, but that Hope had no knowledge of her existence; fear that it was her long-lost twin but she had no interest in her existence; fear that it wasn't her sister at all.

Glory coaxed herself into clicking on the message. She squeezed her eyes closed, breathing out for a count of three before she slowly opened them again.

"Who this?? Am sorry,, I don't know where you mean,, Where is Midland? I want to go to London. Write back pleas."

Glory sighed, and closed the app without replying.

Then she remembered Julian's suggestion—the school uniform. She scrolled through her photo album, locating the images she had taken of the photographs. She zoomed in on the crest embroidered on Hope's cardigan. It definitely said "St" something. She cropped the image so it was just the crest and sent it over to Lará.

"Since you love fonts and letters and stuff, can you work out what the name of this school is?"

A few minutes later Lará responded with the nerd emoji followed by:

"*Do you have this in a higher resolution?*"

Glory didn't and she wasn't sure where in the house her mother might have hidden those photographs now.

"*I can try and scan the original, but I don't know where it is at the moment . . . You can't make anything out at all?*"

"*Hmmm. Give me a little while and I'll see what I can do.*"

Lará ended the message with a detective emoji and Glory thanked her friend.

32

Glory was called in to interview at the agency the following week.

She borrowed money from Faith and made a trip to Primark to buy plain black trousers, a black button-down shirt and flat black ballet pumps. Through the thin soles she could feel each piece of gravel that passed underfoot as she walked up the horseshoe drive and toward the service entrance of the agency's headquarters.

In the small foyer of the converted stately home she was offered water in a plastic cup while she waited with the others. The interview would take up at least half the day, with a one-on-one "conversation," some basic training and a test. They would find out there and then if they had the job.

The others were all younger than Glory and were all women apart from two men. One of the young men looked like he was wearing his school uniform, right down to the short, thick tie bunched around his neck. He sat with one arm draped across the back of his seat, his legs spread wide and feet pouring outward. He chewed gum loudly and tried to make conversation with a girl to his right. She politely responded in three words or fewer, looking concerned, as if his relaxed attitude might be contagious and she might forfeit employment because of a poor choice of seat.

Eventually the group of hopefuls was taken from one waiting room to another, and handed training booklets to read before they were called into the interview room. Glory was interviewed second, and she sat across the table from a woman with wide eyes and a severe ponytail. The woman introduced herself as Sunnie, and offered a firm handshake before running her eyes over Glory's CV.

Glory hadn't been nervous until now, figuring that her previous experience in the company would more or less secure her a role. But as Sunnie ran the tip of her pen over her employment history, she tried to hastily think of a response if the woman were to ask why she was taking itinerant shift work after having once been on a career path. But when Sunnie's eyes found the name Silversprint on the sheet of paper in front of her, she looked up.

"Ah, you've worked here before?"

Glory nodded.

"Welcome back."

The briefest of smiles graced her face.

From then on the interview was a formality. Sunnie wasn't interested in why Glory was going from a salaried role to minimum wage work. All she cared about was how much of the job she could remember and if she still knew what the company's values and uniform were.

"Good luck with the assessment," Sunnie said, rising to shake Glory's hand and signal the end of the conversation. "I doubt you'll need it."

Glory left the room feeling confident.

For the training and assessment they were led to a wing which had retained the home's former splendor. Everyone was quiet and nervous, apart from the boy with the short fat tie who made comments about the paintings and the rugs and how far they had to walk. Glory wanted to tell her potential colleagues to loosen up, but she remembered how high the stakes had felt trying to get her first proper job as a teenager, so she left them to their small anxieties.

They reached a hall set out with four round banqueting tables dressed in white cloth. There was a smaller foldaway table with a place setting laid out and next to it a dumbwaiter loaded with trays, cutlery and glasses. The man who had been leading them silently was tall and thin, with a shadow of gray around his jaw, and when he addressed them he did so in a continental accent.

"I am Franco and I will train you this afternoon." He dipped his head in a slight bow, and the boy with the tie bowed back.

They began by learning how to load trays with champagne glasses, a task that looked simple but was not. Faces turned pink and puckered as trays tipped over and plastic glasses skittered across the floor. Glory, with the advantage of previous training, did it the first time around and spent the rest of the time trying to help a nervous girl with long brown braids whose hands were shaking.

"Always start at the center," Glory said, showing her how to hold her tray with one hand, while the other lined up the glasses. But the girl was too nervous to listen properly, and her tray kept tipping this way and that, glasses tumbling through the air. She was not going to get the job.

The next tasks were learning how to pour champagne, collect and stack empty plates, and lay the table. Some of these skills had served Glory well and impressed her American colleagues when a discussion turned to fine dining and she had been able to guide them through a place setting. They assumed it came from the *Downton Abbey* etiquette training all British people went through. Glory didn't let on she learned it from serving others.

After the training was finished, the hopefuls were given a short break before the assessment began.

"I'm so gonna fail!" the girl with the braids wailed as they went to get more water.

"No, you'll be fine," an elfin girl offered unhelpfully.

Glory would probably never see this girl again, but it was still no use lying to her. She was not good at this. She forgot which way was clockwise when it came to collecting plates and had no sense of coordination, which was sure to send gravy spilling if the plates they had been playing with had any real food on them.

"Is this your first job interview?" Glory asked, and the girl chewed her lip and nodded.

"Then just treat it as a practice run, relax a bit, this isn't life or death, y'know?"

But the girl's watery eyes suggested something else.

"Listen," Glory lowered her voice. "There are literally a million agencies like this in London. If you don't get this job, you just apply for another agency and you've got a head start from this experience."

The girl swallowed and nodded again.

"Don't overthink it and don't rush. Silver service is about efficient service but it's not about being the quickest if it's gonna make you drop soup in someone's lap. Take your time, OK?"

The girl took a deep breath and tried to smile. She looked even younger than the rest of them, and Glory wanted to give her a hug but settled for a light pat on the back. Then they all headed back inside for the assessment.

Glory breezed through the tasks that were meant to test them, and for all his class-clown demeanor, the boy with the short fat tie transformed into another person when the time came for his own service skills to be judged. Franco could barely hide his astonishment. Everyone else was average.

When the task had been completed by all, Franco instructed them to fall into place and he walked the line with his notepad like a general inspecting his troops.

"Tomasz and Glory, you two were very good, I am impressed."

The boy bowed again and this time Franco smiled.

"The remaining—you were OK. You will pass, but you must go home and practice!"

The girl with the braids looked like she had just got through to the next round of *The X Factor*.

"If you want to start work immediately, we have some shifts this week. Oh, and just a note about uniform: black shoes, black socks, black trousers and if ladies wish to wear a skirt it must come down to the knees—no longer, no shorter. When applying for a shift you will be told what color shirt to wear, it will either be black or white, and your appearance must be well kept, no prominent jewelry, and your hair must be groomed." On this last point he looked at Glory's twist-out and the girl with the braids. "We do not approve of dreadlocks or these loud styles." He waved a hand around his head in what Glory assumed was meant to demonstrate the "volume" of her hair.

"Excuse me, sorry, these aren't dreadlocks," the braided girl said.

"Well, whatever they are called, they are not one of the approved hairstyles."

"B–but, I just got these done, it cost me eighty quid." The girl looked upset again.

"Well, maybe you talk to Sunnie about it before you leave," Franco said with a shrug. "Everyone please pick up an employee handbook before you go. Congratulations and welcome to Silversprint."

The girl with the braids found Glory as the group filed out of the room, her fingers anxiously knitted together as she began talking in a hurried whisper.

"I don't want to take my braids out, I got them done especially for the interview, I thought they'd make me look smart—"

"Trust me, it's really not that deep," Glory reassured the girl, but she had already mentally checked out and was ready to escape. She collected her handbook, signed up for a couple of shifts and walked out into the spring sunshine.

Glory moved quickly, not wanting to be forced into conversation with a fellow recruit heading in the same direction. She saw three missed calls from Julian and a message from Faith.

"How did it go?"

"Got the job. Obviously," Glory replied. Then she called Julian back.

"Yooo! Where you at? Been calling you all day!"

His tone was buoyant, as though he hadn't been neglecting her since the day he decided to take in Telly. Glory wanted to point out that three missed calls in the space of twenty minutes did not equate to "calling someone all day," but she bit her tongue.

"I was at a job interview," she said.

"Oh, for real? Where?"

"Just some waitressing thing."

There was a pause.

"Why would you wanna do that?"

"Because I need money."

"That's not money, that's chicken change."

Glory was taken aback by the disgust in his tone. It threw her off momentarily.

"Money's money, innit," was all she said in the end.

"If you need money, you know I've got you like that."

"I'm not trying to be a *kept* woman, Julian. Plus, you've been a bit unreliable recently . . ."

"So?"

"What's going on anyway?" Glory could sense the fight in Julian's voice, and despite her impatience she was not ready to spar with him.

"I wanted to take you out."

Glory was still irritated but she was also hungry, open to a bit of attention, and to be honest, she had missed him.

"All right, let me go home and change, then I can meet you."

"Cool, call me when you're ready."

33

"I can think of five places we could have gone between Peckham and Lewisham. Why did we have to drive all the way here for some Yard food," Julian grumbled as he settled into his seat.

Glory had picked a little Caribbean restaurant in Catford for their date. The inside was dark and cozy, with homely touches like a beaded curtain over the doorway to the kitchen, and reggae playing quietly in the background. They had ordered their food at a counter stacked with flyers promoting family fun days and local raves, before taking a table in the corner.

"First of all, they're probably just takeaways, this is an actual restaurant where we can sit in. Second, I doubt they're as good."

"I dunno about this to be honest. The woman at the till seemed a little too happy for it to be legit." Julian smiled at Glory, but she took a sip of her fruit punch and avoided eye contact. She wasn't ready to make peace just yet.

"How's your new flatmate?"

"Telly?" Julian kissed his teeth. "He's like the younger brother I never wanted."

"How long are you going to babysit him?"

Julian looked up. She held her stony expression. He looked down and twisted the ring pull off the open can in front of him.

"You still ain't told me why he needed to move in and now I can't chill at yours like I used to." Glory watched Julian play with the ring pull. He tossed it to the side and poured the rest of his drink into a glass.

"It's not an interesting story."

"I'm still interested."

He exhaled. "Long story short, Telly's mum found his stash and threw it away. She also threatened to call the police and kicked him out. But it wasn't really his so now he's in debt for it and it's all long."

"And you're letting him stay at your house?" Glory raised an eyebrow.

"Why wouldn't I?" Julian asked, irritated by the question.

"What if the people he owes money to come looking for him or he brings more drugs into your house?"

"He knows not to bring any shit to my house, and anyway, I know the guy he owes. We're working something out."

That did nothing to ease Glory's fears. Her mind was calculating all the possible worst case scenarios, inspired by all the films she'd watched. People lost body parts and loved ones to mobsters for less. Pharoah's had almost been robbed once, even with all of Julian's safety precautions it could be a target again, and a baseball bat under the desk was no match for a gun—Glory was sure drivebys were still a thing that happened every now and again.

The woman who had taken their orders came over with their food. Julian's fat leg of jerk chicken still smelled smoky from the drum out the back, and Glory's curried mutton steamed on her plate. The woman went away and returned

with a large side of creamy homemade coleslaw and two sets
of knives and forks wrapped in napkins.

"Enjoy!" she said brightly as she left.

"Now these are proper portions of food," Julian said with
the grin of a greedy man. "Barely any plate to be seen! Not
like that Mayfair place we went to."

He turned his plate around, admiring the dish from every angle.

"You're the one that chose Maijhun, I chose here, so I
don't know what you're trying to say."

Glory spooned some coleslaw onto her rice.

"Well, I was trying to impress you and now you've impressed
me. Everyone's a winner!"

Glory allowed her chilly demeanor to melt. She really had
missed him.

"What?" Julian asked, catching her stare.

"Nothing," she said, looking down at her plate.

The food was so good they didn't talk. Julian worked his
way through his chicken, abandoning his knife and fork after
a few bites and gripping his drumstick between his fingers.
Glory finished her portion of aromatic stew and rice and peas,
and waited until Julian had cleared his plate, throwing a used
napkin on top and slumping back into his chair.

"You found that Mama Wawo yet?" Julian asked her,
smoothing his hands over his stomach.

"Nope, I told you already, I don't know where to start."

"What about your mum's friends?"

Glory snorted. "Go talking to my mum's friends about
family secrets?"

The idea was absurd, and Julian should have known that.

"You don't have to go into detail. Just find out if they
know this woman. Someone has to know her."

"You're trying to get me kicked out."

"You could move in with me, no problem."

"With you and Telly?" Glory said, cocking her head to one side and giving Julian a sarcastic smile. "You gonna buy bunk beds for us or will we have to top and tail it?"

Julian sighed as his phone buzzed on the table. He picked it up, looked at the screen and placed it back, facedown.

"You can't save everyone, you know," Glory said to Julian, reaching across to take his hand in hers, but keeping her eyes on his phone.

His face darkened with a shadow of aggravation.

"I'm not trying to save everyone, I'm just looking out for someone I know. If I had someone older looking out for me, who knows all the BS I could have avoided? I could be a millionaire by now and living in a nice house off ends."

"Sometimes I feel like you just want more for other people than they want for themselves," Glory said, running a thumb over the back of his hand.

Julian frowned and pulled his hand away.

"Like how I feel about you and this waitressing t'ing?"

Glory paused, feeling the sharp sting of her point backfiring.

"You really want to fight about this waitressing job, don't you?" she eventually asked in a calm voice. "Why?"

"I think you can do better."

"I *know* I can do better. But right now, I'm just doing what I can. My parents didn't raise me to be useless. If I just do this, maybe everything else will fall into place."

It was not lost on Glory that she was directly quoting her mother.

Julian raised his eyebrows and looked away.

Gregory Isaacs whined from the speakers, *"If you wanna be my number one, let me know your future plans, let me know, let me know . . ."*

"You made it out, y'know?" Julian said. "You made it all the way to America and you came back but this place is a trap, this whole place is a trap and I'm not tryna be the only one who makes it out."

Glory puzzled through his passionate statement, trying to decipher the meaning underneath his words.

"It's not hard to do. You could sell the shop, take your money and go."

"It's not that simple."

"It's only as hard as you make it."

"Are you ready to go? I'm done."

Julian pushed his seat back roughly and moved toward the door.

Outside, he walked slightly ahead of Glory until he reached his car. He opened the passenger door nearest the curb and once Glory was in the seat he slammed it shut behind her.

Chatter from the radio filled the car as Julian drove, allowing them both to pretend that there was not an iceberg between them. Julian's fingers danced, tapping out an irritated beat on the steering wheel, and switching from station to station. Glory watched the names flit by on the LCD screen. Light glinted on the chrome accents that circled the dials and heating vents.

"You know, if you sold this car, you could use the money to start a new life wherever you wanted."

The impatient rhythm of Julian's fingers slowed to a steady tempo.

"Only if you'd come with me," he said, his lips softening into a smile.

"I'm done with running. The worst has already happened."

Blue lights flashed through the car and Julian froze. The yelp of a siren followed, but it was hard to tell which direction the emergency vehicle was approaching from. Julian sped up, slamming his foot on the brake when traffic appeared ahead of them. He watched the rearview mirror grimly until a police car nosed its way past.

"Are you all right?" Glory said, rubbing her shoulder where the seat belt had cut in.

He breathed out slowly and deliberately, waiting for the cars in front to start moving.

"What's wrong?" Glory tried again. "It was just a police car."

"*Just* a police car." Julian snorted.

Glory looked around the car.

"Do you have something in here? Did Telly leave something in your car?!" she asked, panic pushing her voice higher than usual.

"Don't be stupid. My license is suspended. That's all. Didn't want them to impound the car."

"Why is your license suspended?"

"Playing chicken with speed cameras."

"You think this is a joke? Why are you driving on a suspended license?"

Julian turned to look at Glory, narrowing his eyes with a curl of his lips.

"Don't talk to me like that."

"Like what?"

"Like I'm a dickhead."

"It's a valid question, Julian! You're paranoid about the police but you're doing dumb shit that puts you at risk. You should be smarter than that!"

Driving a car that he shouldn't have been driving was the reason Victor was sitting in a cell with a conviction for manslaughter. Julian of all people should have understood that he couldn't afford to make a mistake.

For a second, Glory thought he was going to shout back at her. Her choice of words was inflammatory but Julian only kissed his teeth and resumed his drumming. He turned up the volume on the radio, but Glory reached forward and spun the dial until the sound level hit zero.

"Don't do that."

Julian swung around a corner, and Glory lurched in her seat with the tilt of the car. He pulled up behind a parked van and turned off the engine.

"I was in such a fucking good mood today, and I swear to God, I don't need this stress here as well!"

Glory stayed silent, keeping her gaze fixed straight ahead. Julian swore under his breath.

"So you don't want to know why I was in a good mood or why I'm stressed? You don't care about none of that?"

"If you wanted to talk about it, you would have already."

Julian kissed his teeth again, turned the engine back on, and pulled off from the curb. Glory counted lamp posts as they sped by in steady pulses of yellow light.

Her phone chimed loudly and she checked her notification.

"*St. Magdalene or St. Margaret. Sorry it took a while, had to transfer the picture to my laptop, then from the cluster of pixels I had to guess where the terminals of letters might be (it's a serif typeface). Anyway, M, A, G definitely appear in the first few letters, and the name is long enough to be 8 or 9 characters long. Sorry I can't be more helpful. X*"

Glory was grinning.

"*You are a STAR, Lará! I don't get half of what you're saying most of the time, but you have been sooooo helpful. You don't understand.*"

Glory looked over at Julian whose face was still screwed up in irritation. He had been taking rough turns around corners as though he was trying to make the drive as uncomfortable as he could. A part of her wanted to share this amazing news but the other part felt he didn't deserve it. He had plenty of things he didn't tell her about; this would be her secret for now.

When they arrived at her house, she thanked him coolly for dinner and the lift home, before leaving the car without so much as a glance back. As she walked up the steps to her front door, her phone was already in her hand, searching for primary schools in the Kent area.

The first result was for a St. Mary Magdalene secondary school in Tonbridge with an emerald green uniform. There were no St. Magdalene schools anywhere in England—which if Glory thought a bit more about her Sunday school education made sense. So instead she searched for a St. Margaret's and found one: St. Margaret's Church of England Primary School in Sevenoaks. But the uniform wasn't dark like the uniform Hope was wearing in the photograph. It was an electric royal blue jumper.

They must have changed the uniform, Glory thought—that was the only sensible explanation. She was now on her bed, her outside clothes still on, scrolling quickly through the school's website.

When the virtual tour of the grounds wouldn't load, Glory ditched the smartphone and switched to her laptop. She clicked quickly through corridors and classrooms, looking for something that might suggest that this *was* the school she had been looking for. In the assembly hall, there was a display of pictures on a far wall. She zoomed in as far as the tour would let her, but she couldn't tell if the pictures were recent or from a while ago—if they were snapshots of former pupils wearing more somber hues, or it was the same bright color that was worn by the clean, smiling children in the school's prospectus, just caught in the shadow of the hall.

She made a note of the school's telephone number and set an alarm to call them at nine the following morning.

34

"Good morning, St. Margaret's Primary School!" the bright voice of the receptionist trilled through the phone.

Glory's alarm had only gone off five minutes before and her brain still felt clogged with sleep.

"H-hi! I have a bit of a strange question to ask. Did St. Margaret's change its uniform recently?"

"Recently? Well, if you count . . . oooh, it must be twelve or thirteen years now. If you count that as recent, then yeah!"

"Ah, brilliant," Glory said, switching to her "approachable" tone. "Was the uniform darker before? Maybe a navy or a black?"

"I didn't actually work here then," the receptionist said. "But let me just ask someone."

Glory heard the woman cup a hand over the receiver and shout to someone in the background.

"It was a navy blue, we think," the receptionist said when she returned. Glory's heart leaped in her chest and she sat up straighter in her bed.

"Wonderful, my next question is even stranger, if I'm honest, but I'm looking for someone, an old pupil who would have attended in the early nineties, around 1994 or 1995? Her name was Hope Akindélé—I can spell that for you—or she might have been registered as Hope Marksham?"

"Erm, OK . . ." The receptionist sounded a lot less cheerful but she tried to remain polite. "Are you a journalist or something?"

"No, I'm actually her sister. We were separated as children and I haven't seen her since, I'm just trying to find her."

"Oh," the woman said, her suspicions easing slightly. "I'm sorry love, I weren't working here then."

"Do you have like the pupil records or anything? Can you confirm that she attended? I mean, I'm pretty sure that she did now—"

"I'm sorry, I can't give you any information like that—data protection."

Glory's heart sunk and she began to feel tearful.

"What about teachers? Are any teachers from then still around? I've got a picture of her when she attended St. Margaret's, I can send it to you, but I just need to know if any of them know where she moved to after leaving. She's my twin sister, I don't know where she is," Glory pleaded, gripping the phone so tightly it felt like her knuckles would burst from her skin.

The receptionist breathed deeply down the phone.

"One sec, my love, let me ask someone." This time Glory heard the receiver being set down on a hard surface and the voice receded into the background. She waited, praying and bargaining with God all over again. Yes, she had not kept to her previous promise, but this time—*this time*—she would join her mother's church choir if he would just make sure that something here worked out!

"Hello?"

"Hi! Yes, I'm still here," Glory said, her chest expanding with expectation.

"I'm so sorry, we don't have any teachers from then still on staff. Have you tried searching for your sister on Facebook?"

"Yes," Glory said, trying to keep her mouth from breaking open into a sob. "Thanks for trying. Thank you, bye."

She hung up before the receptionist had a chance to respond.

Glory gritted her teeth and inhaled deeply, the air whistling through her clenched jaw. She did not want to cry, she was tired of crying and being so emotional and frustrated. Her NHS therapist had told her that emotions were not good or bad, they were just signals she needed to pay attention to, but she was tired of the signals. She knew what was wrong and, despite everything, she could not fix this or anything else.

She tried to console herself with the fact that at least she had a location now. She picked the phone back up and typed "Joan Marksham Sevenoaks Kent," "Edward Marksham Sevenoaks Kent" and eventually "Hope Akindele Marksham Seven-oaks Kent."

"Of course!" she shouted when the results came back with nothing. At this point Hope didn't even feel real. She could be stuck in an elongated loop of familial delusion or her sister could have died and not even her parents knew. She threw her phone from the bed, flopping facefirst into her pillow and screaming into it until her throat ached.

35

There was one option Glory hadn't explored yet, for fear it would backfire spectacularly: she could go behind her mother's back and talk to one of her friends.

If any one of Celeste's friends knew anything, it would be Auntie Dòtun. She had been around for as long as Glory could remember and, while Celeste regularly suspected her other friends and acquaintances of malice and ill intent, Glory had never heard her mother complain about the woman she often referred to as her sister.

So a few days later, on a Sunday morning, Glory rose earlier than usual and began to get ready. She repurposed one of her work shirts and laid a thick layer of gel on her hair, working it into a tidy and compact bun that would stop any inquiries of when she was going to "do something" with it. Her jewelry was modest and demure and she tried her best to channel Faith—the archetype of respectful.

"Where are you going today?" her mother asked as they passed each other on the landing.

"To church, with you," Glory responded with a sweet smile.

Celeste looked puzzled, then smug.

"God always answers my prayer," she told Glory with a knowing look and wagging finger.

"Amen!" Glory replied, happy to let her mother believe it.

It took awhile for Celeste to get ready. Long enough that Glory had time to wrestle with the wisdom of her plan as she flipped between absolute conviction and thinking of ways to back out.

Finally in the car and ready to go, Glory clicked her seat belt in place knowing it was too late to change her mind.

"So, tell me about America," Celeste began cheerfully as she set the car in motion and, for a brief moment, Glory thought about unbuckling her seat belt and leaping dramatically from the car that was rolling forward at 10 mph.

"What do you want to know?"

"What church were you attending while you were there?"

Celeste already knew the answer to this, Glory was sure, but she played along.

"Erm, I went to Hillsong's once or twice."

Celeste snorted as she checked the car's wing mirrors before making a turn.

"That one is a rock concert, not a church."

Then she turned to give Glory a visual appraisal.

"Is that what you'd wear to Hillsong's?"

"Er—"

"I don't like it. You didn't have anything nicer to wear? Brighter? Like a blouse and skirt?"

Glory shifted in her seat impatiently.

"I don't know where you put my clothes, Mummy. I can't find anything that fits. This is all I had."

"Well, at least you made your hair," Celeste said, and Glory turned obstinately to face the window. If she kept quiet, she might be able to delay feelings of immediate regret for as long as possible.

As they drove down Old Kent Road in silence, Glory counted the churches they passed along the way. Her mother's church was one of many meeting in shop fronts, above restaurants or in unassuming industrial buildings and former warehouses. Celeste's own church, The International House of Praise, rented a whole floor in an old office building, and the drab interior and low ceilings were made over with draped fabric backdrops, an elevated stage, extra lighting rigs and artificial plants. Standing fans turned in perpetual motion trying to keep air moving through the large stuffy room. Even after years of absence, the quiet rattle and hum of their blades were a familiar comfort to Glory as she entered the "main sanctuary."

"Ah, *Glory* be to God in the highest!" Auntie Dọtun said with pleasant shock when she saw Celeste and Glory taking their seats across the room. "The prodigal daughter indeed!"

"Good morning, Auntie," Glory said, employing a bright smile and even dipping into a discreet curtsy.

Auntie Dọtun looked from Glory to her mother in amused bewilderment, the question in her eyes met only by a shrug from Celeste.

"Now you are here," Auntie Dọtun pointed two fingers toward the floor with enough vigor to make the gold bangles on her wrists jangle, "you have truly returned home, ehn? Praise God!"

"Alleluia!" Celeste said.

The worship band took to the stage, the bassist signaling their presence with a few resonant plucks on his strings. A young woman around Glory's age stood forward.

"Good morning, church!" she called into the mic with a voice that was rich and melodic. The congregation murmured back in response as they took their seats.

"The psalmist said, *I was glad when they said to me let us go to the house of the Lord.* Are we glad today, church?"

The response came back stronger and more enthusiastic than before, and the woman flashed a smile, her white teeth set against deep plum lipstick. The drummer counted in the band and they began playing, music filling the room as the congregation joined in.

The lyrics and rhythms came back to Glory like muscle memory. The shrill aunties sliding up and down the scale had been an unforgettable feature of the church services of her youth, but they had been replaced by a well rehearsed and devout band of musicians and singers in their mid-twenties. Glory felt frumpy in front of the women in jewel-toned tailored dresses and heels. Her mother was right, she should have made more of an effort.

When the music ended, the musicians and singers trooped off the stage to take their seats and a man in a sharp suit stood at the pulpit to deliver church notices. He was older than Glory, but not by much, and she wondered where all these well dressed and self-assured young people had come from. They were probably the people her mother had in mind when she lectured her about her own lack of direction.

Soon the man's duties were done and the familiar face of the senior pastor came into view as he took his position behind the pulpit. He stretched his arms out to grip either side of the wooden lectern as he instructed the congregation in a deep and somber voice to turn to the book of Judges, chapter six. Finally, Glory could relax and stop paying attention, the pastor's sermon forming a bed of white noise while she planned her way into a private conversation with Auntie Dọtun.

Glory's opportunity came at the end of the service, when another woman approached Auntie Dọtun to return some coolers she had been lent.

"They are downstairs, but you'll need someone to help you move them to your own car," the woman said.

"I'll help!" Glory offered, before anyone could suggest one of the pious young people milling around the room.

"We can just get one of the boys to—"

"No, no need, I can help you, Auntie Dọtun," Glory said eagerly, so the woman led them both into the corridor, down the tight staircase and into the car park.

At the boot of the woman's car, Glory waited while her arms were loaded with four large Thermos coolers.

"Glory, you can just take two at a time."

"No, it's fine! I can carry them, I just need you to direct me because I can't see."

She couldn't afford to let Auntie Dọtun go back upstairs and leave her to load the boot by herself.

Glory's arms strained to carry the toppling tower, and Auntie Dọtun gracelessly tried to lead her through the car park toward her little hatchback. They spent another fifteen minutes trying to fit the coolers around the rest of the things that lived in Auntie Dọtun's boot, and when they had finally finished and snapped the boot shut, Glory rested against the car to catch her breath.

"How did you find church?" Auntie Dọtun asked her with a hopeful smile. "Will you be coming more regularly now?"

"It was good, yeah—maybe!" Glory said, smiling back at her mother's friend. Thankfully the answer was enough for the older woman.

"I wanted to ask you a question, actually," Glory continued, wiping her damp palms down the front of her trousers.

"Oh? What is it?"

"Yeah, erm . . . do you know someone called Mama Wawo?"

"Who is she?"

"She used to live in Peckham, I just wondered if you knew her."

"Why would I know her?"

"Doesn't everyone know everyone else in Peckham?" Glory said with an uncomfortable laugh, straightening up to her full height.

"Have you asked your mum?" Auntie Dọtun was staring at Glory with a blank look which, given her default state of high emotion, was unfamiliar and eerie.

"No. I don't want to upset her."

"Why would you upset her?"

Auntie Dọtun's eyes were fixed fast on Glory.

"Upset who?"

Glory turned around to see her mother approaching the car, clearly having overheard the last part of their conversation.

"Ah, my sister, don't worry," Auntie Dọtun said quickly, her gaze sliding from Glory to Celeste.

"Upset who?" Celeste asked again, looking from her friend to her daughter.

"Glory was just telling me about a disagreement she had with Faith—no wàhálà!"

Glory stammered in agreement, unsettled by how swiftly Auntie Dọtun had covered the tracks of their conversation.

Celeste snorted.

"I am not getting in the middle of any of your squabbles with your sister! You are both adults, àbí?"

"Yes, Mummy. Of course."

"Please, let us go. I want to go home," Celeste said sounding tired. "Sister Dọtun, I will call you later, sha."

"OK, o!" Auntie Dọtun said cheerfully, patting her old friend on the shoulder and giving Glory a strange smile. As

Glory turned to follow her mother to the car, she was not only convinced that Auntie Dòtun knew exactly who Mama Wawo was and exactly what had happened, but she knew that she was not about to share any secrets with her dear friend's daughter.

36

Glory and Julian's honeymoon period was over. Julian became more and more occupied with "business" at the barbershop and beyond, while Glory filled her days perfecting the art of slicing translucent slithers of prosciutto for the rich. The work was almost hypnotic in its monotony, but it kept the days moving forward, eating up weeks at a time.

Her favorite shifts were at football stadiums, where on special match days young men would tuck a wad of twenties into her palm before they'd even sat down, insurance that she would facilitate their every wish. This usually meant extra portions of gourmet pies and desserts that would have otherwise been thrown away or eaten by the staff. But as long as the customer left feeling like they got their money's worth, Glory could tuck the undeclared tips into her bra without a second thought.

The job was far from the imagined life that had set her American dream in motion, but if she avoided thinking about that, she was fine. It was a means to an end, and kept her busy and mostly distracted while she worked out exactly what that end might be.

It also helped her avoid social media and socializing in general. Even Lará's earnest passion and quiet ambition began to grate on Glory and she slowly withdrew until she was in another self-imposed exile—but one without the envy inducing snapshots to share with her followers.

But at least she had Victor back.

"Your job sounds dead, bruv!" he teased on the phone, after she had finished explaining an intricate technique for sneaking leftover food into the cloakroom to take home at the end of her shifts.

"It *is* dead," Glory said with resignation.

"Well, I'd rather be out there eating stale cake than in here."

"It doesn't get stale if you wrap—anyway! Is everything, OK, Vic? What's going on?"

Victor sighed heavily. "Nothing's going on, that's the problem! I'm trying to get on to education but they have me wrapping headphones for some airline. They've had us on twenty-three-hour lockdown for so long, I don't even know what fucking day it is! Can't go to the gym, can't shower, and the guy in my cell is doing my head in. I think I'm gonna fake a breakdown to get moved to a single cell or something."

He laughed bitterly but Glory felt so helpless she couldn't even speak.

"Do you need money? What can I do?" she asked.

"Nah, don't stress—Michael and Faith keep my canteen stacked," Victor said. "They send me like £150 a month, and I told them I can only use £12.50 a week, but at least I'm prison balling."

"At least he's good for something!"

"Who?"

"Faith's husband."

"Michael? Nah, don't be like that, Glory. He's calm."

"Why is *everyone* in love with Michael?" Glory said with a derisive snort. "Anyway, I don't want to talk about Michael."

"Neither do I. I've got twenty minutes before bang up. Let me go and deal with a few things and I'll call you in a couple days, yeah?"

"Shall I book another visit?" Glory asked. She had dreaded the thought of seeing her brother in prison the first couple of times, but was surprised by how easily she had adapted to this unfortunate new normal.

"Not yet. I'll tell you when to come, yeah?"

"OK. Love you, Victor!"

"Yeah, hundred," Victor said gruffly.

"What?"

"Love you too, sis," he said in a hurried whisper, before hanging up the phone.

The next day was another work day. Silversprint was servicing a national awards ceremony for advertising and design, and Glory and her fellow servers were in a large event hall folding napkins and arranging chairs around circular tables.

"This is an event for people working in the business of visuals," the evening's event manager had briefed them with unnecessary pomp, "so the details are important!"

But as the guests filled up on bottomless champagne and hors d'œuvres, tablecloths were knocked askew, intricately folded napkins were flattened to mop up spilled drinks and the audience resembled little more than a carefully styled pub crowd.

Glory was relieved to find herself assigned to the bar. People were always more courteous to those providing them with free alcohol. At the bar they actually made eye contact, even if it was just half a wink as they held their glasses aloft, their eyes urging her not to cut them off despite their slurring speech and clumsy coordination.

"I did this event last year," a girl called Tannika told Glory as she polished empty glasses. "Someone managed to throw up underneath a table and we found a pair of knickers on another seat."

She curled her top lip, the skin dimpling where she had taken out her lip piercing. Glory and Tannika had been on a few shifts together, and she always turned up with all her facial piercings in, rolling her eyes every time a shift manager told her to remove them, as if she hadn't been told a hundred times before. Glory liked Tannika, she worked well, had a good sense of humor and although she was a few years younger than Glory, she didn't get caught up in the shenanigans of the other staff her age.

At Silversprint, workers fell broadly into two categories: young Londoners on their first job, biding time while they worked out what they were trying to do with their lives, or post-graduate students, often foreign, most of whom were promoted quickly to team leader and supervisor positions.

There was a third category of worker who would show up depending on the event. These were the hostesses, exclusively women, around Glory's age or slightly older, who were dancers and models and actresses by day, supplementing their dreams by being paid by the hour to flirt with male patrons and guests—or at least that's how it looked.

But tonight there were no hostesses working, just servers like Glory, all in androgynous black from head to toe, with ridiculous silver bow ties they were instructed in the sternest of tones to return after the shift had ended.

"Like anyone would want to t'eef these foolish bow ties anyway!" Tannika had said as Glory had tied hers. "Like them stupid things that them men in them silent films used to wear—what are they called again?"

Tannika smoothed a hand over her hair, her dress-code-breaking nail polish sparkling under the light.

"Laurel and Hardy?" Glory said as she finished fiddling with Tannika's collar.

"Yeah, them. Not gonna lie, they were kinda jokes still." Tannika waddled like a penguin behind the bar.

"Nah, I think his name was Charlie Chaplin, "y'know? We learned about him in dance GCSE."

She then waddled the length of the bar, pretending to serve a drink in slapstick fashion, which made Glory laugh and drew sharp looks from two managers.

Tannika made these shifts bearable. They didn't have any kind of official friendship, they hadn't exchanged numbers and spoke little of life besides sarcastic observations of the guests they were serving. Nevertheless, at the beginning of each shift Glory would scan the assembled faces, or look expectantly toward the door every time someone slunk in late. The shifts without Tannika were dull—Glory stayed in her head and worked mechanically—but when she was around a ten-hour shift could breeze by easily.

Tonight Tannika was distracting Glory from the fact that back in LA *she* would have been on the guest list, hoping for recognition for a big-brand collaboration or well executed viral campaign. Instead she was polishing glasses and serving drinks, her thumb wedged in the base of a champagne bottle, praying today would not be the day she dropped it. Julian hadn't brought up her waitressing job again, but as a particularly lairy patron let his glass slip through his hands, laughing as it shattered at Glory's feet, his words came back to haunt her: she could do much better than this.

As soon as the breakage was cleaned up, Glory volunteered to wheel crates of dirty glasses out to the kitchens—anything to get a break from the people hanging around the bar, turning more obnoxious with each passing sip.

As she turned, pushing the stacked crates in front of her, she came upon a group of women huddled at an open fire door, sharing a cigarette. She averted her eyes deferentially from their forbidden act, when she heard one of them call out, pulling her back.

"Glory?"

Glory turned around and saw Lará blowing a spurt of smoke out the corner of her mouth as she handed the cigarette to another woman.

"Oh my days! What are you doing here?"

Lará looked pleased to see her, but Glory felt shapeless at that moment. Lará was wearing a short, sequined shift dress with on-trend block heels. She looked chic in a quirky, cute way and, in the place of her distinctive glasses was a wash of shimmery eyeshadow. Lará was all glitter and smoke, her face wearing the kind of open and warm expression that came with regular laughter and drinks.

"Just working," Glory said, gesturing modestly to the crates in front of her.

The women behind Lará looked uninterested in their conversation, but Lará introduced them anyway as her colleagues.

"Glory used to work in an agency out in LA, but she's taking a break from the industry," Lará said, all smiles, while Glory felt the women's inquisitive looks digesting her uniform and current social standing.

One of them held out a delicate hand and said "enchanté" as Glory took it.

"She's French," Lará said by way of apology.

The other woman flicked away the stub of the cigarette and eased the fire door closed, pulling out a packet of chewing gum and passing it around. Glory felt like she was in school, having stumbled upon the cool girls as she scurried between classes.

"Anyway, I need to get these glasses to the porters," Glory said as she began to steer the unwieldy stack.

"What section are you working? I'll come by," Lará said.

"I'm at the bar."

Lará's colleagues smiled at Glory as they stalked off. Lará let them walk away a few paces before she gave Glory a quick, giddy squeeze.

"How random is this?" she said, showing all her teeth.

"Yeah," Glory said, laughing self-consciously. "Sorry I dropped off the radar a bit, I've been working quite a lot and stuff."

"No worries," Lará said, flapping away Glory's apology. "How've you been though? We should catch up soon."

"Yeah, fine, but I need to . . ." Glory gestured to the glasses again.

"Oh, of course! Sorry, I'll come over and see you in a bit!" Lará said, before hurrying back to her table.

The night droned on. Glory tried to pay attention to the awards in case Lará won anything, keeping an eye out for brown faces as winners took to the stage to hiccup through acceptance speeches.

As the evening drew to a close, Glory thought Lará might have forgotten about her, and self-pity pricked her heart before she saw her walking toward the bar. Lará looked in her element, her face glowing, smiling as if she was laughing at a joke no one else had heard. When she reached the bar she collapsed across it, feigning exhaustion, before propping her head up on her hands.

"There's some stuff happening at that table that I don't want to see." She jerked a thumb in the direction she had come from. "Don't want HR asking me to write a formal statement about what I witnessed tonight—no way!"

Tannika looked at the tipsy woman with an amused expression, and Glory introduced them before Tannika excused herself.

"How's it going tonight?"

"Yeah . . ." Glory shrugged. "Same old same. Don't think I'll be making any tips tonight though. Your advertising lot are stingy!"

"*My* advertising lot? They're your people too!" Lará laughed, but Glory didn't answer as she wiped down the bar with extra vigor, before refilling the straws and napkins.

"Did your agency win anything?"

"Nope!" Lará said, and then she lowered her voice and leaned in with a conspiratorial air. "I was only hanging onto this job because these awards were coming up. They usually get something each year and if my project won something, I thought it would help with moving on to a better role. And of course we didn't win a damn thing." She kissed her teeth and pulled away. "But I'm already planning my exit—life is too short!"

"Mmm," Glory grunted, avoiding Lará's eyes and busying herself with another task.

"Oh! I forgot to ask you about that St. Magdalene thing—was it helpful? Did you get anywhere?"

"Oh, no," Glory said, looking up. "I mean, yes it was really helpful, and it was Margaret, not Magdalene. But I didn't get anywhere in my . . . investigation. I found the school, but I didn't find what I was ultimately looking for."

"Oh, sorry!" Lará's face dropped. "What was it you were looking for?"

Glory laughed nervously.

"My sister," she said in a small voice.

"Your sister?"

"Yeah, I'm a twin—didn't you know?"

"No, I knew! But I always thought she had . . . well, I thought she was dead."

Lará whispered "dead" like the word itself might harm her.

"Who told you she had died? Did your mum?"

"Well, not directly, but I remember if it ever came up it was always this really tragic thing, like she was gone. And where else would she be gone to? Even when my mum found out about your dad she was saying how your mum had lost so much, your sister, your brother and then your dad."

Glory swallowed hard and looked down, staring very intently at the weave in the cloth she had been using to wipe the bar.

"Sorry," Lará said, holding out a hand. Glory didn't take it but instead cleared her throat and looked up again.

"Yeah, well, turns out she didn't die, she's alive and I've been trying to find her. My parents let us go and live with this white couple for a while, but Hope carried on living with them after we left. I have a picture of her in a school uniform—that was the school logo I sent to you. I found the school, but when I called they couldn't tell me anything."

"Wow."

Lará exhaled and Glory's words settled between them.

"Did you check to see if your foster family still live in the area?" Lará asked after awhile.

"Foster family?" Glory frowned.

"Yeah, the white people you were living with."

"No, my mum said they moved away and that's when they lost touch. But we weren't in like, *care* or anything. My mum said she paid the woman, like childminding I guess, but full-time."

"Yeah, I know exactly what you mean, but that's what it's called—private fostering. I think it's illegal now, though."

"I didn't know it had a name," Glory said and Lará laughed.

"What? You thought you guys were the only ones? Nah, it happened a lot. I was privately fostered too!"

"What?!" Glory asked, dropping her cloth on the bar and leaning toward Lará. "When?"

"When I was a baby, just for a little bit," Lará said with a shrug. "It was quite common in the eighties and nineties."

Glory leaned heavily against the bar.

"How did I not know this? Why does no one talk about this?" Glory said, feeling tense and agitated.

"What's there to talk about?" Lará asked, sounding bemused. "Do you remember anything about being fostered? I don't."

"No, bu-but!" Glory floundered, lost for words. "I mean . . . Fostering is one thing, but just leaving your daughter with strangers and not saying anything? Letting everyone believe she had died? That's fucked up!"

"Yeah, but that's . . . survival," Lará said, looking thoughtful.

"Survival?"

"You know, *Keep calm and carry on? Push through the pain?* I bet there's like a million mottoes like that."

"Oh, like repress the bad shit and keep on going?"

Lará nodded.

"Yeah, I'm pretty sure that's the attitude that sent my mum to Maudsley."

"Your mum was in Maudsley? Is she OK?"

"She's fine, but that's a whole other story, Lará, trust me!"

Glory laughed lightly, but Lará was shaking her head silently and for a second Glory felt the shame of her family's dysfunction weigh on her.

"How can I find Hope's foster parents though?" she asked, deciding to change the subject. "Are you still in touch with yours?"

"No."

"Well, that makes sense. Unless you gave your kid away to strangers, there wouldn't be any need," Glory sneered.

"Look, I know this is wild, but privately fostered children living long term with white families is more common than you'd think. It's just . . . yeah, no one talks about it."

"How do you know all this stuff anyway? Is it another one of your nerdy little projects?" Glory asked Lará, sighing and picking up a metal tray and some cleaning spray.

"Ha! No, my auntie was involved in organizing these arrangements, so she used to talk about it all the time with my mum."

Glory was polishing the tray, but froze mid-task.

"What's your auntie's name?" she asked.

"Auntie Níkẹ. But most people call her Mama Wawo."

The tray slipped from Glory's hand and dropped to the floor, a loud clatter signaling the impact. One of Glory's managers turned in her direction, so she held up a hand and bent down behind the bar. She tried to catch her breath from her position crouched on the floor, but when she stood up, she felt light-headed.

"Lará," she began, swallowing a big gulp of air in an effort to keep herself breathing. "Lará, I've been looking for your auntie! I didn't know she was related to you! I've been looking for Mama Wawo!"

"Really?"

"*She's* the one who introduced my family to the Markshams! She's the only bridge I have left!"

Glory slapped her hands excitedly on the bar.

"Er, OK!" Lará said. "I can take you to see her, I guess. She might be able to help."

"Oh my days! Lará, I could kiss you right now!"

Lará smiled, but then looked unsure.

"But, wait. It's been decades, right? Auntie Níkẹ might not be that useful," Lará said, twisting a braid around her finger. "What are you going to ask her?"

"*Anything* she might be able to tell me is useful! If it's a dead end, then it's a dead end. But at least I'll know I've tried. I can't find out you're related to this woman I've been looking for and not even *try*."

Lará considered Glory.

"OK then! Let's do it," she eventually said.

Relief, excitement and nerves surged within Glory.

"Wow!" Glory breathed out. "This is happening!" She reached over the bar and squeezed Lará's wrist and Lará smiled back at her, but their moment was interrupted by a man lurching toward them.

"Vodka limes," he said holding up two fingers of an unsteady hand. He then turned toward Lará.

"Do you know Angela? You look just like Angela. Are you related to her?"

Lará pasted on a polite smile and shook her head.

"You do!" the man persisted. "You look just like her. Here, help me bring these drinks to my table and see Jim, he'll tell you just the same!"

Lará looked from the man to Glory and back again, trying to keep her smile neat and polite, but struggling to contain the laugh that was about to spill out.

"In fact . . ." The man reached into his pocket and pulled out a dirty ten pound note. "Just keep a steady stream of drinks coming to our table. We're a good laugh, our lot. We're a friendly bunch."

The man winked and moved toward Lará, almost knocking himself off balance.

"Oh, I don't work here," Lará said, holding up a hand to the note. "I work for an agency."

It took awhile for that information to seep through and be understood, but when it did he turned toward Glory, still waving his money in the air.

"You work for an agency too?"

"Yeah," Glory said, setting down two glasses of vodka in front of him. "I'm just doing you a favor, mate."

"Oh!" the man said, his ears and neck starting to turn red. "Well, thanks."

He tried to carefully pick up the drinks, but liquid spilled down the sides of the glasses. Glory *might* have overfilled them on purpose, just so she could watch him struggle. Lará spotted the ten-pound note on the bar.

"Here," Lará said and slid it across the bar with a finger. "Reparations."

Glory smiled, slipping the note into her pocket.

"We should celebrate!" she said brightly. "Well, *you* should celebrate—I can't drink but I'll hook you up!"

Glory bent to look at the fridges lined up beneath the bar and Lará leaned over with one hand protecting her modesty as she held down the back of her dress.

"Can you do me a mojito?"

Glory looked up with a sheepish smile.

"I'm not actually a bartender. Do you just want some vodka or something?"

Lará tipped back her head and laughed.

"Go on then, Glory, give me whatever you've got."

37

Lará stayed glued to the bar for the rest of the evening, filling Glory in on intra-office scandals and inter-agency beefs, as Glory kept topping her up, alternating between spirits as a safeguard against detection. She needn't have worried. As midnight sailed by the managers started to forget that they were also meant to be working and placed their own orders, although the waiting staff were still not allowed to drink themselves. By the end of the night, everything had descended into a merry chaos.

Lará eventually pulled herself away and headed home, and the staff began to clear the remains. The scene looked like the aftermath of a raucous house party and as Tannika stacked some chairs she picked something up from the floor, holding it out in front of her between her fingertips. It looked like a small square of tracing paper, but Tannika's face was screwed up in disgust.

"It's an empty cocaine wrap!" she said impatiently when Glory looked unfazed.

At the end of the shift they all waited outside the service entrance, exhausted and bleary eyed, some sparking cigarettes for warmth. As taxis pulled up the shift manager called out the names of who would be accompanying who. When Glory's taxi arrived she squeezed inside with three others and they made their way to south London.

After forty minutes it was just Glory and one other young woman. Her head was lolling against the back window, leaving streaks of hair oil on the glass. Glory waited awhile, and when she felt the other woman was truly asleep, she pulled out her phone and made a call.

Julian picked up, his voice gruff and deep with drowsiness.

"You at home?"

"Yeah. What's up?"

"I've just left work, I wanted to know if I could come by."

"Now?"

"Yeah, now."

"You locked out?"

"I just wanted to talk, I've had some exciting news. I wanted to tell somebody."

"You can tell me over the phone."

"You don't want me to come around?"

"It's late."

"So?"

Julian huffed, it sounded like he was changing position, sitting up perhaps. He was probably on the sofa in front of the TV.

"So, what's the news?"

"I found Mama Wawo, she was under my nose the entire time."

"What, like, sitting on your top lip?"

Glory quietly laughed.

"No, it's easier to explain in person. I'm not alone at the moment."

"Come by the shop tomorrow then. Or I'll swing by yours in the afternoon, we could go out or something."

"Are you serious?"

"What?"

"Why don't you want me to come to your house now?"

"Look, I fell asleep, innit. I'm about to go to bed myself. Let's talk tomorrow when I'm properly awake, yeah?"

"Wow, you're serious!"

"I am."

"OK then."

Glory hung up.

The taxi rolled over a speed bump and the dozing girl's head hit the window with a dull thud. She jerked awake, looked around the back of the car and squinted through the glass before leaning back into the headrest and closing her eyes.

Julian knew how important it had been to find Mama Wawo. A conversation with this woman could change the shape of her family, the landscape of her personal history, but he didn't even care. He was locked into his world, and Glory was feeling more like an accessory than a girlfriend.

She rang him back.

"You act really shifty, y'know? I don't know why you can't be straight with me!"

Julian sighed, moving the phone away from his face while he mumbled something.

"Are you with someone right now?" Glory asked, trying to keep her voice down.

"Chill the fuck out, Glory, you want to come here and start checking underneath the bed or something?"

"If you acted normal then I'd have no reason to worry, would I? I swear to God, it feels like I don't even know who I'm talking to sometimes!"

"You wanna come here? Fine! Come around. Let's talk!"

"You're not listening to me."

"I never am, am I?" Julian said in a voice thick with tiredness and resignation.

"Bye, Julian."

Glory ended the call.

Glory stared angrily at her screen as a message came through: *"You always have to have the last word, right? Lol. Mature."*

"I don't need this shit." Glory began to type, but instead of hitting send she held down delete, leaving her text box blank and Julian's final words unanswered.

When the taxi reached Glory's house and she got out, she realized how tired she was. Her feet dragged on the short walk to her front door, but it wasn't just her physical tiredness from work, the short back and forth with Julian had emotionally drained her. All the excitement she had felt just a few hours earlier talking with Lará had been swallowed up by his limp reaction to her news and her irritation at the nonsense that followed.

Tears threatened Glory's eyes—whether it was exhaustion or frustration, she didn't know. But what she did know was that it was Julian's fault. She had been chasing smoke and running into brick walls but now she was the closest she had ever been to finding Hope and all Julian could do was . . .

"No," Glory told herself forcefully. She hadn't been flirting with the wrath of Faith and her mother to let Julian and his bullshit distract her when she finally had a real chance of getting to the bottom of this. She tried to regain the feelings she had felt as she poured Lará alcohol and listened with good humor to tidbits of gossip about strangers. She had felt like her life was finally aligning in a way that made sense. She could not afford to let anyone steal that from her, not even Julian.

38

"Faith? Is that you, Faith?"

Glory and Faith were in Bromley buying new clothes to send to Victor now he had finally been authorized to receive them.

She was loading bags of overpriced sportswear into the boot of Faith's car when someone called out from across the car park. Two women walked up to them. One of them, short with a blunt black bob, was a friend of Faith's from university.

"Oh, Selina. Long time!" Faith said as she hugged the woman.

Glory continued her task while Faith and Selina exchanged small talk, recounting who they had last seen and when, and what everyone was doing now.

"So what are *you* up to these days?" Selina asked, passing a glance over the car and Esther and Elijah strapped into the backseat.

"I'm just in 'mummy mode' at the moment, looking after my twins, keeping busy," Faith said with a smile.

"You're not working?"

"Keeping up with these two is enough work at the moment!" Faith laughed quickly, tapping the roof of her car in a way that Glory thought was unnatural.

"Lucky you. Must be nice to keep things so simple," Selina said, not with obvious spite but Glory stole a wary glance at her sister all the same.

Faith smiled and let out a hollow laugh. Glory could feel the tension coiling up in her sister's body and she wanted to rescue Faith from the unpleasant turn the reunion had taken.

"We're all good to go here," she said, slamming shut the boot of the car and walking around to the passenger side door.

"Well, let's not hold you up any longer!" Selina said. "Good to see you, Faith."

"Yes, take care."

Faith shut the driver-side door with a little more force than usual. Glory knew that the small success of the morning's shopping trip would now be overshadowed by this short interaction.

Back at the house Glory made herself useful in the way she knew how. She threw some fish fingers in the oven and whipped up a quick mash for Esther and Elijah. Then she found a few yams and got to work on Faith's favorite meal, fried yam and grilled fish.

Peeling yam felt like punishment as a child, but now she was older it felt like meditation. She cut the tuber down into slices, then chopped those slices into thick white fingers. She soaked the fingers in cold water, drained them and tossed them in some salt before warming the oil in Faith's deep fryer.

Glory took the fish fillets she had defrosted in the microwave and basted them in a marinade of spices, oil and fresh lemon juice. She then grilled them until the gray skin of the fish was brown and crisp, and served it alongside the golden chips of yam and fried plantain she had arranged into a little fan. A drizzle of red tomato stew provided the final flourish.

Faith rolled her eyes when she saw the fan of plantain.

"Ten out of ten for presentation," she said with a sideways smile. "But you know I need more stew than this."

"I know, but this is the social media version."

Glory leaned over the plate and snapped a picture before going back to the kitchen and bringing through the saucepan of stew.

Faith was already stacking yam, fish and plantain onto her fork when Glory returned, and soon after Glory had spooned more stew onto her plate, Faith was using the last chunk of yam to mop up its residue. She sat back and sighed in contentment. Glory sat next to her, eating the leftover stew straight from the saucepan.

"Don't eat it out the pot!" Faith sighed, but Glory ignored her and carried on.

"Do you have any regrets?" Glory asked Faith, licking the back of the serving spoon.

"I regret letting you do that already," Faith said, trying to snatch the spoon from Glory's hand. Glory dodged her and shifted along the sofa.

"Serious question. Do you ever look at your life and think, *Things weren't meant to go this way*?"

Faith looked pensive.

"There's always going to be moments when you second guess yourself, but I don't think I have any regrets."

"So you're perfectly happy with the way things are now?" Glory trod carefully, well aware that this could ignite another argument.

"The thing about regret is that it assumes that there could have been a better way for things to turn out. We have to rid ourselves of the delusion that things could have been any different."

Glory thought for a moment.

"That sounds really deep."

"Saw it on Pinterest."

Glory shook her head and laughed, and Faith turned on the TV. When she was on the other side of the world, it was simple moments like this that Glory missed the most. As the self-appointed third parent in the family, Faith could be annoying, bossy and a control freak. But Glory knew that her sister loved her like no one else could, and equally, Glory loved her back. She wanted to say all of this, but she didn't. She hoped Faith knew it anyway.

"I've started seeing someone, by the way," Glory said.

Faith's eyes widened and she sat up straight.

"Who? Do I know him?"

"Yeah, he came to Daddy's funeral. Julian."

"Julian as in Joy's little brother?" Faith said, doubtful.

"He's the same age as you!"

Faith still looked unconvinced.

"Let me see a picture, I didn't get a good look at him at the funeral."

Glory flicked through her camera roll until she found a selfie where Julian looked his best. Faith took the phone from her and examined it.

"He's all right, I suppose, if that's your thing."

"If what's my thing?" Glory asked snatching back her phone.

"A little rough around the edges, tattoos and all that. He looks like he has a silver tooth—oh my days, he reminds me of 50 Cent! You used to fancy 50 Cent didn't you?!"

Faith poked her sister with a sharply filed nail and Glory began to protest.

"I'm sure I remember you having posters of him on the wall and then Mummy told you to take them down because it was idolatry!" Faith cackled, clapping her hands together, and the twins looked up from their task sorting toys on the floor.

"Does he rap as well? I bet he raps too!" Faith got up from the sofa and began lumbering around in her best impression of a rapper's swagger.

"Go! Go! Go, Glory! It's ya birthday!"

Glory shrank back and pulled a cushion over her face.

Elijah got up from the floor and joined his mother in her prancing, bouncing up and down and windmilling his arms. Esther watched them for a moment before joining in, spinning on the spot.

The doorbell rang and Faith stopped dancing to go and answer it. Esther and Elijah paused mid move, watching their mother leave the room and return with a young woman in a headwrap and lots of colorful jewelry.

"Estie, go upstairs and tell Daddy that the tailor is here please."

"No, I wanna do it!" Elijah yelped, leaping up and racing his sister from the room.

Faith showed the tailor through to the rarely used dining room where she began laying out her tools on the table. She did so with an air of professionalism that Glory suspected was there to justify whatever she was charging Faith for the convenience of home service. But Glory couldn't knock her hustle, it beat serving wedges of pungent cheese to the wealthy and wealth-adjacent at silent auctions.

"Who's going to go first?" the tailor asked Faith.

They were all getting measured for outfits for Tabitha's traditional engagement ceremony.

Michael came downstairs, carrying the red and gold lace that the bride's mother had distributed to her guests, with the twins trotting diligently behind. The first time Glory had seen the sumptuous fabric, her mouth had practically watered. There were enough yards for the whole family, although Glory was sure that Michael would find an excuse not to attend.

"Is Mummy going to get measured?" Glory asked her sister.

"No. She's not coming."

"Since when?"

"Who knows. Maybe one of her holy men told her not to," Faith said with a polite, but clearly sarcastic smile.

Michael settled into an armchair with Elijah on his lap, burrowing into his father's body, thumb in mouth. Esther lay on her back at her dad's feet, her legs propped up against him while she played a driving game, twisting her tablet this way and that.

"I'll go first," Glory offered the tailor, who had been waiting patiently for an answer. She stood with her arms out, and the woman wrapped a tape measure around her bust and started making notes.

"Remember Lará? I saw her the other day," Glory told Faith, who was scrolling through her phone looking for the picture of the type of dress she wanted made. "I worked some industry function that she was attending. Her agency didn't win anything though."

"How is she?"

"She's good." Glory paused. "Mummy never mentioned that Mama Wawo is, like, her auntie or something."

Faith looked up from her phone and watched the tailor measure Glory's hips.

"Mama who?" she asked. Her fake ignorance was a warning shot, a chance for Glory to back down.

"Mama Wawo, the woman Mummy mentioned at the house a couple weeks ago."

"Why were you talking to Lará about that?" Faith put down her phone.

"It just came up."

Faith looked around the room as if whatever she wanted to say next was hiding behind the television or on the shelves next to the photo frames and carefully curated books. Esther continued to narrate her gameplay and Elijah had dozed off against his father's chest, but Michael was watching his wife closely.

"What are you planning to do with this new information?" Faith asked, using every ounce of self-control she had to remain calm.

"What do you think I should do?"

"Not go gossiping about family business at the first opportunity."

"It's no big deal," Glory said, trying to keep her tone bubbly as the tailor finished writing out her measurements. "Lará was fostered too."

"Who's next?"

Faith looked from Glory to the tailor and back again, fighting to keep anger from her face.

"I'll be right back!" she finally said, then she left the room and went upstairs.

Glory took a seat, meeting Michael's eyes in the process.

"So what are you going to do?" Michael asked Glory, who was surprised by the fact he had been paying attention to their conversation, let alone was interested in its topic.

"Erm, I'm not sure yet," she said, not attempting to hide her disinterest in his interest.

"I think you should go and talk to this Madam Wawo."

"It's *Mama* Wawo," Glory corrected him. This felt like a trap.

"Well, whatever her name is, she's clearly your best bet. I tell Faith this every time she brings it up."

"What do you mean brings it up? I thought she didn't care," Glory said, replacing disinterest with cautious curiosity.

"Oh no, she cares about it," Michael said, shifting Elijah from one leg to the other. "She cares a lot. She thinks she's protecting your mum, though."

Glory looked from Michael to the tailor, who stood, flicking through her notebook as if she wished she could hide among the pages.

"From what?" Glory finally asked her brother-in-law, lowering her voice slightly.

"Do you want a drink?" Michael asked the tailor. "There's juice in the fridge, clean glasses in the dishwasher—help yourself."

The tailor looked grateful for a reason to leave the room. When he heard the fridge door open Michael continued.

"You know," he said, settling into his seat. "Being the oldest, Faith's seen things from a completely different perspective. She didn't have a shield."

"She's not that much older than me," Glory said, sitting up straighter and looking at Michael directly.

"Well, I think you should see if you can speak to this woman. Let me know if I can help. I mean it."

Glory's instinct was to tell him she'd be fine, that this was her family and she could handle it. But Faith was his wife.

"Thanks," she said in the end. "I'll let you know."

39

Lará lived in a large house in Camberwell with a gate and gardens front and back. Glory found it odd that she would pay a premium to live a twenty-five-minute walk away from her own mother's house, but Lará said she liked the "familiar change of scenery." She lived with four other professionals, one couple who fancied themselves the parental figures of the house, another woman who had called Glory by Lará's name twice within the first hour of Glory crossing the threshold, and a quiet, bird-like man who seemed to flit around, balancing a laptop on his bony wrists.

"He's a programr, or something," Lará had explained as Glory drank her peppermint tea. "Really nerdy and nervous but very intelligent. If you need your computer or smartphone fixed, he's your guy."

Now they were on their way to Elephant and Castle, where Lará said Mama Wawo would be. That Celeste and Mama Wawo could live and work in such close proximity and never come across each other was the nature of London in a nutshell. So many people, so much congestion, but everyone operating within their own separate galaxy.

They weaved between teenagers dawdling on their way to Saturday school or returning home from football. Tall buses queued up like red elephants waiting to unload their cargo, and the smell of hot churros tempted Glory as they walked past one of the huts selling Latin food. They descended the outdoor staircase and made their way through the market, where Glory used to spend her money on Chinese slippers, multicolored leggings or whatever else was the latest trend, while being harassed by young boys in fake Lot 29 and Akademiks tracksuits.

There were still the same shipping container shops and tarpaulin-covered metal frames weighed down by clothing, but the ambience felt different. The vibrancy had left, or perhaps it was Glory's own youthful excitement that was missing. The truth was, the shopping center was caught between two worlds. Eventually this place along with all its memories would be flattened and reduced to broken concrete and twisted metal. Whatever would replace it would be nothing like what came before, and, of course, that was the point.

Lará led the way, passing the café, the WHSmith, the money transfer signs and discount shoe shop, until they reached a unit tucked away in a corner near the Greggs. The old signage was obscured by a white PVC banner, "Virtuous Woman Jewels and Accessorries," the extra "r" turning the final word to gibberish. The inside of the shop was taken up by half empty plastic wrapping and cardboard boxes, but a pair of hands were arranging mannequin necks weighed down with reimagined designer logos in bright gold.

"Good morning, Auntie Níkẹ," Lará called to the pair of hands, and a woman's face ducked around the door frame to see who was greeting her.

"Ọmọlará! Morning, my dear." Mama Wawo reached out for a hug. "How's your mum?"

"She's fine—I brought my friend as I said I would. Glory."

Mama Wawo's neck and wrists were weighed down with yellow gold. Pearlescent lilac eyeshadow stretched from her eyelashes to the hard black lines of her eyebrows. A gold tooth glittered in her mouth among straight white teeth.

"Good morning, Ma," Glory said, dipping into a quick curtsey.

"Good morning, dear," Mama Wawo said with a regal nod.

"We were hoping you might be able to help us," Lará began and a single penciled eyebrow arched upward on Mama Wawo's face.

"You know my mother," Glory said, picking up from Lará's introduction. "Well, you knew my mother, back when I was really small. She was looking for help with childcare and I believe you introduced her to a family—a white family—who looked after me and my sisters for a while."

Mama Wawo squinted, sizing up Glory and what she had just said.

"What's your mother's name?"

"Celeste Akíndélé."

"And you are?"

"Glory Akíndélé."

"I see," Mama Wawo said slowly, turning away to attend to a new task. "So what do you want my help with?"

Glory looked to Lará, who nodded in encouragement.

"Well, one of my sisters stayed with this family, after we left, and I haven't seen her since. The white couple were called Joan and Edward Marksham. I wondered if you knew how to find them so that I could find her."

Mama Wawo turned her head and looked at Lará. She stared at her for a long time until a smile broke across her face and she turned back to Glory slowly, her gold tooth flashing.

"I told her, you cannot question God. Sometimes you just have to wait," she said with a knowing smile.

278

"You told who? My mother?"

"No, I haven't seen your mother in years . . . but I know your family well. You have another sister, àbí? Grace?"

"Faith."

"Yes, Faith. Your parents are Yorùbá but named you all like the Igbo."

Mama Wawo laughed and shook her head like she was revisiting an old joke.

"I think my mum's mum was Igbo . . ." Glory started to say but Mama Wawo waved away the rest of the thought.

"Does your father know you are here?" she asked, suddenly serious.

Glory felt Lará's eyes on her.

"No, he passed actually," Glory said, swallowing the lump that never failed to appear when she had to relay this information to someone new.

"Oh," Mama Wawo said, shocked, but her voice softened. "I'm sorry, my dear. May God have mercy upon his precious soul."

Mama Wawo turned and walked to the small storeroom in the back of the shop. She was gone for a minute, but returned with a worn purple notebook bursting with folded pieces of paper slipped in between its pages. She perched a pair of glasses on the end of her nose, running a fat finger ringed with gold down each page until she found what she was looking for. She ripped off the bottom half of a page and handed it to Glory.

"What's this?"

"Your sister's phone number."

Glory looked up.

"B-but—what? How?"

Glory looked at the scrap of paper again, her lips mouthing each of the eleven digits written in front of her. She then glanced at Lará, who looked just as bewildered.

"The way that God works is mysterious," Mama Wawo said, looking upward as if she was consulting with angels sitting in the rafters. "Your sister came to me several months ago, she had been looking for your parents. I even knew who you were as soon as you came, but I had to be careful."

Mama Wawo's voice began to swim in and out as Glory stared past her into the bare interior of the shop. For so long Hope had felt like mist in the distance, but Mama Wawo speaking of her in the recent past made her seem terribly real.

Glory began imagining what she looked like, how tall she might have been, what clothes she wore when she came and what had even brought her to London? How did Hope come so close—a twenty-minute bus ride away—and Glory didn't know? Was there not meant to be some kind of twin intuition, some sixth sense that would let her know that Hope was looking for her? Or was it because she wasn't in the country at the time, so it didn't work? Or maybe she had switched that part of her brain off since all this time she had thought— she had been *told*, *deceived*, *lied to*—that her sister, the person who had shared a womb with her for nine months, was dead.

She interrupted Mama Wawo's monologue.

"She came here?"

"Yes! I already said that!"

The air around Glory felt thin, like it could not support the weight of her and she was about to crash right through it. Everything around her felt too light and bright and garish, the sounds of people and voices got too loud. Her knees buckled and she was down.

Glory felt the smooth, hard floor beneath her as she came to. Someone had folded her over into the recovery position and she could hear another voice asking if anybody had called an ambulance.

"No, please don't," she managed to croak. "I just need a minute."

She tried to push herself up into a seated position and felt hands lift her weight.

"Don't let her sit there, bring her into my shop."

The stern voice of Mama Wawo cut through the clamor and the same hands carried her into the cool storeroom at the back of the tiny little unit. Glory was lifted onto a stack of boxes, the cardboard sagging beneath her weight.

"Be careful, o! Don't crush my merchandise or I will have to charge you."

But when Glory looked into Mama Wawo's face, she wasn't angry.

"When did you last eat?" Mama Wawo tutted.

She went over to another stack of boxes, which sat next to a small, compact fridge with a microwave on top. Mama Wawo opened the fridge, fiddled around and the microwave made a few beeps before humming into action.

"Oya, Ọmọlará, go buy water!" Mama Wawo ordered. Lará was lingering in the entryway to the storeroom, looking worried, but on Mama Wawo's command she hurried away.

"Was it what I said about your dad? Did that upset you?" Mama Wawo asked Glory gently when Lará had left. There was hardly any light back here, the single swinging fixture was bulbless and bare, so Mama Wawo looked carefully into Glory's face with the light that came in from the front of the shop.

"I didn't hear that bit. I think I was in shock. What did you say about my father?"

The microwave pinged and Mama Wawo opened the door, taking out a paper bag and wrapping a couple of sheets of kitchen roll around it.

"Let it cool," she instructed as she handed it to Glory. Glory unwrapped the paper and peered into the bag at a steaming meat pie.

Mama Wawo folded her hands against her stomach and sighed, she no longer looked like she wanted to talk.

"What were you saying about my father?"

"When Hope first came to me, I got in touch with him. He was not interested."

She pushed out her lips and dusted off her palms with a few claps.

"What did he say?"

"He said that it was not the right time."

Glory's body started shuddering violently, and before she knew it she was crying. Hacking sobs rose from her chest and she gripped the paper bag in her hand so hard the heat from the meat pie began to burn her fingertips.

"Please, please," Mama Wawo said, bringing her hands up and letting them drop again, but Glory couldn't stop, her shoulders shook until they ached. She was heartbroken.

"Here." Mama Wawo handed a wad of kitchen roll to Glory and laid a hand on her shoulder, squeezing lightly. "There's no need to cry, dear. It is well."

"But why? Why did he . . ." Glory's question trailed off into a gasp.

"We cannot question the dead," Mama Wawo said with finality.

Glory wiped her face and felt frantic when she realized she didn't know what happened to the scrap of paper with the phone number.

"Wh-where's it gone?" she asked desperately, setting the meat pie on her lap and feeling through her pockets. "Her number! I don't know where I put it!"

"Here, here!" Mama Wawo pushed the scrap back at Glory. "Ọmọlará picked it up from where you dropped it. Please, calm down, ehn?"

Now it was Mama Wawo's turned to look worried, as though she regretted everything she had said so far.

This was lost to Glory, who stared at the jagged scrap of paper until she was seeing through it, the numbers reduced to a white blur.

"What we name our children is very important, you know that, ehn?" Mama Wawo said after a few moments of calm silence had passed. "When we name a child we are calling forth their destiny."

Glory stayed silent. She folded the scrap of paper and put it into the coin pocket of her jeans, sure that it would not get lost in this small compartment. Then she blew on the meat pie and took a wide bite. The filling was still hot and scalded the inside of her mouth, but she chewed and chewed until she could eventually swallow.

40

"You OK?" Lará asked Glory on the bus back to Camberwell.

Glory had not said anything since they had left Mama Wawo's shop, so Lará had been staring out of the window as the bus worked its way through the traffic on Walworth Road.

"I think I need to go home," Glory said.

Lará nodded.

"Are you going to tell your mum about the number?"

"Eventually. I don't know when though, she's not been—it's just been really hard recently."

"Yeah, of course, with your dad and that . . ."

Glory nodded, but she wanted to tell Lará the full story, about the stain on the living room carpet and why her mother ended up in Maudsley. She wanted to tell her about the midnight prayer session that had scared her so much she still dreamed about it.

"Just take your time, OK? You're allowed to do that."

Glory nodded but kept her face turned in the opposite direction. Tears were burning her eyes again.

They continued the journey in silence until they reached Camberwell Green.

"I'm gonna go home but if you need me, or you want to hang out or something, just drop me a text."

She stooped to hug Glory tight before getting off of the bus. Glory watched her friend watch the bus pull away from the pavement.

She didn't want to go home. She was in no mood to creep around the house with this development weighing on her. What she wanted was to see Julian. But when Glory got to Pharoah's, the shutters were down.

The barbershop was never closed during the day, and to be closed on a Saturday was unthinkable. Even on a slow morning with no clientele, there would still be at least two or three men in there, watching the TV or taking part in a spirited debate. When Glory called Julian's phone twice and neither call was answered, she began walking quickly toward his house.

At the entrance to his building, she rang the bell, holding down the buzzer for seconds at a time until finally he answered. He met her at the door in a creased vest and sagging tracksuit bottoms. He looked like he had just gotten out of bed while his face suggested that he hadn't slept in awhile.

"Are you OK?" Glory asked him as soon as the front door cracked open, but Julian just waved her inside.

Glory sat on the sofa. The TV was on but it only showed a sheet of artificial blue. Julian slumped down next to her and dropped his feet onto the low coffee table. He tipped his head back and raised his hands to cover his face.

"It's fucked," he said from behind his hands, the "d" at the end of the word taking on a hard final edge.

"What is?"

"They've got Telly. They've got him in some hospital in Woolwich handcuffed to a bed."

"What happened?"

Julian sighed as though someone was pressing the air out of him.

"Yesterday we had an argument about something and he just left my house, didn't tell me where he was going or nothing. Then I got a call from him late last night but I didn't answer it because I can't lie, I was still heated. Then he sent me a text saying that he needed to be picked up ASAP, but I ignored it because I'm not a cab service—no apology or nothing, just *come get man*. I went to bed and then next thing I know I'm getting calls from his sister, saying that Telly's in hospital with stab wounds to his head, neck and chest. Apparently he beat up some other guy with a metal pole and his boys came back and stabbed him. He might not even make it out of hospital alive, but they've charged him with aggravated assault. Bullshit."

Julian sucked his teeth.

Glory clutched at her own throat reflexively. She knew what Julian was thinking, she could see it written in the lines on his face.

"This isn't your fault."

Julian looked up at the ceiling, his fingers interlocked and hands resting on his head.

"Not completely."

"It's not at all, Julian!" Glory said, pulling at his arm and trying to get him to meet her eye.

Julian pulled free of her grip, his face still upturned.

"But if I'd just answered that call, he wouldn't be in hospital right now, would he?"

"You don't know if he tried to call you before or after he beat up that boy with a pole. He could have been calling you to come get him because he knew they were coming back, and then you would have been caught up in it too."

Julian shook his head stubbornly.

"Julian," Glory pleaded. "You can't save someone from the consequences of their own actions."

"I'm tired of all of this hood shit!"

Glory tried to make some reassuring noises, resting a hand on Julian's leg but at her touch he got up and started pacing in front of the TV.

"Do you know how many guys I know who are dead or locked up? It's so normal, but when you think about it, it's fucking insane. You watch it happen to everyone your age and you swear that you're going to be that person that us man never had, but then the cycle repeats itself. It's fucking mad, Glory. I'm tired of this shit."

"Julian . . ." Glory searched for something to say. "You did what you could for Telly—you even let him live with you! I know you don't want to hear this, but people have to make their own choices."

"But when you ain't got that many choices in the first place, what fucking choice have you got?"

"But you came from the same background as the people you're talking about, and you made it."

"Made it *where*?" Julian stopped pacing, holding his hands out and looking around the small living room. "I still live in the fucking hood! One false move and police are at my door or they're raiding my shop and then I'm just another black man in the back of a bully van."

"But my point is . . ." Glory frantically tried to think. "My point is you had a choice. You chose differently. You—"

"So what did your brother choose?" The question landed in Glory's chest, making the breath stop short in her throat.

She wanted to say that Victor was different, that it was all an unfortunate sequence of events, but she suspected that the same could be said for any of the young men that Julian had in mind. They probably all had sisters or mothers ready to argue the same thing on their behalf, and where such a blood relative didn't exist, there would most likely be someone like Julian, anger and regret forcing them to wear circles into a different living room floor. So she said something else.

"I'm sorry your friend is in the hospital."

Julian paced until he seemed to tire himself out. Then he sat back down beside Glory, his elbows resting on his knees, his head tucked into his chest and his knuckles rapping on the table.

Glory put an arm around his shoulders and rested her head against his. His hair was unoiled, unbrushed, and the sweet scent of his grooming products was replaced by the tang of his own earthy smell.

He turned to embrace her, burying his face into her shoulder and gripping her tightly.

"I wish there was something I could do," she said into his neck as they remained frozen together.

"Just do this," he said, his voice vibrating through her body. "I just need you to be here."

Glory lay back on the sofa and Julian lay half on top of her, his head resting on her chest. They stayed like that in silence, Glory stroking his head until eventually his breathing slowed and deepened as he drifted off to sleep.

41

Glory was woken by Julian peeling himself off her. His vest was damp where it had been pressed between their sleeping bodies and he pulled it over his head and walked to the bathroom.

"I'm starving," he said. "Let me have a shower, and then we can go and get something to eat."

"I need to tell you something," Glory said, drawing him back into the room. She patted the sofa next to her.

"Don't know how much more bad news I can take right now, to be honest."

"No, this is good—mostly."

Glory reached into her pocket and pulled out the scrap of paper, unfolding it and holding it out.

"I met Mama Wawo and she gave me this."

Julian took it from her carefully.

"That's her number," Glory said.

"Mama Wawo's number?"

"No. Hope's number. My sister is on the other end of that number!" Glory pointed at the paper until her finger started shaking.

Julian raised his eyebrows, his eyes wide.

"Swear down? Have you called it?"

"Not yet."

"Call her now then."

"I don't know what to say."

"There's only one thing to say: *Hi, my name's Glory, I'm your sister.*"

Julian pulled out his phone and typed in the numbers. He pressed the call button and gave the phone to Glory who looked petrified. When she refused to take the device, he pushed it up against her ear.

Glory's heart was beating in her throat as the phone rang and her brain spun through what she might say when Hope answered. To her relief, it rang through to voicemail.

"Oh, erm. Hi. My name's Glory. I got your number from a woman called Mama Wawo. I think I'm—I guess, I mean, yeah. I'm your twin? Sorry. Please call me back when you get this."

She ended the call quickly and threw the phone at Julian like it was burning her fingers. He was sniggering.

"You never gave your number. She's gonna call *me* back."

"Oh shit."

Glory redialed the number and left another halting message, this time reciting her number twice at the end of it. When the call finished her hands were shaking.

"Now you wait," Julian said simply.

Glory breathed in deeply through her nose, trying to steady the pattering rhythm of her heart. Underneath the fear was a small bead of excitement that she could feel growing. She leaped onto Julian and kissed him furiously.

"Oh my God, I can't believe this is happening!" she exclaimed when she finally pulled away from him.

She wanted to tell everyone, her mother, Victor and Faith. She couldn't wait to tell them that she had found Hope. Faith would be happy, she tried to convince herself, her hesitation was because—what was it that Michael had said?—she was trying to protect their mother. She was scared of disappointment. That was it! And Glory was positive that this discovery could cure her mother's broken heart. And if Daddy was still here . . . But on remembering her father, Glory's own heart sank.

"You cool?" Julian asked, watching her face drop from ecstasy to misery.

"Mama Wawo said . . ." Glory was about to start crying.

"Said what?"

Glory exhaled and collapsed into a slouch.

"Do you remember when Princess Diana died? My parents had the worst argument ever about the flag. You know how Buckingham Palace didn't lower the flag like they're supposed to do when one of them dies?"

Julian looked at her, confused, waiting for this tangent to make sense.

"My mum was so upset about it. She was crying."

"About the flag or about Diana?"

"About everything, I guess. But my dad was just angry. He was like *What did you expect? She embarrassed herself and the whole Royal Family! She's a disgrace!* I never understood how they both could feel so strongly about people they'd never met, but I was such a daddy's girl I just agreed with him by default, even when I didn't understand."

Glory shook her head and laughed sadly, brushing fluff from the legs of her jeans.

"He actually sat me down and gave me this lecture about collective responsibility, upholding family honor and how disgrace cannot go unchecked, or something. I was like, what? Seven? Eight? I just nodded along like I knew what he was talking about. Well . . . my mum always says what's done in the dark will always come to light. I think that's from the Bible."

Julian nodded slowly, digesting this long-winded anecdote.

"My mum loved Princess Diana," Julian said after a moment or two.

"They all do." Glory sighed.

"I spent years telling people that my dad was some big shot in Nigeria and that's why he wasn't here. When I finally met him I was really disappointed. He was showing me pictures of his other children and the only thing I could think was, *I should have told everyone he was dead.*"

"How old were you?"

"Fifteen or sixteen," Julian said wistfully. "Seeing your parents for who they really are instead of who we want them to be is one of the shit parts of growing up. But that don't mean everything good we thought about them don't exist either."

"Yeah, well the reason why Hope ended up with that white family is because one day my dad lost his temper and beat her so badly that my mum was scared."

"Shit."

"And Hope tried to get in contact with my parents not long ago, but Daddy basically told Mama Wawo he wasn't interested."

Glory pressed a finger and a thumb into her tear ducts.

"I didn't recognize the man who would do that, not at first. But then I piece together all the different parts of him that I know, some parts I even used to think were good and then I can see it. I can see what Faith is talking about when she says he wasn't as good as I thought he was."

Julian put his hand on Glory's knee.

"But there were still parts of him that were good though, right?"

"What's good about your dad?" she asked him.

"I don't know, I don't know him like you knew yours."

"Sorry."

"For what? It's not your fault." He took one of Glory's hands. "Now I really need to get in the shower, babe, I feel like a tramp."

Julian kissed her knuckles and left the room.

42

When Glory brought home the dress that Faith's tailor had made for her, a fitted floor-length gown with an off-shoulder neckline, her mother changed her mind about attending Tabitha's wedding. Celeste fingered the red fabric, checked the exquisitely laid seams and asked if Faith had bought any aṣọ ẹbí for her. Celeste's ìró and bùbá were whipped up in a couple of days and the three Akíndélé women were good to go.

Faith was so excited by the prospect of their mother socializing that she arranged for a makeup artist to come to the house to sculpt their faces and tie their gèlè beforehand. When the woman had finished working her brushes over Celeste's face, Celeste posed patiently as the artist took photographs and video for her portfolio. She fluttered her eyelashes, even giving the camera a coy smile. She looked beautiful.

Then it was Glory's turn. She vetoed the glittery eyeshadow and asked for a more muted shade of blusher but accepted the bright red lipstick and thick false lashes that made her eyelids heavy. When the woman had finished tying the stiff aṣọ òkè on Glory's head, Celeste asked Glory to take full-length pictures of her outfit on her phone. She turned and twisted under the lights, the sequins shimmering and her eyes bright as she stood next to the large portrait of Glory's father, his face hovering over her shoulder.

When Celeste had finished posing by herself, she turned the camera on Glory. She directed her daughter this way and that, pushing and prodding her with impatient fingers. After a change of earrings, a change of background, and a series of increasingly uncomfortable poses, Celeste had the desired shot of her daughter.

"Don't complain, this one will find you a husband," she said, grinning into the screen when she caught Glory rolling her eyes.

In the car on the way to east London, Celeste pushed in a tape of old Nigerian praise songs and sang for most of the journey. Glory sent Julian one of the pictures her mother had taken.

"*Nice*," he replied with a smiling emoji, but left her follow-up messages unanswered.

They arrived late, which was intentional. Traditional engagement celebrations, or traditional weddings as they were often viewed, were long and unwieldy affairs and despite their lateness, proceedings hadn't even started. They found seats with a good view of the center of the room and got comfortable. On each table was a bowl of chin chin, and Glory crunched her way through two handfuls until her mother hissed at her with a sharp look.

A man in a Liverpool football shirt was walking around with a camera slung from one shoulder, and a large stack of bound dollar bills balanced on the other.

"Buy me some dollars," Glory's mum said, pushing money into her hand and pointing her in the direction of the multi-tasking entrepreneur. Glory exchanged some British notes for a small wad of dollar bills and when she turned to go back to the table, she saw her mother in conversation with two other older women. Not wanting to be besieged by prying questions, she snuck off in the opposite direction.

Glory passed elders she vaguely recognized, smiling and ducking into quick curtsies in return for satisfied nods. She walked by a group of men whose conversation slowed as she approached. One of them greeted her, each of them watching her with lowered eyes. She smiled politely and kept on walking, feeling their eyes follow her path.

The banqueting hall stretched on and on. Tables laid with red satin, gold charger plates and elaborate centerpieces fought each other for attention. A laptop and CDJs stood unattended at one end, the speakers pumping out a playlist of Afropop hits.

Out in the corridor, people were dashing by with coolers of rice and tightly wrapped hampers of cooking equipment that would form part of the gifts the groom-to-be would present to his fiancée during the ceremony.

Glory walked around until she found the toilet, a queue of women in red spilling out of the door and commandeering the accessible toilet as well. A chair was set up directly outside, with women taking turns to have their gèlè tied or retied and makeup touched up by a woman in black.

"Good evening, ma!" Glory greeted one of the women who she was almost sure she knew.

"Ah, good evening, darling! How's your mum doing?"

"She's fine, ma. She's here." Glory smiled, acknowledging the other women waiting.

"We have missed her. How are your children?" The auntie took a seat and offered up her face to the woman in black.

"Oh, I don't have any children. You must be thinking of my sister, Faith."

The woman pulled her chin from the makeup artist's hand, studying Glory's face from where she sat.

"You and your sisters look so similar," she said and turned back. "I'll come and see your mum when I've finished."

Sisters? Glory thought, her stomach lurching.

"OK, ma," she squeaked and she turned and left the queue, returning to the banqueting hall and her mother.

"I see you've been parading around the room," Celeste said as Glory sat next to her. "We will be planning your own traditional in a year's time in Jesus' name!"

"Mummy, please."

"Ah! Say amen now! If you keep complaining I will send your picture to my cousin to go and find you a husband from our village!" Celeste teased, giggling at Glory's horrified protest.

The host for the evening took to the mic, warming up her vocals with a few "one, two"s and greeting the hall in Yorùbá.

"Or I could tell the MC to advertise you during the break. You can do your little parade walk up there like it's market day." Celeste pushed her lips into a mocking pout and shook her shoulders.

"Oh, Mum!" Glory hid her face with a hand as Celeste cackled and clapped her on the back.

"What's the joke?"

Faith arrived at the table, a twin on the end of each arm with Michael in tow carrying her bag.

"Tell your mum to behave," Glory said with her nose in the air. "She's trying to auction me off."

"Mummy, you don't need to worry about Glory, one day she'll surprise us all."

Faith winked at her sister.

When the celebrations finally began, Glory was surprised by how much she enjoyed herself. She even joined her mother to spray the bride-to-be with crisp dollar bills, and the ease with which she wound her waist and dipped her hips to the guttural beat of the talking drum drew inquisitive glances from some of the groom-to-be's friends. Given the occasion, romance was in the air, but it wasn't just romance it was desire: a deep desire for sensuous connection with another human being, the kind that would turn out a community to celebrate the promise of a lifelong bond.

Glory sent another message to Julian, this time a looping gif of her blowing a kiss into the camera lens. He responded with a string of lovestruck emojis and the reply:

"*Where are you? You're gonna make me come get you right now!!*"

Glory was happy with that.

As the night rolled on, heels were kicked off and replaced with flip-flops and sandals, headties loosened and slipped back on foreheads. The groom's agbádá was abandoned when the tribal drumbeat of funky house pounded through the hall and his friends held him aloft like a conquering hero. When "Sweet Mother" came on, the bride and groom each danced with their mothers, swapping partners midway to toast their future in-law, and when the DJ commanded all other mothers to the dancefloor, Faith and Glory followed Celeste's wiggling backside, fanning her and singing the lyrics shrilly: "*Sweet mother, I no go forget you, for dey suffer wey, you suffer for me . . .*"

When the song ended, Faith disappeared to the toilet while Glory and Celeste returned to their table, mopping their brows and gulping cool water. Everything so far had been perfect. Celeste was glowing, Faith was in a good mood and Glory felt, for once, in her element.

"Mummy? I went to see Mama Wawo," Glory blurted out.

Celeste did not react, but continued fanning herself with a lace-edged fan. But as Glory opened her mouth to repeat what she had just said, her mother responded.

"What did she say?" Celeste asked, keeping her eyes fixed ahead.

"She gave me her telephone number. Hope's. She gave me Hope's telephone number."

"She did?"

"Yes."

Celeste breathed in through her nose, closing her eyes slowly and letting her breath hiss through pursed lips.

"I called, but no answer. I left a message. Well, two messages."

Glory could swear she could hear her pulse echoing in her head, and she gripped the edge of the table with sweaty hands.

Celeste turned to Glory, unwept tears shining in her eyes and a strange smile on her face. She reached over and rested a hand on Glory's fingers, which were clawing at the tablecloth.

"It is well, my dear. It is well."

The warmth and weight of her mother's hand felt comforting.

"Sometimes I think about how things could have gone differently." Celeste was talking in a low voice, almost murmuring to herself. "If we had sold the house and moved to Kent when we were going to, then Victor would have had other friends and he wouldn't have been with those boys."

Glory remembered driving with her parents out to places like Chatham and Gillingham to look at houses with full-sized gardens and things called reception rooms. Glory had been adamant that she wasn't prepared to move outside of the M25, but it wasn't her refusal to get out of the car that convinced her parents not to move. Her father was sure that the price of their own house would increase more and the plan was to remortgage to buy the new house, so they could keep the old house and rent it out. The plan never materialized for reasons that a teenage Glory was grateful for, but didn't care enough to investigate. Maybe this was why a faint pang of guilt was working its way across Glory's chest now.

"We never had a chance to rest in this country," Celeste continued, emotion thickening her voice. "From when we got here it was work, work, work, work. The pressure, the stress . . ."

Her mother chuckled, although it sounded like she was holding back tears.

"If we had moved to Kent . . . maybe we could have rested."

"You did the best you could, Mummy, we all know that," Glory said desperately.

Celeste gripped Glory's fingers, her eyes still watery as she smiled at her daughter and shook her head.

"So many regrets. If God spares your life to live as long as I have you will have your own collection. But, you—my dear Glory. The detective."

She laughed and a single tear shook loose and made its way down to her chin. Glory wiped it away.

"Anything you want, you always manage to find it. Ẹní bá ń jẹ òbúkọ tó gbójú, yóó jẹ àgùtàn tó yọwo. Do you know what that means?"

Glory frowned and shook her head and Celeste searched her mind for a loose translation.

"It means when you have already done extraordinary things, of course you would do something like this. That is just who you are."

Celeste removed her hand from Glory's and smoothed her skirt.

"Anyways, I cannot question God. It is well."

Glory cleared her throat and managed to croak a weak "Amen."

43

"It is well."

Something in her mother's voice made Glory believe that it would be.

On the way home, Celeste was in even brighter spirits, singing loudly along to her tapes and Glory even joined in. When her mother stopped at a petrol station, Glory began looking through the videos and pictures she had taken on her phone. She selected one to post and uploaded it, waiting for the likes and heart-eyed emojis to roll in.

When they got home, she reluctantly took off her makeup and undressed. Her legs and feet were gently throbbing but as she lay in bed, her heart was full and at rest. She checked her notifications one last time before she slept.

Julian had gone quiet again on WhatsApp, and he hadn't responded to the Instagram post that was steadily accruing compliments. In a fit of childishness Glory sent him what would be her final message for the night:

"I see you're too busy for me these days. I give up."

The status bar of the message window informed her that Julian was typing a reply, but before he had a chance to say his piece, she switched her phone to Airplane Mode and slipped it under her pillow.

She wasn't sure what time it was when she was woken by the front doorbell. Startled out of her sleep, she reached for her phone, checked the time and then panicked, praying that somehow the new sleeping pills her mother had been prescribed would keep her from waking up.

"Who's there?!" Celeste cried from her room.

Glory stumbled from her bed and out onto the landing.

"I don't know, Mummy. Maybe they're ringing the wrong doorbell," Glory called back, her voice hoarse.

They waited in silence, and just when Glory was ready to go back to her bed, the doorbell rang again. She swore under her breath.

"Don't answer it!" her mother commanded from her room, fear creeping into her voice.

Glory ignored her and crept down the stairs, picking up an umbrella along the way to use as a weapon should she need it.

"Who's there?" she called out when she reached the door.

"Glory?" the muffled voice called back.

"Who is it?" Celeste's voice echoed from the top of the stairs.

"I don't know, Mum!" Glory replied impatiently, before turning back to the door. "Who's there?! Say a name or I'm going to call the police!" she shouted at the door, her mother's fear coloring her own voice.

"It's Julian!"

Glory dropped the umbrella, unlatched the door and pulled it back slightly. Sure enough, Julian stood before her. He was backlit by the headlamps of a car that was parked directly in front of Glory's door, his face thrown into shadow.

"Julian? Are you crazy? You woke up my mum!"

"Who is it?!" Celeste called desperately from the first floor.

"It's OK, Mum. I know them, it's my—my friend."

"What friend?!" the fear in Celeste's voice was replaced by anger. "What time is this that they are waking up the whole street ringing my bell?!"

"Mummy, please! I'm an adult! Let me handle this!" Glory snapped back at her mother, who tutted and retreated to her bedroom mumbling about her rude daughter and her daughter's rude friends.

Julian had stood on the doorstep during this exchange, his head hung slightly as he waited for Glory's mother to leave.

"What the *fuck*, Julian?" Glory said, bristling.

"That's what happens when you think you can send messages anyhow and then turn off your phone."

"My battery died," Glory lied. "But you thought it was a smart idea to come and ring my doorbell in the middle of the night and wake up my mum?"

"And I'm your *friend* now?" Julian said with a mean smile that Glory could just about make out in the dark.

"You really want me to tell my mum that my boyfriend came knocking down her door at two o'clock in the morning?" Glory said in a sharp whisper. "Not the best first impression, *trust* me!"

Julian sighed and shifted his weight from one leg to the other.

"Did you come all this way to argue? I'm sure you've got more important things to be doing."

Glory rested one hand on the door and the other hand on her hip. She looked past him to the parked car. She could make out someone in the passenger seat. A hooded head against the glass, a slack jaw beneath the shadow suggested the passenger was asleep.

"Don't talk to me like I'm some dickhead, Glory."

"I'm really not gonna argue outside my mum's house like we're on *Eastenders*, I need to sleep! I'm going to see Victor in the morning."

Glory took a step back, ready to push the door shut in Julian's face, but Julian's arm snapped out and held the door open.

"You know you've got a big attitude problem?" He was beginning to lose his cool. "You start arguments that you don't wanna finish then think you can act like nothing's happened afterwards."

Julian's assessment of her caught her off guard, and all the warmth she had felt earlier in the evening slipped out into the black night.

"I didn't start any argument tonight," Glory said, keeping her hand on the door even though she could feel Julian's weight pressing against it.

"So why did you send that bullshit manipulative message and turn off your phone if you didn't want something to fight about?"

"If you keep shouting, my mum's gonna come down here and fight us both."

Julian stepped away from the door and went down the steps, beckoning Glory to follow him. He leaned up against the car bonnet and Glory stood in front of him, turning back to look up at her mother's bedroom window. The light was still off and the curtains were closed, but Glory was sure her mother was sitting up in bed waiting for her to return.

"So, you have my attention—is that what you wanted?" Julian had calmed down in the distance from Glory's front door to the car and was trying to sound rational.

"I was just letting you know how I feel," Glory said, wrapping her arms around her body, aware that she was cold and not properly dressed. Julian ignored her discomfort and continued. He took his phone out and reread her last message.

"*I see you're too busy for me.* That's not telling me how you feel, that's trying to provoke a reaction."

Glory was struck by the absurdity of the situation: they were standing outside her mother's house, her in her pyjamas, while he was attempting to cross-examine her.

"Have you been drinking?" she asked, unable to stop the amusement from coloring her voice.

Julian exhaled harshly and turned his head from her.

"You know what? You're fucking impossible to talk to sometimes. Now it's my turn to give up."

Julian pushed off from the bonnet, walked to the driver-side door and opened it.

Glory stood, stunned by his anger. She pulled her arms tighter around her body, her lips forming the words before she had fully acknowledged what she was about to say.

"Fuck you."

Julian had begun to lower himself into the driver's seat but now sprung back up, his face contorted in outrage.

"Fuck me, yeah?"

Glory turned and began to walk back toward her house, as Julian repeated the epithet.

"Fuck me, yeah? Is that what you're sayin', yeah?"

She spun back around and spat out her response as severely as she could without raising her voice.

"You said you give up on me, well I'm saying fuck you!"

She entered her house and as she pushed the door shut behind her, Julian's final retort slipped in with the last gust of night air. She tiptoed to look through the frosted glass that was set in the top of the doorframe. The car engine started and the tires screeched into a violent three-point turn, and then the distorted red beam of the rear lights disappeared into the dark.

Glory waited until her temper cooled off and her heartbeat slowed. She then tried to climb the stairs as quietly as she could, avoiding the floorboards she knew to creak until she was almost back in her room.

"It's very inappropriate," Celeste called from her room. "A man coming to drag a young woman from her bed in her mother's house? It's very inappropriate and I don't like it."

"I know," Glory sighed. "Sorry, Mummy. I didn't tell him to come."

"If he comes again to my house—"

"You won't see him again!" Glory shouted back.

Celeste harrumphed and turned over in her bed, the mattress creaks ringing through the darkness. When her mother had settled, Glory fell into a restless sleep.

44

Glory had been going to the prison long enough to recognize that different days had different atmospheres, depending on the composition of visitors.

Weekends were the liveliest. This was when families with more than one relative in prison would double or triple up, expanding a single visit quota from three adults to six or nine, plus any children. The group would often occupy a corner of the visiting hall, food and drink overflowing from tables and children running between them.

But weekends were also fraught with visits from those estranged from the prisoner in question: disappointed mothers who pressed tissue to drawn faces; shy children brought along by a resentful ex-partner.

Glory had chosen to visit on a Sunday morning because it would be the quietest. She was with a handful of others in the windowless waiting room. This was usually the room where the patience of all wore thin, the room where the clock seemed to tick the quickest, each passing minute eating into the hour assigned. Here, people would get agitated, shouting "Come on!" at the locked door while the frustrated mumbles of others turned into a low drone.

When they were finally let into the hall, the wait continued. The air buzzed with quiet desperation as cups of tea and coffee cooled on tables, and heads turned expectantly toward the door behind the empty command station. A woman walked up to the officer who had escorted the group in and asked what was happening.

"Will we still get an hour?"

The hall was so quiet, Glory could hear their conversation echoing across the space.

"Let me see what's going on."

The officer was gone for a while. Eventually two others came out, then one by one the prisoners began to trickle in. Relief flowed from table to table as the occupants stood to receive the man they were waiting for.

Victor came out toward the end. He pressed his finger on the scanner mounted to the side of the command station and handed over his white slip. Glory rose to greet him, searching his face before he reached the table. They hugged briefly.

"What happened?" she asked as they took their seats.

"Incident on another wing," he said gruffly. "I think someone was having a bad reaction to some spice or something."

"Are they OK?"

Victor shrugged, completely uninterested.

"So it's just you today then?"

"Yeah, we all went to a traditional last night, Tabitha's, do you remember her?"

Victor shook his head.

"Mum and Faith are still recovering and, anyway, I wanted to see you by myself."

Victor nodded.

"How's work and that?" he asked.

"Work's work. They pay me on time, that's what matters. How are you doing though?"

"I'm alive, innit."

Victor looked down, his restless fingers shredding the napkin in front of him. Glory watched his fingers move and then she noticed his knuckles. They were grazed and scabbed over.

"Have you been fighting again?" she asked him.

"What? No," he said sullenly.

"What happened to your knuckles?"

Victor started to pull his hands off the table, but Glory reached out and grabbed one of them in a tight grip. The scabs were fresh, the dark crust of skin only partially covering bloody pink flesh underneath.

Victor kissed his teeth and yanked his hand out of her grip.

"It's minor."

"What happened? Did you fall?"

"Fall? I'm not a kid," Victor said with that new bitter laugh that came too easily to him.

"So?" Glory pressed.

"I was stressed, innit . . ." he said, examining his knuckles for himself and leaving Glory to figure out the rest.

Glory felt sick, then she remembered the fine web of scars she'd noticed across his hands and wrist the first time she had visited him and felt sicker still.

"You, like, punched a wall or something?"

Victor grunted.

"Did you do the, erm, marks on your wrists and your hands too?"

Victor looked at her for a moment, not reacting, but then turned his palms to the sky, stretching his arms out so that his wrists revealed themselves from the long sleeves of his top.

"They've almost gone," he said casually, finally looking at Glory with an expression that she read as defiance. Glory drummed her fingers against the table.

"Chill out," Victor eventually said with a dark smile. "I'm not trying to kill myself or anything. It just helps with the stress. Better than getting into a fight and getting an IEP."

"Do you cut anywhere else?" Glory asked him and she watched his hands instinctively travel to his upper arms, almost protectively.

"Shit, Victor!" she exclaimed, trying not to scold him but needing to direct her anger somewhere. "Why don't you speak to that counselor you mentioned?"

"Because I'm not tapped!" Victor spat back. "I'm not mad in the head like some man you see in here! I'm just stressed!"

"Stress can kill, Vic," Glory said, her voice softer than before. She thought of what her mother had told her the night before about stress and pressure, then she thought of her father waking up one morning only to drop dead.

"You're funny, Glory," Victor said, trying to deflect. "There's nothing wrong with me, it's just stress! If I weren't in here, I'd be fine, you know this."

"But you are here, that's the problem!" she said, frustration pushing its way back into her voice. "I was reading this thing about PTSD in young men who grow up in ends, you know with witnessing so much violence and that—"

"Why were you reading that?"

"Just something happened to a friend of a friend, but my friend's been acting off since then. But anyway, I was thinking about you and like, I know you didn't do anything, but everything that you've been through, from the party until now—"

"Who?"

"What do you mean who? You!" Glory snapped.

"No, who's your friend?"

"Oh, I dunno if you remember him—Julian? Old, old family friend. He owns Pharaoh's Barbershop on Southampton Way."

"You mean your man?"

"Who told you he's my man?"

"Why else would he be trying to get me to talk to you if he wasn't your man?"

"What are you on about?"

"He didn't tell you?" Victor laughed.

"No! What did he do?"

"When I was still airing your letters and that, he must have got in touch through Délé and his sister, innit. Basically trying to convince me to stop ignoring you."

"Did it work?"

"You're sitting here aren't you?"

Guilt made Glory pause for a second.

"Well, he was my man," she said with uncertainty. "But we got into it last night, so right now? Who knows."

Glory gathered the shredded tissue into a pile, squeezing it tight into a ball.

"Got into it how?"

"I don't even know! It started over something stupid and then it ended with me saying *fuck you.*"

"Damn."

"Yeah."

"He was proper riding for you when I spoke with him."

"Yeah, well . . ."

Victor picked up a new napkin and began shredding it.

"It was probably your fault, still," he said.

Glory flicked the paper ball in her brother's direction.

"How the hell do you know it's my fault? You don't even know what's happened! Why can't you be on *my* side for once? First Michael, now you're backing it for Julian—you don't even know him!"

"I know *you*, Glory. You put up all these fronts and shit. No guy wants to be in a relationship with another guy."

"Why is it the girl who has to be emotional? Why don't you lot know how to talk about your emotions instead of getting offended over something small because you're bottling up the stuff that's really bothering you?" Or cutting your body into shreds, she wanted to add, but of course she didn't.

"Well, all I'm saying is if you want to stay with him, apologize for telling him to fuck off, innit."

"I didn't tell him to fuck off, I said *fuck you*."

"Even worse."

Glory felt blood rush to her face.

"Anyway, the only reason I even started talking about this, is because I'm worried about you. Even if you don't want to talk to someone in here, talk to *me*. I know we're not good at talking about stuff as a family, but we have to do better going forward. Please, Vic?"

"You ain't exactly an open communicator."

"I know and that's what I'm trying to change—ask me anything, I'm an open book!"

Victor looked amused, then thoughtful.

"OK. How could you be out in LA just chilling for all that time, when we were going through so much shit here? Didn't you think about us at all?" Victor delivered his question dispassionately, but he might as well have shouted in Glory's face.

"Oh, Vic . . ." she began, her voice weak. "I thought about you all the time, it wasn't that I wasn't thinking about you guys, it's just . . ."

She stopped, ignoring the excuses that flooded her mind instinctively.

"I made a selfish decision—it was dumb and I should have come straight away, but I made that decision and it became easier to go along with it, telling myself that everything would work out instead of seeing that it was a wrong decision to make and doing what I should have done immediately. As soon as I knew your case was going to trial, I should have come home. I wanted to stay because I didn't want to be wrong and it was easier to believe that I wasn't wrong if I just stuck with the stupid decision I'd made in the first place. Does that make sense?"

Victor had been watching Glory carefully, and he watched her for a few seconds more, letting her sit in her discomfort.

"No," he eventually said. "It doesn't make sense, but I understand what you meant."

Glory hadn't realized that she had stopped breathing until she exhaled in relief.

"Now that I'm here, I can't imagine leaving again. Even if things got worse after I turned up! Anything else you want to ask me?"

Victor shook his head.

"I'm sure I'll think of something though. So what's going on? What's new?"

Glory jumped up suddenly.

"That's even why I came to see you!" she said excitedly, remembering what her mission had been before Victor's knuckles distracted her. "I found Hope!"

"You're lying." Victor smirked.

"No! And she had been looking for us too! Well, I don't know if she knows about *us*, but she'd been looking for Mummy and Daddy. I've got her number, so I called and left a message."

"That's good."

Victor held out his hand for Glory to shake and Glory obliged the clumsy little gesture.

"I even told Mummy last night and she was so calm about it. I thought she'd be angry or something but she wasn't. But, you know when I tell Faith, she's going to freak out."

"She really will."

"So what do I do?"

"Try and see it from her point of view."

"I'm not gonna stop now! I've come too far," Glory said quickly.

"No one's telling you to do what she says, just understand where she's coming from, then you'll know how to respond when she reacts."

"When did you turn wise, baby brother?" Glory asked, reaching out to tug at his cheeks. Victor ducked and dodged her fingers, pushing her hands onto the table and looking around.

"I think a lot. All you've got to do in here is think, or smoke, or eat, or work out, or fight over bullshit prison politics. The food's shit, I'm not really trying to fight anyone, and I trade all the tobacco on my canteen for mackerel."

Glory nodded, but she had nothing to add to that. She watched Victor roll up the ripped strips of paper into more balls and line them up in a row, neatly spaced apart.

"You were right about something else too," she said.

"About what?"

"Family's all we've got."

He looked up from the table directly at Glory.

"It is though."

"I know, but I get it now."

Victor smiled, only slightly, then looked back down, trying to hide the satisfied look settling on his face.

Before Glory knew it, an officer was walking around the hall telling everyone to finish up. She checked the clock and pulled a face, sure the hour couldn't be over already, but after she squeezed her brother tight, she almost floated out of the hall.

At the visitors' center she opened up her locker and collected her bag, turning her phone on as she walked toward the bus stop. An alert pinged through: one new voicemail. The stumbling voice in the message had a Midlands lilt to it.

"Hello, I'm looking for Glory? I'm trying to get in touch with Glory—I mean, hi. I'm just returning your call. You left a message a while back, so I'm just returning your call. It's—oh, God! This is so bloody weird . . ." The voice took a deep breath, air escaping directly into the mouthpiece, "Hi, it's Hope. Please call me back."

Glory nearly dropped the phone. She wanted to scream and stamp her feet and run back to the visit hall and shake Victor so hard he would be forced to break into the kind of smile that would show all his teeth. But instead she dropped the phone into her bag while her heart skipped a few beats, and focused on walking in a straight line toward the bus stop.

45

The first conversation between Glory and Hope was as halting and awkward as Hope's voicemail, but at least they were as nervous as each other.

"I got your messages as soon as you left them. But after so long it just took me by surprise. I needed a bit of time before I could call you back. I'm sorry."

Glory was pacing up and down in front of her bed.

"No, it's fine, it's fine," Glory said, her voice wavering. "In fact, there's something I need to tell you."

She stopped, wondering if she was really going to start this relationship by telling Hope how their father had betrayed them both.

"Go on," Hope said with apprehension when Glory let her sentence hang for too long.

"Our dad died."

"Oh." Hope's breath caught in her throat. "Recently?"

"Beginning of the year," Glory said.

Hope drew in a breath.

"I just missed him. Oh God. I'm crying. Am I allowed to cry about this?"

Glory was glad that no one was around to see the tears that were quietly streaming from her own eyes.

"This whole thing is just . . . it's weird, isn't it?" Glory said after she had a second to collect herself, rubbing away the tears. "I don't really know where to begin. Maybe we should meet in person, just us."

"Yeah, maybe . . ."

"Well, I mean, we don't have to do it right away. After all these years, we can wait a little bit longer!"

Glory's joke was lost in how pathetic she sounded and she regretted her words instantly.

"Right," Hope said.

"Sorry, that wasn't funny."

"It's OK," Hope said. "It's . . . fine. Fine. But I need to go—sorry, not the best moment to end the call, but I've really gotta go. I'll call you back later—or maybe tomorrow!"

Glory garbled a goodbye and tried to remain optimistic, but as twenty-four hours turned into thirty-six she put her ego to the side and sent a message that she had drafted and redrafted a number of times before pasting it into WhatsApp and hitting send:

"Hi! Just wanted to say quickly that I meant it about it being fine to wait. I feel like it came out funny, but I was being sincere. Don't feel any pressure. Hope you're having a good week. Glory x"

She regretted the exclamation mark but stood by everything else.

Hope replied a few hours later with a date, a time and a place, so meticulous and abrupt in her communication that Glory felt anxiety run through her. She tried to prepare herself for another potentially tense sibling reunion.

When the afternoon of their meeting came, Glory was at

the restaurant extra early. Between the leather banquettes and the polished marble bar that formed the centerpiece of the room, she wasn't sure where to sit. Sitting at the bar, elbow to elbow, could feel too intimate but sitting opposite each other in a booth would require much more eye contact. Maybe meeting at a restaurant had been the wrong idea from the start, perhaps they should have met in a park or another crowded place where there was enough distraction to fill any silences. In the end Glory sat at the bar with a clear view of the door, crossing and recrossing her legs.

It was like waiting to meet a blind date that she would have to marry later on in the day. Her stomach twisted into knots imagining the worst—what if they didn't like each other? She checked the time once more and realized that Hope was late, only by seven minutes or so, but the feeling in her stomach morphed from nerves to a tight fist of dread. She wanted to call someone for reassurance, but she hadn't told anyone that they were meeting, so instead the specter of disappointment hung so heavily around her, she felt that she would have a panic attack if she was forced to wait any longer.

But then she saw the door to the restaurant swing open, and Hope walked in. Of course she knew it was Hope as soon as she saw the shadowed profile through the glass, because although they were not identical, it was like watching a version of herself enter from a different universe. Hope was around the same height, the same build, the same mushroom-tipped nose and smooth brown skin, but her cheekbones sat a bit higher in her face, making it a little longer, and her long flowing black hair made her resemble Faith.

The open and expressive face that Glory had seen in the old photograph was closed in on itself, like a nervous twitch, two white teeth sinking into her bottom lip as she looked around the room for Glory. When their eyes met there was the spark of recognition, almost like a tangible pull, and she said something to the tall blond man who was with her. When he looked over to Glory there was a moment of shock, then the uneasy laugh of disbelief.

Glory hopped down off the stool as they walked up to the bar.

"Hi!" Hope said, and now her face was open again, luminous, her voice cutting through the din of the restaurant. "Can I hug you?"

Glory nodded and all the angst she had felt evaporated in Hope's quick, self-conscious embrace.

"This is my partner, Mark," she said as an afterthought, and Mark held out a firm hand which Glory shook.

"You can go now, I'll call when we're done."

"Oh, right—yes, of course!" Mark replied, and his cheeks flushed.

Hope looked at Glory and smiled again. Glory felt the fist in her stomach unclench.

"Where shall we sit?" Hope took off her camel-colored trench coat and folded it across her arm, straightening out a chiffon top layered over a plain white vest. Her style was preppy, Glory noted, with close-cut skinny jeans and bright white Converse trainers. Glory had opted for a dark long line T-shirt with a cropped leather jacket and faux leather leggings and boots. All she needed was a nose ring and a few tattoos and she would look like Hope's evil twin, the little devil perched on Hope's shoulder.

Glory pointed to one of the booths against the wall. She wasn't sure how the rest of the meeting was going to go but if for some reason things got emotional, she didn't want to be an easy spectacle for diners to ogle over lunch.

This was the stuff of dreams though—or the makings of a storyline from one of her favorite childhood films or TV shows, the sitcom *Sister Sister* and Lindsay Lohan's breakout turn in *The Parent Trap* to be precise. It seemed incredibly obvious now but she could see why they were such firm favorites to her young self. Long-lost twin sisters, separated at birth by circumstances beyond their control who reunited for fun, frolics and mischief making. Maybe some primal part of her knew more than a child's mind could fully appreciate, or maybe she had manifested this situation, as she heard people in LA say time and again. Either way, it was happening, but there was no laugh track, no bumbling mishaps that were sure to end amicably. Only desperate anticipation.

They started by ordering drinks.

"I'll take a fresh mint tea," Hope told their waitress.

"Same," Glory said, and Hope's eyes met hers and they both giggled.

"I've been role-playing how our conversation would go all morning, but now I've completely forgotten my script!"

Hope laughed nervously, her voice was soft and melodic, free from the blunt force of a London twang. She straightened out the cutlery laid to her right, and realigned her empty glass.

"I should be feeling a lot happier than I am, but when you told me that, um . . . he had just passed . . . I just wish I had got to meet him, that's all."

A prickling sensation began to rise through Glory's body. She couldn't tell if it was excitement or she was about to throw up.

Their waitress returned and set down their drinks on the table. She then took out her notepad and waited patiently for their food orders.

"Can you give us a minute?" Glory asked her.

"I don't even think I can eat anything." Hope laid a hand

on her stomach. "This was a terrible idea. I shouldn't have picked a restaurant."

Glory really wanted Hope to like her and the rest of her biological family. Things were far from black and white, but as long as Glory held back, it felt like everything she would say to Hope would be a lie. If Hope was going to reject them, she would rather it be sooner than later.

"I've been debating whether to tell you this because, well, I don't want you to hate us, but when I spoke to Mama Wawo, she told me that when you first came to her, she told my dad—our dad—while he was still alive, but he never contacted you because he said it wasn't the right time."

Hope's face closed up again and she recoiled as if she had been physically struck. Glory tensed, waiting for her to get up and leave.

"I-I've been so angry since I found out, I can't imagine how you're feeling, but I think I can explain," Glory gabbled.

Hope stirred the mint leaves in her cup, then lay down her teaspoon carefully and precisely next to the teacup and saucer. She blew to cool down her drink and took a small sip.

"I should've ordered an Irish coffee," she said. "OK, go on."

"Well, I suppose the first thing you need to know is our father was a very proud man, and the last few years haven't been easy. There are four of us all together, right? Faith is the oldest, then we were born, then there's Victor, the youngest."

Hope nodded, whether she had already known this or not, Glory couldn't tell.

"Well, erm, a while back Victor was arrested and convicted and sent to prison. I was in LA at the time, but it had a really negative impact on everyone, obviously. My mum's—*our* mum's health—has been up and down, she was hospitalized recently, and I know that this whole situation is a really delicate issue for her. I think our dad was trying to protect her or something, or at least maybe wait until things were calmer."

Hope's mouth was a straight line. She carefully turned her cup around in its saucer.

"Protect her?" she asked, her voice tight. "From me?"

"No, not you," Glory said quickly. "From disappointment in case things didn't work out or you were angry. And of course, I don't know this for sure because my—our—dad never spoke to me about any of this. I didn't even know you . . . well, it just wasn't spoken about so I'm kinda putting words in his mouth, but I just thought you should know. I want to be honest and transparent. No secrets."

No *more* secrets, Glory corrected herself internally.

"Is she still in the hospital?"

"Oh, our mum? No, she's back home. She's doing better, back at work."

"Does she know we're meeting today?"

"No. I told her when I got your number and called you, and she was quite positive and hopeful. But I haven't told her about today."

"Good," Hope said with a finality that made Glory uncomfortable, but if Hope sensed her unease she didn't feel the need to explain what was so good about that.

"Angry . . ." Hope said quietly, sounding each syllable deliberately. "Do you think I've got anything to be angry about?"

She looked Glory in the eye as she asked this and Glory felt like she was caught in the hot beam of a spotlight.

"Probably," Glory replied. "I mean, *I* feel angry, so I would understand if you did. You're entitled to that."

"I'm so sorry about Victor," Hope said. "Do you get to see or talk to him?"

"Yeah, he calls and we go to visit him. He's not actually too far from here."

"That's good," Hope said. She rotated her cup in the opposite direction, stared at its contents and took another small sip. "I'm sorry if I'm not saying much, it's just a lot to take in."

"Please don't apologize. This is kind of why I didn't want to tell you, but I thought it's only fair to let you know what you might be getting yourself into. Give you a chance to change your mind and run." Glory laughed too loudly, again regretting an ill-judged joke. She was acting too familiar, aching to bridge the decades between them.

"Thanks for being honest," Hope said, straight-faced.

Glory took a gulp of hot tea, swallowing quickly then picking up the menu.

"I think I'm actually gonna get something to eat, I don't want anything too heavy though—do you want to share something?"

"No, but you should get the chicken and pomegranate salad, it's really good."

Hope waved over the waitress and Glory placed her order.

Glory watched Hope fidget with her watch and rearrange her unused cutlery again.

"How did you find Mama Wawo?" Glory asked after she had drained her cup. "All this time I thought you'd still be in Birmingham."

"Stourbridge," Hope corrected. "I moved to London for university actually. I studied History at King's."

"Oh, right," Glory said, feeling intimidated by the casual familiarity Hope showed with the prestigious institution.

"I got Mama Wawo's number from my mum. She gave it to me when I first moved to London. I think she thought I chose to move here to find my biological family."

"So you always knew?"

"That they weren't my biological parents? Of course! That's not something you can keep a secret!"

"No." Glory felt embarrassed. "I mean, you always knew that we were here? In London?"

"Oh, yeah," Hope said. "Well, when I was little I used to think that Mama Wawo—or Mrs. Wawo, as my mum would call her—was like a fairy godmother or something. When I asked my parents why they were pink and I was brown, my mum would say that Mama Wawo brought me to them. Then when I was about nine, I realized that she was actually a real person and that my birth family were in London. Then they told me the whole story."

"What did they tell you?" Glory asked slowly.

"That they used to look after me, you and our other sister and then when it was time for us to go home, everyone agreed that it would be better for me to stay with them. Then we moved to Stourbridge to look after my mum's mum, before she passed away."

"Oh, right," Glory said. The words "my mum's mum" bored deep into her brain.

"Is that what you were told?" Hope asked.

"Yeah, pretty much, but I didn't know why you moved."

Hope nodded and looked down into her cup. Glory looked around the restaurant.

"Why . . ." She coughed. "Um. Why didn't they get in touch with us earlier? Like, before you moved to London?"

Glory didn't like how the question sounded once it had left her mouth, and the look Hope shot her suggested she didn't like it either.

"They tried once, just before I started secondary school, but my mum said she couldn't get through. Maybe it wasn't the right time."

Hope held Glory's gaze pointedly, until Glory had to look away, that sick feeling creeping over her body again.

Glory's salad was delivered to the table, but she was no longer hungry.

"Do, erm, Joan and Edward know you're meeting up with me today?" Glory asked, pushing the salad around her plate with a fork.

"My mum does," Hope checked her watch. "She's probably waiting anxiously by the phone for an update."

Hope let out a little laugh, the first genuine one since she had arrived.

"She'll probably tell my dad. Then she'll want a blow-by-blow account when we go and see them in a couple of weeks." Hope rolled her eyes and drank her tea.

"Are you sure you don't want some salad? I'm not going to finish it."

Glory hadn't taken a single bite, but she pushed the plate to the center of the table anyway. Hope picked up her fork and speared some chicken and salad leaves.

"Is it just you? I mean, are there any other, erm, children in your family?" Glory asked.

Hope chewed her mouthful and swallowed, suddenly looking guilty.

"Yeah, I was a right brat growing up. My parents were considering fostering another child, they thought I might want a sibling, but I told them I didn't want one. I wanted it to just be me, and I had Carlene, my best friend, who felt more like a sister anyway. So they never did. Then I got up and left them to come to London, didn't I?"

Hope's strained smile had returned.

Glory scooped up a few pomegranate seeds and crunched them between her teeth. She wanted to know more about this Carlene.

"What was it like growing up? I hope you don't mind me asking."

"It's fine," Hope said, setting down her fork. "Everyone asks, and not so politely either. But besides the fact that I had white parents, there was nothing particularly interesting about it. It was a nice childhood. No horror stories, no identity crises."

"Horror stories?" Glory frowned.

"Well, some black children who have grown up with white parents have these horrible stories, like physical and psychological abuse, or sometimes their foster families or extended families didn't like them that much," Hope said. "When I decided to finally search, I joined this kind of support group online. Some of the stories will give you nightmares. But my childhood wasn't like that. Not at all."

"Well, that's a relief."

"Yes, my parents loved me."

Glory cleared her throat.

"Did you think my—our—parents didn't?"

She was getting caught up in the imprecise nature of possessive pronouns. Her parents were technically Hope's by blood and science, but in any concrete sense they were strangers. Glory knew that rationally, but she couldn't shake the irrational irritation she felt at Hope's insistence on referring to Joan and Edward as her parents. She couldn't ignore the way Hope sidestepped referring directly to the parents they shared.

"I . . ." Hope started, pushing her fork aimlessly around the plate. "I don't know what I thought, to be honest I tried not to think about it too hard."

Melancholy crept into her voice, so Glory nodded and allowed the moment to breathe before carefully changing track.

"What's Stourbridge like compared to London, then?"

"It's calmer, friendlier. People actually talk to their neighbors." Hope pulled a face that Glory couldn't read.

"Are there many black people there?"

"Not as many as London," Hope said. "I didn't have my first black friend until I was eight."

Glory's face must have revealed the shock she was feeling because Hope started grinning.

"Are you serious?" Glory asked, trying to imagine a childhood where none of her friends looked like her.

"Yeah. There was a girl in my primary school from Zimbabwe but we basically hated each other—that's awful, isn't it? But they would always lump us together or pit us against each other and we took out our frustrations on each other, so she doesn't count as a friend. Then I met Carlene when I was eight. She was black, but Jamaican. I didn't have my first Nigerian friend until I came to uni. That's when I learned how to say my surname properly."

"You kept your surname?"

"In secondary school I thought about changing it because I was tired of all the teachers struggling to say it," Hope confessed. "But then I found out the translation."

Glory had never even thought about what her surname meant.

"It means 'valor comes home' or something, doesn't it?"

Glory nodded as if she was certain of that fact.

"And, I dunno, I just liked the bit about coming home."

"I searched for you online, but I couldn't find you anywhere, not even Facebook."

"Oh no, I stay off all of that stuff. Facebook, Twitter, Instagram. Not my thing at all. I mean, I had a Facebook profile once but I deactivated it a few years ago."

"Good for you. I basically live on Instagram and I kinda hate myself for it."

"Let me see your Instagram profile!" Hope said suddenly, a glint flashing in her eye that struck deep at Glory's heart as it reminded her of Victor.

"Oh, no—not in front of me! That's just awkward. I'll give you my username later and you can pree when I'm not around!" Glory said with a smile.

"I'm sorry," Hope said, returning the smile. "I just love living vicariously through my friends—especially dating apps! Oh my god! I love a good Tinder swiping session."

Glory laughed through teeth that were stopping her from asking who Hope's friends were, what they were like and if she could see pictures of them. She wanted to soak herself in every minute detail of her sister's existence, do some vicarious living of her own. If this was a film—and if they had been identical—they would plan to swap lives for a week, slipping into each other's skins and learning about the other from the inside out. Despite herself, Glory felt exhilarated at the prospect.

Hope was still smiling when she picked up her fork and took another bite of the salad that sat between them. Glory decided to try a proper mouthful. The sweetness of the pomegranate seeds next to the salty chicken and toasted walnuts tasted divine on her tongue, and she had refilled her fork before she had swallowed the first bite.

"Good isn't it?" Hope said as she picked up a salad leaf to nibble at.

"Mmm," Glory hummed through another mouthful.

"Do you like Nigerian food?" Glory asked when half the plate was gone.

"I do actually. I don't cook it, but I think I've worked my way through the entire menu at this Nigerian restaurant near our flat."

Glory perked up at this.

"What's your favorite?"

"Erm, fried rice and moin moin. Sorry, I'm pretty basic."

"I thought you were going to say jollof rice—*that's* basic."

"Jollof rice is overrated to be honest."

When Glory clutched at her heart and gasped, Hope quickly clarified.

"It's nice, I'll eat it, but it's not worth going to war over. Same with Supermalt."

"You don't like Supermalt?!"

Hope pretended to retch, sticking out her tongue and shuddering.

"Carlene couldn't believe that one either, but it's disgusting. I really can't."

"Does Carlene still live in Stourbridge?"

"No," Hope said, her voice falling to just above a whisper. "She died about eighteen months ago."

Glory stopped mid-chew.

"I'm so sorry."

"Car accident. On the motorway."

Glory swallowed hard. She needed water.

"How old was she?"

"Twenty-four."

"Wow, I'm really sorry."

"You go to bed one night and then you wake up the next morning and your best friend is gone. I know that death is never easy to deal with, but if she had been ill or something, it wouldn't have felt so violent."

"Our dad died suddenly too. He just collapsed out of the blue. Pulmonary embolism."

"It's never easy."

"No."

Hope reached into her bag and took out her phone.

"Oh! Mark's texted me, like, five times."

She dismissed the notifications and tapped at her screen, eventually setting it down on the table to face Glory.

"That's Carlene."

Glory leaned over and looked at the picture. Hope had her arms wrapped around another woman, she was very slim, very pretty, with long straight black hair. Glory could see how these two could be mistaken for sisters. Carlene had one hand on the side of Hope's head pressing it into her cheek. The other hand held a bottle of wine or champagne. It looked like someone's birthday party.

"She was always telling me that I should look for my bio family, she used to joke that I might be related to African royalty—her dad was Rastafarian—but in my head, I always thought, I'm fine. It felt like if I went looking it meant I wasn't happy or satisfied with my life, like my parents had done something wrong."

Hope stopped and exhaled, pressing a knuckle to the inside corner of one eye.

"When she died I thought, well, I have to now, don't I? Because you just never know. You never ever know."

Glory wanted to tell her that it was a death that started her on this path too, but the fullness of that story felt too bitter to deliver. They had talked through enough hard things for now.

"Oh God, it's Mark again," Hope said when the image on her phone was obscured by another notification. "Let me just call him."

While Hope made the call, Glory finished what was left of the salad. She was exhausted, physically and emotionally. She called the waitress to deliver their bill as Hope ended her conversation.

"I'm so sorry, he's so protective. He's literally just been loitering around, waiting for us to finish."

"It's OK." Glory smiled.

When the bill came, Hope took care of it, waving away Glory's offer. Mark appeared at the window like an apparition. Glory could see him scanning Hope's face for any indication of how their reunion went, but Hope was still burdened by the thought of Carlene. Instead Glory offered a bright smile in his direction.

The long-lost sisters hugged again, this time tighter and for longer. Mark looked satisfied.

"I'm sure we'll meet again, Glory," he said as he waved goodbye. Hope grasped his hand, smiled at her sister one last time and the couple walked away from the restaurant, a low sun against their backs.

46

The first meeting was always going to be hard, Glory told herself on her way back south. Still, she was happy and needed to share the news. She was glad to finally have something good to tell Julian, something which might erase their last few arguments. Julian would be happy for her, she'd say she couldn't have done it without him, and their relationship would be reset. Even her calls going unanswered didn't dampen her spirits, and she made a detour to stop by Pharoah's.

Julian wasn't in the barbershop, he was across the road, standing outside the newsagent laughing with a woman that Glory didn't recognize. This woman was short with long blonde cornrows adorned with little gold hoops. Julian said something and the woman laughed, placing a hand on his forearm and shaking her head, the twinkling hair jewelry taunting Glory.

When Julian looked up from his companion, he saw Glory outside the barbershop. He said something to the woman, touching her lightly at the elbow and she turned and looked in Glory's direction. Julian crossed the road and Glory tried to stay bright.

"I won the lottery!" she said, throwing open her arms as he walked up to her.

Julian leaned in to give her a loose hug, looked past Glory and into the shop, and rubbed the end of his nose. He steered her in the direction of Burgess Park.

"Lottery?"

"Yeah, and I'm gonna buy you that ugly car you love so much. What's it called again? It looks like it's wearing a muzzle."

"Bugatti."

"That's the one."

"Cool."

Glory linked arms with him and they walked on.

"Who was that?" she asked, turning to look back at the woman.

"No one," Julian said gruffly.

"What's wrong?" Glory asked after a few minutes of dead air had passed between them. He was killing her vibe.

"I told you I was gonna buy you a Bugatti and you barely reacted."

"I know you're lying, Glory."

"*Lying?*" Glory was offended. "Wow, so we can't joke around any more?"

"I'm not in the joking mood—but what's going on anyway?" The question was impatient.

They were at the edge of the park where boys on bicycles were executing wheelies. They nodded at Julian who returned the greeting as he stopped at a park bench. He hopped onto it, balancing on the backrest with his feet on the seat. Glory sat down carefully and more conventionally beside him. From this position she was looking up at him, but he kept his gaze looking forward.

"I met up with Hope today."

When the name registered, Julian dropped his indifferent demeanor for just a second.

"For real?"

"Yeah, it was good, a bit awkward at times, but she's really nice."

Glory had forgotten all the excited things she had originally wanted to tell him.

"Cool."

"Julian, what's wrong? Are you still upset about the other night?" Glory asked.

"Shouldn't I be?" Julian said, his tone flat.

"I've apologized already, can we just move on?"

"Have you though?" Julian finally turned to look down at her, square on.

"Yeah, we've talked since then, haven't we?"

"And in which conversation did you apologize?"

Glory raced through her memories.

"OK, I'm sorry, Julian."

"What for?"

"For whatever I've done that's so bad that you're still holding it against me!"

He snickered cynically.

"Wow . . ." Julian shook his head, a mean smile stuck to his lips.

"Who were you flirting with in broad daylight outside the barbershop, anyway?"

Julian kissed his teeth.

"Don't change the subject. You think you can argue, tell me to fuck off and all sorts and then we're gonna just pick right back up like nothing happened?"

"It's not even that deep, Julian," Glory said, a whiny note leaking into her voice. This wasn't how the conversation was meant to go.

"To you, Glory. And that's where we have a problem. You want everything on your terms."

334

"I'm sorry, Julian, I really am. I shouldn't have told you to fuck off and I should have apologized earlier." She turned toward him and tried to turn on the charm. "Can we kiss and make up now, please?"

"You've been moving mad, for real. Got man looking crazy out here."

"There's more to life than how things look."

"Nah, you don't get it. You disrespected me."

Glory was losing patience.

"For God's sake, Julian! What do you want me to do, to get down on my knees and grovel? To kiss your feet like those women in the painting in Pharoah's? I've said I'm sorry!"

Julian shook his head, stood up and hopped down from the bench.

"Where are you going?" Glory snapped, louder and more aggressive than she would have liked.

"You're talking to me like I'm a dickhead again," Julian said. "When you've fixed your attitude, come and find me."

"Is your ego that fragile? You've got issues!" Glory spat after him, and he stopped mid-stride, turning slowly to face her.

"Yeah, I'm the only one with issues here, right?" he said, sarcasm dripping off of every word. "I forgot that Glory's always right, and no one can tell you any differently. You see problems where there aren't any, and when you don't want to see an issue you don't. It's always everyone else with the problems, me, Faith, your mum, your brother-in-law."

"What the hell has Faith, Michael and my mum got to do with anything?"

Glory rose and the two were in a stand-off, a stretch of path between them.

"OK, let's take Faith's husband for example—what has he actually ever done to you?"

Glory opened and closed her mouth like a goldfish, and for a second Julian looked amused at her speechlessness.

"This argument isn't about Michael, it's about us! Don't pretend you've been the perfect boyfriend. I'm always having to come and track you down because you never pick up the phone. Sometimes you're not even at Pharoah's when you should be! Jumping in and out of black vans, running your "errands" across London—I'm not dumb, Julian, I don't forget these things."

Julian laughed, but the laugh was sad and slow. He looked down at his feet, rubbing a hand over his hair, brushing it forward.

"You wanna know what I'm doing?"

He looked up at Glory, his eyes clear.

"I'm paying off a loan. My uncle owns a construction company and he lent me the money to start Pharoah's. I'm paying him back by working for him."

"Oh." Glory felt like she had fallen off of her righteous horse.

"And the woman I was talking to earlier? Her name's Gabrielle. She wants to open her own shop, hair and beauty, so she came to ask for some advice."

"OK."

The air crackled around them.

"But why don't you just *talk* to me," Glory now pleaded. "Instead of making me assume all these different things."

"No one made you do anything."

Glory wanted to dig her heels in, but she felt she was losing ground.

"It might seem like a minor to you, but what you said the other night really hurt me. I'm not gonna lie."

There was nothing fraught in Julian's tone, he just sounded resigned, but the vulnerability of his admission hit Glory in a tender place. She opened her mouth to respond to that, not with an excuse or deflection, but something similarly honest. Before she could, Julian started talking.

"We're both going through a lot, and I don't think now is a good time for us. I need some space."

"Space?"

Julian nodded soberly. Glory could only look at him. This was definitely not the way that this conversation was meant to have gone.

"What happened? Because it can't have been just that."

"*Just that*? You really don't get it, do you?"

"I can't read your mind."

"And I can't read yours."

"What's that supposed to mean?"

Julian threw his hands in the air and let them drop with a sigh.

"I dunno, man. I think we've both got too much pride, right now. Honestly."

"And you think this is the best way to deal with it?" Glory tried not to sound as distraught as she felt.

"This is just how I need to deal with it."

"Ah, so that whole, *It's not you, it's me* thing," Glory said, curling her lip.

Julian let out a laugh of disbelief.

"Nah, it is me, but it's definitely you too."

Glory slumped back onto the park bench.

"Fine."

"I need to get back to the shop, are you gonna be all right?"

"Yeah," she said, not looking up. She could already trace back in the conversation to where she could have said something that might have steered them both differently. Even now, there was still time to say it, but instead she tracked Julian's path with her eyes as he turned and walked away.

Glory sat on the bench, unable to move because her arms and legs felt like they were filled with lead. A light drizzle began to fall and still she didn't move, until she felt a drop of rainwater slip into her collar and down her back.

She called Faith.

"I can't move, Faith, I keep telling myself to get up and go home, but I feel stuck on this bench. I just can't . . . move," she gasped into the phone.

"Are you having a panic attack?!" Faith said, panic in her own voice. "What happened just before you started feeling like this?"

"Julian broke up with me."

"Oh, Glor'!" Faith wailed. "I'm so sorry, Glory. What the hell? Did he tell you why?"

"He did, but that's not important right now, I just want to go home, Faith, but I can't move. It's raining. I feel like someone's kicked me in the ribs. Should I call an ambulance?"

"I think you're just heartbroken, sis—no, not *just*, because heartbreak is a big deal—what I mean is, you need to get home, get into bed, and just stay there. Can you do that? Do you want me to call Mummy and ask her to come and get you? I'm still at home, but I can come around this evening?"

"No, don't call Mummy." Glory took a deep breath and pushed herself slowly to a standing position. "I'm up, I'm going home."

"OK, let me know when you get there—make sure and don't forget like you usually do and let me think that you've collapsed on some backroad in Peckham!"

Glory managed a faint laugh and they said their goodbyes.

When she got to the house, Celeste was waiting for her in the living room.

"Glory?" her mother sprang up when she entered. "Faith said that you're not well, what's wrong? You're so wet!"

Celeste held a hand against Glory's forehead, then helped her out of her damp outer layers.

"I'm OK, I just want to go to bed."

"Yes, go upstairs and get into bed. I'm going to make you pepe soup, ehn? And you must eat it all, even if it makes your nose drip because that's how the sickness will leave your body."

Glory pulled herself up the stairs and peeled off her clothes, putting on her pyjamas and falling into bed with her phone in hand. She changed the string of multicolored hearts next to Julian's name to a single red, broken one, then put her phone on Airplane Mode and left it on the side table next to her bed.

It was when her mother brought in a tray of steaming pepe soup, the broth smelling hot and potent, that Glory remembered Hope. She hadn't told anyone else besides Julian about their meeting.

Celeste stood over her daughter until Glory gingerly took a sip, panting slightly as the taste of scotch bonnet pepper tore through her tongue. She sniffed. Celeste sighed in satisfaction and sat down heavily next to her.

"Faith said it was to do with a boy," Celeste said, her voice a gentle purr.

Glory took a breath, ready to deny all notion of romance in her life.

"Was it that boy who came to my house in the middle of the night?"

"Yes, Mummy."

"Well, good riddance!" Celeste said sternly. "You have to be careful who you attach yourself to in this life. The wrong man will ruin you."

Glory spooned up a piece of shaki and chewed carefully.

"Did Daddy ruin your life?" she asked, too weary to tread softly.

Celeste stiffened sharply, ready to take offense on her late husband's behalf but then she looked at Glory, still looking damp and miserable despite her dry clothes and hot soup.

"Glory," she said finally. "You cannot judge a man by his weakest moments. Do you judge me by mine? Shall I judge you by yours?"

Glory sniffed again but did not answer, her concentration fixed on removing a tender chunk of meat from the bone.

"Why are you making excuses for him?" she replied like a petulant child.

"Excuses, kẹ?" Celeste said with a sharp laugh. "Can a man do anything if God did not allow it? Should I start blaming God too?"

When Glory did not answer again, Celeste clapped her hands impatiently and stood up.

"For every bad thought you hold against your father you are just as stubborn as he was!" Celeste said tapping a finger vigorously at her own temple. She watched Glory take another silent, insolent sip and left the room.

47

When Faith got pregnant the first time, the time that nearly sabotaged her studies, she broke the news to their father over steaming hot bowls of draw soup and pounded yam—*a spoonful of swallow to help the shame go down*, as Glory had described it. There was one moment when it seemed like their father might be choking, but, as their mother had predicted, he didn't turn over tables, shout or hector. He ate his food in silence and allowed his anger to cool to a stony rage that sat high in his chest and prevented him from talking to Faith for nearly three weeks. By the time he broke it was already too late, Faith had miscarried.

When Glory decided to abandon her degree, Faith coached her through her own "bad news meal."

"You need to find the stats on employment for your degree subject," she had begun. "And also look into the employment rates and pay prospects for black female graduates in the UK—I'm sure I read about this somewhere—and then when you tell Mummy and Daddy, you need to present the case that you're no worse off out of university. Bring the facts! He will appreciate the facts."

That meal—jollof rice and stewed chicken—had not worked out so well, so maybe Glory's method of delivery for the latest piece of life-changing news was more to do with family tradition than efficacy.

But also, this was not bad news.

The menu for the evening was ẹ̀fọ́ rírò, the rich and spicy spinach stew that her mother loved. Glory had gone all out, buying fresh cuts of beef and rich palm oil to try and make it as authentically as possible, just as Celeste had once taught her.

The fragrant stew was simmering in its final moments of perfection when Faith let herself in through the front door.

"What are you making?" Faith asked, removing her jacket and entering the kitchen.

"Ẹ̀fọ́ rírò and pounded yam."

"Mmm," Faith breathed deeply, taking in the aroma. "What's the occasion?"

Glory pretended she hadn't heard her, and dipped a wooden spoon into the pot, tapping the back of her wrist in the way she had watched her mother do a hundred times before. She then blew on the small puddle of stew on her skin and tasted it.

"Is that my world-famous ẹ̀fọ́ rírò that I smell?" Celeste called from the stairs. She sauntered into the kitchen, scooping up a thick chunk of beef straight from the pot with two fingers long immune to the heat of cooking.

"I taught you well, my dear!" she said as she smacked her lips, and blew on the beef to cool it.

"What's the occasion?" Faith asked again, leaning more heavily into the question.

"I have some news that I want to tell you both."

Glory thought she sounded casual as she worked another wooden spoon around and around, mixing the pounded yam.

"What has happened?" Her mother tensed.

"Nothing bad, Mummy, I'll tell you when everything's ready."

"Are you going back to LA?" Faith chipped in.

"No—"

"Then what is it?"

Their mother's face folded up with concern and, taking recent history into account, Glory could see how unfair the suspense was. Faith's expression mirrored Celeste, her hands on her hips, fearful and ready to react to any of the worst case scenarios playing through her mind.

Glory sighed and set down the spoon. She turned and addressed their mother directly.

"Hope called me back. We met up. She's here, in London."

Her mother went rigid, and for a long, drawn-out second Glory thought she was about to keel forward like a plank of wood.

"What are you talking about?" Faith asked, but Glory ignored her and kept her eyes fixed on her mother.

"*Jesu!*" Celeste finally breathed after a few moments of tense silence.

"Glory, what are you talking about?" Faith was moving in on her.

"Mummy, do you want to meet her?" Glory asked meekly.

Celeste began to beat lightly on her chest and mumble under her breath. It sounded like a prayer.

"Meet who?" Faith insisted.

But Glory knew the question was a stalling tactic. She could feel Faith searching for ways to shut down and contain the situation.

"How does she just turn up out of the blue? What did you do?" Faith's eyes narrowed; her tone was accusing.

"I didn't do anything!" Glory replied, finally acknowledging her sister. "I went to speak to Mama Wawo and she told me our sister had been in contact with her. *She* was looking for *us*."

"Why were you going to speak to Mama Wawo?"

343

"Does it matter? Hope is here in London and I met her! That's the most important thing!" Glory waved her arms around and knocked the lid off the pot on the stove. It landed with a clatter on the kitchen floor and the sound knocked their mother out of her trance.

"How is she?" Celeste finally asked.

"She's good, Mummy. She's really good."

Her mother swayed back and forth on her feet. Her lips twitched, as though she was trying to say something, or maybe not cry out loud. Faith moved toward her.

"Mummy, are you OK? You need to sit down."

Faith offered her an arm and Celeste gratefully took it.

"Let's go upstairs."

Glory made to follow her sister and mother out of the kitchen but Faith snapped her head back toward Glory.

"You need to stay here!" she hissed and the venom in her voice rooted Glory to the spot.

Faith led their mother from the kitchen and Glory heard the stairs creak as they climbed them. A few minutes later, Faith returned, filled a glass of water without a word and took it upstairs.

The low whir of the extractor fan and the bubble of the stew were the only sounds in the kitchen. Glory picked up the lid that still lay at her feet, rinsed it under the tap and returned it to the pot.

Faith reappeared and pushed the kitchen door to. The old swollen wooden frame wouldn't let it shut completely.

"What does she want?" Faith asked.

"Who?"

"You know who I'm talking about."

"What do you mean, *what does she want?* What do you think she wants?"

344

"Don't you think Mummy's been through enough recently without more drama? Are you trying to kill her?"

"You know, some people would call this a happy ending! Mummy was fine when I told her that I had tried to call Hope. She was *pleased*, even."

Faith hung her head, a wall of wavy hair obscuring her face. She drummed her nails into the countertop and sniffed.

"I can't believe you went behind my back and did this."

"I didn't realize I had to ask for your permission. She's *my* twin!"

Faith sniffed again, and looked up at the ceiling.

"Don't pretend like you don't care, I know you talk to Michael about this."

At the sound of her husband's name, Faith landed a hard glare on Glory. Her nostrils were flared and her face darkened with rage.

"Don't you fucking dare!"

Faith never swore.

"Don't you fucking dare talk about Mi— Oh my God! I can't believe you!"

Faith hit the countertop. The sound made Glory flinch.

"You waltz around here thinking you can do whatever the hell you want and the rest of us just have to put up with you. You have no idea, no fucking idea of what this family has been through while you were doing whatever you wanted over there! *I'm* the one that had to hold everything together, to pick up the pieces every time she broke down, and now you think *you* know what's best for her? For us?"

Faith was quivering with rage. Each sentence modulated in volume as Faith got very close to losing control before remembering herself again. Glory had never seen her sister raise her voice at anyone. All Esther and Elijah got was a carefully worded admonishment, delivered through gritted teeth. Faith seemed unhinged, or as close to unhinged as it was possible for her to get. In this moment, she reminded Glory of their father.

Faith raised her hands to her temples, pushing hard against her skull with her fingertips. When she looked at Glory, angry tears were spilling down her face.

"Faith . . ." Glory started, trying to keep steady even though alarm bells were ringing in her head.

"Faith—" she tried again but her sister cut in.

"Don't talk to me!" Faith spat. "You didn't even want to live with her. You were gonna let her stay in this house all by herself and now . . ." She let out a laugh soaked in derision, and when Glory reached out to her sister—just a hand, and she was not sure why she thought to do it—Faith winced and pulled away.

"Just don't burn the food," Faith said, looking past Glory and turning away.

When the kitchen door slammed behind her, rebounding off its misshapen frame, something shook loose in Glory and she began to cry hard. She pushed her knuckles into her mouth trying to stifle the wails that were coming thick and fast as her heart felt overwhelmed by everything: Julian, Faith, Hope, her mother, her father . . . her father . . . her father . . .

When she was calm enough to eat, Glory filled a bowl with èfọ́ rírò and ate alone at the kitchen counter.

Halfway through her second bowl, she could hear her name being called. It was faint and frail and came from her mother's bedroom.

Glory followed her name up the stairs and into the room, and as soon as she entered Faith walked out.

The curtains were open and Celeste was sitting up in the double bed, her hands folded on top of some papers in her lap. She directed Glory to sit. Glory perched on the edge of the bed.

"I don't want you to think that I'm not happy, you've done well," her mother said, lower than necessary, Glory thought.

"There's that saying, *you cannot question God*. Well, I've told you before, I grew up in a very polygamous family, and my father's wives and children treated him as God. No one questioned him! That was how I understood things to be. But when you treat your husband as God, you cannot be his helper, because God does not need a helper, àbí?"

Glory nodded.

"Your father needed a helper. He made some bad choices that affected us all. He was just a man, it's to be expected, but he needed a helper and I failed in that way as a wife—as a *mother*."

"How did *you* fail, Mummy?" Glory asked. "You're not the one—"

"I could have been firmer! I could have done something. Kúnlé needed to correct the path he had set, but I was so lost after I had Victor. I was . . . afflicted."

Celeste's voice cracked over the final word that sounded strangely stilted and formal in her mouth. She cleared her throat.

"Anyways, sha. I am not afraid for you in that respect. I am more concerned that your husband will return you to this house because you cannot stop correcting him."

Her mother chuckled and cupped Glory's face with a hand. Her palm was warm and soft.

"We will meet her soon, by the grace of God. Very soon."

Her other hand was still laying on top of the papers in her lap. Glory could see a child's face—Hope's face—peeking between her fingers. She wanted to study the photograph, it looked like one she hadn't seen before in all her snooping, but instead she smiled at her mother. Celeste smiled back and pinched Glory's cheek.

"Now go and bring me food."

Glory left her mother's room, nearly running into Faith who was standing directly outside the door, eavesdropping.

Glory wiped her eyes and offered a smile to her sister, who looked straight past her and went back into the room.

48

Glory thought she might have lost Faith for nothing. Hope's responses to her WhatsApp messages were verging on monosyllabic.

"My mum's not even mentioned meeting Hope again," Glory told Lará when they finally met up for lunch.

Glory had invited her to a small Italian restaurant she had read about on Bellenden Road that served fresh homemade pasta and gelato. She still wasn't a fan of all the changes in Peckham, but she had to reluctantly admit that gentrification had its perks.

"I don't get it, she's not angry with me, but whenever I try to force the conversation she's not interested. I'm sure if I could tell Hope that my mum was ready to meet her, she'd be more responsive."

"You can't force your mum or Hope to do anything that they're not ready to," Lará said, looping tagliatelle around her fork. "You've been working toward this for months, you've had time to process everything."

"I guess," Glory said, her own pasta untouched. "It just felt like I've done all this stuff, fighting off Faith who didn't want any of this to happen, and now, nothing."

"It's not nothing, it's just not moving as fast as you'd like. You can't micromanage something like this."

Glory nodded and finally began to eat. "How's the job hunt going anyway?"

"Ooh, good! I've got an interview for a type design position at a foundry right here in London. My dream job, basically!"

Glory nodded enthusiastically, despite not quite understanding, as usual.

"I'm happy for you, Lará! I have no idea what a foundry is, but it sounds like . . . yeah!"

Lará laughed until she was nearly choking on a mouthful of pasta.

Glory kept Lará's advice about micromanaging at the front of her mind every time she was ready to broach the topic again with her mother or dial Hope's number and ask her what the matter was. It was good that Hope wasn't on social media, or Glory would have lost hours of her life lurking on her profiles.

Thankfully, a few days later, she called.

"I'm sorry," she began. "It's just—I'm sorry. Work and stuff."

"I never even asked where you worked," Glory said, trying not to sound as giddy as she had felt when Hope's name popped up on her screen.

"Nowhere interesting, I'm an executive personal assistant to the CEO of a charity. What about you?"

"Oh, I'm between things at the moment. Just doing shift work while I have a bit of downtime."

"Oh, cool," Hope said. "Well, I was wondering if you're free on Saturday?"

"I'm meant to be working, but I can get out of it."

"Are you sure? We can do next week or something—won't they need you?"

Glory snorted.

"I work silver service, I'm just a body in a uniform. They'll survive without me."

"Oh, sorry," Hope said.

"No need to apologize, not your fault."

"Mark is always telling me I apologize too much," she said. "Sor— You know what, forget it!"

Glory laughed.

"Apparently I don't apologize at all, so maybe I should be taking notes from you. What do you want to do on Saturday?"

"You can come around to ours, if you don't mind."

"Sounds good!" Glory said, hoping that Mark wouldn't be there.

Hope lived in a stylish box on the fifteenth floor of a brand-new tower in the Isle of Dogs. The apartment was shiny and spare, with an open plan kitchen and living area, a wrap-around balcony and an incredible view.

"This is nice!" Glory said, looking out from one of the floor-to-ceiling windows. "I need to change careers."

"To be honest, this is all on Mark's salary," Hope said, looking around as if she was seeing the flat for the first time.

"What does he do?"

"He works in finance. That's where I met him actually, I used to PA for his boss. Do you want a drink?"

"Just some water, thanks."

"Still or sparkling?"

"I was thinking tap, but sparkling is fine."

Hope handed her a chilled bottle.

Glory sat on one of the low chairs in the front room, pulling a glass-topped coffee table toward her. She laid out the things she had brought with her: the program from her father's funeral, pictures from Faith's wedding, other photographs she had found from their childhood, and a few more recent images she had printed out from her phone.

Hope sat on the floor to her right, curling her legs underneath her. She picked up a picture of Esther and Elijah when they were babies.

"Are these Faith's kids? They're so cute!"

"On paper. They're a lot more trouble in person."

Glory handed Hope a more recent photograph. Elijah was smiling at the camera, his reluctant grin looking like a grimace. Esther was side-eyeing her brother.

"You know fraternal twins are genetic right?" Hope looked up from the image. "We could end up with a set of twins each. How mad would that be?"

"I didn't actually know that."

"I guess you don't obsessively research these things like I do, then?"

Glory smiled, but she was embarrassed by her ignorance yet again.

Hope reached for the funeral program.

"I actually learned a lot about Daddy after his death when I was compiling the program," Glory said. "I had no idea about some of the details in there."

"He was a chief?" Hope asked in a reverent tone as she read.

"Yeah, we went back to Nigeria when he was being installed or whatever they call it. I was like twelve. I didn't enjoy it though, we weren't allowed to do anything fun and our Nigerian cousins constantly took the piss out of us."

"Woah." Hope breathed. "So Carlene was right. Imagine that."

"I don't know if it counts as *royalty* royalty," Glory said quickly. "There are lots of chiefs. The actual kings are called something different. Can't remember what now."

"Ọba," Hope said.

"Yeah, I think that's it."

Hope was looking through the photographs printed in the program, studying each one carefully.

"So, you don't speak Yorùbá?" she asked, not looking up from the page in her hand.

"No," Glory said sheepishly. "I can understand it a bit, usually when Mum's angry and cussing someone."

"I was meant to be taking lessons from Auntie Helen—the woman who owns that takeaway I was telling you about—but it's quite intimidating to be honest."

"They don't make it easy, I know that much," Glory said, remembering her Nigerian cousins and the way they would mock Faith and Glory's attempts to assimilate.

"You really look like her," Hope said, pausing on a picture from their parents' wedding day, her finger resting next to their mother.

"You do too!" Glory said. "Well, I guess it would make sense, as we definitely look alike."

Hope turned a few more pages, a satisfied smile on her face.

"Is that Victor?" she said, pressing a finger to a picture of their father with his arm draped around their younger brother.

"Yeah, back when he still felt like my baby brother."

"Is it OK to ask what he went to prison for?" Hope asked, pausing to look at Glory.

"Erm, yeah. It's fine."

If Hope wanted in with her biological bloodline, this was as in as you could get.

"It was manslaughter—but by joint enterprise," Glory said. "He was with some others and one of them got into a fight with someone they knew. One of his friends bottled the victim. I think it was an accident. I mean, I don't think he meant to kill him, but Victor and the others all got charged too."

"That's awful," Hope said quietly, looking back to the funeral program.

"Victor's not violent at all, well he was never violent before . . . but it is what it is."

"Mark's sister is a solicitor. She deals with white collar crime, mostly, but she's always got these stories of, like, injustice and stuff."

This moment of simple empathy was precious. They sat quietly. At first the complete silence of the flat unnerved Glory, but she got used to it. Hope continued examining the program and picking up photographs.

When she was finished she pulled her knees up to her chin and sat still like that for a while. Her hair was tied up into a high ponytail that curled at the bottom. She looked like a child.

Glory couldn't tell if Hope was sad, angry or just thoughtful, and it bothered her. These were the things you were meant to know about your sister, especially your twin.

She gathered up the photographs from the coffee table and began sorting them.

"You can keep these ones if you like."

Glory put a few of them back down and pushed them toward Hope.

"It's OK."

"No, I printed them especially for you to have."

"That's a nice thought, but I'm *fine*."

"Oh." Glory drew the pile back toward her. "Sorry, I just thought you might want some pictures of your family."

"I already have a family. Always have."

Her words sliced through Glory.

"I know, I was just thinking . . . well, I mean I wasn't trying to say . . ." Glory fumbled as the atmosphere grew tense.

"When you grow up how I did, people look at you like you're half-formed because you don't know how to cook jollof rice," Hope eventually said. "But I'm fine. I know how to cook rice and peas, I have more than enough rice in my life."

Glory didn't know how to respond to that, so she just kept her mouth closed and listened.

"As soon as I discovered Pink hair lotion and Jamm gel, I was fine. In secondary school, you would never have known I was brought up by white parents. But by then I wanted everyone to know."

"Why did you want them to know?" Glory asked.

"Because my parents did an amazing job. They aren't perfect, but they did the best they could, and it was more than enough. But sometimes you have black people thinking I'm lacking something fundamental, but then you have white people acting as if my parents aren't my parents but my generous benefactors, like I was plucked out from an orphanage in the middle of Africa and saved from a life of poverty. When I wasn't, I was . . ."

Glory felt the hair on the back of her neck rise at this unspoken thought. She held her breath, waiting.

"You know, this could all be very straightforward but people—and I don't mean you—but other people make it hard when they bring their assumptions. I can be a bit defensive sometimes, I'm sorry. Thanks for printing those photographs for me," Hope said eventually, smiling at Glory, but the smile didn't quite reach her eyes.

"No worries." Glory put the photographs back on the table. "I'm glad that your . . . I'm glad Joan and Edward gave you a good childhood."

355

"They really did."

"But we're not a bad family. We're a bit . . . dysfunctional but you probably would have been fine if you grew up with us."

"Probably. But I didn't make that choice, did I?"

Glory was sure that Hope knew more than she had let on, but this was not a conversation she was equipped to have.

"So, erm, how long have you and Mark been together?"

Hope looked up as she counted under her breath.

"Three . . . four years, now I think? We've been together for four years, but only living together for about two."

"Are you going to get married? Shit! Sorry! I'm sounding like one of Mum's friends—forget I asked!"

"Did you go through a rebellious stage?" Hope asked, ignoring Glory's question but turning to look at her.

"If I'm honest," she replied. "I feel like the last ten years have been my rebellious stage."

"You're lucky," Hope said quietly. "I couldn't afford to have one."

"Well, it's never too late," Glory said with a smile, and Hope finally smiled but shook her head.

"It would've been nice to explore all my options, but I'm OK with where I've landed."

"Rebellion is not all it's cracked up to be anyway. You're not the one working silver service."

"You've not failed or anything," Hope said with alarming clarity. "You've just chosen differently."

"Well, at some point different starts to feel like wrong."

Hope's phone rang and when she looked at the screen she gasped.

"It's my mum!" she said. "I bet she's calling because she knew you'd be here. She's such a busybody—one sec!"

Hope stood up in one smooth motion.

"Mum! Hiya!" She walked over to the kitchen and turned her back toward the living area. The conversation dropped to a mumble. Glory took out her own phone and began looking through it, she was straining to hear every word said across the kitchen but didn't want to make it obvious.

". . . Oh, Mum . . . don't make it awkward, please . . ." she heard Hope say, before she turned and began walking over to Glory. "OK, let me ask her."

Hope rolled her eyes and dropped the phone away from her face.

"My mum wants to speak with you, do you mind? Feel free to say no!"

"N-no. It's fine," Glory said, feeling the breath being sucked out of her. Hope handed over the phone and Glory held it up to her ear.

"Hello?"

"Hello, Glory, I'm so happy to speak to you after all these years." The voice was warm and the woman on the other end talked with a disarming familiarity. "How are you, love?"

"I'm fine, thank you."

"I was so sad to hear about your father passing away. He was such an intelligent man, so brilliant and hardworking. We admired him very much."

"Th-thank you."

"How's your mum doing?"

Glory took a breath and steadied herself.

"She's getting on OK. Getting better with time."

"Of course. Hope'll probably tell me off again, so send her my love."

"I will, thank you . . ." Glory didn't know what to call her. Calling her by her first name felt inappropriate.

"Is she still cooking all the time? She used to bring us these big tubs of rice and chicken and beef. Oh, I missed that when we moved. Anyway love, I'll let you go. I'm so glad you girls have found each other."

"Thank you, so am I. Bye."

Glory handed the phone back in a daze. The rest of the conversation between Hope and Joan faded into the background as Glory wrestled with the new feelings within her.

"I'm sorry," Hope said when the call had ended.

"No, she sounds really nice."

"Yeah, well, she's insisting that I send her a picture of us together. Are you ready for your close up?" Hope brushed a hand through her ponytail, pulling it over her shoulder. Glory stood next to Hope and Hope pulled her closer, clicking away as the two of them grinned into the tiny lens, making slight changes to the angle of their heads with each shutter click.

After a few seconds of posing, Hope reviewed the images.

"I like this one," she said, handing the phone to Glory.

Glory looked at it and nodded, her mouth was too dry to talk. Seeing their identical smiles frozen in time, sent butterflies through her stomach. She gave the phone back to Hope and looked away.

"Oh, hi Glory!"

Mark emerged from the bedroom in a T-shirt and shorts, hair tousled and eyes bleary from sleep.

"Hey."

Glory felt it necessary to avert her eyes.

He walked over to Hope and gently pulled her head back by her ponytail. He leaned over and kissed her on the lips.

"Don't forget dinner with my family tonight. I'm going to get in the shower, you should start getting ready."

"OK, honey," Hope said.

358

"You don't want to go, do you?"

"Well—"

"Glory, do you want to celebrate my mum's birthday? You won't need to pay for your meal," Mark said, not waiting for Hope to finish.

"Mark! You can't just invite Glory without speaking to your mum, it's not your money."

Hope mouthed an apology to Glory.

"Thanks, but I can't," Glory said before Mark could object to Hope's objection.

"OK, but could you encourage this one to at least get ready," he said, tugging at Hope's ponytail again. She pulled it from his grip with a tut and pointed in the direction of the bathroom.

"I need something stronger than sparkling water," Hope said when she heard the shower turn on.

She got up and took two wineglasses from a cupboard over the sink and half filled them with rosé. She handed one to Glory and led her into the master bedroom.

One wall was the mirrored door of a built-in wardrobe. Hope slid open one of the panels and revealed a rack of brightly colored clothes. She pulled out a couple of dresses by their hangers and laid them carefully on the bed.

"What's Mark's family like?" Glory asked, running a hand over a shift dress whose sequins were black or blue depending how the light hit them.

"They're nice. He's the youngest, can you tell?" Hope said drily. "But his friends on the other hand . . ."

Hope made her eyes wide behind the rim of the wineglass. Glory waited for her to complete her thought.

"Well, one of them always asks me if I've heard whatever new thing Drake has released, and there's another one who went to Harrow and uses every available opportunity to remind you."

"No way," Glory said, taking a sip of her wine. "I've never asked you what kind of music you like actually, what do you listen to?"

"A bit of everything. My dad's really into The Clash, so I listen to a lot of that kind of stuff."

"The Clash?" Glory asked, her nose wrinkling.

"This band from the 70s." Hope waved away Glory's confusion. "What about you?"

"Erm . . . Drake?"

The two women fell about laughing, Hope almost sloshing her wine over the dresses on the bed.

"Next time Will asks me, I'm going to give him your number and say, *"Talk to my sister about it!"* Hope laughed some more before sitting up straight and taking in a breath. *"My sister!* Wow. Never thought I'd be saying that."

She got up from the bed and sat on a stool in front of one of the mirrored sliding doors and began removing her makeup with damp cotton pads.

"I really should have a shower too, but I can't be bothered," Hope said as she wiped carefully at her hairline.

When she was sure her skin was clear, she began trying on dresses, Glory giving her feedback as she twisted and turned in front of the mirror. Glory suspected that Hope wasn't indecisive about what she wanted to wear, she didn't seem like the type, but instead she was enjoying the process, the sisterly conspiracy and easy giggles.

Hope finally settled on a burnt orange sleeveless A-line dress. She laid it on the bed and put away the other options.

She then sat back on the stool and began remaking her face. Glory wanted to map out every detail of her sister's features.

Watching her hands flutter and stroke, she was drawn back to the funeral and Faith doing her own makeup that morning.

"Death is another type of beginning," the pastor had said during the sermon. On the day it had merged into the mush of empty platitudes being passed around, but who could have known everything that would follow?

Hope was outlining her lips when Mark walked into the bedroom, hair dripping water onto the shoulders of his dressing gown.

"Perfect," he said, trying to land a kiss on Hope's cheek.

"Don't mess up my makeup," Hope told him, ducking out of his way. "Did you remember to pick up the present?"

Mark paused, his grin stiffened.

"I didn't."

Hope let a moment pass before saying, "I knew you'd forget, don't worry I did it."

Mark looked relieved then puzzled.

"What did you get her again?"

"You're bloody useless. It's in the bag by the door, go look."

And when Mark had left the room, she turned to Glory, lowering her voice.

"He should pay me for being *his* executive assistant."

"I like that color," Glory said as Hope filled in her outlined lips with a deep pink.

"It's not too much for someone else's birthday meal?" Hope asked, trying to dab off some of the pigment. "Don't want to upstage his mum."

"Trust me, it's fine. But even if it wasn't, Faith always says that as Nigerians, being extra is our birthright."

Hope smacked her lips together, the corners of her mouth pulling them into a smile.

"My birthright," she repeated. "I like that."

49

Glory didn't leave until the last possible moment. She hung onto every morsel of conversation and Hope reciprocated, brushing and rebrushing her hair, replaying her act of indecisiveness when it came to choosing her shoes and accessories.

When Mark poked his head through the door one too many times, Hope told him off in a flash of irritation that reminded Glory again of Faith. She tried not to smirk outwardly when Mark hung his head a little.

"Apologies!" he said, addressing Glory after Hope had handed him the shirt he was after. "She's the better half of my brain."

Glory felt a twinge in her chest, like a sharp tug on her heart that she only recognized as jealousy after she had left Hope and Mark. An adoring partner could be found or created, but she only had one twin sister and Mark was the one with access to half of her brain.

"What's she like?" Victor asked when he called the following day.

"She reminds me of Faith so much! You know how Faith is very organized and particular? She rolls her eyes a lot like Faith too. But then she reminds me of you, because she's quieter than Faith. I think she's got more of your sense of humor—she looks like Mummy, though, definitely!" Glory said in an excited burst.

"Argh, I wish I was there, man," Victor said in a rare display of vulnerability. "Do you have a picture of her? Send me a pic."

"She can come and see you! Add her to your list," Glory said.

"Nah," Victor said. "I don't want the first time I'm going to meet her to be in here. Dead that."

"Fair enough."

"Have you been back to Daddy's grave yet?" Victor asked.

"No . . . Can't bring myself to, to be honest."

"Too creepy?"

"Nah, I'm still angry at him—that's bad, innit?"

"It's understandable."

"I feel like I don't even know who he was," Glory said. "How do you keep a secret like that from your children? At first it was the beating Hope thing that I couldn't get my head around, but fair enough, he mellowed out—"

"Mellowed out?" Victor asked with a laugh. "You must have a selective memory, Daddy never mellowed out."

"He never beat me though, not once that I can remember!"

"He beat me, boy!" Victor said, still laughing. "I carried all the licks until I was about thirteen. When I got arrested, I swear he was about to take off his belt and beat me again, but Mummy stood between us and wouldn't move."

"No way!" Glory said in a gasp. "I didn't know."

"You were his favorite, Glory, obviously."

"Does that make you hate him? I'm scared I might hate him now."

Victor hummed as he thought.

"If you care about someone and you find out something bad about them, you're either gonna blindly defend them, not believing anything, or you're gonna be so angry that they did something so bad, that your love might turn to hate for a bit. That was exactly both of their reactions when I got arrested, Mummy was blindly defending me, Daddy hated me for a little bit, but it's fine. We were on good terms by the end."

"You had the opportunity to talk it through, though. I don't. I'm scared I'm going to be stuck hating him just a little bit forever."

"Talk it through? Glor," are we even talking about the same man right now?" Victor was chuckling in disbelief. "We didn't talk it through, he just started talking to me again. The end."

"Well, looks like you inherited that nonverbal gene from him. You won't talk to a counselor and you won't talk to me."

"I'm cool, Glory, I promise you. I'm feeling better now that I'm on a course."

"Are you still, y'know?" Glory asked carefully, aware that the call might be monitored.

"Nah, I told you, it was just stress. I'm not stressed any more."

"Well, you still need to talk. It helps."

"Yeah, well we were talking about Daddy, and you'll eventually forgive him. We always do."

As comforting as Victor's words were, the blind spots in Glory's impression of their father and their childhood disturbed her. It scared her that her memory might have always been selective, and if it had, what did that mean for her perspective of everyone and everything else?

After her conversation with Victor ended, she scrolled through her contacts. When she found the name she was looking for, she pressed call, her chest tight as she waited for the other person to answer.

"Hi G—"

"If you're with Faith, don't let her know I'm calling, please!" Glory interrupted quickly.

"No, I'm not with her. What's going on?"

"Is Faith still mad at me?"

"Yes," Michael replied with certainty.

"How do I get her to stop being mad at me?"

"Tell her you're sorry and she was right."

"But she's not—not fully!"

"I know, I told her that myself."

"What did she say?" Glory asked.

Michael hesitated.

"Nothing worth repeating." Glory's heart sank.

"Are you OK?" he asked, after giving Glory some time to recover.

"I saw Hope again yesterday," she said. "Second time. I even spoke to her . . . Joan. The lady."

"Well, that's great news!" Michael said.

"Yeah . . . but I think Hope really needs to meet Mum now, and Mum says she's open to it, but Faith is the only person who can convince her to actually do it."

"Mmmm . . ." Michael said, sounding thoughtful. "OK, leave it with me. Let me see what I can do."

"What are you going to do?"

"Don't worry, we'll make this happen, OK?"

"OK," Glory said, allowing a little bit of optimism to surge within her heart.

"And Glory?"

"Yeah?"

"You absolutely did the right thing."

50

The following Sunday, Glory waited until her mother had left the house before setting up camp in the front room. The TV was showing reruns of *Come Dine With Me* and Glory's thumb was stuck in an endless scroll over her various feeds, when her phone began ringing. She couldn't help feel her stomach leap with excitement when she saw Julian's name. She cleared her throat a few times before answering, trying to sound as casual as possible, but Julian bypassed the pleasantries.

"Are you still working that waitressing t'ing?" he asked.

"Yeah, why?"

"Listen, I've got something you might be interested in—well it's not me, it's my boy actually, he's launching this—what's it called again?" He called off to someone in the background. "Yeah, that's it, it's like some pop-up restaurant for Nigerian food, but not like a takeaway? I dunno man, but he's looking for someone to help with marketing and I thought of you."

The words "I thought of you" echoed in Glory's mind, but "pop-up restaurant" was the thing that really made her pay attention.

"Is it paid?"

"Come on, Glory!"

She felt the familiar comfort of his laugh.

"You think I'd try bring you in on some internship? 'Course it's paid, you're legit, that's why I suggested you. I know you don't really wanna do the social media thing, but I thought being as you're a foodie, this might change your mind."

"It does sound interesting."

"Calm." Julian sounded satisfied. "I'll give him your number."

"All right, then."

"You good, though?"

"I'm OK, yeah. How are you?"

"Man's here, y'know. Livin'."

There was a pregnant pause, enough space for Glory to tell him about Hope, to impress him with her tenacity; enough space for one of them to declare something that might push open the door of possibility.

"Anyways, let me not take up any more of your Sunday. My boy will be in touch—his name's Ayọ̀, yeah?"

"OK, no problem," Glory said with an ease that sounded convincing. "Take care, Julian."

"Always," was his response and then the line went dead.

Glory lay back and let her mind wander. She thought of the restaurants she'd read about that started off as pop-up sensations. She imagined herself posing in *Time Out*, next to this Ayọ̀ and the rest of the team, in an article singing the praises of this new venture. She imagined a launch party— with Julian there, of course, it would be a genuine excuse to see him. But then the front door opened and Glory nearly jumped out of her skin.

"Hellooo?" Faith called into the house and Glory cycled through fear, relief and confusion.

"It's just me!" she called back.

"Ah, good," Faith said, entering the room and surveying Glory stretched out on the sofa, the coffee table littered with plantain crisps and a single bottle of Supermalt.

Glory put her phone down and watched her sister sit carefully in one of the armchairs. Faith rubbed her palms together, stood back up, took off her jacket, then sat back down.

"Where are the twins?" Glory asked.

"Michael offered to take them out," Faith replied, her eyes fixed on the television screen. "He said you went to see her last week."

Glory tried to remain charitable but this refusal to say Hope's name felt childish and cruel. Hope was the only one in all this that had done nothing at all.

"I did. I spoke to the woman too. Joan."

Faith held her poker face.

"So, what does that mean going forward?"

Glory didn't know how to answer this question, so she said nothing for a moment. When one of them finally spoke, the other did too.

"Look—"

"I—"

Faith gestured for Glory to continue.

"I'm sorry. I've been thinking about everything you said before and you were right about so much. But I had to do this. I just *had* to."

Faith's face stayed blank.

"I think the fact that I wasn't here for so many of the important things made me feel like I had to try and fix this one thing, and I know now that it could have backfired and been the most horrible thing to happen on top of everything else, but I needed to feel like I was doing something to help.

You've done so much for us, Faith. I'm sorry I ran away from it all and you had to do it alone."

"Thank you," Faith said, but her body language didn't change.

"And you know what?" Glory said with resignation. "I've chatted a lot of shit about Michael over the years, but he's not actually that bad. He's a good lad."

Faith was so shocked by this concession that she forgot to maintain her emotional distance, and didn't suppress the confused smile that appeared on her face.

"I checked the weather this morning, but it didn't say anything about pigs flying!" she said, now trying to regain her aloof position. But it didn't work, the wedge between the two sisters had dissolved.

"What's your plan for this big reunion then?" Faith asked Glory, sitting forward in her chair slightly.

"Well, I was thinking maybe a neutral environment, like going for coffee or something."

"Er, no," Faith said. "It needs to be at home or Mummy won't be comfortable."

"But it would be a bit intense don't you think?" Glory asked. "Just putting myself in Hope's position, that's all."

Faith thought this over.

"She should come with Joan, then. I'm sure Mummy would be happy to see her as well."

Faith tossed out the name with an easy familiarity. Glory's tongue still tripped clumsily over what to call the only woman Hope had known as "Mum."

"You sure?"

Faith nodded.

"And how do *you* feel about it?"

"The wheels were in motion long before you poked your nose in this," Faith said. "I should have expected it, really."

"You knew," Glory said, as the realization dawned on her.

"Sort of."

Glory was swamped with questions, but she reined them all in. There would be time for all of that, she reminded herself. Nobody was going anywhere.

Faith picked up a handful of plantain crisps, settling in to get comfortable and watch the TV.

"You're turning into Daddy, y'know," she said to Glory after swallowing a mouthful. "He used to do this every Sunday after church, remember?"

"Watch *Come Dine With Me*?" Glory said doubtfully.

"No, sit on the sofa and drink malt and eat plantain crisps."

Glory paused to think, and yes, it was a scene that came easily to mind. She grunted and sat up straight.

"You can have the rest of the Supermalt if you want."

Her phone started ringing again and when she read the caller display, she rushed to show it to Faith. It was Hope.

"Do you want to speak to her?" Glory whispered excitedly.

"No," Faith said calmly. "She's phoning to talk to you. You answer."

And she sat back, turning her attention to the TV.

"Oh my God, Glory!" Hope exclaimed when Glory answered. "I told you Mark's sister is a solicitor, right?"

"Yeah, why?"

"He was with her last night and apparently she was talking about work and I don't know, but one thing lead to another and Mark mentioned something about joint enterprise—I don't think he mentioned Victor or anything, I mean, he knows, I told him, I hope you don't mind, but I don't think he would have—anyway! Eliza mentioned that there had been a Supreme Court ruling on it."

"On what?" Glory asked.

"Joint enterprise! Mark looked it up this morning! I'll send you a link now!"

Hope ended the call and not two seconds later, a link had appeared on Glory's screen.

"What's up?" Faith asked, wondering why the call had been so short.

"I'm not sure, one sec," Glory said as she loaded the webpage.

A headline appeared in solid black type: "Joint Enterprise Law Wrongly Interpreted For 30 Years, Supreme Court Rules."

Glory's eyes scanned hungrily over the article, her throat constricting after each sentence.

"Faith! Oh my God, Faith! Look at this!"

Glory leaped up and onto the arm of the chair Faith was sitting in, holding the phone out.

Faith's eyes widened as she read, her hand held midair, holding a plantain crisp that hadn't quite made it to her mouth.

"Does this mean—"

Glory was already calling Hope back.

"Hope? You're on speaker, Faith's here too!" Glory held the phone between the two of them.

"Oh! Hi Faith, you all right?"

"H-hi Hope," Faith said, for once not sounding self-assured.

"What does this mean, though?" Glory asked, afraid to allow herself to come to any conclusion.

"Was that Glory or Faith?" Hope asked. "You both sound so similar! Sorry!"

All three of them laughed.

"It was me, Glory."

"Right, well, it means we'd need to get him a lawyer and then appeal it, I think? Oh my God, I don't know. Do you want me to ask Mark's sister?"

"Yes, please!" Glory said hurriedly, then looking at Faith she added: "We can call Michael as well, Faith's husband—he's a lawyer too!"

"Oh, perfect! Let me try her now and call you back."

"Mad, innit?" Glory said to Faith, taking a deep breath and rubbing a hand over her face. And, for once, Faith was speechless too.

51

Any lingering doubts Faith had disappeared after Hope's call. She was completely on board with Glory's reunion project, but convincing their mother was a trial in and of itself. Celeste refused to commit, reverting to pseudo-religious jargon about waiting "on God's time." Eventually, Faith drafted in Michael.

Celeste came down the stairs one day to see the three of them—Michael, Faith and Glory—sitting expectantly in the living room. She eyed her children suspiciously.

"What is it?" Her gaze shifted from face to face trying to decipher the circumstances of this obvious intervention.

"Ma," Michael said, standing up and gesturing with a broad palm for his mother-in-law to take his seat.

Celeste sat slowly, perched on the edge of her armchair.

"Yes?" she asked again, looking up at her son-in-law.

"There is a matter that has been ongoing for some time now, circumstances have presented themselves and we can all gain some closure on this topic," Michael said, addressing Celeste in a deep lawyerly baritone and the authority of a much older man.

Celeste nodded and her shoulders relaxed, clearly knowing where this was heading.

"We have thought long and hard about it, and we have been prayerful in our approach—"

Glory nearly laughed at this statement, never having seen Michael in church past his wedding day, let alone prayerful about anything.

". . . it is not about the details of why things are as they are, but your daughter is ready to meet her sisters, and your other daughters would not do something like this without your blessing and your presence. Of course, Hope will want to meet you as well, and we know that there is nothing more that a caring and loving mother as yourself would want than to meet her daughter who she has been separated from for such a long time."

Celeste considered all that Michael was saying, nodding slightly to affirm certain parts of his speech.

"So we request humbly that you would not only give us your blessing for this reunion, but that you would be present to receive Hope and her foster mother when they arrive. It is important to Faith and Glory, but it is also important for this family. This is good news after many months of trials."

Seeing Michael in action, it made sense to Glory why he was loved and adored by the older generation. He addressed them on their terms, their contrived propriety, the saccharine flattery—he spoke like a Nigerian politician, so it was clear now why he always got what he wanted.

Celeste was convinced by his performance, but put on one of her own, the expression on her face chosen to show that she was considering all that was said and coming to her own conclusion.

"Yes, you are right," she eventually said. "God's timing is best and it is now time."

All Michael had done was repackage everything Glory and Faith had been telling their mother, but Glory let the annoyance that she felt be overwhelmed with delight in hearing her mother finally agree.

Then it only took a week and a half to synchronize diaries, book train tickets and to go far enough with the plan that it would be hard for any party to back out.

Glory was grateful for Faith's support in the planning, although, if Glory had left it completely up to Faith, she was sure there would be place names, menu cards and a section for diplomatic gift exchange. But the idea to have small gifts for Hope and Joan was still a nice touch.

Celeste finally let Glory properly begin the process of clearing out the house. After a few days of work, Glory had only managed to clear the area around the dining table, but it was still a relief to see Faith drive five bin bags of junk away.

On the morning of the reunion, Glory was in the kitchen putting the final touches on the food, although it was Celeste who had done most of the work at her own insistence. Glory was mixing up shop-bought salad with tuna, boiled egg and salad cream when Faith, Michael and the twins showed up, carrying a new tablecloth for the newly recovered dining table.

"I wasn't sure if Joan took tea or coffee, so I bought both," Faith said, quickly unloading a shopping bag onto the kitchen counter.

"I could've just asked Hope," Glory said, wrapping the tray of salad with clingfilm.

"No! It's nicer when it's unexpected!" Faith said, fanning her face.

"It's just tea."

"It's not just anything! It's the details, the details matter!" Faith snapped and, on hearing his wife's raised voice, Michael came into the kitchen, placing a large hand on each of her shoulders and gently kneading them.

"It's going to be fine, Faith," he said in a soothing voice, but a noise from the living room made Faith jump and crane her neck to look around him.

"What are the kids doing? They better not mess up the—"

"I'll take them to the park, OK?"

Faith nodded, biting the tips of her manicured nails. Glory was sure she hadn't even been this wound up at her own wedding.

She relaxed once the door shut behind her husband and children, but only marginally.

"You seem really worried about this going right, for someone who at one point was sure this shouldn't happen!" Glory joked, but Faith didn't smile. It looked like she was wearing a groove into the tip of her acrylic nail extension with her front teeth.

"Joan sounded lovely on the phone, and Hope is really chill, like Victor—not like either of us," Glory said with half a smile.

Faith nodded, but her teeth still worked away.

"They're ten minutes away!" Glory hollered through the house when the text from Hope came through.

Faith sprang into action, going upstairs to help their mother with anything that might delay her in joining them. Esther and Elijah got up and started dancing, for some reason, and Michael tried to settle them down before Faith came back and their unruly energy worked her up some more.

Glory checked the time. Victor was due to call any moment from now, she just hoped he would call when Hope and Joan had arrived and everyone was settled.

Glory went to the kitchen and put an anxious hand on the coolers of food set out next to the cooker. Everything was perfect serving temperature. There was a tray of chin chin and drinks ready to be brought through. She filled the kettle and started the water boiling so that they wouldn't have to wait if anyone wanted tea or coffee. Faith's forward planning was beginning to rub off on her.

When the doorbell rang, Celeste was still only halfway down the stairs. Glory rushed to answer it, Esther and Elijah at her side, ready to see who these secret guests were.

Glory opened the door. Hope stood on the doorstep, chewing on her bottom lip. Joan stood next to her, older, more wrinkled and perhaps ever so slightly stooped over, but still recognizable as the woman with the warm smile and frizzy halo. Her hand was looped through the crook of Hope's elbow, exactly how Celeste would loop her hand through Glory's arm.

"Hey!" Glory said in an excited rush. "Welcome! Welcome!"

But Esther and Elijah stood in the way, their little faces puzzled as they looked at these strangers, one who looked so much like their mum and aunt.

"Hello, little ones!" Joan cooed in a sugary voice. "You must be Esther and Elijah!"

That broke their trance and they scuttled back inside to the arms of their parents, throwing suspicious looks over their shoulders as Hope allowed Joan to enter ahead of her.

"My, my! Look at you, Glory!" Joan reached out and Glory hugged her awkwardly.

She stepped to the side to allow Joan to enter and Hope to follow, but Hope hesitated.

"Oh my!" Glory could hear Joan call out behind her. "Celeste! So good to see you after all this time!"

Celeste laughed, for a moment unable to speak, and the two older women hugged each other tight. Time froze as everyone waited for the connection to break and when they finally pulled away from each other, both of them had eyes shining with tears.

Celeste was gripping both of Joan's hands in her own and mouthing the words "thank you," her throat still choked with emotion. Joan was shaking her head so hard the tears fell loose. They hugged again.

The house was silent, entranced by this spell. After releasing Celeste a second time, Joan reached into her handbag, recovered a tissue and pressed it against her eyes, turning to see Faith standing next to Michael.

"My little Faith!" she exclaimed. "You're a woman now, with two beautiful children, and I suppose this handsome man is your husband."

Joan chuckled and Faith dipped into a curtsey before remembering herself and opting for a hug instead. While she was introducing Michael to her former foster mother, Glory realized that Hope hadn't moved two steps beyond the threshold of the front door.

"Come," she said quietly to Hope, holding out a hand, and Celeste, momentarily distracted by the sight of the woman she had trusted to look after her three precious children, pushed past Glory, pulling Hope away from the door and into the living room.

She gasped, cupping two trembling hands around her daughter's face, who had to bend slightly to allow her to do this, but then she was weeping freely. Hope started crying too, so hard she looked like she might collapse. Sensing this, Celeste gripped her tight, holding her up against her bosom.

By now, tears were freely exchanged between everyone in the room. Still hanging on to her daughter for dear life, Celeste struck up a praise song, her voice cracking from the weight of her tears and joy.

"Olúwa Olúwa wa, Ọlọ́run Olọrun mi, Olówó orí mi, ẹ mà ṣeun, modúpẹ́ tí ẹ kó mi yọ . . ."

She repeated her shrill refrain until she eventually released Hope, a sodden patch on her blouse where Hope's face had been against her shoulder.

"You know what that means, ehn?" Celeste asked and Hope shook her head, sniffing and trying to dry her face with her sleeve.

"It means, *My God, my Lord, the lifter of my head, thank you, I'm grateful that you delivered me.* Do you understand now?"

Hope nodded quickly, then Celeste turned to look around at everyone witnessing this.

"Because he delivered me, didn't he?" she didn't wait for anyone to respond. "My enemies thought I was cursed, they thought I would never be happy again, but Baba God delivered me from that dark place and I am here with my daughters. All three of my daughters! He brought Hope back to me!"

She started up the chorus again, this time with a bit more vigor. Glory and Hope both started laughing, and Esther and Elijah hopped down from their parents' arms to join their grandmother in her thanksgiving dance.

52

No one wanted to leave or be left. Glory noticed how Hope opened up more with Joan around, the reticent shell that she would suddenly retreat into unfurling to reveal a playful woman who could happily roll on the floor with Esther and Elijah, or allow herself to fall back into Glory when she was laughing at a funny childhood story.

Glory noticed her mother's hands often finding Joan's, their fingers interlocked as they sat side by side, laughter lining their eyes, leaning into each other. *If you were going to leave your young child with anyone*, Glory reasoned, *you would trust them with someone like Joan.*

"Hope, pet," Joan began. "It's getting late and I can feel my bones creaking. I'm not young and spritely like you youngsters!"

Hope pouted, and Glory could see the stern little face of the child in the navy school uniform in the photograph. She felt such a violent rush of love that she wanted to wrap her arms around her sister and never let her go.

"OK," Hope said with a sigh, gathering a sleeping Esther from her lap and handing her over to Faith.

"This was so wonderful, though!" Joan said, edging along the seat of the sofa, bracing herself to stand.

"I'm just so grateful," Celeste said, offering an arm to steady Joan as she pulled herself up carefully, her face still broken open with joy.

Their reluctant goodbyes dragged out the farewell process, but soon Hope and Joan were stepping into the night and heading toward the car, gratefully accepting Michael's offer of a lift back to Hope's flat across the river.

Glory stood on the doorstep, long past the point when the car pulled away. She wanted to bottle up the day's happiness and keep it forever. The thought crossed her mind to call Julian, as it often did. She even went as far as opening up their last conversation, reading back through the messages, a mixture of inane details, distracted flirting and passive-aggressive jibes. But she thought better of it and texted Lará instead:

"BIG success!!!!!"

Back in the house, Celeste was on the sofa, sinking into sleep next to her grandchildren. Faith was in the kitchen stacking plates in the sink and soaking pots.

"Can't remember the last time I saw you wash a plate," Glory said, approaching from behind.

"Neither can I!" Faith replied, rolling up her sleeves with slow precision. "I've been telling Mummy she needs a dishwasher. I even offered to pay for it."

"You should get Michael to tell her. I'm sure he'll convince her. He's probably charming the pants off Joan right now—not literally of course! But he does have a way with aunties."

Faith stopped scrubbing the plate.

"I thought you and Michael were cool now?" she asked Glory.

"We are! I was just admiring his powers of persuasion. Well, I guess he is a lawyer!"

"He is indeed."

"Michael's cool," Glory continued. "I was just not happy with him being gone all the time. I thought he might have a mistress or something."

"A what?" Faith spluttered into laughter. "He's not cheating on me, Glory! Yeah, he's gone a lot but . . . he's just not very emotionally intelligent. I'll say that much."

"Fine, but just don't let him walk all over you, will you?" Glory said sincerely, gently pushing Faith to the side so she could take over scrubbing the pots.

"You mean like Daddy?" Faith asked wiping her hands on a tea towel and examining her nails for any soap-inflicted damage.

"Yeah."

Faith tapped away at her smartphone while Glory scrubbed, rinsed and set out the clean crockery and cooking pots to dry.

"Faaiith . . ." Glory began. Faith stopped tapping and looked up from her screen.

"Yeah?"

"When did you know about all this? With Hope and Joan and stuff? Did you always know?"

Faith set down her phone on the side and straightened up.

"I was too young when it happened, so I wouldn't say I knew then, but it was like a thing I always got stuck on. I didn't piece the whole story together until a few years ago when that Mama Wawo tried to get in touch. Daddy told me about it and we had a massive argument because he wouldn't tell Mummy. I told him that he should let her decide what to do, as she is not a child, but he wouldn't hear it. He got *mad*. Michael had to come and calm him down."

"But if you knew and you were mad at him then why were you so against me when I was trying to figure this all out?"

"I was scared, Glory—maybe if this had all happened before,

I would have felt differently, but I was petrified for Mummy. It felt like I watched everything fall apart in front of my eyes. I was there the day they sentenced Victor, I watched them take him from the dock! I was in the hospital after Daddy died, I saw his body! When Mummy collapsed, it was *me* Auntie Búkì called first. Then you wanted to come and blow things up some more."

"I was trying to make things better, Faith. Don't you think I felt bad too? I was trying to help."

Faith shook her head, a tired smile spreading over her face.

"Glory, you help in very . . . confrontational ways. You fix things with a sledgehammer. I'm not saying things don't get fixed, but you're not delicate in your method."

"You can question my method, but you can't question my motive."

"That's what Mummy said about Daddy when I finally spoke to her about all of this."

"Well, that's not someone I really want to be compared to." Faith snorted.

"The only reason you're so disappointed in him is because you had such high expectations. You've just got to accept people for who they are, not be angry at who they're not."

"Are you talking about Daddy or Michael?" Glory asked with a smirk.

"I'm talking about everyone, OK? Even you!"

Faith threw a tea towel at Glory's head and Glory ducked out of the way and flicked water in Faith's direction.

"Speaking of disappointments, how's Julian?"

Glory shrugged, wiping her hands on the back of her jeans.

"Not spoken to him since he called about his friend's pop-up thing."

"You know what that was, right?"

"What?"

Faith sighed.

"He didn't have to call you about that, he called because he wanted an excuse to talk to you. That was him leaving the door open for the two of you to make up."

"No, it wasn't."

"How do you know?"

"I just know!"

Faith arched an eyebrow but said no more, turning her attention back to her phone.

Glory took out her own phone and opened up WhatsApp, her thumb hovering over Julian's picture.

"Hey stranger," she eventually typed. *"I've been meaning to say thank you."*

Julian's reply came a few seconds later:

"What for?"

Glory began her response, remembering all the different ways Julian had nudged her toward reuniting with Hope, and Victor too. But then she highlighted the lengthy paragraph and deleted it.

The cursor blinked expectantly on her screen.

"Can I call you? It's easier to explain on the phone." She added a smiling emoji and clicked send.

Acknowledgments

This book might not exist if it wasn't for Christina Demosthenous planting the seed of possibility in my head way back in 2016. Thanks to my fairy godmother/agent Juliet for holding my hand through this process, and my editors Sam and Rachel for your enthusiasm, your guidance but above all, for getting it. There are so many other people involved in turning a manuscript into a real life book and I'm grateful for every single encouraging comment and excited exchange that kept me going whenever doubts crept in.

The artist's work mentioned in Chapter 25 is *Whip It Good: Spinning From History's Filthy Mind* by Jeannette Ehlers, which showed at Autograph ABP's gallery in 2015.

APPRECIATION

The Black Ballad community: for being my guiding star. I wrote this for myself first, then you lot next. To Tobi and Bola for seeing us, making space for us—and giving me the time off to work on this!

Flow and Tols: for the tea, the advice, the memes and the

podcast-length voice notes. For being the first civilians to read an early draft and for not hating it.

Lauren and Karen: for our summer salons, the M&S food, the book chat, the feedback and encouragement, for sharing your talent and making me want to get better.

Rasheed and Opeyemi: for checking and double-checking the Yorùbá.

My family: for my sis and my cousins for keeping me young, my aunties and uncles for being our support, my grandmother for the life-affirming prayers. Rest well to those we love and miss—Grandpa, Grandad, Granma, Auntie Bola, Izzy.

My dear mother-in-law/love: for taking the kids so that I could rest and write and rest some more, for your unwavering support and for everything that you do for us.

Mom, Dad and Josh: for making me who I am. Words aren't enough.

Sean: for believing in what I couldn't yet see.

Anaiah, Amari and Ace: for being the lights of my life.

I wrote this book during a period of my life that was a bit mad, to say the least, but I have an army of friends from Brum to Manny to LDN to Joburg (with plenty of stop-offs in between) that carried me through the ups and downs. Without you lot checking in on us and making sure I was good in general, writing this would have been a myth! You are God's love made manifest.

TO GOD BE THE GLORY